28 Days in Berlin

Joan Strobel

Barnes & Noble Press

Printed in the United States of America
by Barnes & Noble Press
122 Fifth Avenue, New York, New York 10011
ISBN 979-8-9875403-1-2
ISBN 979-8-9875403-2-9 (ebook)

© 2023 Joan Strobel

For Mark, my Volodya

*For the people of Ukraine ...
May you live in freedom.
Sláva Ukrayíni!*

A sincere thank you to my extraordinary editor, Ashley Casteel, for your help in greatly improving this manuscript. I learned so much from you. In the words of the character, Iza, (spoken in a different context), "After all our work together, I feel as though I've known you for a long time already."

Thank you to my talented designer, Sabir Shah, for the creative cover design.

Finally, a special thank you to my husband, Mark, for his encouragement and patient reading of the early drafts of this manuscript.

Wednesday, October 12 (Day 1)

The plane touched down with a bump, jolting Iza awake. Much to her surprise and embarrassment, she'd briefly dozed off during the last hour of the flight. Russ, the middle-aged businessman seated next to her, had been talking continuously about government contracts and the global supply chain since shortly after the meal service. *That's what I get for mentioning my new job as a consular affairs officer, and forgetting to pack my headphones in my daypack,* she thought. It had been a struggle to feign interest in the mostly one-sided conversation, but she hoped he wasn't offended that she'd fallen asleep. As the plane taxied toward the gate, she glanced eagerly out the window, checking her phone to see that it was already after noon in Berlin.

"Looks like we've arrived, Iza," Russ said as he began to gather his things.

"Yeah. Sorry I fell asleep there for a while. It was nice hearing so much about your work," she said, trying to sincerely express what she didn't feel.

"No problem. After all these years, I still get nervous when I fly, and I need to prattle on. I appreciate that you listened. When is your first day at the embassy again?"

"This Friday."

"Good luck to you! I think you'll like Berlin. It's a fun place for an attractive young woman like you," he said with a wink.

She forced a polite smile.

Iza was seated near the back of the plane and noticed several passengers ahead of her struggling with their carry-on luggage. *Come on people, between this seat assignment and my full bladder, I can't get off this plane fast enough,* she thought. She'd only taken her small running daypack aboard the flight. Her worldly belongings were packed in her blue hardside suitcase. She'd purchased it three weeks earlier from the department store where she'd worked after completing her graduate studies in May. She'd thought the bright blue color would be easy to pick out from the typical sea of black luggage on the baggage claim carousel.

After disembarking, Iza rushed to the restroom, moved through the passport control line, and then placed a call to Washington.

"Ellen, it's Iza. I'm in Berlin!"

"You did it, Iza! Tony and I are *so* excited for you, and we're proud of you. Did I tell you that too many times already?"

"No. I need to hear it a few more times. I can hardly believe I'm here."

"Did you call your mom to let her know you arrived safely?"

Iza's cheery voice suddenly turned somber. "No. And I'm not going to call her either."

"Come on, Iza. You can't be angry with your mom forever. I know you wanted her to come to the airport to see you off, but the Vermont trip with Günther just came up. You need to understand; she *had* to go."

"Why am *I* always the one who needs to understand? She knew three weeks ago when I was leaving. I moved back to her house this summer after I graduated to spend time with her before this move and she spent *all* of her free time with Günther instead. We barely saw each other. I almost never ask her to do anything for me, Ellen. But this was important to me. I don't know when I'll get home next time to see her or if she'll visit me here."

"Your mom's been alone for thirteen years. Having Günther in her life is a blessing. Just call her. You know . . . you and I are like peas in a pod. We're both 'pleasers.' In the end, we want everyone to be happy. We were born to choose kindness, even if at times we loathe ourselves for it. Call your mom. Honestly, I think she'll appreciate it."

"Well, I'm not calling her. Maybe I'm going to stand up for myself more in the future and not be so focused on making other people happy at my expense."

After a brief pause, Ellen said, "I'm sorry, Iza. I didn't mean to ruin your excitement. Tony will be back in town later tonight, and I'm sure he'll call you at some point next week to see how things are going with the new job. He's been crazy busy with work; I've barely seen him lately."

There was a long pause, as Iza immediately regretted her outburst.

"Ellen . . . I'm sorry if I sounded like an ungrateful brat. I'm not going to call, but I'll send Mom a nice text. I promise."

"You won't regret being kind to your mom. We love you, Iza."

"I love you and Tony too. Thanks for always being there for me."

Iza sent her mom a brief text with a heart emoji, then strolled toward the carousel where luggage from her flight was offloaded. *Wow, it looks like most of the luggage is already gone,* she observed. The carousel was still turning, but she wondered where her suitcase was.

As Iza walked closer, she noticed a short, heavyset man with a craggy face kneeling over an open blue suitcase in a corner near the carousel. Her eyes opened wide at the sight of her belongings scattered on the floor, and she ran toward the man. "Hey, that's my suitcase! Help! Stop! Somebody stop that guy!"

The area beyond the carousel was bustling with people, but the man ran into the crowd and disappeared from her view. No one paid attention to her calls for help. Iza weighed her options. *If I chase him, someone could steal my stuff. And what would I do anyway if I caught the guy? Hit him with my daypack? I'd have to find the airport* Polizei *first.* She decided to just gather her things and refer to the packing list on her phone to figure out what had been taken.

11

How strange, she thought when she finished her inventory. *Nothing is missing and he didn't put anything in my suitcase either. I wonder what that was all about?*

As she approached Customs and tried to determine which line to enter, Iza thought she saw the man ahead of her. But in an instant, he was gone again. She wanted to report the strange incident to an airline representative, but the customer-service line snaked on for meters and she was tired. On the long flight from Washington, D.C., she'd only slept an hour. She sighed. *It'll be Friday by the time I get to an agent.* With her suitcase in tow, she headed toward the exit. *What could customer service do anyway? Nothing was taken,* she reasoned. *One thing's for sure, I'll remember that guy's face for a long time.*

Iza took a taxi to her apartment building in the Mitte borough. The €50 price of the taxi ride was a splurge but worth it. The incident with her suitcase had only added to her fatigue and made her feel unsettled, no matter how much she tried to downplay it in her mind.

Her semi-furnished apartment was on the third floor of an older apartment building. When she arrived at the building, an entry information sign directed her to an apartment on the ground floor. There, she met Frau Böhmer, the owner and *Vermieterin* of the building. Frau Böhmer spoke only halting English, so Iza transitioned to German. Iza guessed that Frau Böhmer was in her mid-seventies. She was a plump, gray-haired woman with a pleasing face, and Iza found her to be delightful to talk to. She seemed to be someone who knew everyone's business yet was still discreet in dealing with her tenants.

"*Komm bitte,*" Frau Böhmer said, inviting Iza into her apartment for *"Kaffee und Kuchen."*

"Tell me about yourself. Why did you come to live in Berlin? Won't your family miss you?"

"I'm from Washington, D.C. My dad was a Foreign Service political officer for the State Department, assigned to

European embassies for twelve years and then eventually for two years in the Middle East. His first assignment was in Berlin. I'll be working at the Berlin embassy for my first assignment too. I'll be a Consular Affairs officer. I was *really* close to my dad, and I want to follow in his footsteps—to a point. He was murdered in an ambush attack on his way to a meeting in Iraq when I was fourteen. But my mom is still living in Washington. Maybe I'll talk her into visiting me here someday."

"You poor little girl," Frau Böhmer said sincerely. "I'm sure you will make your Papa proud."

After they spent more time visiting, Frau Böhmer took Iza on a building tour.

"The building entrance door is always open, but I recently had a security camera installed to monitor the entrance. It uses the latest technology. It's not that anything has ever happened near my buildings—only petty crime. You're really very safe living here.

"This small laundry area in the basement is always open for your use, and here is something quite unique. This passageway joins our building to the adjacent building that I also own. You can travel indoors to the next street if there is bad weather." As they walked on the tour, Frau Böhmer told her the nearest apothecary, drug store, and grocer locations.

Iza's apartment was sparsely furnished. The kitchen had a tiny dining area with a table and two chairs near a small window. There were also cabinets, a small sink, a refrigerator, and a gas range. The living area included only a sofa, built-in shelving, and a chandelier; being on an interior wall, that room had no windows. The bedroom had a large bed and an armoire but no lighting or bedding. The bathroom was small but had been recently remodeled. Frau Böhmer showed Iza how to adjust the heat on each radiator. The water was centrally heated in the basement, then distributed to the radiators in each apartment through a network of pipes. She explained the third-floor apartment might take longer to heat for that reason.

Iza was distraught as she looked over the meager furnishings in the chilly apartment. *The online advert indicated this place was fully furnished, but there's almost no furniture,* she thought. *And it's freezing in here. But Frau Böhmer seems like such a nice lady; I really can't complain and hurt her feelings.* Instead, she said, "It's perfect."

"Here is your key. Stop by any time for a visit or if you need something." Frau Böhmer disappeared down the stairway, the *klomp, klomp, klomp* sound of her shoes fading as she descended.

Iza unpacked her suitcase and slid it beneath the bed. She was disturbed as she recalled the man searching through her belongings at the airport, and again she felt the urge to tell someone. *Maybe I'll call Tony . . . or Roger . . . and tell them about my suitcase. They've both worked for the State Department for a long time; they'll get why it's bothering me so much.* First, she hung up her clothes in the armoire and then left briefly to eat at one of the nearby restaurants Frau Böhmer had recommended.

As she ate, Iza made a list of the items she would need for her new place. *I'll have a lot of shopping to do tomorrow. Hopefully, I can get the apartment set up before I start work on Friday.* She glanced at her phone to check the time and weighed her options on who to call about the suitcase incident. *Even though Tony treats me like a daughter, I can't bother him. His job is so demanding, and he's got bigger things to worry about. Ellen said she's barely seen him lately. It's not like the guy at the airport took something or did something more serious. But if I call Roger instead, he'll just go to Tony. I'm not calling Mom on her vacation. I'd only make her worry. I'm trying to be so independent with this move and new job—starting my adult life—but I'm kind of freaked out. I guess I'll leave Tony a message tomorrow morning. That way, at least he'll know something weird happened to me.*

Thursday, October 13 (Day 2)

"Ugh, that was a short night," Iza moaned when the alarm on her phone woke her at 7:30. She rolled over on the bed, covered in the two bath towels she'd brought with her. It was 1:30 a.m. in Washington, D.C., but she left a brief message for Tony anyway.

"Tony, this is Iza. I'm so sorry to bother you, but I need to talk with you. Something weird happened yesterday when I arrived in Berlin. A guy was going through my suitcase at the baggage claim. It's not like he'd made a mistake and grabbed the wrong one. He took *everything* out like he was looking for something. He ran away when I hollered, but he didn't take anything. I keep trying to think of a logical explanation. I didn't pack anything super valuable. Maybe nothing I had was good enough to take? It's just bugging me. Please call me."

She dressed in jeans and a sweater and grabbed her lightweight jacket. She had a lot she wanted to accomplish, including figuring out how long it would take to walk to the U.S. Embassy, but first she was off to the Hackescher Markt.

After getting some groceries, Iza made short trips back and forth from the apartment, dropping off her purchases of home goods throughout the day. She selected bedding, a blow dryer and curling iron, a coffee maker, a bedroom lamp, and some accent pillows for the sofa. *Fully furnishing my apartment will take more time and money than I have right now,* she thought, *but a few small things will make it feel more like home.* By the time she was finished shopping and visiting the embassy, it was nearly sunset.

As she approached the apartment, Iza was startled by who she saw standing near the entrance of the building. *Oh my*

God! That's the guy from the airport! She slipped into the outer vestibule of the building next door to hers and cautiously peered out, setting her bags down in the entryway behind her. A sleek black sedan pulled up in front of her building, and the man spoke with someone inside the vehicle. But in the increasing darkness, she started to doubt if it was the same man from the airport. *Maybe this is only my imagination. I can't see his face clearly. I'm probably just freaked out by what happened yesterday,* she thought. *In fact, I know I'm freaked out by what happened yesterday.*

The man abruptly turned away from the car and scurried off in the opposite direction, his short, heavy frame gradually disappearing from her view. The sedan sat idling for a moment, then slowly drove forward in Iza's direction. She peeked out from the vestibule as it rolled by and observed the license plate: 0 140 35. *That's a diplomatic plate,* she realized. The vehicle drove off and vanished into the growing darkness.

Iza walked around the block and entered the adjacent building, then walked through the basement-level passageway to her building rather than taking the direct route to her apartment. She slowly crept up the stairway and checked her apartment door. It was still locked. She carefully unlocked the door and slipped inside, using her phone flashlight to light the way.

Everything appeared as she'd left it after her previous return trip. She locked the door, switched on the living area chandelier, and then slowly sat down on the sofa, her mind racing. *Diplomatic plate numbers are assigned, and every country has a system for that,* she recalled. *Dad had one.* Iza looked up the German system for assigning diplomatic plate numbers for Berlin embassies on her phone. *The zero means the vehicle is assigned to an embassy diplomat. The final number is sequential—car number thirty-five. The middle number on the plate is the country code.* She scanned down the list until she reached 140. The country was Russia.

"Iza, you're freaking yourself out. What you just saw has *nothing* to do with you," she said aloud. "That guy outside your building couldn't have been the same guy from the airport. How would he know where you live? And lots of people who work at different embassies live in the Mitte. This area is close to a bunch of embassies. That car from the Russian Embassy could have belonged to someone who lives around here.

"Besides, you don't have anything that anyone would want, unless they're looking for some young woman's clothes, which no craggy-faced guy wants unless he's some kind of pervert. That guy at the airport probably mistook your suitcase for his and wondered why a bunch of woman's shit was inside it. He must have realized he'd opened the wrong suitcase, and then you scared him when you yelled. It's *nothing* more than that."

She calmed herself as much as possible, put away her purchases, ate a quick supper, and got to bed early, thinking that the next day would be long and busy. In addition to her mandatory new-employee orientation, she'd been invited to attend a formal embassy dinner-and-dance event with her new supervisor on Friday evening. The formal event was sponsored by the U.S. embassy, and the guest list included personnel from the embassies of all U.S. allies in Berlin. Iza was apprehensive about attending the event because she didn't own any formal attire and didn't have the money to purchase something suitable to wear.

As she tossed and turned trying to fall sleep, she planned to leave another, much more urgent, message for Tony, because she didn't actually believe a word of what she'd told herself about the man and the sedan that she'd seen in front of her apartment building.

Friday, October 14 (Day 3)

Before walking to the embassy, Iza left an urgent message for Tony, describing what she'd observed the previous evening. The incident at the airport had seemed legitimately suspicious, but she was hoping for some validation that the man and the car she saw yesterday had nothing to do with her. *I hope you return my call, Tony. With everything else you have going on in your work, maybe this seems pretty minor. But I'm freaked out. I'm not sure what you can do to help me, but it'd be reassuring to talk.*

The new-employee orientation at the U.S. Embassy was about to begin. Iza had just been issued her entrance pass after having her embassy photo taken, and she'd proudly clipped the pass to the lanyard she'd been given, which was embroidered with the words "U.S. Embassy Berlin." *I hope I make you proud, Dad,* she thought as she referred to the embassy map for the location of the orientation conference room, smiling at the picture in her mind of her dad looking down on her with pride.

To Iza's dismay, the orientation was exceptionally dull. *Ugh. This guy is so unenthusiastic. He just keeps talking like Russ on the airplane—droning on about all these embassy policies and procedures. I'll never remember any of this. This is the kind of stuff you have to learn through experience.*

The orientation was supposed to run until 15:00, but with the excitement of the embassy dinner-and-dance event at the fore, the presenter cut the session short and let the five new employees "graduate" at noon instead.

Iza was eager to find her new office in the Consular Affairs department but decided to stop and say hello to her supervisor first. She'd only talked with Claire Daniels briefly by phone a week earlier and wanted to make a good first impression. Claire looked up from her lunch as Iza hesitantly peeked inside her office. *Great, perfect timing,* Iza thought, trying to cover her embarrassment with a pleasant smile.

"You must be Iza," Claire said cordially, excusing herself for talking with her mouth full of salad. She walked around to the front of her desk and extended her hand to Iza in greeting. Iza guessed that Claire was about forty. She was a very attractive woman and wore her dark brown hair in a severe bob with full blunt-cut bangs. Her classic black pantsuit and heels complemented her tall figure. And her heavy eye makeup and bright red lipstick were impeccable. Her obviously artificial nails were a bright, shiny red.

Claire's friendly demeanor made Iza feel somewhat at ease, but she still felt guilty about intruding on her while she was trying to eat.

"I'm sorry for interrupting your lunch, Claire," she said as she shook her hand in greeting. "The orientation ended early today. The presenter seemed more enthused about the dinner-and-dance event tonight than the orientation. I just wanted to stop in and say 'hello'; we can talk more later this afternoon, and of course this evening." Iza inched back toward the door, hoping she could manage to excuse herself quickly.

Claire laughed softly, then became serious. "Iza, I'm *so* sorry. David and I won't be able to attend the event with you this evening as we'd discussed on the phone. Our son came down with a fever at his nursery this morning. David picked him up, but he just called and told me his temperature has been rising."

"I'm so sorry about your son, Claire. I hope it's nothing serious." Iza tried not to let her disappointment show as she thought about navigating the event on her own. She figured she probably wouldn't know anyone there, except for perhaps a few people who knew her parents.

"Thank you. I'm sure everything will be fine," Claire said kindly. "I *so* wish I could be there to point out some of the noteworthy people in attendance, but you'll still have a great time." She glanced at her watch and continued, "Since you're here, let me show you your office. I also put together a new-employee packet for you. Our general orientation isn't the most riveting way to start your new assignment here. The Berlin Embassy is actually a very interesting place to work, and I think you're going to like it here in Consular Affairs. I've been here ten years now. Every day provides a new challenge."

Iza instantly liked Claire. She appeared well organized, enthusiastic, and genuine—all traits that Iza appreciated. But as they walked to her new office, Iza couldn't help dwelling on the evening ahead. *I don't do well socializing in large crowds, but I probably should make an appearance. I can always slip out after the dinner. It's not like I have anything else to do tonight. At least it'll keep me from thinking about the airport guy.*

◆

When Iza arrived at the event center at 18:00, the hallway leading to the main ballroom was already crowded with attendees. She filled out a tag with her name and work affiliation after showing her identification.

Iza wore a very short, black, long-sleeved dress and low heels—the only dressy dress she owned. Although she was only five feet, six inches tall, she looked taller because she had the slender body of a long-distance runner. *Wow, do I feel out of place*, she thought as she entered the ballroom. *The other women here are so much more formally dressed than I am. They're all wearing perfectly contoured makeup and look like they've spent hours at the salon.*

Iza had curled her long, straight brown hair into beach waves that, along with her feathered bangs, gave her a somewhat casual appearance. She wore minimal makeup, although what little she did wear highlighted her expressive blue eyes and her full lips. *Geez, I feel like a little girl attending an adult event.* But instead of succumbing to the feeling of inferiority, she held her head high and confidently strode through the crowd to the bar. *Come on; you can do this, Iza.* While her short dress was less formal than what the other women in attendance wore, she felt comfortable and attractive in it. Iza took a glass of white wine from the bar and then stood leaning against a side wall not far from the bar, surveying the crowd. She tried to guess the country of the attendees near the bar area by their dress and mannerisms and hoped she might recognize an old friend of her parents.

Iza periodically sipped wine from her glass and finally checked her watch. Only fifteen minutes had gone by. She scanned the event program displayed on a large screen at the front of the room. She could make out that wine and cocktails would be served for one hour, followed by dinner, brief remarks from the U.S. Ambassador to Germany, and then dancing and an open bar until midnight. *I hope I'll eventually see somebody who I recognize as a friend of Mom and Dad. That would help make the time pass more quickly,* she thought. *At this rate, I don't know if I'll make it through the dinner.*

Volodya had been watching the woman in the short, black dress standing near the wall for some time, trying to decide if she was alone, and if so, if he could muster the courage to introduce himself. He was attracted by her natural beauty, and by how different she seemed from the other women in their fancy gowns with their stiff-looking hair and mask-like faces. *She looks like someone who knows how to have fun.* He'd glanced at her hands to see if she wore a ring, then around the bar area to see if anyone was coming to join her at her position near the wall. As he performed his reconnaissance, he thought to himself, *Volodya, you are so pathetic. War makes you not know how to approach women anymore. You are so nervous. Where is self-confidence you once had?*

He tugged at the cuffs of his rental tuxedo, loosened his collar, took a deep breath, and finally walked over to her. "Hello," he said as he held out his hand in greeting. "My name is Volodymyr Korsun from Ukraine, but my friends call me Volodya. I saw you standing along wall and wondered if you are waiting for someone or if you are also alone. I am actually attending in place of my boss. I do not know *anyone* here."

"My name is Izabella Carter, but my friends call me Iza. I'm pleased to meet you, Volodya," she said as she grasped his hand in greeting and turned her name tag in his direction. "I'm new at the U.S. Embassy. In fact, this was my first day of work here in Berlin. I don't know anyone here either."

Volodya held her hand an especially long time, captivated by the softness of her skin and the warmth of her smile. She looked at him with such interest on her face and in her expressive eyes that he suddenly felt as if he were the most important human being she'd ever met. He looked away briefly and noticed that her wine glass was nearly empty. "May I bring you another glass of wine?"

"Yeah, thanks," Iza managed to get out before Volodya took the glass from her hand.

"Which varietal are you drinking?"

"Well, I think they only have generic white or red wine—as far as I can tell. I didn't see I had a choice other than color." He smiled at her and immediately walked to the bar, letting out a nervous sigh.

Volodya, this girl is beautiful, but you have been out of dating scene far too long between graduate school and war. You will not get another chance with woman like her, so do not mess up this chance tonight.

Volodya returned with another glass of white wine for Iza and a glass of red wine for himself. She was charmed by the bright, kind, but also somewhat mischievous smile on his face.

"Budmo," he said, offering a toast in his deep, pure voice—a voice she wouldn't have expected from someone his size. She guessed that he was only about three inches taller than she was, and though he was quite thin, his muscular upper arms were visible through his well-fitted tuxedo.

She looked into his piercing dark brown eyes and felt as though they were searching her soul. "Budmo," she said as she clinked her wine glass together with his, thoroughly intrigued by this mysterious man from Ukraine.

He had moderately long, dark brown hair, a stubble beard, and a mustache, which set him apart from the other men in attendance, who mostly had short, well-groomed hair and were clean shaven.

I might be in trouble, Iza thought as she sipped her wine. *I've always had a thing for men with facial hair, and his accent is so sexy. I'm definitely not looking for a relationship right now, but it can't hurt to chat with him for a while. It might even make the time go by faster tonight.*

"So, Volodya, may I ask you some questions about yourself?"

"Of course, but only if you promise to let me ask same questions of you."

"That's fair," she replied. "I'll start with something easy. Where are you from in Ukraine?"

"I was born in Mariupol, Ukraine," he replied. "And you, where are you from?"

"I was born in Washington, D.C., but I didn't live there very long as a child. Did you grow up in Mariupol?"

"Yes, my family lived in Mariupol until two years ago. My parents both worked at Azovstal steel plant in Mariupol. My dad worked in plant, and my mom in office. They actually met each other there. I have older brother, who also worked at Azovstal. He is thirty-eight years old—ten years older than me."

Before he could ask the same question of Iza, she followed up with another question. "So—your family moved before the devastation there?" she asked with concern.

"My parents retired two years ago from Azovstal, and they move near Kyiv to enjoy their retirement. Unfortunately, they move to Bucha. I do not want to ruin our evening. I will only tell you that they were killed by Russian soldiers there in March." He paused briefly. "And my brother—I have not spoken to him since we learned our parents died. He is—how do you call it—ultranationalist. He is in Ukrainian army fighting somewhere."

For a moment, Iza didn't know what to say. "I'm so sorry for you, Volodya," she finally replied very quietly. Her eyes filled with tears. She took a deep breath and tried to shake her mental image of the terror at Bucha. She'd read that hundreds of Ukrainian civilians were brutally tortured and murdered by Russian soldiers there.

"Please, it is okay. I have to accept they are gone. Believe me, it is *not* easy for me. But I have to live on for them." He smiled at her again and asked, "How about you? Where did you grow up?"

"My dad was a Foreign Service officer, and my mom is an interpreter. They met at the State Department in Washington, D.C., where I was born. My dad was transferred to a lot of different places while I was growing up. We mostly lived in Europe—Berlin, Paris, London. Then he was transferred to the Middle East for a couple years. My dad was killed in an ambush attack in Iraq thirteen years ago when I was fourteen. My mom and I moved back to Washington the next year."

Volodya bit on his upper lip as he listened to her story. "Iza, I am so sorry for you too."

"At least we understand each other, right? We've both suffered that kind of loss." Volodya sadly nodded his head in agreement.

Iza's face brightened as she changed the subject, "Where did you go to school, and what did you study? What were you interested in?"

"I was good student in math and science, and my parents made sure I could go to University. I graduated from Kharkiv National University. I studied computer science. My PhD thesis project was in applied artificial intelligence. I majored in history too—history of Ukraine, Poland, and Russia."

Iza could tell he was proud of his academic accomplishments. "Wow, that's impressive! I'd like to understand more about artificial intelligence. You know, the world lacks wisdom these days, so maybe artificial intelligence can help save us from our stupidity." She smiled again, and Volodya grinned in return.

"And you, Iza, where did you go to school?"

"When I came back to the U.S. with my mom, I was lost for a while in school. It was a culture shock . . . I mean . . . to be a teenaged girl accustomed to a very different way of life in Europe and the Middle East; it was difficult coming back to life in the U.S. I started riding horses and running to cope with my dad's death and with being a misfit in my school. I was actually a pretty good runner. I got an athletic scholarship to American University in Washington because of that. I got my undergraduate degree in International Studies and my PhD in International Relations there."

"And what are International Studies and International Relations? Those are not so familiar to me."

"Well, International Studies looks at the social and cultural aspects of countries and International Relations looks more specifically at global affairs related to politics and economics—those sorts of things. I wanted to eventually work for the State Department, in a way, to be like my dad."

"What will you do for your work at embassy?"

"I'm starting in Consular Affairs here in Berlin. I don't actually know everything about the job yet, but it's a public-service job. I'll be helping people solve problems. What do you do for your work? I noticed it wasn't on your name tag. Do you work at the Ukrainian Embassy on artificial intelligence?"

"No, no. I actually work for joint-venture company between Ukraine, U.S., and Germany. My boss is—was—supposed to be guest of Ukrainian Ambassador, who is also his friend from Kyiv. But when he could not come tonight, my boss canceled also and told me to go instead. My company uses artificial intelligence in new applications, and I do general programming and . . . other things."

"What kind of applications? Or can't you say . . . I mean, if they're proprietary?"

"Oh . . . applications to determine when equipment needs repair or how to get certain machines to make some simple decisions without person there. It is hard concept to explain and probably not so interesting."

"How long have you been working for your company in Berlin?"

"About three months so far—not really very long time yet."

"Do you like the work?"

"I do not think it is what I want to do for my life work, but it is pretty important work right now, so I need to do it."

"What's the name of the joint-venture—"

Volodya abruptly changed the subject without letting Iza finish asking her question.

"I know you speak English and probably German since embassy assigned you to Berlin. Do you speak other languages?"

"Yeah, just a little Farsi."

"Oh! I guess that is hard language to learn."

"It is for an English speaker," Iza smiled. "That's why I only know a little. So, I know you speak Ukrainian and English. Do you speak any other languages?"

"Yes, I also speak Russian—kind of need to know that if you grow up . . . or is it grew up . . . in Mariupol."

"Grew up."

"I try to improve my English by learning slang and idioms. I read if you know those, then you really understand English. Sometimes, I may ask you what you mean if I do not understand something you say. I hope you do not mind."

"Of course not!"

There was a lull in the conversation as they each sipped on their wine and looked intently at each other. *I feel so at ease around him*, Iza thought, *and I already feel a strong connection with him—an attraction. There's something vulnerable in his eyes that's so endearing.*

"How would someone describe you, or how would you describe yourself?" Iza asked suddenly as she thought of a new topic for discussion.

"I am not sure what you mean."

"So, are you a happy person or an honest person? That sort of thing."

"Oh, okay. My mom always told me that my older brother got all good looks, and I got all kindness within me. My brother is tough guy, but he is very handsome. Maybe I am not so much."

Iza scrunched her nose. "Well, I think you're *very* good-looking." He smiled broadly at her compliment. "Moms say those kinds of hurtful things sometimes I guess . . . or at least my mom does."

"So maybe I am kind and honest and little quiet. And maybe little funny, do you think? I like to be happy and to have fun. What about you, Iza?"

"I like to be happy too, and I like to make other people happy." *I hope that didn't sound suggestive,* she thought.

"Our family friend, Roger—my dad's best friend—always says I'm too independent, too honest, too organized, too quiet, but *way* funny."

Volodya grinned at Iza and glanced at his watch. "It is almost time for dinner to start. Will you sit with me?"

Wow, talking to Volodya really did make the time fly by! "Yeah, I'd love to," she said. But first they stopped at the bar to refill their wine glasses.

◆

The round dining tables were set up to seat ten. Iza and Volodya scanned the room for available seats and saw a table with three British couples sitting next to each other, leaving four seats in a row empty on one side. Volodya and Iza asked if they could join the table or if the seats were taken. One of the men replied, "By all means, please join us." But then the women sitting next to the vacant chairs on each end of their group immediately set their purses on the empty chairs next to them, requiring Volodya and Iza to sit with an empty chair on each side, separating them from the other couples. Volodya rolled his eyes, and Iza winked back at him. They were happy to avoid small talk with the other couples and continued chatting together through the entire dinner service.

"What are your hobbies, Iza?"

"Hmm. I love running, classical music, and some popular music from the 60s and 70s. I like art. And languages. And I love to cook too."

"Do you play instrument or paint?"

"No! I'm a patron of the arts." Iza grinned. "I'm *not* talented. Now you know what I'm going to ask you," Iza said, nudging Volodya with her hand.

"I like to run too, although I admit my running program has been interrupted quite much this year. I love classical music. Rachmaninoff's Piano Concerto No. 3 is my favorite work. It is really passionate and romantic. It is music to listen to when you make love. I mean . . . romance and passion build as you listen, and by third movement, you cannot resist what Rachmaninoff has expressed. *Oh Volodya. That was dumb thing to say when you just met her! Don't scare her away.* But I like Ukrainian and American folk music as well. I study history also."

"I love that concerto too," Iza responded, obviously suppressing a smile. "It's definitely on my list of favorites. Do you play an instrument?"

"No, I think I am also patron of arts," Volodya replied with a warm, mischievous grin, grateful that she had overlooked his awkward comment. *She seems like such nice girl,* he thought. *She is smart and interesting and independent. And she is making me feel like I am important guy.*

"Iza, what is your favorite classical work?"

"Mussorgsky's Pictures at an Exhibition—Ravel's orchestration. "The Great Gate of Kyiv" is my favorite 'picture.' It evokes something so powerful. I envision storms and majestic mountains when I listen to it."

"I have heard that work before, but it is not so familiar to me. I will need to buy that CD."

"Wow, you're so lucky if you've got a CD player! I want to buy a good one for my apartment, but I can't afford it right now. People who download music files don't realize how compressed the downloaded files are—how much of the sound quality is lost. CDs are the best for enjoying music, especially classical music."

"I can see that you love music as much as I do. I hope you will come to my place some day and listen to CDs with me. I mean . . . until you can get your own player for your apartment, of course." *And I will make love with you while we listen to Rachmaninoff.* "Oh, I forget—forgot—to say that I like to eat. So, you know, if you like to cook, I will like to eat what you prepare."

"I'll keep that in mind."

"Do you have other family or close friends besides your mom and Roger?"

"Well, I'm quite close to Tony and his family."

Please tell me he is not your boyfriend.

"His wife, Ellen, and their two kids are like family to me. He's actually the Assistant Secretary of State for European and Eurasian Affairs, so he gets to Berlin fairly frequently. You know . . . he's the boss at my embassy here . . . and for all of Europe actually. I hope you can meet him. What about your family and close friends?"

"I just have my brother. My family was split by war; my uncles support Russia's cause."

Iza asked quietly, "Did you have to fight in the war like your brother?"

He hated everything about the war and wanted to cut off this part of their conversation as quickly as possible. "Yes, I fought about five months or so in Kharkiv Oblast after basic training. I was excited about doing it until Russians started shooting at me."

29

He was relieved when she quickly changed the subject, as she sensed his unease. "What's your favorite color and why?" she asked with brightness in her voice.

"I like brown. It is color of earth, of soil. And Iza likes?"

"I like green. It's the color of life."

They continued chatting, and their conversation turned to serious topics: overpopulation, the world energy-supply situation, climate change, and the state of democracy in the world. They were each impressed with the other's insights. But Volodya was glad there was no more talk about the war in Ukraine.

Shortly after the tables were cleared, the U.S. Ambassador to Germany made some brief and unmemorable remarks to the crowd that were translated into several languages on the large screen at the front of the room. The live music started shortly thereafter.

Iza was surprised when Volodya turned to her and said, "The music is going to start and they will play waltz. Will you dance with me?" *I'd love to dance with him, but I don't want to make a fool of myself in front of these stuffy Brits,* she thought. *Those women were so unfriendly toward us.*

She whispered into Volodya's ear so the British couples couldn't hear, "I would love to, but I don't know how to dance the waltz."

"But you do not have to know how; I will push you," Volodya whispered back.

Iza giggled. "I think you will *lead* me, not *push* me." She then showed Volodya what push meant by shoving him with her hands, and the two laughed.

"English verbs like that are hard for me. Iza, I want to tell you beforehand though, I will have to hold you very close to me to lead. Is that okay with you?"

How close can that really be? "That's fine. I just hope I don't step on your feet too often."

When they got on the dance floor, Volodya pulled her in *very* close to him; from his upper thigh to his chest, the two were in intimate contact. His right arm went around Iza's back at her shoulder and he instructed her to place her left arm and hand around his neck at his shoulder. Their opposite hands were clasped together at Iza's eye level. *I'm so glad the lights on the dance floor are dimmer than near the tables because my face must be bright red. We have our clothes between us, but it hardly seems to make a difference; he wasn't kidding when he said he'd be holding me close,* she thought to herself as she nervously breathed in and held her breath momentarily.

◆

Volodya skillfully led Iza around the dance floor, relishing how close her warm body was to his. They smiled at each other as they danced. As the waltz ended, Iza said, "Thank you. Where did you learn to dance like this?"

"From my mom. I do not know where she learned. My dad would only dance when he drank too much vodka. My brother was too big, and she could not force him to dance. I was not so big—she could force me to be her dancing partner." Iza laughed and Volodya continued, "We did not go to dances. We danced in our house—mostly waltzes and folk dances—in main room or outside in garden, especially at all holidays."

The music changed to an American rock number. They continued to dance and stayed on the dance floor until the musicians took their first break. When they returned to their table, the three British couples were gone, so they were alone. The two were perspiring heavily from dancing in the warm ballroom. Volodya removed his tuxedo jacket and laid it on the chair beside them. The underarms of his shirt were damp with perspiration, and he could feel sweat dripping along his hairline. He noticed that Iza's bangs were wet and the underarms of her dress were sweaty. *She seems to not worry about her looks because she is having fun. I like that. We are laughing and being silly with our dancing now. She does not need to run to restroom every few minutes to fix her makeup and her hair.* He went to the bar again and brought them each sparkling water and another glass of wine.

They spent the remainder of the evening either dancing or chatting. The musicians finally called that it was the last dance, which was another waltz. They were both surprised that it was already midnight. Volodya held Iza's hand as he led her to the dance floor to dance the final waltz. "Volodya, after all of our talking tonight, I feel as though I've known you for a long time already."

"I feel same about you, Iza. Have we met once before in different life?" he smiled his mischievous smile. *Volodya, I think you did okay tonight. Will she see you again though?*

◆

Large groups started leaving the Embassy party at the same time, creating long lines for taxi services. Volodya offered, "Iza, may I walk you back to your apartment house? Of course, I assume you do not live in Potsdam, in which case, you will need taxi," he laughed softly and she did too. "I do not think you will find taxi any time soon."

"I live in the Mitte borough, not too far from here. I accept your offer, Mr. Korsun."

As they strolled toward her apartment, they continued talking and laughing along the route. Iza's pulse increased when Volodya reached out unexpectedly and held her hand. She realized that she'd never felt so strongly attracted to anyone before. Not when she dated in college or not even in grad school when she'd dated Taylor on and off for two years. *And I'm not the type of woman who falls for every guy who looks at her,* she thought. *Could this be something real?*

When they neared the entrance to her building, Iza saw Frau Böhmer outside near the doorway while an ambulance crew and officers from several squad cars of the Berlin Polizei were huddled on the sidewalk in front of the entrance. A portion of the street was cordoned off. As a feeling of dread

overcame her, Iza ran up to Frau Böhmer, pulling Volodya along, and asked with concern in German, "What *happened*?"
Frau Böhmer was visibly shaken. "A man was killed just outside the building about half an hour ago. I have not been able to get any information from the Polizei."
"Oh my gosh, that's terrible! I'll ask around the embassy on Monday and see if I can learn anything." *Why did I say that?* she thought, immediately regretting her offer. *I don't think I can learn anything about a murder in the Mitte from the embassy, but I don't know what else to say. Frau Böhmer looks so distraught.*
She turned to Volodya and explained in English that a man had just been murdered. Iza then noticed Frau Böhmer eyeing Volodya. "He's a colleague from the embassy, and we're returning from an embassy party. No taxis were available, so he offered to walk me to my door," she again responded in German. Frau Böhmer then smiled at Volodya, apparently satisfied with Iza's explanation.
"Are you okay to stay here alone, or are you worried that someone was killed here?" Volodya inquired with concern in his voice.
"I'm not sure, Volodya. I mean . . . it's disturbing and terrible . . . but I don't think it involves me. At least I hope not. I'm a little afraid. *Is this somehow connected to my suitcase?* she wondered. *God, I hope Tony returned my call.* "You're one of the few people I even know in Berlin. Who else knows I'm here?"
"You can always come with me to my place and stay there for tonight."
"Thanks, but I think I'll be okay here. It looks like the Polizei are everywhere. We should get off the street though."

◆

Volodya walked Iza to the door of her apartment. He felt as though he'd been holding his breath up all three flights of stairs in anticipation. *Volodya, you must have courage,* he thought. "Iza, can I see you again?" he asked quietly, still a little fearful that she'd say no.

To his relief, Iza smiled brightly. "I hope so! I'll give you my phone number, and could I have yours too?" Volodya took the receipt for his tuxedo rental from his pocket and tore it in two pieces. They exchanged cell phone numbers.

Volodya pressed, "Can I see you again on Sunday? I have work tomorrow."

"Let's text each other sometime tomorrow and plan what we should do."

Volodya ran his hand down Iza's cheek and then kissed her cheek. "Thank you for such fun evening. I have not enjoyed anything like this in long, *long* time."

Iza touched his hand and smiled as she stared into his searching brown eyes. "I haven't either."

He couldn't resist any longer; he put his hand behind her neck and pulled her close, kissing her lips. They stood kissing at her door until they were interrupted by the *klomp, klomp, klomp* of Frau Böhmer's shoes in the entryway below.

"I should let you go if you have work tomorrow. See you Sunday," Iza whispered. They broke apart and Volodya sprinted down the stairway, quietly singing "The Night Is So Moonlit," one of his favorite Ukrainian love songs, in his deep, pure voice as he quickly exited the building.

As Iza tucked her shoes beneath the bed and then hung her dress in the armoire, she thought, *Well, that was unexpected. What a cool guy! I've never met anyone like him. He's so fun and so sweet.* She quickly washed up in the bathroom and brushed her hair, smiling at the memory of Volodya's touch as they waltzed. *I'm like hugely attracted to him. I hope he really does text me tomorrow.*

Then she felt a sudden pang of guilt. *I'll bet this isn't how Claire thought I'd be spending my evening though. I probably should have circulated in the crowd and introduced myself to people. But,* she rationalized, *I'm terrible at doing that, so I guess I wouldn't have done a lot of mixing, even if I hadn't met Volodya.*

That's not a good excuse, Iza, her conscience scolded.

There was no message from Tony.

Saturday, October 15 (Day 4)

Volodya left Iza at her apartment door after 1:00. *Volodya, you are seriously in love with this girl. She is who you have been looking for. Maybe God changed your bad luck to good tonight.* By the time he'd walked back to his apartment in the Kreuzberg neighborhood, it was nearly 2:00. He had to be at work by 7:00 for the daily briefing. He'd *never* missed a briefing.

Volodya was so tired that he didn't even shower before bed. He set his alarm for 5:30. Thinking ahead that he might oversleep the alarm, he wore his work jeans and shirt to bed. He left his leather jacket and wallet on a kitchen chair and his cell phone on the table nearby.

When the alarm sounded, Volodya awoke with a pounding headache. He didn't recall having had that much to drink and wondered if he could be dehydrated. He decided to sleep for a few more minutes, but when he next looked at the clock, it was nearly 7:15—he was late for work!

Volodya jumped from the bed, grabbed his wallet, slipped on his running shoes and jacket, and ran out the door. When he was halfway down the staircase to the apartment exit, he turned and ran back up to his apartment. He picked up his cell phone from the kitchen table and was off again running. He briskly walked into the data center at 8:00.

Ten Americans, five Germans, and three Ukrainians were on "the Team." The three Ukrainian members were Volodya, Petro Yurchenko, and the commander, Dmytro Melnik.

Everything about Dmytro Melnik was big, except his height. Dmytro had a big personality, a booming voice, a raucous laugh, an impressive girth, and a stellar resume. Volodya and Petro revered him, even though he often came across as brutish. He could be brutish if he thought that the other members of the Team were not being fair to "his guys." He was middle-aged with short, dark hair that was graying at his temples. Dmytro was a brilliant programmer. He'd run his own successful programming firm in Kyiv until the war began. He temporarily left his wife and two teenagers in Kyiv to work on the Team.

Petro was thirty-five, married with a newborn son, and had been an artificial intelligence programmer for the most advanced and well-known grain-export transportation firm in Odesa. He sent his wife and son to live in Berlin when the war started. The opportunity to work on the Team meant that he could reunite with his family in Berlin, which he was thankful for. Petro was tall, quiet, and studious.

Although Volodya had the most formal education of the three, he had the least practical experience. He had only graduated shortly before the war began. His work with the Team was his first full-time job, and he was the youngest member of the entire Team. Of the three Ukrainians, he was the only one to have any real military experience.

The Team as a whole did their work together in English, but the Ukrainians and the Germans spoke in their native languages when talking amongst themselves. The Ukrainians were especially animated and often bantered good-naturedly back and forth in Ukrainian at the start of the workday or when they took a break together. As Dmytro explained to Petro and Volodya, "Sometimes it is useful *not* to be understood."

After Volodya signed in at the data center security desk, he grabbed two bottles of water from the canteen and flew into his workstation chair. He had barely hit the seat when Dmytro hollered out to him in Ukrainian from across the room, "Fuck you, Volodya, you are late. You missed briefing."

Usually, Volodya was passive around Dmytro, but this time he yelled in his direction, "Fuck you back, Dmytro." Petro stopped working, sat back in his chair, and grinned.

Dmytro strode over to Volodya's chair. "Is that any way to talk to your commanding officer?"

Volodya remained seated with his back to Dmytro and responded loudly, "It *is* when commanding officer fails to notice his subordinate was wounded in line of duty." Dmytro looked surprised. Petro was now chuckling at his workstation.

"And how were you wounded, soldier?"

Volodya stood up and faced Dmytro, saluting and responding, "You forget your subordinate attended embassy dinner on your behalf last night."

Dmytro looked Volodya up and down and burst into raucous laughter. Volodya's uncombed hair was tangled, oily, and matted on the side he'd slept on. His eyes were bloodshot and watery; his eyelids and upper cheeks were swollen. His wrinkled clothes had obviously been slept in; his shirt was only half tucked into his pants, he'd forgotten his belt, and his running shoes were untied. By this time, Petro was now laughing loudly too.

"Volodya, so how was party?" Dmytro asked in a severe tone as he edged nearer to Volodya's face while trying not to laugh.

"It was fun, sir," Volodya shot back, now slyly grinning at Dmytro. He knew Dmytro had expected the embassy dinner to be boring and that he'd been glad he didn't have to attend.

Dmytro looked surprised. "Really?"

Volodya responded, "*Really*."

Then Dmytro shook his head, laughed loudly again, and left Volodya with a stack of satellite images.

"Did you meet girl at dinner?" Petro whispered to Volodya with a wink. "You would not look like *this* if you sat at stuffy embassy dinner with our ambassador's staff person."

Volodya raised his eyebrows and shrugged, pressing his lips together in a suppressed smile. He and Petro went to work marking and analyzing images.

One of the American Team members sitting nearby shook his head, having no idea what had been said. "Crazy Ukrainians."

◆

At 10:00, everyone on the Team took a short break. They weren't allowed to smoke, eat, or drink anything other than water in the main work areas. There was also a ban on personal cell phone use. There was always a rush to the canteen or to the outdoor courtyard of the data center building at break times.

Volodya walked outside. He wanted to send Iza a clever text message, but he couldn't think of what to write. Although, in general, he didn't like to use emojis, he finally decided to simply send her a smiling face. Then he went back to his stack of images.

Iza awoke later than usual. She'd fallen asleep quickly but then woke up two hours later in a sweat. After that, she'd only slept intermittently. *I can't recall drinking that much wine,* she thought in the morning, *but it sure feels like I did. I'll go for a run to clear my head.*

On her run, she thought about what she could do with Volodya on Sunday . . . *if* he called or texted her as promised. *We could run together on the Tiergarten trails. I could make an "American-style" brunch—he said he likes to eat. Or I could reserve us art museum tickets—maybe to the Gemäldegalerie and the Urban Nation Museum. Or we could have dinner together.*

And why hasn't Tony called me? she wondered as a squad car passed by. *At least the Polizei are everywhere around my building today doing their investigation. I feel pretty safe for now.*

She showered after her run, and just as she finished wrapping her hair in a towel, an incoming text message pinged on her phone. She saw the smiling face emoji from Volodya and grinned. She sent back a winking smiling face emoji and SUNDAY?, eager for his response. At noon, she got another text from Volodya asking if she could plan something fun for them to do on Sunday. He wrote that any time, even the entire

day, was good for him. After going back and forth, they decided they'd meet at Iza's apartment at 8:00. Volodya promised to make chicken soup with galushki—a recipe his mom always made—for supper. They'd spend the entire day together.
    At 12:30, she left another message for Tony.

Much to Dmytro's and Volodya's delight, Petro's wife, Iryna, had baked loaves of a traditional Ukrainian rye sourdough bread for each of them. Petro gave them the loaves when they went to eat in the canteen at noon. Volodya decided to save his loaf for his dinner with Iza on Sunday, even though he was extremely hungry. He hadn't had time to pack a lunch, and there was no food available in the canteen. He didn't have the time or money to go to any nearby restaurants to eat.
    At 16:00, the Team leader, Lloyd T. Austin, told everyone to call it a day. Volodya stopped at a market on the way home and purchased the ingredients he'd need for the soup. He was too tired to prepare anything to eat, so he ate an apple for his supper.

At 16:00, Iza heard her phone ping, signaling another incoming text. It was her mom, Elise. HOW R U? Iza wondered aloud, "Do you really care, mom? Do any of you care? I haven't heard from you since you left for Vermont with your awful boyfriend, Günther. I left Tony three messages, and he hasn't called back. I'm alone and I'm scared." But she texted LOVE YOU, MOM, along with a heart emoji. There was no further response from her mom—or Tony.

Sunday, October 16 (Day 5)

Volodya knocked on Iza's apartment door at precisely 8:00 on Sunday, after waiting ten minutes in the entryway of her building to avoid arriving early. "Whoa, let me help you!" she said as she opened the door. He was carrying a soup pot, two totes of groceries, and his gym duffel bag.

He handed Iza the soup pot and carried in the totes and duffel bag. "How are you today, Iza?" he asked, flashing a broad smile. *You look even prettier in your running shorts and long-sleeved T-shirt than you did on Friday*, he thought as he brought the totes into the kitchen and emptied them on the table. Chicken, onions, carrots, dill, and white wine went into the small refrigerator in the kitchen. The galushki and Iryna's rye sourdough bread were moved to the counter. Vodka went into the freezer.

"I feel so much better today than yesterday. I didn't think we drank that much wine on Friday, but my head told me otherwise yesterday."

"Yes, my head was pounding yesterday too. I did not have most productive day at work." Volodya said as he changed into his running clothes. "I only had time to eat apple yesterday. I admit I am looking forward to breakfast more than our run." Once he was ready, they immediately left the apartment for the Tiergarten trails.

Volodya remembered that Iza had mentioned she was a "pretty good" runner at the embassy dinner on Friday, but he suspected she was probably more than pretty good since American University had paid for her schooling based on her athletic ability. He enjoyed running but hadn't been able to keep up a consistent training schedule since his deployment to Kharkiv Oblast. During his military training, he'd run the fastest of his trainee class while wearing full gear, but that was different than running for exercise and pleasure. Iza had mapped out a ten-kilometer route that began at the Brandenburg Gate and made a figure-eight loop through the park. They also had to run about two kilometers from her apartment to the Gate and then back.

It didn't take long for Volodya to confirm his suspicion that Iza was a gifted runner. While he was starting to feel winded, she didn't seem to be breathing hard at all. He checked his watch and saw they were on a four minute per kilometer pace. She seemed to be quite a competitive runner, too. Whenever he felt like he was getting into a rhythm, Iza would increase the pace. There was no talking; he had to concentrate on keeping up with Iza while she was running in her own little world. When he finally felt sure trying to match her pace would kill him, they made the turn out of the park back toward Iza's apartment.

Iza called out, "Let's slow our pace for the return run so we can talk."

Volodya responded while breathing heavily, "Maybe then I will live long enough to enjoy your breakfast." They both laughed. He was visibly dragging by the time they turned onto the street to her apartment. "You are more than pretty good runner, Iza, I think," Volodya called out to her.

When they reached the base of the stairs to her apartment, Iza shouted, "Last one to the apartment does the dishes!" as she sprinted up the stairs. Reinvigorated by the challenge, Volodya started running up the stairs after her, but he immediately clutched his hamstring and called out in pain. Iza wheeled around and ran back down the stairs. "Are you okay?" she asked in a concerned voice. Then Volodya suddenly sprinted up the stairs ahead of her. "Mr. Korsun, you're disqualified; you're cheating!" Iza yelled after him as she sprinted up behind him. "No fair," she hollered up the stairs in protest.

"You did not say there were rules to this game," Volodya hollered back down the stairs at her. He was laughing and panting at her apartment door when Iza reached him. She giggled as she caught her breath but wasn't nearly as winded as he was. He grabbed her and kissed her cheek.

"Mr. Korsun, getting sweet with the judge will *not* change the ruling that you cheated. You're disqualified."

"But you did not say there were any rules," he protested.

She glared at him, then started laughing. "Smart move, Mr. Korsun. Playing on my sympathy. Grrr," she growled at him.

"Iza, what does 'getting sweet' mean?"

"Sorry. It's slang. It means you're attracted to me—you know, like romantically—but in this case, you're just pretending to be so I don't disqualify you."

"What if it is true?"

Iza looked intently at Volodya for a moment, then started laughing, not knowing quite how to respond. *I'm so attracted to you, but do you really feel the same way about me? You're probably just being funny. It'd be so awkward if I responded and you didn't really mean it that way.* She decided he was just being funny and playfully pushed him out of the way to unlock the door.

As she opened the door, the two of them fought to get into the apartment first. The moment slipped away as they both stumbled inside, neither the clear winner of that round.

Iza showered quickly so she could begin preparing breakfast, but she couldn't stop thinking about the way Volodya had looked at her after their race up the stairs. *I wonder if he really could be attracted to me?* She smiled to herself as she recalled the way Volodya had kissed her after the dinner-and-dance. *Oh, Iza, what are you thinking? You're acting like a lovestruck teenager when you should be a serious adult.* She shook her head to try to refocus her thoughts. *But, I honestly can't help it. There's something about him that's so alluring.*

Volodya started the soup preparation while Iza was in the shower, and then he showered while she prepared their breakfast. When he came out of the bathroom, the apartment was filled with the delicious aromas of Denver omelets, oven-toasted sourdough bread, and speck, because Iza hadn't been able to find any American-style bacon.

Iza was wearing a loose-fitting, pale greenish-yellow pullover, jeans, and a pair of distinctive teardrop earrings. Volodya noticed them and asked, "Iza, what is stone in your earrings? They are beautiful."

"The stones are citrine; it's a form of quartz. Roger gave me these earrings when I graduated earlier this year. He said citrine is a symbol of happiness and positivity, and that's how he thinks of me. I was so touched. When you meet Roger, you'll see he doesn't seem like the kind of guy who would be so thoughtful. He's *always* joking around. But he really is a good, kind man." *Why did I just blurt out that he'll get to meet Roger?* Iza wondered in embarrassment, hoping Volodya hadn't noticed. *I have no idea if or when Roger will come visit me in Berlin. We'd have to be in a pretty serious relationship for Volodya to fly home to D.C. with me. Come on, Iza—get your head out of the clouds!*

As they ate, they talked about their experiences moving abroad, and Iza debated whether or not to bring up all the weird things that had happened since she'd arrived in Berlin. Volodya seemed like someone she could confide in, but she didn't want him to think she was paranoid or overly dramatic. *But who knows when Tony might call me back?* she thought.

"Volodya, there's something I didn't tell you about since we just met on Friday and it didn't seem appropriate," she said tentatively. "And maybe it isn't even appropriate now, but I called my friend Tony about it, and he hasn't called back. I'm actually scared."

"You can tell me. What is it?"

"When I got off the plane in Berlin, I didn't get to the luggage carousel right away. When I did, I saw a man with *my* open suitcase in a corner near the carousel. He was going through it like he was searching for something. All my stuff was on the floor. I yelled, and he ran away. I would have chased him, except all my things were laying out on the airport floor. When I repacked, I realized he hadn't taken anything and he didn't put anything in my suitcase either.

"Then on Thursday, when I came back here around sunset after shopping, I thought I saw the same man outside my building, but I wasn't sure. The man was talking to someone in a car, and when the car drove away, I saw it had a diplomatic license plate. I looked it up, and the car was from the Russian Embassy. Then Friday night . . . well, you already know someone was murdered outside my building. That was only half an hour before we got here. We could have been caught up in whatever happened. I don't know if these incidents are at all related, but I'm worried. Does that sound crazy?"

"No, not crazy at all. I understand why you are worried." His serious expression made Iza feel both relieved and anxious. "Sure, it could be all things that are independent of each other and maybe only airport incident involved you. Even that might have innocent explanation. But if not, then there is reason to be scared. I would be scared. Anything that involves Russia these days scares me.

"I think we can go to museums today and eat here early before it is too dark. Then maybe you should not stay here after dark and maybe not until you talk to your friend Tony. He could help us figure out who is man murdered outside your apartment, since Tony probably has contacts in German security agencies. We can make plans while we look at museums today, okay?"

"Honestly, I don't expect you to get involved with any of this. I just needed to tell someone who'd actually take me seriously. Thank you for listening."

"Iza, I will help you. I promise you."

◆

They arrived at the Gemäldegalerie just before the 11:00 opening time. Volodya could tell that Iza was looking forward to touring this museum by how happily she raved about it on the walk there.

"The Galerie is one of the top galleries in the world for European paintings from the thirteenth through eighteenth centuries, spanning everything from early German works, Rembrandt and the Dutch Golden Age to the Italian Renaissance. Most museums in the world would be happy to have even one of the paintings on display here. We'll see *sixteen* Rembrandt paintings, although my favorite isn't in this museum. I've never actually seen my favorite Rembrandt in person—the latter of Rembrandt's two paintings of Lucretia, exhibited in the Minneapolis Institute of Art in the U.S. I studied that painting in detail in one of my undergraduate art-history courses."

"Why is this painting your favorite Rembrandt?"

"I don't actually know why; maybe it's because Lucretia committed suicide to defend her honor. The painting shows her just after she stabbed herself in her heart. She's still holding the dagger. It's a beautiful painting."

Iza and Volodya spent almost three hours touring the Galerie before they realized the time and hurried to visit the Urban Nation Museum.

On the way there, Volodya said, "Iza, I think you will come with me to my apartment after our dinner. You can stay at my place until we figure out if you are safe at your apartment. You can pack for few days, we will eat, and then we can leave just when it turns dark so no one will see us."

"You're so kind, but I can't do that. I can stay at my place. I'm probably just overreacting. Although, I felt a little better about staying there yesterday while the *Polizei* were still around doing their investigation. They're gone today. But, I'll call Tony again tomorrow. I'm sure there's a good reason I haven't heard from him."

"We will see tonight; you can still decide to come with me."

◆

They liked much of the contemporary art and graffiti on display in the museum but were getting tired of touring until they came upon a collaborative exhibit that invited visitors to add their own contributions to a wall mural. Iza and Volodya stood close together for quite a while as they discussed what they would add. They finally decided to paint a hand in a tight fist but giving the peace sign overlaying the Ukrainian flag. Iza sketched out the fist, fingers, and flag outline on their allotted portion of the mural and then expertly colored the hand, graffiti style. Volodya spent most of that time finding the correct colors for painting the Ukrainian flag. When he finally returned to where Iza was working, he was impressed.

"Wow, Iza! I thought you said you had no talent for art."

"I've done a little drawing and painting in the past. I'm not Rembrandt though."

"But you *do* have talent, and you do not need to be another Rembrandt. *I* am impressed!"

"I suppose I shouldn't use Rembrandt as my standard, but that's just the way I'm wired. You know—I never think I'm good enough—at anything, actually. It's sort of how I was brought up—at least after my dad wasn't around any longer. He used to be my biggest fan."

"Maybe I can be your biggest fan now," he replied as he looked into her eyes. Before she could reply, he questioned, "What does 'way I'm wired' mean? Is that way to say it is your personality?"

"Yeah. It's like my brain is a network of computers and there are all these chips and wires and cables inside that make me think the way I do."

"Then we need to reprogram your computer so you understand that you are special just way you are."

She grabbed a paintbrush from him and smiled.

They painted broad brush strokes of blue and golden yellow to fill the flag outline that she'd sketched behind the hand. They stood back and looked proudly at their work of art. A passing couple stopped and applauded them. Iza and Volodya took a selfie smiling in front of their artwork. Volodya said, "I do not like selfies, but *this* one I like. If I had anyone to send it to, I would." It was nearly 17:00 when they walked back to Iza's apartment; Volodya again took Iza's hand and held it as they walked.

◆

Excited yet tired from their long day, they ate the delicious soup with large pieces of bread slathered with butter and drank vodka and water. They talked nonstop about the paintings and their graffiti artwork. Afterward, as Iza cleared the dishes, Volodya packed a tote and his duffel bag, placing them on the kitchen table. It was just after civil twilight, and he was about to plead again with Iza to pack and come with him when her apartment suddenly went dark.

"Oh!" Iza looked out the kitchen window. "That's interesting. The other buildings around here all have lights on. It must be something in this building."

"Hmm, my phone battery is low; I have no flashlight. Maybe power outage will not take long to fix." The street lamp outside the building dimly illuminated the kitchen. The living area was in complete darkness. They each felt their way toward the entry door and listened. They could hear Frau Böhmer and a downstairs neighbor talking animatedly, although Iza couldn't hear what was being said, and Volodya didn't understand German. The conversation grew quiet, and they heard the *klomp, klomp, klomp* of Frau Böhmer's shoes fading away. Then they heard the heavy footsteps of someone slowly ascending the stairs. Iza wanted to open the door to see who was coming, but Volodya instinctively held her back. It could be nothing—only a neighbor—but he felt a wave of fear wash over him. Volodya whispered to Iza, "Is there somewhere you can hide?"

Iza responded almost inaudibly, "Under the bed?" Her eyes had adjusted to the darkness, and she saw him shake his head no. "Kitchen broom closet?" He touched her hand to signal her to go. She quietly slipped back into the kitchen, grabbed her paring knife from the counter, and squeezed into the broom closet, pulling the door closed behind her.

Volodya heard a scratching sound in the entry door lock, but it was not the sound of a key. He could hear a tensioner wrench and a rake working to pick the lock. Whoever was on the other side of the door knew what they were doing. He hoped whoever it was *didn't* know that he and Iza were in the apartment. It was incredibly dark near the entry door, and Volodya decided to move behind the door when it opened so that he could assess the situation before charging the intruder. He heard the lock pop, and the door slowly creaked open.

The light from a flashlight illuminated the living area sofa and shelving. Volodya could see the outline of a very tall man stepping slowly into the apartment. The man left the door partially open. The flashlight now scanned the shelving near the sofa. Iza had no other furniture or decoration in the room yet. Volodya guessed that the man was more than two meters tall, and his upper body appeared large and powerful. Volodya quickly decided he wasn't strong enough to fight the intruder, so he remained in the shadow of the entry door and watched.

The man trained the flashlight toward the kitchen and bathroom but seemed uninterested in those rooms, instead stepping slowly forward into the bedroom. It was dark again in the living area, giving Volodya time for his eyes to readjust. He could hear the man rummaging through the armoire in Iza's bedroom. He heard the thunk of her laptop dropping onto the bedroom floor, then the sound of papers being strewn about. He could also hear Frau Böhmer hollering something indistinctly from below.

Suddenly, the lights in the kitchen and bedroom came on. The rest of the apartment remained cloaked in darkness. Volodya slipped back behind the entry door. He could hear Frau Böhmer calling indistinctly to her tenants from below, presumably letting everyone know that the electricity was restored.

The man walked briskly out of the bedroom and exited the apartment, slamming the door closed behind him. Volodya breathed a sigh of relief that the man hadn't noticed him hiding behind the door. He could hear the man's heavy footsteps as he ran down the stairway. Volodya slid down the wall near the door and locked it. He crawled to the kitchen and turned off the light, letting his eyes readjust to the dim light, then crawled to the broom closet and quietly called out to Iza, letting her know it was safe to come out. She crept out of the closet, knife still in hand, and saw Volodya on the floor. She quickly joined him on the floor, and they held each other close.

Iza whispered, "A thief?"

Volodya shook his head. "I do not know. Come with me to bedroom. I thought about confronting that guy, but he looked much bigger and stronger than me. I think I would have met my end with him."

Iza's clothing and work papers were strewn about the bedroom floor. They sat cross-legged on the floor near the side of the bed next to the lamp. Iza checked her wallet, but nothing was taken. Her new work laptop and phone lay on the floor. Volodya wondered aloud, "What kind of thief comes to apartment like yours? Would guy not observe that your neighbors have more to steal than you do? What kind of thief leaves your money, your phone, your laptop?"

Iza shook her head. "I don't understand either, Volodya. This is the second time someone has searched my stuff without taking anything. Why?"

Volodya's eyes opened wide as he put his arm around Iza's shoulder. "Iza," he said in a very serious tone, "you *have* to get out of here, honestly. Maybe you have something you do not know about, and these guys want it. We can think about that later. You should not stay here tonight and maybe not for long while. That guy may come back."

"But where will I go? I don't have the money to stay in a hotel."

"You will come to my place, like I said earlier."

"No! I don't know what's happening, but *you* can't be involved. I don't want you hurt because of me. That man could have *killed* you!"

Volodya refused to listen. "No more lights on, in case someone is watching apartment right now," he ordered sternly. "I do not think so because that guy did not know we were here, but maybe someone is out there. Get your toiletries, laptop, phone, papers, and clothes for few days." He started picking up her papers and laptop and retrieved her phone. Iza hurriedly stuffed her toiletries and some of her clothing into shopping tote bags.

"Is there another way out of this building besides front door?" Volodya asked.

"When I moved in, Frau Böhmer showed me. There's a basement passageway connecting this building to the one next door. I used it once. The entrance to that building is on the opposite street."

"Come quick then. We need to go!"

They took their things and followed the passageway to the adjoining building. They walked cautiously toward the sidewalk, then continued down the street as if they were a young couple returning from a shopping trip.

Volodya's apartment was modest, with a single small bedroom, a combined living/kitchen/dining area, and a tiny bathroom featuring a pedestal sink, small mirror, a toilet, and a small shower stall, His furnishings were sparse. The kitchen/dining area had only a tiny table and two worn and discolored vinyl-covered chairs. The living space had a long, deep sofa decorated with multiple colorful pillows of various sizes and shapes. There was a shelf across from the sofa where Volodya had an old receiver, a CD player, two small speakers, and a stack of CDs. There were two piles of history books on the floor near the shelf. The small bedroom had a large bed and a small armoire for clothing storage; there was room for little else.

Volodya went to the bedroom and tossed his clothing from the small armoire onto the floor.

"Iza, put your clothing into armoire."

"No. I don't want you to throw your stuff on the floor."

"You can sleep in my bed, and I will sleep on sofa."

He left Iza in his bedroom, then lay on his side on the sofa, still wearing his clothes, tossed some of the throw pillows over himself for warmth, and immediately fell soundly asleep.

Iza put on her nightshirt. It was 22:00. She curled up on Volodya's bed under the comforter but felt cold and afraid. Her mind was racing. *What could I have that would make someone break into my apartment? Who was the man searching through my luggage? Is there any connection to the man murdered outside my apartment on Friday night? What are they looking for? Who can I ask for help? Why isn't Tony calling me back?* All these questions kept running through her head as she tossed and turned, unable to sleep.

She finally walked into the living area, hoping that Volodya might be awake so she could assuage her fears by talking to him. But in the dim light from the window, she saw that Volodya was sleeping peacefully on the sofa. He didn't have a comforter to keep warm, and she saw that he'd stacked the throw pillows atop himself. Iza dragged the comforter from the bed to the sofa and carefully removed the pillows surrounding him, covered him with the comforter, then lay down beside him on the sofa, pulling half the comforter around herself. She slipped his arm around her waist. The sound of his regular breathing and the nearness of his warm body finally lulled her to sleep.

Monday, October 17 (Day 6)

Volodya woke up with a start at 5:00. He hadn't moved his position the entire night. His neck was stiff, and his shoulder was sore. He suddenly realized that Iza was lying next to him on the sofa. Her hair had fallen gently onto his face and shoulder, and her warm body touched his. His arm was around her waist—his hand touching her abdomen. He could feel through her nightshirt that she was naked underneath. He could also feel himself getting aroused. *Volodya, this cannot happen!* Extricating himself from Iza as gently as possible, he rolled over her body onto the floor with a loud thud. While changing into a shirt that wasn't quite as wrinkled as the one he'd just slept in—his cleanest dirty shirt pulled from a pile on the bedroom floor—he moved into the kitchen to make strong coffee for the two of them.

Iza awoke slowly, wondering where she was. She smelled coffee and sat up, wrapping herself in the comforter. Volodya smiled at her and handed her a steaming mug. "Thank you," she said, smiling warmly back at him. "I'm sorry I didn't sleep in the bed last night; I hope I didn't disturb you. I couldn't sleep. I was *so* cold and afraid. I promise I won't do that again."

"It is okay, Iza," Volodya replied as he sat next to her. "Last evening was stressful for both of us. I was so tired . . . I forgot you were here when I first waked up. Now we need to make plans for today."

Iza looked imploringly at Volodya. "You don't have to help me, Volodya. You don't need to be involved. I don't know what this is all about. But for sure, I don't want you to get hurt."

Volodya set his coffee mug on the floor next to the sofa and spoke quietly as he caressed Iza's cheek. "Iza, you tell me that guy Roger says you are too independent, yes? You are being too independent. Two people can figure this out better than one. I can help you, and I *want* to help you." Volodya hesitated for a moment, then continued sincerely, "Iza, in these couple days, I learn that I care for you very much. Please . . . let us end this discussion. We need to make plans for today before I go for work."

Iza set down her coffee mug and held Volodya's hand between hers. Her eyes teared up. "I care a lot for you too. You're a kind man, Volodya." She got up from the sofa and returned with paper and a pen to take notes.

"I remember the face of the airport man so well, but how do we figure out who he is? He was short and heavyset too."

"Then he could not have been guy at your apartment last night because that guy was really tall. He was not heavy, but had broad, muscular shoulders. I think guy was over two meters tall. He probably weighed hundred or hundred ten kilos compared to my sixty-two." He paused briefly, then said, "You know, Iza, maybe we can figure out who airport man is. If he was at luggage area between Passport Control and Customs, he had to be on incoming flight, right? Otherwise, he could not be in there."

"Yeah, you're right. He had to come in on an incoming flight that landed before noon last Wednesday. I'll bet airlines have to keep flight manifests with passenger names for some period of time. And, I wonder if international flights keep track of passport photos."

"Can your friend Tony find out for us?"

"Well, probably, if he ever returns my calls. I'll try calling him again today."

"And what about man murdered outside your apartment building on Friday. In Consular Affairs, I assume you have to help Americans if someone is injured or killed here. Does

Claire know contact from Berlin Polizei who could help? That dead guy probably wasn't American, but maybe same contact could help with information on who he was."

"I'll tell Claire I need the information as a favor for my landlady. I'll call Frau Böhmer late in the day and tell her I had to go out of town for the embassy for a few days too. Maybe she'll watch my apartment."

"Then I will go after work to your apartment building and look for security surveillance equipment. You said there is camera near entry door. I will look for video recorder if it is stored in building. Maybe I can steal security footage to learn more about this tall guy from last night."

"Should I go to the Polizei and report the break-in? The man didn't take anything, but I just don't think it could have been at random that he showed up at my apartment and went searching through my stuff."

Volodya hesitated, and Iza immediately sensed his unease at the mention of the Polizei. "I think you will need to ask your friend Tony for his advice," he said, then quickly changed the subject. "And Iza, maybe someone watches for you at embassy when you leave there. Since we do not know if these guys know who you are or where you work, you need to be careful when you leave embassy and come back here. No one should follow you."

With their action list agreed upon, Volodya gave Iza the extra key to his apartment and left for work.

Iza dressed hurriedly and was en route to the embassy by 7:30. *Why am I feeling so upbeat when I should be feeling angst?* she wondered. *I must be crazy.* Then she realized it was because Volodya had confessed that he cared for her. She cared for him too. *Is it possible for two people to fall in love in like two days? I've never felt such an intense connection with anyone before.*

◆

Iza had barely removed her jacket when Claire appeared in her office doorway.

"How's your son, Claire?"

Claire laughed. "It was a stressful night on Friday. Sometimes I wonder why I had a kid. Since Sunday morning, he's been running around like the wild child he is." Iza grinned.

"How was the Embassy dinner?" Claire inquired apologetically.

"I met a few interesting people at the dinner, particularly a man from the Ukrainian Embassy. It was informative to learn about Ukraine from his perspective," Iza replied not quite truthfully. *I can't exactly tell her I didn't even try to socialize with anyone else there, like I undoubtedly should have,* she thought. *Claire probably wouldn't be too happy with me if she knew I just spent the whole night dancing and drinking with a cool Ukrainian guy I met there instead—who I slept with on his sofa last night and might be in love with. Oh Iza, what are you doing?*

Claire's voice shook Iza out of her reverie. "Iza, I want to show you how we process visa applications for Ukrainians who want temporary parole in the U.S."

"May I ask a favor first?"

"Of course."

"On Friday night a man was murdered just outside my apartment building—only thirty minutes before I returned there from the embassy event. My landlady hasn't been able to learn anything from the police about the circumstances, and she's obviously concerned. I am too. If I'd arrived home a half hour earlier, I might have been caught up in whatever happened there. Is there a way to find out any information about the incident using our embassy connections?"

Claire thought for a moment. "This'll be a good challenge for you. We typically help U.S. citizens injured in Germany or assist family members of U.S. citizens who die here. As a start, I'll give you my contacts at the Berlin Bundeskriminalamt and the Berlin Polizei. Look up the procedures to follow in the new-employee manual I gave you. And remember, if this doesn't involve a U.S. citizen, they don't have to give you any information. So, don't be disappointed. I'll check back with you for lunch; I hope you'll join me. Then this afternoon, I'll show you how we process those visa applications for Ukrainians who want temporary parole in the U.S."

"Thanks so much, Claire." Soon after Claire left her office, Iza received an email from her with the contact information for the Berlin BKA and Polizei.

First, Iza decided to call the Berlin Polizei office of Gerhard Hoffman. She introduced herself as an employee of the U.S. Embassy working for Claire Daniels but realized that he somehow already knew from the phone connection that she was calling from a secure U.S. Embassy phone line. She made her inquiry.

"Yes, Frau Carter," he confirmed, "my department has been investigating the murder. Unfortunately, I cannot supply you with additional details. I am quite sorry. Perhaps you should contact the Berlin Bundeskriminalamt instead."

Iza expressed her disappointment. In the ensuing silence, she could sense that Gerhard wanted to tell her more. She prodded further, "Are you sure there isn't *anything* you can tell me about the murder?"

Gerhard sighed loudly into the phone and offered, "The man was a German citizen; the case investigation is sealed for security reasons. I'm sorry, but even that is more than I *should* tell you." With that, Gerhard hung up. Iza was stunned by his disclosure—a sealed investigation for security reasons!

She quickly dialed the direct line to the Berlin BKA office of Wilhelm Kühn. He answered immediately. "My name is Iza Carter. I'm an employee of the U.S. Embassy here in Berlin, and I'm calling on behalf of our Assistant Secretary of State, Tony Brooks. He's interested in learning the circumstances surrounding the murder of a German citizen in the Mitte borough on Friday night, wherein the investigative details are sealed for security reasons. Tony authorized me to meet with you to discuss the case and report back to him. Is it possible to set up a meeting time this week?"

There was a long silence on the line. Herr Kühn asked her for her name again, and Iza could hear him, presumably, writing it down. "Iza Carter," he replied, "Tony Brooks is a good friend of mine. But I will need to consider this request. I will get back to you in a few days." She thanked him and hung up. *I'm a total fool! Tony will either fire me or kill me—maybe both—if he ever finds out I used his name like this.*

◆

Following lunch, Claire explained the embassy procedure for processing Ukrainian visa applications, and Iza launched excitedly into the task.

She dialed Frau Böhmer while on her afternoon break from processing applications. Frau Böhmer sounded delighted to help Iza by keeping a watchful eye on her apartment. Iza also informed Frau Böhmer that she'd inquired about the man murdered in front of her apartment building on Friday night and that more information about the man's identity might be forthcoming.

The embassy closed at 17:30, and Iza returned to her office to place another call to Tony. He didn't answer. She left a message informing him of the break-in at her apartment. She also inquired about getting flight manifests to possibly identify the man who'd searched her suitcase at the airport, and begged him to return her call as soon as possible.

Iza returned to Volodya's apartment, taking a circuitous route. She purchased spaghetti, a jar of sauce, and a prepackaged salad for their supper at a grocer along the way; they wouldn't have much time for cooking this evening.

Volodya and Petro had a productive day, analyzing hundreds of images to identify the coordinates of several vital targets for the Ukrainian military. It was nearly 17:00 when Lloyd called it a day for the Team.

Volodya verified that sunset was at 18:12 and that civil twilight ended at 18:48. He grabbed a large paper clip from his workstation before departing and reconfirmed that he had his Swiss Army tool. Before catching the S-Bahn to the vicinity of Iza's apartment, he stopped at a tobacco store and purchased a pack of cigarettes and a lighter. He strolled the remaining distance to her apartment, arriving shortly before sunset.

As he leaned against the wall of the apartment building across the street and a few doors down from Iza's building, Volodya took out a cigarette and lit it. He had only smoked a few times and didn't like it, but it was a necessary action this evening. He was trying to look inconspicuous, like a guy whose wife had sent him to smoke outdoors instead of in their apartment. He scanned the street in both directions from Iza's apartment.

It was a beautiful, warm mid-October evening when most people would want to enjoy the fresh air outdoors before dark. He watched carefully for anything out of the ordinary and lit another cigarette. It was nearly 18:40 when he noticed the faint glow of a cigarette on the driver's side of a sedan parked along the street among a long line of cars. It seemed unusual for a person to be sitting alone in a parked vehicle on such a beautiful evening. Volodya didn't know for sure, but he suspected that someone in that vehicle was watching for Iza. He crushed out his cigarette and wandered toward Iza's apartment building.

He'd already observed the location of the security camera at the main entry. He'd worked for a summer installing commercial security systems while on break from his undergraduate computer studies in Kharkiv. He surmised that Frau Böhmer wouldn't have wanted the network video recorder stored inside her apartment. Then he remembered that he'd seen a laundry room near the downstairs passageway they had used to get out of the building Sunday evening. He'd noticed other closed doors farther down the hallway from the laundry. That would be the place he'd begin his search.

Volodya entered the building and observed a second interior security camera near the main entryway, then bounded down to the lower level. As he passed the laundry room, he checked inside; no one was there. There were two doors beyond the laundry. The clatter of utility equipment emanated from the first room. The second room was quiet, and it was locked. With his Swiss Army tool and paper clip in hand, he worked on picking the lock, stopping periodically to check if anyone was coming. Within minutes, the lock popped open, and he was in the room. Volodya felt along the wall until he found a light switch; a single bulb illuminated the tiny, warm room. Seeing the video recorder on a small desk inside, Volodya closed the door and locked himself in.

Frau Böhmer's system used artificial intelligence video-search technology, eliminating the need to scan through useless video footage. This search technology was rapidly becoming the standard for new commercial installations. By simply entering the date, the time range, and "tall man" onto the search screen, every frame of a tall man appeared. Volodya didn't take time to peruse the footage but downloaded it onto his phone.

Next, he deleted the footage of his own entrance into the building.

Now feeling lucky, Volodya began a search for the footage from Friday night—the night the man was murdered outside Iza's building. This search took a bit longer since he had neither a description of the man nor the exact timeframe when the man had been near the building. Volodya was getting warm and increasingly nervous in the tiny, enclosed space. He sat quietly when he heard someone walking down the corridor, but then, whoever it was entered the laundry area. The swoosh of a washing machine echoed in the hall. A "No results found" message popped up on the screen. The security footage from Friday evening into early Saturday morning was missing.

Just as Volodya exited the search screen, he heard the unmistakable *klomp, klomp, klomp* of Frau Böhmer's shoes in the basement corridor. She hollered out—perhaps in greeting to someone in the laundry room—and then the klomping continued past the laundry area. Already warm in his leather jacket, Volodya started sweating profusely. *Fuck,* he thought.

There is nowhere to hide in here. If she opens this door, what can I say to her? Fuck, I cannot say anything; I do not speak German! What will she do when she sees long-haired Ukrainian punk stealing her building security footage?

He listened as Frau Böhmer inserted a key into the lock and heard her heavy breathing on the other side of the door. With a loud click, the lock popped open. She was opening the door. Volodya's heart was racing as he breathed in deeply and held his breath, preparing for her entry. Then, he heard a sudden shriek from the corridor. Someone cried out to Frau Böhmer. She abruptly pulled the door closed and relocked it. Volodya heard the receding *klomp, klomp, klomp* of Frau Böhmer as she hollered something in German. He momentarily fell back into the chair, heaving a sigh of relief.

Volodya cautiously opened the door, then slipped out of the building through the passageway. As he quickly strode past the laundry room, he glanced inside and observed that a waterline had broken, and the floor in the laundry was flooding. Once outside, he threw the cigarettes and lighter in a trash bin, strolled a few blocks, then hopped the U-Bahn back to the area of his apartment. It was 19:45.

The salad was tossed, but Iza hadn't dropped the spaghetti into the pot of boiling water since she didn't know when Volodya would return. Shortly after he entered the apartment, she added the spaghetti and started heating up the sauce in a pan. The two discussed what they'd learned when Volodya saw the pasta water boil over.

"Ahh, shit, shit, shit!" Volodya yelled out as he instinctively grabbed the metal handle to slide the pot from the heat, burning the palm of his left hand. He put his hand under cold running water and grimaced in pain.

Iza watched with concern. "I've got some gel bandages I use for heel blisters and some bigger coverings too. I grabbed them last night with my stuff. Let me get them for your hand."

Once Volodya's palm was cool, Iza knelt and carefully dried the blistered area, covered it with the gel bandage, and then applied a larger bandage to protect the area. She kissed the back of Volodya's hand. "If I kiss it, it will be all better," she said with a grin.

Volodya smiled and kissed her cheek as he looked at her intently with his piercing brown eyes. "Thank you, Iza."

Iza suddenly stood, her lips pressed together. She said nothing as she looked raptly at Volodya, thinking, *I'm so scared with all this stuff going on, yet I've fallen madly in love with you. And your eyes . . . the way you look at me . . . I'm losing control of myself . . . and . . . I want to love you.*

"Is something wrong?"

She shook her head, then whispered almost inaudibly to herself, "I need to take a cold shower."

Volodya looked at her with surprise, not fully grasping what she'd faintly whispered. "Can you wait for shower? We should eat first."

Iza didn't answer. The spaghetti sauce spat onto the stovetop, and she dashed to pull the pan from the heat.

◆

It was 22:00. They looked at the images Volodya had loaded onto his phone. The security camera produced excellent-quality images; the exposure having adjusted well to the darkness of evening. They could see the tall man in more detail. They decided that he was over two meters tall, as Volodya had estimated. He was well-built, perhaps in his early- or mid-thirties, and with light blonde hair.

"So, what did we learn today? The murdered man was a German, and the details of his death investigation are sealed for security reasons. That means we're not going to read about his murder in the newspapers. There's probably someone watching for me at my apartment. And, we have a better description of the tall man from last night. Let's call him 'the tall, blonde man'. It's a good start," Iza said with a sigh.

"What if Frau Böhmer had opened door to see me stealing her security camera footage?"

Iza thought for a moment and burst out laughing. Then, realizing how late it was, she changed the subject. "Volodya, that sofa was not comfortable last night, and I really don't want you to sleep there again. But I don't want to sleep there either. Look here," she said as she pulled him by his uninjured hand into the bedroom. "I stacked the throw pillows down the center of the bed. Maybe we can both sleep in your bed. This could be my side of the bed, and that could be your side," she proposed.

"This might work. The sofa was not comfortable last night. My neck was stiff all day, and my shoulder hurt also." Volodya nodded his head affirmatively, as if he were carefully pondering her proposal. *But I do not think it will work for very long, Iza.*

Tuesday, October 18 (Day 7)

Volodya glanced over the pillow barrier and saw that Iza was still sleeping peacefully. He quietly slipped out of bed and selected a pair of jeans and a wrinkled shirt from the small pile of his clothing on the bedroom floor. *Later today, I really need to do laundry. We can discuss what she brought with her to Berlin while we are at laundromat. What does she have that these people want?*

Volodya arrived at the data center early and proceeded to the briefing room. He sat alone for a few minutes, pondering the events of the past evening. One of the American Team members, Bobby Scruggs, sauntered into the room and sat next to Volodya. Bobby was in his early forties, a lanky native Alabaman. Although Volodya often had difficulty understanding him because of his accent, he liked Bobby because he was always ready with a joke. He seemed like a happy guy. Volodya leaned over in his chair and asked, "Hey Bobby, I overheard some American guy say he needed to take cold shower. What does that mean?"

Just then, two other American Team members walked into the room. Bobby grinned from ear to ear, "Shit, y'all, that's funny." He leaned over and whispered in Volodya's ear.

Volodya's eyes opened wide in surprise, and he started laughing. "Really? That is funny." He and Bobby chuckled together while the other Team members slowly wandered in for the morning briefing. *Funny . . . but interesting.*

Dmytro led the briefing. After discussing the plan for the day, he shared that the Ukrainian military had had a major breakthrough in Russian defenses north of Kherson overnight. They were driving south. The news buoyed everyone's spirits.

◆

Claire sent Iza to assist Jack Malone, another Consular Affairs officer, for the day. He was to instruct Iza in interviewing U.S. passport applicants who'd been unable to use a mail-in application form for one reason or another.

Jack was in his mid-thirties, a friendly and patient man with a ready smile. While they waited for the first applicant to arrive, Jack mentioned that he and his wife had been living in Berlin for the past three years. They were originally natives of the Boston area. He and Iza got along well, discussing various topics during the short breaks between applicant interviews.

At their lunch break, Jack said, "If you ever need recommendations for fun stuff to do in Berlin or just outside of the city, let me know. Sarah and I made a list that I hand out to our new employees—at least those who show an interest."

"Unfortunately, I don't really have time to do anything right now, but maybe someday soon I will. We seem to share a lot of the same interests. I'll definitely ask for your list in a couple of weeks."

It was past the 17:30 Embassy closing time when the last interview concluded. Iza stopped briefly at her office and was surprised that Tony had left her three messages. They were simply requests to call him as soon as possible, but Iza could sense a bit of irritation and possibly even anger in his voice, which seemed to intensify in each successive message. Herr Kühn had obviously called Tony, meaning he now knew that she'd used his name without his permission. Iza shook her head, thinking, *I really am an idiot, but at least he finally called. Maybe that's what it took for him to finally take me seriously. It's so unlike him though. He's always made time for me in the past. He had to hear how upset I am.*

Iza tried to reach Tony again, but there was no answer. She left another message: "Tony, please call me. I need your help. I don't know what's going on here, but I think I'm in danger. Please call. Call my cell phone any time. Or call my work phone. I need to talk to you."

♦

Iza and Volodya hurried to the neighborhood Waschküche laundromat and take-out diner. "Tony finally called me, but I wasn't working in my office today. He left three messages, but I could never reach him. Maybe he'll call me on my cell phone tonight or at the embassy again tomorrow."

While Iza was reading the washing machine directions, Volodya stuffed a machine with all of his dirty clothing. He was about to add soap and pay when Iza walked over and looked at him quizzically. "You can't wash whites with colors or towels with jeans!" she said as she pulled his clothes out of the machine.

Volodya was amused. "What are you doing?" he asked with a grin.

She sorted the items by color and fabric type, then set them in piles with her corresponding clothing. "I'm doing laundry," she responded with a smirk. They giggled as they looked sternly at each other. Iza had four loads compared with Volodya's one load.

"My way is cheaper."

"Only today. My way is cheaper in the long term. You'll wear out your clothes faster and discolor them doing it your way."

Volodya bowed to Iza and stepped back. As the four machines were running, they purchased salads and sparkling water at the take-out diner, then sat at a table near the washers.

They inspected her detailed packing list on her phone. She'd brought clothing, towels, kitchen towels, shoes, short winter boots, two light jackets, a winter jacket, and various toiletries. She'd packed a small framed photo of her parents, a travel mug, a headlamp for running after dark, and a few kitchen utensils. Volodya realized she'd indeed brought nothing to Berlin that would interest a thief—or anyone but her, for that matter.

"Are your citrine earrings valuable? Could someone want those?"

"No. Citrine is a kind of quartz. It's not that expensive and it's fairly common. It just has sentimental meaning and it's pretty."

"What about your suitcase?"

"It's a hardside case with a fabric interior. I bought it three weeks before my flight at the department store where I worked after graduating. I didn't notice any pockets in the suitcase. It just has dividers between the two halves, but no place to hide anything—at least no place that I know of. Honestly, I bought it because it was huge and bright blue, but I didn't study the specs or anything."

"Could man at airport have put something into your suitcase?"

"No, I checked carefully. I even took the frame apart on my parents' photo."

"Who knew you were coming to Berlin?"

"My mom, Roger, Tony, Ellen, their kids, Greta and Tony Jr., I'm sure some people at the State Department and at the embassy here, and Günther Kohler. He's my mom's boyfriend."

"Are you sure that is everyone?"

"My mom did have a party at our house with some of her coworkers and a few people from the German Embassy two weeks before I left. I'm not really sure who was there. But I don't think she mentioned my new job to any of them, although I'm not positive. I wasn't home . . . I was working and then I stopped at Tony and Ellen's house on my way home. The people were gone by the time I got home."

"What about this guy, Günther?"

"Well . . . my mom met him through work. She's a German and Russian interpreter at the State Department, and he was in a meeting where she was the interpreter. I think she met him four or five months ago, right around the time I moved out of my apartment and back to her house. He works for the German Embassy in Washington, but I don't know what his job is. I only talked with him a few times one-to-one.

"Um . . . what else? I don't like him at all. I think he's arrogant and egotistical. And, um . . . he supports Russia's cause in the war in Ukraine. I can't forgive that."

"I can understand that you would not like him."

"I guess he makes my mom happy. You know, my mom and I didn't really interact very much when I was living at her house again because we were both working a lot, I was doing final interviews for my job, and when she wasn't working, she was always with Günther. She stayed at his place pretty often."

Volodya rubbed his stubble beard, thinking. "What is model and what company made your suitcase?" He took out his phone and searched for information about it. He scrolled through the specifications and suddenly stopped at one line. "Look here, Iza," he said excitedly. "It says there is one fabric pocket in interior lining." They stopped eating and stared at interior photos of the suitcase. There was a fabric pocket running the width of the case on one of the interior sides; it was nearly invisible because the pocket ran along a seam in the interior fabric lining. The pocket was advertised as providing secure storage.

While their clothes were drying, they made their plan. "I have to work late tomorrow on big project, but I can go to your apartment to check suitcase pocket on Thursday after work. You should not go there; it could be dangerous," Volodya said.

The dryers stopped, and he began forcefully stuffing their clean clothing into a laundry bag. Iza looked at him sternly again, so he redeposited the clothing in the dryer. She handed him underwear and socks. "I'll trust you to sort these," she said with a smirk. There was a steam iron near the dryers, and Iza used it to iron Volodya's shirts. She carefully folded the items and placed them in the laundry bag in neat stacks.

"You know, Iza," he said quite seriously, "no one at my work will recognize me tomorrow." They both laughed.

Abruptly changing the subject, Volodya said, "Iza, Saturday is my birthday. Will you come to my party?" Iza was surprised, and slightly disappointed that he hadn't mentioned anything about his birthday or a party earlier, but then she suppressed a smile as she recalled that they'd only met on Friday! *Come on, Iza—in Europe, it's normal to plan your own birthday party. Yet, I'm a little worried. Maybe he's invited his coworkers too. I hope I'll fit in.*

"Sure, I'll come to your party. Who else is invited?"

"Just you. Maybe you will plan something fun for us to do. I have whole day off."

"Maybe I will."

Before they left the laundromat, Iza checked her phone again. Tony hadn't called.

Wednesday, October 19 (Day 8)

Volodya awoke to see Iza staring at him. He smiled at her from his side of the pillows. "Iza, remember I have to work late today. I will not be back here until at least 19:00, or even later. If you can wait, I will make dinner for you."

"You don't need to do that. I'll make a late dinner for us. Just knock when you get here, and I'll open the door for you." Iza smiled and reached over the pillows, taking his left hand gently into hers. "Do you need a clean bandage on your hand?" she asked with concern.

"I think this one is still okay. I will make coffee."

Within a few minutes he returned with two mugs and sat next to Iza.

"I read there will be big storm late tonight. They say it will rain and get very cold for October. It is not usual. Is this sign of climate change?"

"I don't know, but our climate *is* changing. Is tonight just weather, or is it climate?"

Volodya kissed her cheek. "I will see you tonight." He turned to exit the room.

"Come back here." She sat up in bed and pulled him down, then kissed him intensely, not letting him go.

"Iza, pretty soon, I will not be able to go for work," he chuckled as he pulled away from her embrace. *Iza, you make me crazy. I know I love you and now I am thinking maybe you love me.*

"Thank you for helping me."

Iza skipped breakfast and strolled to the embassy, arriving a few minutes before opening time, unsure if she should be concerned that someone was surveilling her. She carried her waterproof daypack, which she'd packed with her headlamp and other running gear. *If the weather is still decent by the end of the workday, I'll run back to Volodya's apartment for stress relief. I'm driving myself nuts,* she thought.

Iza placed another call to Tony's office. "Tony, this is Iza. It was so nice to hear your voice yesterday. I'm pretty scared . . . in fact, *terrified* is a better word. We're trying to figure out what's going on, and it would help us if we knew more about a man who was murdered outside my apartment building last Friday. That's why I tried to get a meeting with Herr Kühn. I know you're really busy, but I hope you'll have time to talk soon. Please, please call me."

Claire stopped by promptly at 8:30 with a stack of papers for Iza. "Iza, today you'll be working to locate and assist the next-of-kin of Frank Masters. Here's the info I have. He died unexpectedly while vacationing in Berlin. He was seventy-nine and had been traveling alone through Europe for about a month before he passed." Claire warned, "This is one of the more difficult assignments you'll have as a Consular Affairs officer. It's pretty stressful dealing with families when someone dies like this, and they'll have lots of questions for you. If you have any of me, I'll be working in my office all day."

Just then, Iza heard the ping of an incoming text on her cell phone. The use of personal cell phones during working hours was not allowed, but she glanced to see if it was Tony. It was a text from her mom. She'd have to wait until lunchtime to respond. *Wow, that's an odd time for Mom to text.*

She then quickly dialed Jack Malone on her embassy phone. "Jack, how are you?" After chatting briefly, Iza asked, "I hope this isn't too short notice, but can you recommend something for a friend and me to do on Saturday? I hadn't expected to make any social plans for a few weeks, but I'm suddenly in need an idea."

"How about picking apples at an orchard? I think Saturday is supposed to be a beautiful day. My wife and I are close friends with a German couple we met in our neighborhood. The man's parents own an apple orchard about forty kilometers southwest of Berlin, near Potsdam. It's a fun destination. His parents *always* look for an extra helping hand on weekends when their paid crew is off. Personally, I think it's just fun for them to have visitors from the big city. I have an old beater car I loan out to friends on occasion. It's parked in the Clayallee embassy parking garage. You could certainly borrow it. Otherwise, Potsdam or Dresden are possibilities. You'd need to buy train tickets for either of those, but they're not super expensive."

"I like the apple orchard idea. My friend spends a lot of time in front of screens—he's a programmer at a company here in Berlin. It'd be a nice break for him to be out in the sunshine for a day. And I'd enjoy it too."

"Do either of you ride horses?"

"I do! I'm not sure about my friend."

"The Bauers have horses, and I'm sure they'd let you ride for an hour or two if you want. You don't need to decide that until you're there. Tell you what, I'll make the arrangements and get back to you by Friday morning at the latest. What's your friend's name, so I can tell them who's coming?"

"His name is Volodya Korsun. He's from Ukraine, and um, this will be a nice treat for him."

"I'll be in touch soon."

"Thanks, Jack. You're so kind."

At last, Iza skimmed through the paperwork Claire had dropped off and made a task list for dealing with Frank Masters and his family. It wouldn't be a fun day.

◆

On her lunch break, Iza called her mom. It was 6:00 a.m. in Washington, but her mom was usually an early riser. However, Elise sounded as though she were still in bed when she answered. "Iza dear, how are you?"

Iza bit her lip. *I've only had a one-line text from you until today. You didn't even come to the airport to see me off; you went to Vermont instead. Do you actually care how I am?* Instead, she replied, "I'm good, mom."

"Iza, I'm thinking of visiting Berlin with Günther. Maybe later this month."

Oh no—I can't have you in Berlin now! And even if none of this stuff was going on, I don't want to spend time with Günther. "Mom, my apartment isn't really set up very well with furniture yet, and I'm still so new at this job . . . I can't take time off for a visit in the next two weeks. Can *you* come for Christmas?"

"Well, Iza, we'd really like to come sooner. But I guess you're too busy to spend time with your mother."

"Mom, it's not that I'm too busy. I only want your visit to be fun, and—"

Elise cut Iza off. "Iza, Günther has a son in Berlin, and he'd like you to call his son to say hello. His son has a good job at an energy firm there. Maybe you'll even like him. I'll send you his contact information so you can get in touch."

Yeah right, she thought. *Any son of Günther is probably a member of the Hitler Youth.* But instead, she responded sweetly, "I'll definitely look for that info, mom." *So, I can delete it!*

Just then, Iza heard a man calling for her mom in the background and realized that Günther was there. Given the early hour, Iza guessed that he was sleeping with her mom at her house this time. *Mom, I want you to be happy. I know how much you miss Dad and how hard his death was on you. I want you to have someone to love again . . . but I just don't like Günther. I know I have to learn to accept him because he's who you love. I need more time.*

Elise started to say something, but Iza suddenly interrupted. "Mom, I have to get back to work. I love you. Let's talk more on Sunday." She turned off her phone. Lunch break was already past, and she'd missed eating at the canteen.

Throughout the day, Iza checked periodically for messages from Tony between calls to local funeral service providers to learn the cost of cremation, an urn, or a coffin. She checked on prices for returning the body to the U.S. Then she called Frank Masters's son. He was devastated on hearing of his father's death, and Iza had a hard time holding herself together. Her mind flashed back to the day when she and her mom had learned of her own father's death. Consoling his son had been stressful. By 17:30, she was ready to leave work. But the fact that Tony hadn't called weighed heavily on her mind.

She knew his job demanded that he make countless decisions with limited information in stressful and difficult situations. He possessed the skills and the position at the embassy to help her. She also knew that he loved her like a daughter. *At least he tried to call me yesterday. There must be something going on in Washington that I don't know about. He'd call me if he could. But when he calls, Tony always needs convincing. If only I had tangible proof of the strange things afoot in Berlin! If only I knew what these people were looking for!*

Her thoughts turned to her suitcase. *Volodya can't check the pocket until after work tomorrow. But if I can check it tonight, I might find something concrete to share with Tony. Maybe if I'm super careful, I can safely stop at my apartment for just a few minutes. I still have my apartment key in my wallet.*

Iza left her work clothing, jacket, and phone in a drawer in her desk so she'd have plenty of available space in her small daypack for whatever she might find in her suitcase—if anything.

There were ominous-looking clouds in the sky as Iza began her run, but it wasn't raining. She stopped about a block from her apartment building and cautiously walked the remainder of the route, scanning the area for anything suspicious. It felt cooler and was windier outside than she'd expected, but she wasn't worried. *I'll quickly change into my thermal training jacket and tights once I'm in the apartment. I didn't think to take them when I was in a hurry to pack Sunday night since I didn't expect to need them.* At the moment, she was only wearing her running shorts and a long-sleeved shirt.

Seeing nothing unusual in the area, she entered her building, and rapidly ran up the stairway to her apartment. She swiftly slipped into the bedroom and pulled her suitcase from beneath the bed. Inside, she felt along the lining near where she and Volodya had seen the hidden pocket in the luggage specifications. She found it! Then she discovered a slim, sealed packet inside the slit in the suitcase lining. Iza tucked the packet into her daypack and slid the suitcase back beneath the bed. She was elated but suddenly worried. Maybe this packet held the answer they'd been searching for, but she had to be careful. She couldn't let whoever was looking for it get it from her. She cautiously peered out from the corner of the bedroom window just in time to glimpse the back side of a blonde-haired man walking briskly in the direction of her building. Her heart started to race. She didn't know if he was "the" tall, blonde man, but if it was and she ran down the stairway to leave the building, she'd meet him at the base of the stairs. If he actually came to her apartment, she'd be trapped inside. She had no time to put on her training suit. She raced out of her flat and locked the door, wondering what to do.

A petite Asian woman and a young boy were laughing as they ran to an apartment beyond Iza's. They were obviously racing each other from the stairway to their door. Iza guessed that the woman was a mom who'd picked up her school-aged son from a bus stop. She rushed up to them, edged close to their doorway, and hurriedly inquired in English, "I'm your neighbor down the hall. I misplaced my apartment key, and I can't reach Frau Böhmer to get in. I'm not really dressed to sit in the cold hallway to wait until she returns. May I sit in your apartment for a few minutes until she gets back?" The woman smiled brightly at Iza as she opened their apartment door; Iza realized that she didn't understand English.

The boy said something to his mom. He was translating. The woman smiled again, grabbed Iza's hand and led her into their apartment. Iza sat quietly on a chair near the door, breathing a sigh of relief.

The boy spoke to Iza. "I'm Jinping," he said.

"I'm Iza."

"Daddy works at the Chinese Embassy," he said, "but he's in Beijing now."

Iza said, "Thank you and your mom, Jinping, for letting me wait here."

Jinping and his mom went about their usual after-school routines while Iza waited. She checked her watch. It was 18:50. With the thickening clouds in the sky, there wouldn't be a long twilight. Iza finally decided it would be dark enough to leave the building safely. She profusely thanked her two neighbors and then slipped out their door, walking cautiously down the stairway to the basement passageway and into the adjoining building. She put on her headlamp and emerged from the door.

The weather had changed dramatically since she'd run to her apartment from the embassy. The wind was gusting, and it was already drizzling. The temperature had also fallen since Iza first entered her building. She felt cold but hoped that she'd warm up once she was running again.

When she turned the corner past her building, her headlamp illuminated the unmistakably massive body of the tall, blonde man. He was only meters away, standing near a sedan and talking with someone inside. The light from her headlamp caught his attention, but she kept running, trying not to attract scrutiny. However, the tall, blonde man had been watching for her, and now he recognized her distinctive body shape in the dim light of the street lamps. He gave chase.

Iza was absolutely terrified, but she knew she needed to calm herself internally and think rationally. She needed a strategy, and she thought through her options as she ran the empty sidewalks of her neighborhood. *I'll head back to the embassy. There's usually a guard outside, and I can ask for help. If no one is outside, then I can't stop there because I don't know if my employee entrance pass works outside of regular operating hours. If I stop to find out, the man could catch me. I don't have my phone, but I can't stop to call 110 for help anyway. I can't run directly to Volodya's apartment because then the man will know where I'm living. I can try to find an open shop and duck inside, but that's risky. Most shops are closing soon, and in any event, the man could follow me inside a store. I can't hop on a train; I'd be trapped in a train car. What are my chances of finding the Polizei? Running where there's heavy traffic is risky because I might have to stop and he'd be able to catch me.*

If there isn't a guard outside at the embassy, I'll head to Tiergarten Park. I know the paths aren't well-lit, but the darkness and rain could work in my favor. There are so many intersecting paths in the park that it'll eventually confuse him. And I memorized the figure-eight route Volodya and I ran on Sunday. I can repeat at least a portion of that route and lose him. I know I can outrun most guys on an average day, and all this adrenaline should give me a huge advantage.

But she soon realized that the tall, blonde man was also a serious runner. He wasn't gaining on her, but he wasn't falling behind either. She knew this was a race she had to win.

The rain increased in intensity, and the temperature dropped further. Iza was still warm from the exertion of running but realized that she needed to pay attention to her body temperature in these conditions. The rain had already thoroughly soaked her.

There was no guard outside of the embassy in the deteriorating weather, and the usually busy sidewalks were empty, so she crossed into Tiergarten Park. The tall, blonde man was still behind her but wasn't getting any closer. She couldn't stop to check her watch but eventually guessed that she'd been running for nearly an hour. She couldn't run as fast as usual in the dark and rain, but she had been keeping up a reasonable pace and was happy that she hadn't had to stop anywhere. Iza finally looked back and saw that she'd lost him. No one was on the trail, so she slowed her pace.

Iza was exhausted from the run, the difficult weather conditions, and the fear that her life was in danger. She began to shiver. She had to slow down even more as she left the park for fear of slipping on the icy patches that were forming in places on the sidewalk. She jogged carefully toward the busy intersection near the Potsdamer Platz and hoped to return to Volodya's apartment from there. But two blocks from the Platz, she saw the blonde-haired man again. He was waiting near the curb, perhaps for the sedan to come pick him up.

Oh God, she prayed as tears streamed down her face, mixing with the rain pouring off her, *please help me.*

The man saw her and gave chase again. They were the only two people outside in the deteriorating weather. When Iza came near the intersection, the lanes of heavy traffic were moving slowly but still fast enough that it was too dangerous to cross. She had to stop to wait for the signal. The man was rapidly closing the gap between them. Iza made the split-second decision to jump out into the multiple lanes of traffic. She dodged the oncoming cars, slipping between them while irate drivers honked their horns. In moments, she emerged safely on the opposite side of the street. She glanced back and saw that the backup of slow-moving traffic had suddenly loosened. All of the cars accelerated forward in a sudden burst. The man had to stop and wait. Iza kept running; she had gotten away.

Volodya arrived at his apartment. It was 20:15. He'd taken the U-Bahn to a nearby stop and had run through the onslaught of cold, icy rain. He knocked on the door, but there was no answer. When he entered his apartment, it was dark. He turned on a light and checked his phone; there was no message from Iza. He checked the kitchen counter and table for a note; there was none. "Where could she be?" he asked aloud. "If she had to work late, she would leave message. If she went to grocer, she would leave note. Would she have gone to her apartment without me? She is so independent . . . I wonder." He paced back and forth until it was nearly 21:00.

She still hadn't returned.

The rain became torrential, and the wind howled. Sheets of cold, icy rain pelted Iza's bare skin. She had been shivering while she was running, but the shivering stopped. She was rapidly losing body heat. As she neared Volodya's apartment, she slowed to a walk, then began to stumble. She started mumbling nonsense to herself and finally fell beneath a streetlamp several doors from Volodya's apartment building, suddenly wondering why she was there. Unable to move, she sat on the sidewalk in the freezing rain, only wanting to sleep.

◆

Volodya decided he simply had to go to Iza's apartment to look for her. Maybe she'd gone there and had then stayed when the weather deteriorated. When he left his building, he saw Iza in the dim light of the streetlamp, sitting on the sidewalk. He ran to her and instantly knew she was hypothermic. He'd learned to recognize and treat mild and moderate hypothermia in his basic military training since it sometimes happened to troops exposed to cold and wet conditions. Time was of the essence, and he was thankful that she was still awake and responsive to his voice. Instead of spending precious time getting her to a hospital, he knew he could start treating her immediately, before her body temperature fell any further.

Iza couldn't stand up, so Volodya picked her up and gently carried her to his apartment. Once inside, he saw that her skin was pure white. He asked her to help him remove her wet clothing. She couldn't help, but she didn't resist as he rapidly, yet gently stripped her wet running clothing from her body. He tossed her daypack into a corner. Using towels, he gently dried her skin and hair. He couldn't put her under the shower. He needed to warm her core first: her heart, neck, and head. If her extremities were warmed too quickly, it would push cold blood to her heart and brain, potentially causing death.

He put his wool cap on her head and wrapped her tightly in his down comforter, leaving only her face exposed. He carried her to the bed, laid her gently on the mattress, and covered her chest, neck, and head with every warm piece of clothing he could find in the armoire. He lay very near her to transfer his body heat to her core. He wanted her to stay awake to ensure she was rewarming, so he softly sang Ukrainian folk songs to her. He sang in a deep, pure voice. Then he was overcome by his emotions and started crying. "I just find you, Iza. Please . . . *please* do not die!" And then he prayed.

Thursday, October 20 (Day 9)

At about 2:00, Volodya finally measured regular pulse and respiration rates for Iza. Once those had begun to increase earlier in the night, he knew she was likely out of danger, but he kept checking to be absolutely certain. He stayed near her to continue supplying warmth to her body.

Volodya drifted into a deep sleep, dreaming of Iza in a flowing white dress, her skin pure white. She was walking away from him through a field of golden, ripened grain while the sky above was a brilliant blue. The golden field set against the blue sky resembled the Ukrainian flag. He cried out to Iza to return to him, but she continued walking away. He tried running toward her but could never reach her; the faster he ran, the farther away she moved.

He awoke at 5:00, drenched in sweat as though he'd been running. He heard Iza's regular breathing next to him and realized it had only been a dream. Iza's face felt warm and dry. He was overcome with a sense of contented relief that she was alive—and that she was sleeping next to him.

Iza will be weak, and she might suffer temporary memory loss. I remember it is typical in cases of hypothermia. I want to know what happened, but I do not want to upset her by asking all my questions, so I will wait to see how she is feeling. Since the Team had worked late the previous evening, the morning briefing was scheduled for 9:00. He'd insist on traveling with her on the U-Bahn to drop her off at the embassy if she felt well enough to work, and then he'd return at the end of her workday to accompany her back to his apartment. They'd previously planned that he'd check inside her suitcase at her apartment directly after work, but he decided to wait and go there later in the evening instead. He slipped out of the bedroom, his plan now formulated.

◆

Iza awoke remembering only that she'd encountered the tall, blonde man somewhere, had run from him, and became intensely cold from exposure to icy, wind-driven rain. She couldn't recall much of anything else. Her brain felt sluggish, as if it had separately run its own race outside her body and now needed time to recover from the exertion.

Whoa, I can't get out of bed! I'm so unsteady. And why am I nude? She sat on the bed and wrapped herself in the down comforter. Volodya heard her stirring in the bedroom and brought her a plate of toast with honey and a mug of warm, sweetened lemon water. Iza looked pale and exceptionally tired. She devoured the toast, gulped down the warm drink, and then smiled at him. "I'm starving . . . what happened to me?"

Volodya sat on the edge of the bed and looked at her curiously. "I do not know, Iza. You tell me."

"I feel like I was run over by a truck. I think it hit my brain because I can't think straight. But I have to get ready for work."

Volodya threw Iza her nightshirt. "Let me see you get out of bed and walk to shower. Then we can decide if you will go for work today or if you will stay here." He left the room, and Iza put on her nightshirt. She tried to get out of bed to walk, but she was unsteady and weak.

"Volodya," she called out, "come back." When he returned to the room, she giggled. "Please walk with me to the shower, Mr. Korsun." He came to the bedside, helped her up, and then walked with her to the shower. She kissed his cheek. "Thank you." She enjoyed the hot shower for a *long* time.

◆

Volodya sat on the sofa, drinking his coffee, and watched as Iza made her way back from the bathroom to the bedroom after her shower, using the wall to help steady herself. She came out a few minutes later dressed for work. She wore a very short black skirt with black tights, the pale greenish-yellow oversized pullover she'd worn to the museums, and her teardrop citrine earrings.

"I do not think truck hurt you very much. You look beautiful."

"Flattery will get you somewhere," Iza responded as she dropped beside him on the sofa. "What time is it? Are you back from work already?"

"Iza, I think your brain is . . . how do you say it . . . foggy? Should you really go for work today?"

"Yeah, I think I have to. Jack will be angry with me if I don't show up."

"Iza, you work for Claire."

Iza shook her head slightly as if to remove some cobwebs from her brain and then grinned at him, "Yeah, that's what I meant to say."

"Did you go to your apartment last night?" he questioned while smiling at her so she wouldn't feel as if he were interrogating her.

"Yeah, I think so . . . maybe. I . . . I don't remember for sure what happened." She paused, obviously trying to recall the events of the past evening, then turned to Volodya and said, "I think a little boy from China helped me."

"A little boy from *China* helped you," Volodya repeated Iza's words slowly, with both surprise and concern. *Iza, if you think little boy from China helped you, I do not believe you are thinking so well.* He decided to wait until later to ask her more of his questions.

"Where's my daypack? Let's go."

He brought her the daypack and set it on the sofa next to her.

"Iza, are you *sure*? I mean . . . your brain seems *very* tired. I think you need to stay here and rest today."

"I can't—I'll lose my *job* if I don't show up! I'll be okay. It'll just take me a few minutes to wake up better. I *have* to go." Tears welled up in her eyes.

Volodya relented, and they left for the U-Bahn station. He wanted to know what had happened Wednesday night, but her mind was incapable of putting together a coherent timeline of events. On the walk to the station, he put his arm around her shoulder and held her, ostensibly as a sign of affection, but it was actually a necessity because she was still unsteady. Once on the subway train, Volodya kept his arm around her shoulder and held her hand, but he spent most of the ride looking out the window, deep in thought. *Volodya, you only know her for few days, but you love her. You cannot wait in case something happens. You need to tell her.*

He walked at her side with his arm around her shoulder until they arrived at the main embassy entrance. Then Volodya abruptly turned to face Iza and passionately kissed her on her lips. The kiss was so long and intense that she nearly lost her breath. "I will call you later today. And I will see you here tonight," he said. He quickly turned and walked in the direction of his workplace. Iza stood at the Embassy entrance watching him walk away. After he'd crossed the cobblestone plaza in front of the Embassy, he turned around and looked back. Iza was still standing there watching him. She blew a kiss in his direction. Volodya pretended to catch it and put it into his pocket. They waved at each other, and then he was off as she unsteadily ambled into the embassy.

As she entered her office, Jack Malone called. He'd arranged for Iza and her friend to visit the Bauer apple orchard on Saturday. They should plan to arrive by 8:00 and could stay as long as they wanted. Jack asked Iza if she'd like to meet for lunch at the canteen to pick up his car key and to get directions. *I'm not quite sure what he's talking about, but I'd better agree to meet him,* she thought. They agreed to meet at the canteen entrance around noon. Iza hoped she'd be walking at a normal pace and be thinking more clearly by that time.

Claire looked at Iza with surprise and sat across from her. "What happened to you?" she asked in a concerned voice, noticing Iza's pale skin and the look of exhaustion on her face.

Iza sat for a moment, uncertain how to respond. An excuse suddenly flashed into her addled brain. "Food poisoning. That'll teach me never to eat sushi again."

"Oh, you poor dear," Claire responded in a sympathetic voice. "If you don't feel well by the afternoon, take off early and head home."

Wow, I must really look bad today.

At noon, Iza met Jack for lunch. She was feeling stronger and thinking much more coherently, but he took one look at her and asked, "Are you okay? You look *so* pale and tired."

"Food poisoning. Bad sushi," she lied again. *I guess my appearance hasn't improved. At least my brain is functioning a lot better.*

"I'm telling Sarah about you; she eats a lot of sushi. Personally, it's not for me." Jack gave her the key to his old car, which he'd parked in the lower-level garage of the Clayallee U.S. Embassy building. "It's an old, gray beater; you won't miss it among the Mercedes in the garage," Jack said with a laugh. He also gave her a map with driving directions to the Bauer apple orchard near Potsdam. The drive was only about forty kilometers. After thanking Jack, Iza excused herself early from their lunch, then slowly walked back to her office to call Roger.

I'm such a hypocrite, she thought as she dialed his number. *Here I am, angry that mom has barely been in touch since I got to Berlin, and I haven't called Roger once. Roger is always in the office early. I hope I can reach him before any meetings.* He answered the phone immediately.

"Iza, I thought you'd forgotten about me," he said, sounding as though he were mortally wounded.

"Roger, what's new with you?" she inquired in her most upbeat voice.

"Well, Healthy Meals has a new frozen dinner out, and it's pretty good."

Iza jokingly questioned, "When did you get a dog?"

"Ha, ha, ha," Roger responded in a staccato voice.

"I can't help it, Roger. That name always sounds like a brand of dog food."

"So, kid, tell me about Berlin."

Iza told Roger a little about her work, the embassy event, and the museums she'd visited. *I can't tell him about what's been going on here. He'll worry, and there isn't anything he can do. Only Tony can help me. And, should I mention Volodya? Roger is a pretty laid-back guy, but would he think I'm crazy to be living with a guy I just met a week ago, even though it's only a temporary arrangement?*

She also confided in him that she'd likely made Tony angry with her by using his name to get access to information before asking his permission and now he wasn't returning her calls.

Roger asked incredulously, "Iza, didn't your mom call to tell you? Tony's mom *died* last Friday. She had a massive brain aneurysm on Thursday. Tony and Ellen were in the hospital with her. The funeral was Tuesday. Your mom and Günther came back from Vermont early; they were at the funeral. On top of that, Tony is under a lot of pressure at work. Those House Freedom Caucus members are a real pain in the ass. He's been testifying before Congress about something or other yesterday, and he'll be there again today. Those assholes don't know that the 'freedom' in their name comes in part from the hard work of people at State like Tony. He's probably not angry with you—maybe just frustrated with work and grieving too. Anyway, I ran into him in the hallway yesterday on his way back in after his testimony, and he said something about being in Berlin on Monday."

"I'm so sorry. I didn't know." Iza suddenly felt overcome with guilt. *Here I've been thinking he's ignoring me. He must have called me Tuesday from the funeral home or the church. Why didn't Mom tell me? She was probably planning to tell me, but I cut her off because Günther was there. Oh God, forgive me. I'm sorry, Tony. I'm sorry, Mom.*

"But kid, tell me. Who is this 'we' that you keep mentioning?"

Iza bit her lower lip. She hadn't realized that she'd repeatedly used "we" instead of "I" while telling Roger about the things she'd been up to in Berlin. "Well . . . I met a nice guy at that embassy event I was telling you about."

"Is he an American or a German boy?"

"No, he's Ukrainian."

"A Ukrainian kid. Well, I'll be. What's his name and where's he from?"

"Volodymyr Korsun. He's from Mariupol." She could hear Roger inhale loudly at the mention of Mariupol. Iza had always had a good rapport with Roger and felt free to talk with him about her personal life. She decided that she wouldn't hold back. She wanted his advice. "Roger . . . I think I'm in love with him. Do you think that's possible? We just met last Friday, but I've never felt this way about anyone before. He's so kind, and we have a lot of the same interests, and he's smart. He knows a lot about the world, and he cares about that kind of stuff—like I do. And . . . I'm really attracted to him too . . . I mean, like, um . . . physically attracted." She stopped short of telling him that she was living with Volodya.

Roger chuckled. "Iza, in my sixty-plus years of living and in my thirty-five years at State, I've seen that people are capable of *anything*—good and bad. My advice, kiddo, is follow your heart. Mind you, don't do anything stupid. But don't overanalyze, either. You know, you're prone to think too much, Iza. Everything has to be so planned out and organized for you. Have some fun and see where this goes."

"Roger, will you come here to visit for Christmas?"

"Hey kid, I'd really like that. But I promise you, I won't let you win any board games we play like I used to when you were younger."

Iza protested, "But I always won fair and square. You didn't *let* me win."

"Hey Iza, I gotta go here. I gotta grab my briefing packet and get to a meeting in five. You be good. Don't do anything stupid, and call me again before I forget who you are."

"Love you, Roger."

Iza sat for a moment feeling horrible for Tony and his family. She realized the fog had lifted from her brain as the day progressed. She now sat back in her chair, running through the conversation with Roger in her mind. She suddenly recalled something Roger had mentioned. *Briefing packet . . . packet . . . oh! The packet!* She yanked open her desk drawer and unzipped her daypack. She'd absently taken her employee entrance pass from her daypack in the morning and her wallet from the daypack at lunchtime, but her mind had somehow overlooked *the* packet. As she pulled it out and held it, all of her memories from the previous evening came flooding back into her mind. She recalled everything.

She tried calling Volodya, but he didn't answer—it was too late to reach him on his lunch break. He'd left an earlier message, wondering how she was feeling. She tried to reach him again when she guessed he'd be on his afternoon break, but he still didn't answer.

"Volodya, I remember what happened last night; call me. I have what we've been looking for!"

Later in the day, Iza was dismayed to realize that he had tried calling again when she'd stepped out of her office to use the restroom. He'd left another message but didn't answer when she tried to call him back. Iza sat at her desk, about to open the packet, when Claire stepped into her office.

"Iza, if you're feeling well enough, can you help process visas the rest of the day?"

Iza slipped the unopened packet back into her daypack.

It was 16:00 when the Team wrapped up their work for the day. Volodya and Petro stopped at a table in the canteen to drink coffee together before leaving the building. Petro leaned over and whispered to Volodya in Ukrainian, "I know I asked you before, but you only smiled last time. Did you meet girl at embassy dinner last Friday?"

Volodya whispered back, "Does this show on me somehow?"

Petro grinned. "You seem happier these past few days, and your clothes are neatly pressed. I know *you* could not do that. I only wonder."

Volodya scrolled through his phone then handed it to Petro. The screen displayed the selfie of Iza with him in front of the mural at the Urban Nation Museum.

Petro nodded his head positively, "She is very pretty."

Volodya took the phone back. "She is *more* than pretty."

Volodya met Iza at the embassy entrance at 17:30. She started to tell him what had happened the previous evening, but when they arrived at the U-Bahn station, she whispered, "I'll tell you the rest when we get back to your apartment. There are too many people here." As they rode to his Kreuzberg neighborhood, Iza held his hand, squeezing it excitedly, yet he could see sadness in her eyes.

When they were inside his apartment, she said, "Before we look at what I found in my suitcase, I need to apologize to you. I'm incredibly sorry, Volodya. Please forgive me for being so stupid yesterday. I felt desperate. I used *such* poor judgment. I caused you a lot of unnecessary stress. I promise, I'll never do anything like that again."

"I understand. I am just happy you are okay. I mean that." He squeezed her hand.

"I called Roger today. Tony hasn't called because his mom died last week and then he's been testifying in some contentious hearings before Congress the past two days. I wish I would have known. Roger told me Tony will be in Berlin on Monday."

Iza took the packet from her daypack, and they moved to sit cross-legged on the floor near the sofa. Volodya cut it open using his Swiss Army tool. There were four photocopies of blueprints inside the packet. They laid the photocopies out on the floor and pored over them. The writing on the prints was in German. Iza started translating.

"They're stamped 'Top Secret'," she said with fear in her voice. The lower edge of each print was stamped "Kurfürstendamm 23."

Volodya ran his hands through his hair. "Oh, Jezus!"

"What is it?" Iza asked.

He knelt and carefully looked over the blueprints. "Jezus," he repeated again quietly as he fell back into a sitting position.

Volodya sat composing himself as tears welled up in his eyes. "Iza, I have to tell you something. *Please*—will you forgive me?"

"I don't understand," Iza responded in a confused tone.

"Remember I tell you I work for joint-venture company between U.S., Germany, and Ukraine here in Berlin? That I do artificial intelligence programming, general programming?"

"Of course, I remember."

"My employer is not company, Iza. It is Ukraine. I am still in Ukrainian military. I am still soldier."

Iza took his hand in hers and caressed it tenderly as she listened to his story.

"I enlisted in army when I graduated with PhD late last year. There were no jobs for me. People were too worried to hire. We all knew that Russians coming to our border would invade. My brother told me I should enlist; I could get training from U.S. guys. Maybe later, when we are at war, there would not be time for good training. We learn in classroom, but mostly in field under combat conditions. I learn how to fight hand-to-hand combat, how to shoot Malyuk rifle—we have target practice, play war games, keep in shape, and I did maneuvers with my unit."

"You told me you fought for five months."

"Yes. After training, I go—I went—back to Kharkiv with my unit. I fought in battle for Kharkiv. Iza, I have *never* been so scared in my life. They hit us with so many artillery shells and missiles. Buildings were burning. People were blown up. They attack Kharkiv University, schools, hospitals—they want to kill all us Ukrainians. Every day I wake up, I wonder if this is day I will die.

"There was heavy shelling many days, from start of battle into May. When shelling started, guys in my unit were so scared. Regular people could go into underground subways or into cellars to hide. We had to stay out there and fight. It was only time in my life when I smoked cigarettes. Just few times. I did not like it, but it made me calm down. By end of May, after we pushed Russians back toward border, some Ukrainian military guys figured out I can help them do this work in Berlin. At first, I did not want to leave my unit. But then I agree that I can make bigger contribution using what I know, and of course, in military, I did not have choice anyway. I have to go where they tell me to go."

"What do you do for your work?"

"I analyze satellite images and drone footage, then select targets for Ukrainian military planners. I figure out when equipment needs maintenance and keep track of where some important weapons are located on battlefield. I send them coordinates for doing artillery strikes and missile strikes. Our guys do not always use what I send, but they get 'opportunities' to choose from.

"I could not tell you this before because it is supposed to be secret. Even our guys who are married, their wives do not know what they do. Please forgive me for not telling you—and please, remember it is secret—it is *only* for you to know."

Volodya looked pleadingly at Iza, but she didn't seem surprised by his revelation, only by the horror of the war that he described. "It must have been so hard for you," she said quietly. "I can't even imagine how horrible it was . . . and still is. In the U.S., unless you serve in the military, we just don't have anything in our experience to know what it's like to be bombed—to have our homes destroyed—our families and friends killed.

"Volodya, I understand about your work. Sometimes there are things that we can't reveal about our work. I didn't always know what my dad did for the State Department. Sometimes, he couldn't tell us.

"But I already suspected you weren't telling me everything. You need to be to work at specific times, but you're a professional. Even a start-up company doesn't dictate hours for professionals like that. I tried to understand how they would let you leave the Ukrainian army after only five months to work for a company in another country. I wondered if it was because of what happened to your parents—maybe they'd let you go because of that. And then you said you didn't like your work, but it was important work and that you *needed* to do it. Most people would quit a job they didn't like and find something else. But your long hair really threw me," Iza smiled sadly. "I thought you'd have to have short hair to be in the military."

Volodya took Iza's hands in his. "I am sorry."

"Will you have to go back to fight?" Iza asked with sorrow in her voice,

"I do not know. At least not for now." There was a long silence as Volodya looked at her with sadness in his eyes.

Iza looked down again at the photocopies and asked, "Why are you telling me this tonight?"

Volodya pointed to the Kurfürstendamm 23 stamp. "Iza, *this* is address where I work." Iza's eyes widened in fear as he continued, pointing to a room on one of the blueprints. "Look on this photocopy. I sit here." Volodya paused, then tried to think through all the unknowns and estimate the origin of the blueprints. "These are photocopies of blueprints. Are there more copies like this? Where did someone get these? These are highly classified documents. The language is German, so somewhere in Germany? I have to warn my work guys about this; maybe someone wants to target us. Maybe these prints were meant for our enemy. But how can I show these to anyone? Would I say, 'Hey guys, I got these from my girlfriend's suitcase?' Would they think you are traitor? That I am traitor?"

Iza was now trembling. "Who put these in my suitcase? The man at the airport? The man murdered outside my apartment? Someone I actually know?" Iza sat staring at the photocopies, trying to calm herself. She breathed in deeply and sat pensively.

"Volodya, what if you just bring up security to your co-workers in one of your meetings without telling them anything about these prints? One night you told me you were making progress at work. Would it be unreasonable to think someone from the other side might figure out the ways the Ukrainian military is getting targeting information? Ask if there should be a larger security review for your safety. I have to think the other people where you work would share your concern if you talked about it."

They gathered the photocopies and put them back into the packet, then hid the packet in the kitchen. Afterward, they sat on the floor again in silence.

"Come lie next to me on sofa," Volodya said suddenly. "I want to listen to Rachmaninoff before we go to bed. We need to sleep after stress of last night and tonight, but now we can listen together to relax."

As they cuddled on the sofa, he asked Iza about the night they met. "Do you remember what I said about this music?" he whispered.

"Yeah," Iza giggled. "I thought it was a clever pickup line for a classical music fan." She did an exaggerated impression of his voice. "Come listen to Rachmaninoff at my place; it's music to listen to when you make love."

Volodya chuckled at her teasing. "Why did you not say something to me about what I said? Like maybe telling me that was dumb thing to say."

"Because I could tell you were really nervous. And I thought you were cute. You were trying to be so charming."

"What does 'pickup line' mean?"

"It's something a guy says when he wants to start a conversation with a woman he doesn't know. His motive is to pursue a relationship with her—usually just for sex. But sometimes, he's looking for a long-term romantic relationship . . . I guess if he's really captivated by her."

"Okay. I mean, I know you already. But how about if I say this line to you? 'Will you make love with me someday soon'?"

"That's a pretty funny pickup line."

He looked at her with his piercing eyes. "What if I mean it? But not 'just for sex'—for lifelong romantic relationship with you."

"Then I'd say yes." They stared at each other; their eyes full of longing.

By the end of the first movement of the concerto, the sexual tension between them was palpable. Volodya ran his hands beneath her sweater and caressed Iza's breasts. They rolled together on the sofa, touching each other and kissing, trading positions, their breathing becoming rapid and irregular as the third movement reached the toccata climax. As the concerto ended, Volodya dropped off the sofa and shut off the receiver and CD player. They needed sleep.

Friday, October 21 (Day 10)

Volodya lay in bed watching Iza as she carefully took his left hand and began replacing the bandage. It reminded Volodya of when she'd whispered under her breath that she needed to take a cold shower and then of his subsequent conversation with Bobby Scruggs. Every time he looked at Iza, it made him laugh all over again at what Bobby had said to him. She gave him a quizzical look. "What are you laughing at?" But he couldn't answer without laughing harder, which made Iza laugh. "What's this about?" she demanded in amusement.

"Nothing," but then it made him laugh all the harder. He finally pulled Iza down on the bed and hugged her tightly. "I love you, Iza."

She pulled away, then propped herself up on her elbows, staring into his eyes and smiling as she lay on top of him. "I love you, too."

Iza, you did not have to say it; I can see in your eyes now that you love me.

"Let's run away together right now," she continued with a half-playful smile. "We'll leave those silly blueprints in the kitchen and disappear."

"Where do you want to disappear to?"

"I don't know. Wherever you take me."

"I will think about what you propose and get back to you. I admit I am intrigued by your suggestion."

They ate a quick breakfast and avoided discussing the blueprints or Volodya's confession, and then they each left early for work. Iza expected a busy day and was glad she felt much better than she had on Thursday. In addition to her full schedule at work, which consisted of processing visa applications the entire day, she needed to call Frau Böhmer with an update. And shopping for Volodya's birthday was high on her after-work to-do list. She always had her lists.

Iza had been processing student visa applications for about an hour when a call came in on her work phone. It was Tony. *Wow, it's 3:30 a.m. in Washington,* she thought as she picked up the phone. "Hi Tony. Roger told me about your mom yesterday. I'm so sorry. How is your dad doing? No one called to let me know what happened; I feel terrible that I left so many messages for you."

"I'm leaving for Berlin tomorrow."

Oh no, he's in a bad mood. "Tony, can I meet with you while you're here?" she asked hesitantly. "Can we talk about what's been happening to me?"

Tony replied briskly, "I was planning on being in Berlin in three weeks for meetings, but I changed plans to come sooner. I'm coming in part because of you, Iza. I'll meet Wilhelm Kühn on Monday to discuss your 'dead man.' The rest of the week, I'll be in meetings with our German counterparts to discuss Europe's economic and energy situations. I'll have time for dinner with you on Monday evening at 19:00 in one of the private dining rooms at the embassy. My admin will get back to you with details on Monday morning—D.C. time. I can let you know about the meeting with Wilhelm then."

"Can I go with you to the meeting?"

"Absolutely not. Why is knowing more about this dead man so important? I hope this isn't a waste of my time."

"Please, Tony! We've been trying to solve this on our own, but it's too complex. We need access to information we can't get."

"Who is 'we,' Iza?"

"Well . . . I met a nice guy at an embassy event here last Friday, and he's been helping me. I'm actually staying with him right now."

"Iza! *Living* with him? You've only been in Berlin for a week!" Iza could hear the astonishment and offense in his voice.

"Don't say anything to my mom, okay?"

"Why? Are you embarrassed by your promiscuity?"

"Tony, it's *not* what you think! I don't go around randomly hooking up with guys; you should know that! I . . . I don't think my mom would understand." Iza continued, "I'm staying with him *just* for right now. I think my life is in danger if I go back to my apartment."

"What's this guy's name?"

"Volodymyr Korsun. He's from Ukraine. He works for a joint-venture company here in Berlin." Iza could hear Tony writing something—perhaps Volodya's name. *I'm not going to tell Tony he's in the Ukrainian military. Volodya begged me not to tell anyone.*

"Ukraine. Hmm."

Iza explained everything that had happened over the past week, including their harrowing encounters with the tall, blonde man. "My friend is helping me, Tony. I don't have the money to live in a hotel, and I can't live in my apartment until this gets settled. I don't have anyone else here to help me. I didn't have anywhere else to go, okay? I *tried* calling you." Iza's voice quavered. There was a long silence, and she could hear Tony's breathing on the line.

Iza kept talking. "Is your line secure?"

"Yes."

"The documents I found in my luggage are photocopies of blueprints. Tony, they're all labeled 'Top Secret' and are all in German," she whispered into the phone. "I don't know how they got in my suitcase. This is confidential between you and me, but there's a special military operation here in Berlin that's supporting the war in Ukraine. The blueprints show the location and the building layout. And they list all the equipment in the building. Maybe these copies were meant for someone who wants to take out that operation. You don't have to believe *me*, Tony." The pitch of Iza's voice rose with emotion. "If you don't already know something about this, check with your contacts at the Pentagon to verify I'm telling you the truth. I'm scared as hell! I didn't do anything wrong, and *you* don't have the right to judge me! I needed someone to help me." Iza started to cry.

"I'm sorry, Iza; I'm sorry this is happening to you. Don't be afraid, honey. I'll follow up. You've dropped a boatload of information on me. I get this all the time—but not from you—not from someone I love as family. I need time to think about all of this, to make sense of it, and to make some calls. I'll be there on Monday, and we can have dinner together. If your *friend* is as involved as you say, you can invite him to dinner too. Iza, I'm really sorry. Don't cry. We'll figure this out; I'll help you," Tony said sincerely. "But Iza, don't make any more *stupid* decisions before I get there." Iza was taken aback by his comment but said nothing in reply. *What would you be doing if you were me, Tony? I've never been through anything like this and I'm scared! I'm doing the best I can.*

Iza worked through her lunch break, processing a tidal wave of student visa applications. She took a break in the mid-afternoon to place a call to Frau Böhmer. She transitioned to German for their conversation. "Frau Böhmer, this is Iza Carter. I wanted to check in with you. I'm still away at the Consular Office in Düsseldorf for a while longer. Unfortunately, I don't have more information yet about the man killed in front of our building last Friday."

"I will keep looking after your apartment until you return." Just before Iza said goodbye, Frau Böhmer said, "Oh, I almost forgot. There was a man here yesterday looking for you. He was very friendly. He was a tall man—quite good-looking actually—with nice blonde hair. He said he's a distant friend of your family, but it was funny. He couldn't remember your name. He was so embarrassed when I finally had to tell him. I told him you're away for a few days for work. He said he'd come back later."

"Did you tell him where I work?"

"Nein, nein. Das ist private Information."

"Have a pleasant afternoon." *If she told him my name, pretty soon, he'll know where I work.*

Dmytro, rather than Lloyd, led the morning briefing for the Team. He announced that Ukrainian forces attacked Russia's hold on Kherson on Thursday, and fighting was intensifying. Moscow-appointed authorities abandoned the city, fleeing to other Russian-held areas. Ukrainian forces were surrounding Kherson from the west and were now attacking Russia's foothold on the west bank of the Dnipro River. Ukrainian forces had destroyed dozens of Russian ammunition storage depots and command and control centers behind enemy lines. "Our work is helping," he said proudly. Dmytro brought vodka. He poured small glasses for each Team member and offered the toast, *"Sláva Ukrayíni!"* Even though it was only a few minutes after 7:00, the eighteen Team members downed the shots.

Following the briefing, Volodya approached Dmytro and Petro and asked in Ukrainian so that the others couldn't understand, "Guys, what do you think about security here? I mean, only having couple Marine guards. We are making progress on battlefield. Some of our work here is paying off. Would it be unreasonable to think someone from Russian side might figure out how Ukrainian military is getting targeting information? Do we need review of our security here for our safety?"

Dmytro started to downplay the importance of a security review, but Petro nodded in agreement. "I worry about that for long time."

"I will raise security issue immediately," Dmytro promised.

◆

After 17:30, Iza ran from the embassy to the Trüffelschwein men's clothing store, hoping she'd make it there before they closed. On her first shopping day in Berlin, she'd seen a winter jacket in the store window that she'd thought about buying for Roger for Christmas but decided it would be too costly to ship. She wanted to get it for Volodya as a birthday gift instead.

The clerk was about to lock up for the day when Iza arrived. "Please, I'm not here just to look. I want to buy the winter jacket in the window," she begged. To her relief, the clerk opened the door and allowed her inside.

The jacket was a dark brown duck cloth piece with a heavy, warm-looking quilted lining. The cuffs and stand-up collar were lined with dark brown sheepskin. It also had a detachable hood fully lined with the same sheepskin. Iza gasped when she saw the price: €450. She charged the jacket on her credit card, trying not to think about how long it would take her to pay it off. *I want this to be the most fun and memorable birthday Volodya has ever had. Life has been so hard for him the past year. He's lost so much. And I want to show him how much I love him.*

Her next stop was a pastry shop. The shopkeeper showed her a cut slice of a Prinzregententorte—a chocolate-covered cake that had chocolate buttercream filling between its multiple thin layers. It looked delicious, so she bought it for Volodya's birthday cake. She then stopped at a bakery and a grocer before making her final purchase at an apothecary and walking briskly back to the apartment. She didn't know if anyone had been watching her since she left the embassy, but she thought, *I've been in and out of so many places, I'm sure I've lost anyone trying to follow me—at least, I hope.*

As they ate supper, Iza recounted her phone call with Tony. "He said he'll be here on Monday. He's meeting with Herr Kühn in the morning and invited us to dinner at the embassy in the evening. Will you go with me? It's at 19:00, but I don't know any more details yet."

"Of course, Iza, I will go. Tell me more about Tony. You said he is Assistant Secretary of State for Europe. How do you know him?"

"Well, let's see. My dad and Roger were best friends in college. I guess they were quite the pair." Iza smiled, as she imagined younger versions of her father and Roger making mischief together. "They both got jobs interning with the State Department, and that's where they met Tony. He was an intern there too. They all got jobs at State eventually. My dad met my mom and Tony met Ellen there. The five of them did a lot together.

Then my dad got his assignment in Europe. Tony and Roger ended up in the Middle East. Tony rose up faster than my dad and Roger, and he eventually became their boss. After my dad was murdered in Iraq, Tony and Roger transferred back to the U.S. He's been in this job for . . . I don't remember . . . maybe five years. He's a smart guy. He can think on his feet like you wouldn't believe."

"What does 'think on his feet' mean?"

"Sorry. It means he can think and react quickly with good answers when he's bombarded with questions. The few times I've seen him in action, he's a smooth diplomat."

"He sounds like impressive guy." *I wonder what he will think of guy like me,* Volodya worried to himself.

"He is . . . but no more impressive than you."

Volodya grinned at her kind words.

Suddenly Iza blurted out, "I got so distracted between work and planning your birthday surprise, I can't believe I forgot to tell you this! I called Frau Böhmer this afternoon. She told me the tall, blonde man stopped by and asked about me! She didn't tell him where I work, but she gave him my name. Whoever these people are, they didn't know who I was before she told them. They must have only known what I look like. Now that they know my name, they're going to figure out where I work."

"I promise I will try my best to protect you. Tony will help us too. We need to be careful, Iza."

Saturday, October 22 (Day 11)

Iza checked her GPS app. It would take forty minutes to drive from the Clayallee U.S. Embassy garage, where Jack's car was parked, to the Bauers' orchard. "I have a surprise for your birthday," Iza said on the way to the garage. "I hope this sounds fun to you. If it doesn't, just say, and we can do something else instead. We're going to drive to an orchard about forty kilometers from here to pick apples, and we're spending the whole day outdoors. It should be safe to go. The people who own the orchard have horses we can ride too; do you know how?"

"Yes! My grandparents had farm and horses. I have not ridden for some years now, but I know how. This sounds fun! I am so tired of looking at screens all day, Iza. To be outdoors in sunshine with you will make me happy."

He looks so excited to go. I hope it's as fun as Jack said. "First, we just have to find Jack's car," Iza added.

"How will we find Jack's car in parking garage?"

"It's the only beater car there."

"What does 'beater car' mean?"

"You'll know when you see it."

When they arrived at the garage, they split up on the lower level in search of the car. Volodya rounded a pillar and saw the 2004 Citroën Saxo parked between two Mercedes. "Beater car," Volodya said aloud. He hollered out for Iza to come.

When she saw the car, her eyes opened wide, and she started to laugh. "Let's hope we get to the orchard and back!" They climbed in and barely got the doors to close. After a few tries, Iza got the car started. Since Volodya didn't have a German driving license, she'd be the chauffeur for the day. They sputtered out of the garage and eventually entered onto highway A115 towards Potsdam. Volodya was the navigator for their drive, and also the lookout—to ensure they weren't being followed.

◆

At 8:00, they drove up to the farmhouse to meet Karl and Ingrid Bauer. They were in their early seventies. Karl was tall, with thick shoulders and large, powerful hands, arms, and legs. His face was lined from age and sun exposure. He had long salt-and-pepper gray hair tied back in a loose ponytail. He greeted them in a loud voice that exuded joy. In contrast, Ingrid was quite short and thin, with long silver-white hair pulled back into a neat bun. She was talkative, friendly, and motherly. Iza told them that Volodya couldn't speak German. She would act as translator. Karl took them on a tour of the farmhouse grounds. They had two Hanoverian horses: a young stallion, Lothar, and an old mare, Lilli. Although Lilli was past her prime, both horses still looked elegant with their pure chestnut-brown coats. Karl mentioned that they could ride the horses later in the day if they wished.

Ingrid looked over their clothing—jeans, long-sleeved T-shirts, and running shoes, and shook her head with a laugh. She brought them to a shed full of coveralls, rubber boots in various sizes, and work gloves. Once they were properly outfitted, Karl drove them out to the orchard on his tractor.

Their job was picking and crating Braeburn apples, the last apple variety of the growing season. Karl told Iza that he employed field workers to do this work on weekdays, but on weekends, they hosted city folk who wanted to escape urban life for a day. Volodya became the apple picker, and Iza was the packer. As she filled crates, Karl would periodically drive by on his tractor to palletize them.

In the afternoon, Karl and Ingrid drove out on the tractor with lunch; a hearty vegetable soup, dark bread, and apple Kuchen. Ingrid brought warm cider and strong coffee to drink. The four sat on the tractor or ground enjoying the food and the beautiful day. Karl asked if Volodya knew any Ukrainian folk tunes, and through Iza's translating back and forth, they coaxed him into singing for them. Volodya sang "The Duckling Swims" in a deep, pure voice.

"Iza, tell them this is farewell song. The duckling crossing waters symbolizes death and going to other side. The folk tune is beautiful lament that speaks to dangers and price of war."

◆

Karl eventually picked up Iza and Volodya on his tractor and drove them to the horse paddock. He'd saddled up both horses but warned Iza that Lilli had been hard to motivate lately. Volodya was set up first to ride Lothar. He tentatively walked Lothar around the paddock, then transitioned to trotting, and finally to a full-out gallop, practicing turning and stopping. Iza had also ridden as a teen after she and her mom returned from the Middle East following her dad's death. Iza was set up to ride Lilli, but Lilli did not want to be ridden. The old mare walked around the paddock slowly and showed no interest in even breaking into a slow trot. Volodya rode up to Iza on Lothar and asked what was wrong. Iza replied with a shrug, "My pony won't go no more."

Karl returned from the barn carrying a double saddle. He called Volodya over, and they resaddled Lothar. Volodya had to sit in the forward position since he weighed more than Iza. She sat on the back extension saddle and held on to Volodya's waist. They each had their own stirrups. Lothar trotted around the paddock. Then Volodya got Lothar into a full-out gallop. When Karl saw they were comfortable riding, he told them how to get to the back fields for open-field riding. They headed out and eventually raced back and forth through the open fields, Lothar enjoying the freedom as much as Volodya and Iza. The ride was exhilarating. When an hour had passed, they returned to help Karl with brushing Lothar, said their warm goodbyes, and were driving on A115 back to Berlin by sunset.

◆

"Thank you for such fun birthday party, Iza."

"Your party is just starting!"

He smiled broadly, wondering what else she could possibly have planned.

It was 19:30 when they returned Jack's car and cautiously made their way back to the apartment. While Volodya showered, Iza prepared *belegte Brote* for supper. She cut thin slices of dark bread, topping each piece with a unique and artful combination of thinly sliced cucumber, sour cream, dill, sausages, cheeses, red onion, or tomato. She splashed a touch of vinegar on one of the open-faced sandwiches, placed a small piece of leftover basil on another with tomato and soft mozzarella cheese, then thinly sliced sausage, and arranged the slices with red onion and a touch of whole mustard on yet another. She continued until she had a dozen open-faced sandwiches. Then she creatively arranged the belegte Brote on the cutting board.

Iza poured them large glasses of water and small glasses of vodka. She raised the vodka glass and toasted, "Budmo. *Z dnem narodzhennya.*"

Volodya picked up his glass and replied, "Budmo."

Next, she brought out the beautiful Prinzregententorte that she'd hidden in one of the kitchen cupboards. "I don't have candles," she said, "but you can close your eyes and make a wish anyway."

"Can I have two wishes?"

"Maybe; it depends what they are."

"Can I have three wishes?"

"Don't be greedy."

"Okay, I'll make two." Volodya closed his eyes. *I wish for end of war in Ukraine—that my country be made whole again—to become European nation and NATO member. And my personal wish is for this life with Iza to work out for us.*

He opened his eyes and looked at Iza. She smiled.

"My wish did not come true."

"How so?"

"You still wear clothes," he said, laughing.

"You're terrible, Mr. Korsun!"

Slices of the delicious torte disappeared quickly.

Afterward, Iza led him over to the sofa. "Sit here, close your eyes, and hold your arms about a meter apart. No peeking!" She brought in the shopping tote with the winter jacket and rested it in his hands. When Volodya opened his eyes, he was shocked, but thrilled, to see the jacket.

"Iza, I cannot take this from you! You must spend your whole paycheck on such gift."

"Try it on."

He snapped on the hood and tried on the jacket; it fit perfectly. The dark brown color matched his hair and eyes. Volodya modeled the jacket for Iza, then snapped off the hood but left the jacket on, obviously pleased with her gift.

◆

They eventually lay in bed on opposite sides of the central pillow pile. Volodya propped himself up on one arm and turned, facing Iza. "Thank you for best birthday in my life. It was so fun. I am always happy since I met you." He reached his hand over the pillows and caressed Iza's hair, then leaned forward and kissed her. He and Iza looked intently at each other, and after a long pause, Volodya said, "Iza . . . I think I need cold shower."

Iza's eyes opened wide in surprise, and she started laughing softly. "Oh, Volodya . . . I think maybe we both do," she whispered. There was another long pause as Iza lay in bed thinking, Volodya still training his piercing brown eyes on her. *Iza,* a voice within her mind cautioned, *you need to think carefully about what you're doing here.* Another voice inside her replied, *I can't help it. I just can't help it. I love him.*

Iza threw back the comforter and tossed the center line of pillows off the bed, then unbuttoned her nightshirt. She lay on the bed with her nude body exposed to Volodya. He took his index finger and middle finger together and started at her lips, slowly running his fingers down the midline of her body, stopping to kiss her lips, neck, breasts, navel, and abdomen. They continued to intimately touch each other for several minutes. He eventually turned away and picked up something from the floor. Iza suddenly did the same. They met again in the middle of the bed, each holding a condom packet. They laughed quietly as they both realized that the other had expected this moment.

Iza whispered, "Yours or mine?"

"Yours."

Iza opened the packet and rolled the condom on Volodya. He moved Iza on top of himself. They made love passionately. Finally, Iza dug her fingers into Volodya's shoulders and inhaled deeply. "Oh," she breathed out. He breathed heavily seconds later. They both laughed quietly.

They lay together for a few minutes, then rolled apart. Iza laid her head on Volodya's chest as he caressed her hair.

"I need to wash off in the shower," Iza whispered.

"Me too."

They went to the shower. Volodya told Iza that he'd lead her, like dancing. He led her under the showerhead with him and turned on the water. A splash of cold water made them both shiver and then the warm water poured over them while they kissed each other. They eventually lay in bed holding hands but not saying anything for some time.

"I have thought about your suggestion to run away together and disappear," Volodya said finally.

"I didn't really mean it. I'm not leaving Berlin and neither are you."

"I know you were just kidding, but I also decide it is not possible. We will stay here together to face whatever comes our way."

"Do you think we should destroy the prints now? I've been arguing it both ways in my head."

"I am thinking, at some point, yes. But first, Tony will need to see them, and he will need to show them to whoever he knows in German security apparatus, then maybe to his U.S. contacts also. We need to find out where they came from.

Then we can destroy them. But even after we destroy them, these guys who are trying to find you will not know that. They will come for you. And when they do, we need to be ready."

They again lay in silence, still holding hands.

"Do you want me to put pillows back between us?"

"I don't think those pillows will work anymore."

"Be honest, Iza. Did you really think that they would—that you could share my bed with me with only little stack of pillows between us?"

"In my defense, I only thought I'd be here a day—or two at most."

"Do I need to put razor wire between us instead?" he asked, chuckling.

"That probably wouldn't work either. Happy birthday, Volodya."

Sunday, October 23 (Day 12)

At the briefing, the Team learned that the Russian military was pulling their elite units and officers from the west bank of the Dnipro, leaving only those soldiers considered "expendable." They also received intelligence that Iran was supplying Shahed-136 kamikaze drones to Russia. The intelligence indicated that members of the Iran Revolutionary Guard Corps were actually on the ground in Crimea, training Russians in the operation of the Shahed-136. Recent attacks on civilian infrastructure in Odesa and Mykolaiv had been attributed to bombardment with Shahed-136 drones, likely originating from Crimea; Ukrainian artillery didn't have the range to reach Crimea.

After the briefing, everyone went to their respective workstations. About an hour into the workday, Petro called out to Volodya in Ukrainian, "Hey, hey, hey, Volodya, quick, come here and look at this. Is this what I think it is?"

Volodya rapidly rolled his chair over to Petro's workstation and looked at the image area. He zoomed in. The image showed drones, but the GPS coordinates were not for Crimea. The images were from the southern Kherson region. Was it possible that the Iranians were training Russians *in* Kherson Oblast? The team leaders of the three countries met at Petro's workstation: Dymtro; the German, Max Meyer; and the American, Lloyd. Petro showed them his finding while Volodya looked on. Max ordered, *"Bitte, töt die Ficker!"* They sent their Ukrainian military contacts an urgent encrypted message with the GPS coordinates.

At their first break, everyone except Volodya evacuated to the canteen to eat or outdoors to check their phones. Volodya stayed in the main work area but moved to Lloyd's workstation. What he was about to do was strictly forbidden—

using his cell phone in the work area and running defense software for personal use. And he was about to hack into his Team Leader's workstation. *Volodya, do not get caught. You could be disciplined or worse.*

Each member of the Team had access to a powerful facial-recognition software program. They'd constructed a database of Russian Ministry of Defense officials—generals of all levels, senior officers, and field-grade officers. They'd searched open-source and downgraded classified documents for photographs of the people holding those positions. The Team continued to add photos as new material became available. Every photographic addition built the system's knowledge. The facial-recognition software was used to confirm the deaths of Russian officers in the field. The Team received photos of Russian officers killed in action to compare with photos in their database. The information was useful as a propaganda tool for the Ukrainian government, but also for Ukrainian military planners. If the Team could confirm that high-ranking Russian officers were in the field in a specific area and had been killed there, that told military planners something about Russia's military intent and troop readiness.

The facial-recognition program could also access open-source photographs of any person from the internet. The program could identify a person only if they'd had sufficient photographic media coverage.

It is not likely I will learn anything, but footage of tall, blonde guy is still loaded on my cell phone, and this is something I need to try for Iza. He watched the entry door to the work area in case anyone returned from break early. He didn't want to use his own system in case the inappropriate use of the software could be traced. Volodya slipped over to Lloyd's workstation. It took him only minutes to hack into Lloyd's computer.

Volodya loaded the security camera images of the tall, blonde man into the program from his phone when prompted. He was already nervous, then imagined that he heard someone walking into the main hallway, but he saw no one as he looked up from Lloyd's station. With the footage loaded, he started the facial-recognition program.

Volodya's fingers tapped nervously on Lloyd's keyboard as he impatiently waited for the output of his search. He kept looking back and forth between the screen on Lloyd's system and the entry door to the work area. At last, the program displayed the output of photographs. Volodya quickly scanned through them. Most were not close matches—a film actor, an American football player, a Swedish diplomat—people having some facial features similar to the tall, blonde man. But several photos interested Volodya. He zoomed in on these images for a better look. He eliminated several images from consideration but was getting increasingly anxious; it was near the end of their break time. He quickly copied the web addresses of the several remaining images onto a scrap of paper, stuffed the paper into his shirt pocket, and then rapidly logged off Lloyd's system.

Bobby walked through the door just as he was about to get out of Lloyd's chair. The two men made eye contact. *Shit,* Volodya thought. A spontaneous idea came to mind, and he called, "Hey, Bobby, come here." Volodya had a good rapport with Bobby, but he noticed that Bobby walked cautiously to Lloyd's work area.

"What y'all doin' at Lloyd's workstation?" he asked suspiciously. Bobby glanced over seeing only a blank screen at Lloyd's station.

Volodya replied casually, "I stayed behind here at break to try other chairs. Mine makes my back hurt so bad. I like Lloyd's best. Think I can get one?" Lloyd had a Wilkhahn 3D In Chair, a German-made luxury computer chair that cost over €2.600.

Bobby shrugged his shoulders. "Might could," he responded.

Both Bobby and Volodya knew there was absolutely no way that Volodya could order a chair such as Lloyd's. In reality, the German and American members of the Team had arrived on-site at the data center two weeks ahead of the

Ukrainians in mid-June. They'd taken all the best furniture for themselves, and Volodya knew that Bobby had surely taken his share. If the timing had been reversed, Volodya was also certain that the Ukrainians would have done the same. As it were, Volodya had only a green, vinyl-upholstered desk chair that he guessed was a holdover from the World War II era.

Bobby then suggested with a broad smile, "A guy could help you adjust your chair."

Volodya could see that Bobby was no longer suspicious, and took that as his opportunity to get out of Lloyd's chair. "Okay," Volodya nodded his head in agreement. The two walked over to his workstation. He and Bobby worked on adjusting the old desk chair as the other Team members slowly filtered back into the work area.

At 15:00, Dymtro strode over to Petro's station. "Petro," he said, slapping him on the back, "congratulations on your find this morning. Petro, Volodya, tomorrow we have security safety review. Lloyd, Max, and I will be here, but neither of you nor any others are allowed. See you both on Tuesday." Volodya grabbed his leather jacket, said a quick goodbye to Petro, and was out the door.

Volodya waited outside the data center until the courtyard was deserted. One by one, he typed the website addresses from his facial recognition search into the web search bar on his phone. The screen eventually displayed a smiling Evgeny Petrov. Volodya read that the Russian biathlete won the bronze medal in the fifteen-kilometer mass-start biathlon race at the 2014 Sochi Olympics. In the photograph, Evgeny was wearing a beanie cap, so his hair was completely covered. Volodya scrolled further down the page and learned that the International Olympic Committee had stripped his medal following a doping scandal, and he was banned from further participation in the sport. Evgeny was twenty-seven in 2014, which would now make him thirty-five—in the correct age range that he and Iza had guessed from the security camera footage they'd previously viewed. To Volodya's eyes, the tall, blonde man now had a name—Evgeny Petrov—a disgraced, former Russian biathlete.

Iza returned from her laundromat and grocery shopping expeditions on Oranienstraße with totes she could barely carry. She emptied the laundry bags into the bedroom armoire, making neat piles of their clothing, and noticed that Volodya had hung up his new winter jacket in the armoire—the only piece of clothing that she'd ever known him to hang up. Everything else was simply thrown in a jumble in the armoire or on the floor. After cleaning the apartment, Iza finally said aloud, "Okay, Iza, you're trying to avoid calling Mom. And admit it to yourself—it's all because you're worried Günther will be there."

When it was 15:30 in Berlin—9:30 a.m. in Washington—Iza dialed her mom's number. Elise answered the phone immediately.

"Iza, how are you?" she inquired. "I was planning to call you later today. I have some news to share about Tony."

"I'm okay Mom; how are you? What's new?" She already knew the terrible news.

"I'm so excited, Iza. Günther and I just made plans to be in Costa Rica for Christmas!"

"Oh?" Iza responded, a bit startled. She was expecting the news about Tony. She quickly responded, "I thought you might be coming to Berlin. Didn't Günther want to visit his son here?" *Don't you want to visit me?*

"We hadn't made plans back then, and now we have. Costa Rica sounds more exotic than Berlin. It'll be warm there, too. I might even get to wear a sundress." Elise continued, "Did you get the cell number for Günther's son that I sent? Günther wondered if you saw it."

"I did, Mom. I just haven't had time to follow up, but I promise I will."

Elise abruptly changed the subject. "I'm sorry, Iza. I wanted to call you while we were still in Vermont, but the phone service was so poor where we were staying, and then I simply forgot. Tony's mom died last Friday, and the funeral was on Tuesday. I gave a memorial gift from the two of us."

"I actually talked with Roger late last week, and he told me the news. Thanks for including me on the memorial gift, Mom. Let me know how much I owe you for that. I wish I'd known sooner."

"I'm sorry. I've just been so busy."

They chatted about the funeral and the fall colors in Vermont. "Iza, before I forget, Günther has two questions for you about your new suitcase. He needs to buy one for our Costa Rica trip."

Iza's eyes opened wide, and she inhaled deeply. "What does he want to know?" she asked quietly.

"Well . . . remember the time you met Günther here at the house when you'd just brought your new suitcase home from the department store? He told us he liked the blue color because he thought it'd be easy to find on a luggage carousel. Neither of us can remember how large it is. And, he wondered if there are any storage pockets on the inside."

Iza tried hard to be considerate of her mom, but she was suddenly growing suspicious of Günther. It took her a few seconds to answer.

"Well, are there?" Elise asked again.

"No, Mom," she lied. "If he needs that kind of storage space, he'll have to buy a toiletry bag or something. But the suitcase is good sized."

"I'll be sure to tell him. You *do* still have the suitcase at your apartment, right?"

"Mom, where else would I have it?" *Does Günther want to know where my suitcase is stored? Is he somehow involved with the blueprints?*

Elise replied, "*I* don't know. Maybe in one of those scary Berlin basement storage rooms like your father and I used to have. Günther wondered in case he has any other questions

115

about it for you. You know, for the exact measurements. That's all."

Iza relaxed. "Sure, Mom. Let me know if he has any other questions about it. I can measure it for him." *Maybe I'm just being too sensitive, but this is so disturbing.*

Elise then turned the conversation back to Günther's son, but Iza didn't want to hear more about him. "Mom, I have to go; someone's knocking on the door here. Let's talk again soon. I love you, Mom." Before Elise could respond, Iza turned off her phone.

When Volodya arrived at the apartment, Iza was already dressed for a run. "Will you run with me?" she asked.

He quickly changed, and they set off on a ten-kilometer running route that Iza had planned through the Kreuzberg neighborhood. She set a blistering pace, and Volodya eventually dropped back behind her. When she finally noticed he was far behind, she slowed down and returned to him. "I'm sorry, Volodya. I talked with my mom this afternoon, and parts of her call really bothered me."

After they returned to the apartment and showered, Iza described Günther's questions about her suitcase.

"You know, Iza, maybe Günther actually wants to purchase similar suitcase for their upcoming trip. It could be nothing, but it could also be something. We need to keep him in mind. Would Tony know what his job is at German Embassy?"

"I don't know. He hasn't been around that long. But we can ask Tony."

"I had very stressful experience illegally using facial recognition program at data center for us today."

"I told you that you shouldn't have gotten involved with this, Volodya. You could be in trouble if anyone discovers you used that software."

"But Iza," Volodya revealed, "I think we now know who our tall, blonde man is. He is Evgeny Petrov. I do not know his work now. Maybe your friend Tony can help us find out." He opened the photo of Evgeny Petrov on his phone. Iza's eyes opened wide. "He was bronze-medal biathlete in 2014 at Sochi."

"No wonder he could run so well!" She shuddered at the thought of the harrowing chase.

"Iza, there will be security review for data center on Monday, and I do not have to be there. Tomorrow, I have whole day to think long and hard about encounters you had with each guy. Maybe I can make good story for Tony when we meet him later tomorrow."

They eventually went into the bed and lay close to each other, holding hands, each separately wondering about the connection between the man from the airport, the man murdered outside of Iza's apartment, Evgeny Petrov, and the blueprints.

Monday, October 24 (Day 13)

Volodya had a restless night. Since he'd learned of his parents' deaths, his grief was absolute. Yet he realized that he didn't want his parents' lives to be defined by the cruelty of their deaths, nor did *he* want to remember them only in death. Even though he'd tried to keep happy memories of them at the fore, he'd had a recurring nightmare in which he watched as his parents were tortured and killed because they had photos on their cell phone of him and his brother wearing their Ukrainian military uniforms.

In the nightmare, he saw Russian soldiers burning his mother's face with a lit cigarette. He saw them tie his father's hands behind his back while he was standing, then beat him with a club on the back of his knees until he could no longer stand. He saw the Russians assault and rape his mother, laughing as his father looked on, unable to stop them.

Volodya would always awaken from this nightmare in a disturbed state, distressed that the atrocities of Bucha weren't just a terrible dream. A neighbor had witnessed his parents' torture and murder and had told Volodya how they died. The soldiers eventually shot each of his parents in the head at close range and buried them together with others in a shallow, mass grave. The neighbor had been spared but still had the scars of cigarette burns on her face.

Thankfully Iza is still sleeping, Volodya thought. He did not want to burden her with why he was sometimes unable to sleep and hoped he'd never have to tell her about his nightmare. He didn't want to share his despondency with her. His sense of hope in life was returning simply because, for some reason, she loved him. She made him happy, and he wanted to be happy again.

He left for an early fartlek training run to erase the disturbing images of his parents from his mind, reasoning that a run at his usual pace interspersed with high-speed sprints would tire him until he could no longer think.

When he returned to the apartment, his head was clearer. Iza was still sleeping, so Volodya showered, trimmed his stubble beard and mustache, then combed his long hair to make it less of an unruly mess. He examined himself in the mirror, wondering if he looked suitable enough to attend a dinner at the U.S. Embassy with Iza's friend, Tony. He stood dejectedly before the mirror.

Volodya, you do not have dress clothes—jeans and long-sleeved shirts are all you have. You only have one pair of old running shoes. Ukrainian government cannot pay well. At least U.S. government pays your rent to live here and fee for your cell phone. Dymtro and Petro can supplement their meager salaries from their savings, but you do not have any savings since you have not worked normal job yet. You are such pathetic character. You are already twenty-nine years old and you still have no job, no money, no place of your own to live, and now no family either. All your possessions are secondhand junk. War has taken whole year from your life already, and there is no sign when it will end or how. What kind of life can you offer to Iza? Why should she even love you?

◆

Volodya gently shook Iza awake. "Iza, time for work. I have coffee for you."

Iza sat up in bed, yawned, and smiled broadly at him. She drank the coffee he offered as she looked over his combed hair and trimmed beard. "You cleaned up real good," she said brightly, then rolled off the bed, headed for the bathroom, and eventually dressed quickly.

"Volodya, Tony's admin is supposed to call me today with details for our dinner. We'll have to figure out how to get you in the building. I'll call as soon as I hear, but I'll be in meetings most of the day. I might have to call after 17:30."

Iza took a tote from the kitchen and put her long-sleeved black dress and black shoes inside. She planned to change into the dress before the dinner. As she was about to exit the apartment door, she suddenly dropped the tote bag, rushed over to Volodya, and kissed him. "Thank you again for helping me," she whispered. She tousled his hair with her hands while laughing softly. With that, she picked up the bag and ran out the door to work.

On her walk to the embassy, Iza stopped at a flower stand. She purchased a large bouquet of sunflowers. When she arrived at work, she hurried to Jack's office to return his car key and to thank him for arranging the visit with the Bauers. Jack wasn't in his office yet, so Iza left a note with the bouquet.

"Iza, today we're attending the starting session of that week-long meeting I told you about. Diplomats from France, Italy, and Spain are here to discuss their economic and energy situations with the Germans in relation to Russia's war in Ukraine. There's a European Union-wide meeting in November in Prague; this is sort of a pre-meeting of the big four EU countries to stake out their positions. Take careful notes; Tony asked me to aggregate everyone's notes into an interim report. The sessions are all scheduled at the Auswärtiges Amt . . . the German State Department."

Claire and Iza walked the several blocks from the U.S. Embassy to the Amt. In the morning session, the Germans presented their plan to subsidize natural gas prices for their consumers and businesses. This plan raised questions from France and Italy. The Spaniards empathized with the Germans: "The Germans have a pressing need to find alternatives to Russian natural gas," they argued. "The consequences of the war in Ukraine impact us all, but they *clearly* have a greater impact on Germany, which has a higher dependency on Russian carbon-based fuels. Remember that Germany is Europe's leading economy; it is in all our best interests that Germany continues to do well."

◆

Iza and Claire proceeded to the coffee station during a thirty-minute break to refresh their cups. While standing in line near the station, a man approached Claire.

"Claire, how nice to see you!" the man proclaimed with a broad smile while holding out his hand in greeting. He was a nice-looking, friendly man who appeared to be in his early- to mid-forties, with sandy blonde hair and bright blue eyes.

"Alex, it's great to see you, too," Claire responded as she firmly shook his hand, carefully balancing her coffee cup in her other hand. "Alexander Schröder, I'd like you to meet a new coworker of mine from the embassy. This is Iza Carter."

Iza smiled, "Hello Alexander."

Alex looked closely at her nametag and then again at her face. "Oh," he exclaimed, "I would not have recognized you." Iza and Claire looked at him curiously. "I'm sorry," he responded. "About a month ago, when I was last in the U.S., I was actually at a party—I believe at your house, Iza. Is your mother Elise Carter?"

"Yes, Elise is my mom."

"I saw a photo of you with your dad hanging on the wall there. Of course, you were a lot younger then, but you have also changed a lot since that photo was taken. All for the better." He smiled again. "So very nice to meet you and to see you again, Claire," he repeated as he continued on to his seat.

Claire whispered to Iza, "He's an up-and-comer in the Social Democratic Party; he's a member of the Bundestag from Berlin—a real schmoozer. Remember his name. We'll be seeing it a lot in the future."

Iza and Claire refreshed their coffee, then returned to their seats. But Iza nearly spilled her coffee as they walked. She knew the photo that Alex was referring to. It was hanging in the hallway near her bedroom, where she'd left her open suitcase for packing.

◆

Volodya sat at the kitchen table, deep in thought. He began scribbling summary notes for the upcoming meeting with Iza's friend, Tony. He first wrote, *Who is guy at airport who searched through Iza's suitcase?* He and Iza had discussed the incident and were sure he was not a random thief. He must have arrived that morning on an international flight—possibly even on the same flight as Iza.

Beneath the first question, he wrote another: *How many international flights arrived in Berlin on the twelfth, including Iza's flight?* He and Iza had previously planned to ask Tony to access the airline passenger manifest for Iza's flight first. He'd searched on his phone and learned that U.S. airlines are required to keep passenger manifests for three months, which meant the manifest would still be available for Iza's plane. He hoped they could use it to identify men within a specific age range who were traveling alone on her flight. Better still would be if Tony could find photos of the passengers. He knew Iza had a pretty good description of the man from the airport, and she remembered his face in some detail. If she couldn't identify a man fitting that description on her flight, then they'd need access to passenger manifests and passport photos for the remaining flights.

His next question was: *Who was guy murdered outside of Iza's apartment building?* Iza had learned that the man was a German citizen and that no further information could be given out for security reasons. Volodya looked up murder statistics for Berlin. In 2021, there were only one hundred murders in and around Berlin. It seemed an unlikely coincidence that a man would have been randomly killed immediately outside of Iza's building right after her encounters with the man at the airport. Her apartment was located in a relatively safe neighborhood in Berlin—at least safe from violent crime, such as murder. As he sat thinking, he suddenly wondered aloud, "If further information is unavailable for security reasons, then what does this mean for guy's identity? Was he security threat or guy involved in some aspect of German security apparatus?

Who killed him and why?" Volodya had to admit that they wouldn't be able to make further progress without having more information about the man from the German authorities.

Volodya now thought about the tall, blonde man, Evgeny Petrov. He wrote: *What is Evgeny's line of work now?* They knew he was a Russian. He had broken into Iza's apartment after creating a diversion by shutting off the power in her building. It appeared that the tall, blonde man did not know exactly what he was looking for, and he also seemed reluctant to remain in Iza's apartment when the power was restored.

Volodya said aloud as he continued writing, "Was Evgeny afraid that he'd be seen near Iza's apartment? Does he have any connection to murdered man? Did he kill German guy?" Perhaps Evgeny himself had to be careful.

Evgeny had also chased Iza on the night that she'd returned to her apartment to check inside her suitcase. Volodya wrote: *Why did Evgeny chase Iza?* Again, he summarized aloud as he wrote, "He must have suspected Iza had already discovered what was originally in her suitcase, and he thought she came to get it that evening. He must have decided to seize her that night and force her to hand it over."

Volodya became increasingly distressed as he continued to scribble his summary questions: *If tall blonde man is Evgeny Petrov from Russia, then does he actually work at Russian Embassy?* This was likely a question that Tony could help answer, since the CIA would possess intelligence on employees of the Russian Embassy in Berlin.

Volodya's mind was now racing. *Russians like Evgeny are ruthless. If Evgeny finds Iza, he will do anything to her to get what Russian government wants. And once he has that information, he will kill her.* Volodya sat back, unable to focus for several minutes.

At last, he wrote his final question: *Who would have placed blueprints in Iza's suitcase?* He again wondered aloud, "Iza's mom's boyfriend, Günther Kohler? Günther had asked such specific questions about Iza's suitcase. But then, what is Günther's motivation? Is he spy for Russians? She said he supports Russia's cause in Ukraine. Or, is he simply Iza's mom's boyfriend, who Iza does not care for? Who else could have done this?" He wrote a big question mark.

Volodya was now even more anxious about Iza's safety and about the safety of his work Team than he had been. He hoped that Tony could help fill in some of the blanks. He and Iza would have to depend on Tony's help. He completed his notes, incorporating everything he'd thought about, and then waited for Iza's call.

Iza called just after 17:30 and left a message. "Hi Volodya. Can you meet Garrett Dennison inside the Embassy entrance at about 18:50? He's one of Tony's aides, and he'll escort you to the private dining room."

Volodya packed his notes into a grocery tote. He thought about bringing along the blueprints but changed his mind. They'd be safer where he and Iza had hidden them. He left early and walked to the U.S. Embassy, waiting outside on the plaza until 18:50. Garrett greeted Volodya at the Embassy entrance, where they met with Embassy security personnel to get an entrance pass issued.

Iza changed into her black dress and dress shoes, then walked to the dining room. Being the first to arrive, she toured the room. It was split into two areas, as defined by the furniture placement: a sitting area with a low, round table between four upholstered club chairs and a dining area with a round dining table and four dining chairs. The dining table was located farther from the door. The décor was all in muted shades of grey. Several framed prints hung on the walls around the sitting area. The prints showcased famous sights of Berlin, such as the Brandenburg Gate lighted at night and the Memorial to the Murdered Jews of Europe. She strolled around, looking at the prints.

Tony arrived next. Iza recognized his tall figure right away, though his conservatively styled, thick light brown hair was sprinkled with more gray than she remembered. He wore a navy cashmere blazer, grey wool slacks, an open-collared blue-and-white striped dress shirt, and polished black wing-tip shoes. His relatively large laptop computer case overflowed with papers. "Tony!" Iza smiled as she ran over to give him a warm hug. They made small talk. She could immediately tell that Tony was *not* in a good mood. His hazel eyes spoke volumes. His flight into Berlin had been rough, he hadn't slept much, his Monday in Berlin had not gone well, and he was still grieving the unexpected passing of his mother. He appeared impatient and a bit sullen—not his usual diplomatic self.

Garrett escorted Volodya into the room. Iza brought Volodya over and made the introductions. "Tony, this is Volodymyr Korsun. Volodya, this is Tony Brooks."

Volodya extended his hand in greeting and smiled warmly at Tony, "It is my honor to meet you, Mr. Brooks."

Tony's response was a curt hello and a tepid handshake. As they sat in the club chairs around the low table, Iza excused herself to use the restroom. Volodya sat across from Tony, looking him directly in the eyes but saying nothing. He could sense that Tony was judging his appearance, which he immediately resented. It was also apparent to Volodya that Tony didn't trust his intentions. Volodya thought, *Tony needs to understand that I am helping Iza. I am not here to take advantage of her.*

Tony finally broke the silence, "Volodymyr, how long have you known Iza?"

"Eleven days."

"I've known her since she was a baby. I've been in her life for twenty-seven *years*."

Volodya sat staring at Tony for a moment, somewhat confused, then thoughtfully replied, "Time is one measure of commitment, but not only. You also commit when you help your friend when she has need. You commit when you show your friend courage when she is afraid, even though you are also afraid. Even in short time, you can make big commitment to someone."

They sat uncomfortably, staring at each other across the low table. Volodya did not understand why Tony was treating him so rudely. *I cannot help that I have no better clothes to wear. I have no money.*

Finally, Volodya questioned Tony. "Iza tells me this will be working dinner. We will discuss blueprints found in her suitcase and events since she arrived in Berlin, yes? We will need help from someone; of that, I am sure." His tone grew more defiant as he said, "If this is not true and you are unable to help us, I will leave so you can enjoy your dinner with Iza."

Tony scowled.

Dismayed, Volodya thought, *Tony does not seem like friend that Iza thinks. I will leave soon and find place to eat near embassy. She can have dinner with him, and then Iza and I can figure out new plan on our walk back to my apartment.*

Iza returned to the room and immediately sensed the tension between the two men. An attendant came into the room to take their drink orders. While Iza ordered an unoaked Chardonnay and Tony ordered a French Bordeaux, Volodya requested only a glass of water. Iza questioned, "Don't you want a red wine?"

"No, thank you," he answered quietly, smiling at Iza.

Just then, Tony's aide Garrett came back into the room. "Tony, you have a call from Tim in Washington." Tony excused himself and took the call on a secure phone located at the back of the dining area, far from where Iza and Volodya were seated.

"Yes Tim," he answered.

"Tony, I'm sorry this intel is late. Let's just say it's been a hectic few days in D.C., and Ukrainian translators are hard to come by right now; they're all busy. But I got the intel you asked for on Volodymyr Korsun."

"Thanks, Tim. Your timing is perfect."

While Tony continued listening, he glanced over to see Iza and Volodya laughing softly as they sat at the low table together. He eventually nodded, then ended the conversation. "Thanks, Tim. Appreciate your follow-up on this. See you in a week."

Tony walked back to the sitting area. Iza could see Volodya tense up as he returned. Tony asked, "Volodymyr, would you please step out of the room with me for a minute?" He slowly followed Tony out of the room, and Tony closed the door behind them. Iza wanted to know what was being said. She put her ear to the closed door but couldn't hear anything, so she started pacing worriedly around the sitting area.

◆

Volodya was prepared for Tony to tell him that he should leave, but to his surprise, Tony apologized. "Volodymyr, I'm sorry for my behavior toward you this evening."

Volodya looked Tony directly in his eyes but said nothing.

"I'm overly protective of Iza, to be honest. I needed to find out who you really are. I normally would have had that information before we met, but I just got it now. I apologize. Iza told me you were working for a joint-venture company here in Berlin, and that just didn't fly with me. It didn't seem logical that you could be legitimately working for a company in another country while there's a war going on in Ukraine."

Volodya continued to stare at Tony, insulted by the insinuation that he'd lied to Iza about who he was. *Yes, I could not tell her entire truth about why I am in Berlin. It was not intentional lie; it was necessary. And now she knows real reason. But I am not some criminal from Ukraine.*

"I don't know if she told you how her dad died?"

"She did."

"Well, *I'm* the one who assigned her dad to the mission that got him killed. I'll carry that guilt to my grave. I know she's a grown woman, but I don't want to see her get hurt again. Granted, it's no excuse for my behavior toward you. I'm supposedly a diplomat. Please . . . I ask for your understanding. Frankly, sometimes I'm such a dick." Tony held out his hand to Volodya.

Volodya stood for a moment, looking intently at Tony. "Okay, I understand," he replied slowly. "But I want you to know that Iza is special person to me too, Mr. Brooks . . . not only to you."

"Please call me Tony," his hand still offered to Volodya.

Volodya took Tony's hand and shook it. "My friends call me Volodya."

Just then, Tony's aide Garrett came jogging up the hallway. "Tony, you've got an important call. I've got you set up to take it in the adjacent dining area; that room is empty tonight. It should only take five or ten minutes." As Tony rushed to the adjacent room, he said, "Volodya, I'll be back in about ten minutes. You two go ahead with the drinks if they bring our orders before I get back."

Only Volodya came back into the room where Iza was waiting. He immediately whispered to her, "What does it mean when someone says 'I am a dick'?"

Iza was shocked. "Tony called you a dick?"

"No, no, no. A guy says *he* is a dick. What does that mean?"

"Well, he'd never say that, if he were really a dick. A dick would *never* admit he's a dick."

"I do not understand."

"It wouldn't be 'dickish.' You usually call another guy a dick—like in second or third person."

"But what does it mean, Iza?"

"In your example, it means the person isn't happy with his own behavior. He knows he's been rude or not very nice. But a real dick would *never* admit that, which is why you call someone who's a jerk a dick. Oh . . . do you know what 'jerk' means?"

"Yes."

Iza whispered as she leaned close to Volodya's ear, "Dick is also slang for your penis." Volodya started to laugh, and it made Iza laugh too.

"Really? That is funny."

◆

Tony eventually returned to the room. The three sat around the small table. The attendant returned with the Chardonnay and Bordeaux wines and a glass of water for Volodya.

"Could I change my mind? I think I would like glass of Bordeaux also."

Iza realized that whatever had transpired between the two men before, it now appeared that the tension had dissipated. Volodya had refused to drink with Tony until they'd returned from the hallway, and she wondered what had been said. Someone had been a dick—at least momentarily—and she guessed that someone was Tony.

Tony insisted they not discuss the events in Berlin until after their dinner. He told Volodya funny stories about Iza, his family, and himself, slipping into his usual diplomatic persona that Iza remembered, and the mood of the evening lightened.

After dinner, Volodya laid out his notes and began describing what had transpired so far and the questions that remained, beginning with the man at the airport. He asked Iza to fill in if he forgot anything. Tony grabbed a yellow legal pad from his computer case and took notes of his own.

Tony agreed that it was likely that the man had come in on an international flight, but he wasn't convinced that he was necessarily on the same flight as Iza. He told Volodya and Iza that it would be an easy task to get manifests from flights arriving in Berlin from the U.S. that morning, but perhaps a bit more difficult for flights originating in other countries. He agreed to assign an aide to create a list of relevant flights and obtain the manifests, when possible. His aide could comb through the list, and provide a smaller subset with passenger identification photos for Iza to review.

Volodya moved on to the man murdered outside of Iza's apartment. He presented what they knew about the man, then Iza turned to Tony and asked, "Did you learn anything from Herr Kühn today?"

"Frankly, not a lot, but something. I told him that we knew the man was a German citizen, and we wondered if he was somehow involved with a 'joint secret program' between Germany and the U.S. that I was aware of. Mind you, I'm not aware of any joint secret program. I asked him this just to see if he'd bite."

Volodya looked quizzically at Iza and silently mouthed, "Bite?"

Iza grinned and made a mental note to explain the expression later.

Tony continued, "Based on Wilhelm's discomfort around the topic and his answers, I'm guessing this guy was one of his."

"*Really?*" Iza exclaimed.

Volodya questioned, "So, 'good' guy?" Tony nodded his head in the affirmative. Volodya added to his notes. *If he was good guy, then what was he doing outside Iza's building on Friday night? Was he there to warn her? Or, was he there to retrieve what Iza later found in her suitcase? How did he know that Iza had this information?* Tony waited patiently as Volodya wrote his notes.

Next, Volodya laid out what they'd discovered about the tall, blonde man. He showed Tony the security photos and the Sochi Olympics photos. Tony interrupted him to ask how they'd gotten the security camera footage and how they'd found access to facial recognition software. Volodya admitted that he'd stolen the security camera footage from Iza's apartment building but didn't answer Tony's other question. Volodya conveyed his suspicion that the man might be working for the Russian Embassy—and that he'd recently learned Iza's name. In time, he'd learn where she worked so he could surveil her—or worse.

Iza explained how she retrieved the blueprints from her suitcase. "I told you this over our secure phone lines. Volodya and I discovered what the blueprints show."

Tony stopped her. "Iza, that can't possibly be printed on the blueprints, correct? How did you come to this conclusion? After we talked on Friday, I called my Pentagon contacts. Even *I* couldn't learn anything about such a program. How do *you* know about it?" he asked again stridently.

Iza looked uncomfortably at Volodya while she squirmed in her chair. Finally, Volodya responded, "It is where *I* work. Our address is marked on blueprints. On blueprints, I even see where I sit."

Tony's eyes widened, and he let out a loud sigh. "My God," he finally said quietly. "Iza, Volodya, my priority is your safety. I've got to get you two out of this mess."

Volodya responded with a wry smile, "I am in Ukrainian military. That is my job. Even if I wanted to, I cannot leave Berlin."

Iza added, "Tony, I've worked *so* hard to get this embassy job in Berlin. It took a year and a half of effort. I'll never forgive you if you transfer me to a different country. Berlin is a big city—we can blend in here. I'll be careful when I'm around the embassy. There are *always* a lot of people coming and going from the embassy. I can walk out with other people. And, Volodya's work group had a security review today. He'll hear tomorrow what actions they're taking to improve on it." Iza continued, the pitch of her voice rising with emotion, "Tony, someone in the U.S. got these blueprints, presumably from Germany, because all the writing on the blueprints is in German. And then they sent the prints here in *my* suitcase. How'd they get in there? Somebody is a spy and a traitor. We need to figure out who that is, and we need to stop them from doing any more damage. Kühn's man already got *killed*."

Tony sat in silence. He suddenly turned to Volodya and said, "Now I understand your earlier comments about commitment. I thought you were being insolent, but I realize what you meant. You are demonstrating courage."

Iza looked at both men in confusion, guessing that Tony was referring to their conversation in the hallway earlier in the evening.

Tony scribbled some notes on his legal pad, then looked up at Iza and Volodya.

"I need some time to come up with a more detailed plan for us. I'll likely get the CIA involved and FBI Counter-espionage, if they're not already working on this and I just don't know about it. We've got intel on Russian Embassy personnel here in Berlin. As I said, I'll get one of my aides working on the flight stuff."

Iza questioned, "Tony, when will you have time? You've got the European meetings this week. I know you can delegate some things, but you can't change the meeting schedule. And you're leaving early on Saturday morning, right?"

Tony thought for a moment. He looked at Iza and Volodya and said with a sly smile, "I just tested positive for COVID."

After the table had been cleared, Volodya excused himself to look at the framed prints of Berlin hanging in the sitting area. As he walked away from the table to view the prints, Tony said quietly, "Iza, Volodya's an impressive young man. I'm sorry I was hard on you during our call on Friday. I should know by now you've got a good head on your shoulders. I've simply been under too much stress lately. I'll do my best to help both of you."

Iza hugged Tony as she replied quietly, "Thank you, Tony. I'll try not to make any more stupid decisions, but there's no guarantee." He grinned and gave her a hug.

Outside the embassy entrance, Volodya and Iza bid Tony good night. Tony promised to keep in regular contact with the two of them throughout the week until his "case of COVID" resolved, and of course, would also stay in contact when he returned to Washington.

"I'll need those blueprints. And I hope we can have dinner together again before I leave; maybe I'll be feeling better near the end of the week," he said as he nodded at the two of them and then walked briskly in the direction of his hotel.

Volodya put his arm around Iza's shoulder as they strolled back to the apartment, carrying their tote bags. Along the way, he asked, "Iza, can you find out from Tony if he knows what Günther's job is at German Embassy? I was afraid to ask him tonight, but I think maybe we need to know that."

"I completely forgot to ask. You're suspicious of him too, aren't you?"

"Yes, I admit I am little suspicious."

It was late when they arrived back at the apartment, and they needed to sleep. But when they stepped into the bedroom, Iza kissed Volodya intensely. They rolled in the bed, kissing each other. "I love you, Volodya," Iza said quietly, "and, I'm sorry."

Tuesday, October 25 (Day 14)

Iza watched Volodya peacefully sleeping next to her. Before arriving in Berlin, she'd mentally mapped out her future life in great detail. But her life had taken an unexpected turn over the past eleven days. She'd never met anyone like Volodya before and had never expected to. He was someone with whom she felt a strong connection; he shared her interests, cared about the big issues facing humanity, was kind and thoughtful, a hard worker, and shared her sense of humor. Being thrown together by this intrigue and facing the reality of the war had accelerated their developing relationship, yet she knew in her heart that it seemed right. Then she remembered Roger's words: *"Don't overanalyze . . . You're prone to think too much, Iza . . . Follow your heart."*

Volodya awoke suddenly, rolled out of bed, picked his jeans and shirt off the floor, and stumbled to the bathroom. He brought coffee to the bedroom, and they sat together at the edge of the bed, discussing what they expected the day to hold for them. Volodya suddenly glanced at the time. "Iza, I will be late!" He grabbed his leather jacket off the floor, kissed her cheek, and ran out the door. A minute later, he rushed back into the apartment to grab his cell phone from the kitchen table and then disappeared out the door again.

Lloyd presented the results of the security review and the resulting changes. He shared that the reviewers believed the location of the data center was still perfect. It was located in an area of Berlin that was flush with other information technology firms, start-ups, and design firms.

How can I tell my Team about blueprints? Volodya thought as he listened to Lloyd's overview. *In theory, data center location might be perfect, but someone is trying to compromise our operation by revealing site location to Russians.*

Even though their location was deemed acceptable, Lloyd went on to explain that many other security measures had been found lacking. The site required additional closed-circuit television camera surveillance, an expanded monitoring station for security personnel, additional Marine guards, secure phone lines, a prohibition on using personal cell phones, and "something else" that he promised to describe shortly in greater detail. The current policies requiring that each Team member live in a different area of Berlin, remain unaware of their colleagues' housing locations, and abstain from socializing with other Team members outside of the data center would continue as previously instituted.

Finally, Lloyd introduced Janie Monroe—the "something" that he'd promised earlier. She was the current Chief of Disguise for the U.S. Central Intelligence Agency Office of Technical Service. She was fortuitously in Berlin for a special consultation on another matter and was available to help their group. She brought along a team of CIA disguise experts from the U.S. Embassy in Berlin to work with her, along with multiple boxes of her "props."

Janie was a tall, fit-looking woman, perhaps in her late forties, who carried herself well as she confidently strode to the front of the briefing room. Her long, curly blonde hair, large tortoiseshell glasses, and rather heavy makeup added to her persona. Following her introduction, Janie excused herself, explaining she'd inadvertently left something she needed for her presentation in the canteen. She returned in several minutes, except no one recognized the woman entering the room as Janie. She was now shorter, a bit heavier, and perhaps in her early sixties. Her short hair was a greyish-brown color, and her clothing was nondescript. She tentatively stepped to the front of the group.

Janie began her presentation by telling the Team that good disguises are hard to pull off. "A wig and makeup don't make a new person. A complete transformation requires an attitude adjustment," she said. "You'll notice how I first confidently strode to the front of the room but stepped tentatively into the room on my return. It wasn't only the wigs, heel-lifts, makeup, and stuffing materials that made me look different between my first and second entrances. It was also how I carried myself. We're not here today to give each of you a temporary disguise; rather, the objective is to make adjustments to your appearances and how you carry yourselves to help you look like IT entrepreneurs at a Berlin start-up company.

"Lloyd, you just presented that your location is perfect because your data center is nestled on busy Kurfürstendamm with other IT firms. But you guys need to blend in better with the people who work at these other firms as you come and go from this data center. Anyone looking for your location is going to find it because the majority of you look like soldiers coming to work here at 7:00 every morning." Her gaze turned to Lloyd with his military regulation haircut.

Observing the eighteen Team members, Janie suggested that the bulk of her work would be with the Americans. They needed to look and act more European and less "martial," as she called it. However, her group would evaluate each Team member.

Following Janie's presentation, Max and Dmytro briefed the team on the status of the war. During the past twenty-four hours, Ukrainian aviators had carried out more than thirty air strikes. Twenty-two areas of weapons concentrations and military equipment, five ammunition warehouses, and the positions of nine anti-aircraft missile systems of the enemy were destroyed. Artillery and missile forces hit six areas of concentration of manpower, weapons, and military equipment, two ammunition depots, an anti-aircraft missile complex, and a radar station. Not all the targeting information for these strikes came from the Team, but their contributions were significant. Max wished everyone assembled "happy hunting" as the Team members filtered out to their workstations.

Janie first called Dmytro. She looked at Dmytro's impressive girth and confessed that there was little that they could do to make him look thinner. She and her group of experts asked Dmytro to stand as he normally would, then to walk back and forth in front of the group. Janie looked at the greying hair on his temples. They dyed Dmytro's greying hair to match his hair color, checked out his lip configuration to find a temporary mustache that would match his natural facial hairline until he could grow out his own mustache, and trimmed his brows, nose, and ear hairs. He was given a pair of straight-legged, relaxed-fit black jeans; a long, dark gray, button-front shirt to be worn untucked; and a funky-looking black field jacket. He looked like a generic, heavyset Eastern European tech entrepreneur. Dmytro walked back into the workroom and directly over to Petro and Volodya. They had to admit that Dmytro looked at least five years younger. Dmytro responded in Ukrainian, "When Katya sees me next, she'll think I found girlfriend here in Berlin."

Next, Petro was called. Janie quickly established that Petro would need little alteration in his appearance. Petro's thick, black, horn-rimmed glasses were replaced with a pair of round, gold, John Lennon-style wire rim glasses. An identical pair with prescription lenses would be delivered by the end of the week. That was her only recommendation for Petro.

Volodya was the last of the Ukrainians called. Janie took one look at him and remarked, "Well, you certainly look like a young, techie buck already." Volodya had no idea what she meant. They evaluated his walk and his stance. Janie remarked, "Stop pressing your shirts. A few more wrinkles in your shirts will give you just the right messy look." He returned to his workstation unchanged but grinning. He couldn't wait to tell Iza about his shirts.

Janie moved on to the Americans, and her group began with Lloyd. He was a tall, trim, Black man with a military regulation haircut. Like typical Americans, he had a particular way of standing with his weight on one foot or the other, unlike Europeans, who tended to stand firmly on both feet. Janie told him that if he wanted to pass himself off as a European, he'd have to practice walking like a European male and standing squarely on both feet with his arms at his sides. "Observe the people out on the street; imitate their gaits and their mannerisms."

She and her team decided to shave Lloyd's head completely, then added an ear piercing to his left ear. They glued on a chinstrap beard and a mustache, then recommended that he try growing that style. They fitted him with a pair of charcoal-colored men's skinny jeans, a black pullover turtleneck shirt, a relatively wide black belt, and black fabric running shoes. They chose a black double-breasted pea coat and a tight-fitting skull cap for outerwear. Lloyd was not at all comfortable with his new look. But, the other members of the Team were amazed at how different he appeared.

Janie's team worked throughout the day in this manner. Finally, they came to Bobby. Janie decided that her team would need more time to decide what to do with Bobby, and promised to return the next day with an answer. "His look just screams 'Alabama'," she said. By 16:00, she and her team had departed for the day, leaving their wares in the canteen.

It was 8:15. Before leaving her office, a call came in from Tony on her secure phone line.

"Tony, how are you feeling?" Iza asked with mock concern.

"Actually, not too bad," he replied with a laugh. "Maybe this will pass quickly." He continued, "Iza, I left a message with Tim in D.C. to get going with the flight details and manifests from your travel day to Berlin. I told him to focus on your incoming flight first. He can probably have that intel to me by the end of our day today. If we don't find the airport guy on your flight, Tim can get going with the other flights and manifests tomorrow. I'd like you to stop by my hotel room on your way out tonight to look at any photos he sends. I'm checking with the CIA at the embassy to see if they can get you in to review Russian Embassy personnel photos yet today. That might be this afternoon. Keep your cell phone handy for my call."

"What do I tell Claire if I have to leave the meeting early?" Iza asked.

"If you have to leave, I'll talk to Claire. Don't worry. I'm also thinking ahead that the CIA may want to pull you completely out of your apartment, just to be safe. They can set up a window-washing crew or some other building maintenance people to grab the rest of your belongings and get them out."

"What about my lease with Frau Böhmer?" Iza questioned.

"If that's what they decide, they'll take care of the details. You don't need to worry."

"Any other thoughts about the man who was murdered, and how to get more info from Herr Kühn?"

"Iza, I'm thinking about confronting him with the blueprints."

"Tony, *seriously*?"

"Yeah, what if I meet with Wilhelm and bring along your German blueprints? I'll confront him. If I don't get his cooperation in figuring out where these came from, I'll run this up to our CIA Director and someone high up at the Pentagon. He's got to know more than what he told me yesterday, which was pretty much nothing. We may have a problem in D.C., but he may have a bigger one here. Like we talked about yesterday evening, I'm pretty sure it was one of his guys who was murdered."

"Tell me about Kühn. I only talked with him once, but he seemed like a different guy. He's your friend, right?"

"Yeah, I've known him quite a few years. He's the most dedicated public servant I've ever met. He can be friendly—he is with me—but his 'business' is always foremost in his mind. And that business is protecting the security of Germany. He can be demanding and tenacious."

"He sounds scary."

"He can be, but he can also be a big help."

"Do you know what Günther Kohler does for his job at the German Embassy?"

"Why is that important to know?"

"He asked some unusual questions about my suitcase the last time I talked to Mom. It made me wonder if he's somehow involved with the blueprints."

"I actually don't know his exact job title. I mean . . . I think he has some middle-management-type job . . . in administration. Seriously, I'm not completely certain. But I *highly* doubt he could be involved. He doesn't seem savvy enough to be involved in something like this. Are you sure that's your motivation in knowing more about Günther? Your body language when you've been around him makes it pretty clear you don't like him. Is that the real reason you've let yourself be suspicious of him?"

"Well . . . if you can discretely find out what he does there, let me know," Iza replied, not answering Tony's questions.

"I can do that when I get back home next week. I'm sure our CIA people in D.C. know."

"What about Volodya? I don't know if I'll hear from him at all during the day. They're supposed to have their security review results today. It might be good for you to hear what his people had to say. I don't even know if the lead people he works for are aware these blueprints exist. If he calls, should I invite him to meet with us at your hotel room?"

Tony hesitated, then replied, "Yeah Iza, that's probably a good idea. If you hear from him and he has time to get here, have him stop over too. By the way, I'm in Room 410 at the Hotel Adlon Kempinski."

Iza wrote down the hotel name and room number. "Tony, I'll look for your call later today. If I get to the hotel by 17:30, is that reasonable?"

"Sure, I'll see you then if I don't talk to you beforehand. Be sure to knock loudly in case I fall asleep while I'm recovering here," Tony laughed softly again.

"Tony, I'm so grateful for your help. Love you."

◆

The natural gas supply situation in Germany, France, Italy, and Spain was again the planned focus of the sessions at the German State Department. Today the countries would exchange the policies they intended to propose at the upcoming E.U. meeting in Prague.

As they walked to the meeting, Claire asked Iza, "Did you hear? Tony contracted COVID. He won't be at any of the meetings this week."

"Wow, Claire, that's terrible! I hope he doesn't get too sick." Iza feigned concern, knowing that Claire wasn't aware of her dinner with Tony the previous evening.

At the 13:00 lunch break, Iza excused herself to make a call to Frank Masters' family. She'd just completed the call and was ready to arrange the transfer of his body when a call came in from Tony.

"Tony, what's up?"

"I've got you set up with the C group at the embassy, Room 110, at 14:30. They'll be expecting you." *He knows my phone line isn't secure*, Iza thought, recognizing his code for CIA.

"And you're going to call Claire?" Iza questioned.

"Yeah, I'll do that as soon as we're finished here."

By the time Iza returned to the meeting room, Claire had already turned off her phone after talking with Tony. "Wow, Iza," she said, "Tony sounds horrible."

Iza stifled a laugh. "That's too bad."

"He asked if I'd mind if you ran a few errands for him. I guess he needs another 'gofer' today. I told him that'd be fine. Hope you don't mind."

"That's fine, Claire. I'd like to hear more from the meeting here, but I want to help Tony too."

◆

Iza arrived early for her meeting with the CIA. She was fascinated by the complete dossiers the CIA had on every employee of the Russian Embassy in Berlin, which she paged through until she recognized the tall, blonde-haired man. However, he didn't have blonde hair in the CIA photo. His hair was very dark brown. The CIA assistant told her that wasn't unusual; people working in those positions often changed hair color or other identifying features to throw off any potential surveillance. His name was different too—Mikhail Dobrynin—an Embassy Security Attaché. But there was no mistaking him, even if his name and hair color were different.

Iza said, "His name is different than what I expected."

"Sure, you might have seen his real name—Evgeny Petrov. After his embarrassment at the Sochi Olympics, they changed his official name when he moved into this job at the Russian Embassy. He's been assigned to Berlin for about five years now."

The CIA assistant also informed Iza that they'd recover her belongings from her apartment in the coming week. They'd close out her lease for her as well. When she inquired how that was done, the assistant simply told her not to worry about it. They'd contact Tony or her to arrange a time to deliver her belongings.

Iza returned to her office and saw a text from Volodya; he was returning to their apartment. "Volodya, can you come to Room 410 at the Hotel Adlon Kempinski at 17:30 to meet with Tony?" she requested, using her secure phone line.

Volodya met Iza outside Tony's hotel room. Tony's aide had sent passport photos, names, ages, and occupations for all males between thirty and sixty-five years of age and traveling alone on her flight from Dulles to Berlin. There were forty-eight men. Iza slowly paged through the passport photos. She had only seen the man briefly, and that was nearly two weeks ago. However, it was such a shock to see someone rummaging through her suitcase that she remembered the man's appearance in detail. She came to a photo that caught her eye, and she eventually convinced herself that *this* was the man who'd been searching through her suitcase. His name was Johannes Brandt, aged fifty-eight, a sales representative for imperative Energie GmbH. They all agreed that his line of work and employer were not what they'd expected. Tony questioned, "Iza, might you have misidentified the man?"

"It's a possibility, Tony," Iza responded, "but if your aide sends more photos from all the other flights that day, I don't think I'll do any better. This photo is *very* close to what I remember."

After Tony set aside the photos, she recounted the information she'd garnered from her meeting at the embassy with the CIA assistant. "The tall, blonde man, Evgeny Petrov, bleached his hair blonde. They changed his name to Mikhail Dobrynin. He's a Security Attaché at the Russian Embassy. The assistant also told me they'd recover my belongings from my apartment and close out my lease next week."

Iza looked discreetly at Volodya, and he smiled at her. She was glad she could continue living with him, and could tell that he was glad too.

Volodya told Iza and Tony in general terms about the security review results. He couldn't divulge much information, only that he'd be unable to use his cell phone while at the data center. They'd eventually have secure phone lines there, but that wouldn't be until the end of the week.

Finally, Tony turned their conversation to Herr Kühn and the man who'd been murdered. He'd already arranged for another meeting with Wilhelm on Thursday morning. "I'll need the blueprints for that meeting," he said, assuring Iza and Volodya that he was working on a plan to confront Wilhelm with the blueprints. He told them to "stay tuned." Volodya looked curiously at Iza; she knew he didn't understand the expression, but she'd explain later.

◆

The meeting with Tony had lasted two hours.

"We should take U-Bahn," Volodya suggested. "It will be faster than walking and we need to eat."

"Do you think it's safe?"

"It is not as safe as walking, but maybe tonight it is okay. I do not see anything unusual outside here. I do not think anyone is watching for you."

They sat down together in the subway train car. There was only one other couple in the car with them. At the next U-Bahn stop, the other couple suddenly exited the car, laughing and holding hands as they walked past Volodya and Iza. A solitary, tall man entered the car, partially blocked from their view by the exiting couple. It was Evgeny Petrov.

Volodya noticed him immediately after the couple exited. *Fuck. I did not think. U-Bahn line passes near Russian Embassy. He is probably just going home from work.* Iza was looking out the window and hadn't seen Evgeny enter, but Evgeny caught sight of her immediately in the empty car and a sinister smile spread across his face.

Volodya stood, hoping to draw Evgeny away from Iza. Volodya wanted to tell her to exit the car before it pulled away, but the words didn't come fast enough. Iza looked over when Volodya stood up and saw Evgeny approaching. Her eyes opened wide in terror. It was too late.

Evgeny punched Volodya in the upper abdomen, knocking the wind out of him with his well-aimed blow to the solar plexus. Volodya fell to the subway car floor, kneeling and clutching his midsection while gasping for breath. Iza grabbed Evgeny's jacket and tried to pull him away from Volodya, but he was immoveable. She screamed in horror, as Evgeny came again for Volodya, knocking him completely down and stomping on his rib cage. Volodya writhed in agony on the floor of the subway car.

Evgeny then grabbed Iza by her forearm. She tried to pull away, but he was far too strong. He dragged her toward the subway car door as she struggled to resist him. The U-Bahn pulled away from the stop. Evgeny was momentarily distracted by the sudden movement of the train, and Iza took the opportunity to bite his forearm above his wrist, drawing blood. Evgeny let go of her and screamed in Russian, "You fucking bitch!" He hit her above her right eye while throwing her back into a seat, causing a small gash and a deep purple bruise.

Volodya saw Evgeny strike Iza and was overcome with intense rage, adrenaline surging through his body. He knew Evgeny would take Iza if he could, and once he had the information he wanted, he'd kill her. *You will not take Iza from me without killing me first,* he vowed. Still lying on the subway car floor, he quickly pulled his Swiss army tool from his leather jacket and flicked open the knife blade. Volodya stayed low on the floor, keeping the blade concealed. He knew the Russian would attack him again to prevent him from following them off the subway car at the next stop.

Evgeny grabbed Volodya by his hair and pulled him up, laughing mockingly as he bent his tall frame over Volodya, preparing to crash his foot into Volodya's midsection. Volodya lunged forward and stabbed Evgeny in the neck, using both hands to apply as much force as possible, then dragged the knife through his flesh. Evgeny clasped the long, deep gash in his throat and fell backward into a seat, stunned that he'd been stabbed. He attempted to hold his throat together to stop the blood from spurting out, but it was everywhere. Volodya's leather jacket was spattered with it, and his hands were crimson. Iza looked on in shock, unable to move as the U-Bahn pulled into the next stop.

"Iza, we get off here," Volodya quietly ordered her. "Keep head down, hair over face. I walk right behind you, with head down and hands hidden behind you."

They exited the train, Volodya hiding his bloody hands from sight. He whispered to Iza, "We take escalator out of station. Stay close to me. Keep face covered." Iza did as she was told, still in a state of shock at what had just happened.

Her eye was rapidly swelling shut. Volodya's adrenaline rush subdued the pain of his damaged ribs.

"Will he die?" Iza asked quietly as they slowly moved out of the station.

Volodya whispered, "Maybe, maybe not. It depends how fast he gets help." They heard sirens wailing nearby as they continued walking slowly away from the station exit.

"I need to wash off my hands."

"I have a water bottle in my daypack," Iza whispered back as she scanned the plaza ahead. "Let's walk over to those shrubs by the Berliner Dom. I can pour the water over your hands there, and none of these people will see us."

They stepped off the sidewalk into the shrubs. Volodya washed the blood off his hands and knife as Iza slowly poured water over them.

They casually turned and walked in the direction of Volodya's apartment, glancing back to see the Polizei and an ambulance crew racing toward the U-Bahn station entrance.

◆

When they got to the apartment, Volodya threw his jacket on the floor and quickly brought a cloth soaked in cold water to clean Iza's eye. It was nearly swollen shut, and the skin around it was a deep purplish-black color. He looked at the cut above her eyelid; it didn't look as though it would require stitches. He rubbed an antibiotic ointment over it. Volodya sat on the sofa and opened his shirt to see that the right side of his rib cage was already severely bruised. He felt along his ribs; it didn't seem as though anything was broken, but time would tell. He wasn't looking forward to the pain that would flood over him once the adrenaline fully broke down in his body, which he estimated would be within minutes to an hour or two at most.

"Should we call Tony?"

Volodya shook his head sorrowfully. "Not if I killed Evgeny. Yes, it was self-defense and Tony would understand I was defending you. But we are in Germany, and Tony cannot protect us here. I could be arrested and charged with assault or murder. You might be arrested too because you were with me. We cannot tell anyone. Hopefully no camera saw us."

Wednesday, October 26 (Day 15)

Iza awoke around 2:30 to use the toilet, and her eye throbbed in pain. She looked in the mirror to discover that her eyelid was so swollen, she couldn't even force it open. Volodya had given her his pillow, but even with the elevation their two pillows afforded, her lid had continued to swell. *It'll probably be bad for at least a couple days, and then it'll take a couple weeks before the color fades,* she thought with dismay.

When Iza returned to the bedroom, she noticed that Volodya was curled in a fetal position, and she could hear that his breathing was abnormally shallow. Iza knelt at the side of the bed, realizing that Volodya was awake. "Iza, I hurt so bad," he said quietly.

Iza went to the bathroom, drenched a towel in cold water, wrung it out, and laid it over Volodya's bruised rib cage. She tasted his salty tears as she caressed his face and kissed him. He was crying from the pain. Iza massaged his forehead and ran her hands through his hair, trying to calm him and lessen the pain sufficiently so he could sleep.

How can we function tomorrow? Iza thought. *I'll have to go to the meetings at the German State Department. What can I tell people? Maybe I'll say I ran into the edge of a door or I fell on an evening run and hit my eye on a metal bollard. Should I put a bandage over my eye so no one can see how terrible it looks? And what about Volodya? What can he tell his coworkers—if he can even get to work? At least one of us has to drop off the blueprints tomorrow before Tony's Thursday meeting with Herr Kühn. If Tony finds out what happened and sees me, he'll transfer me out of Berlin. There won't be anything I can say or do to convince him otherwise.*

She looked down at Volodya and saw he'd finally drifted off to sleep. She took the towel and drenched it in cold water again, wrung it out, then laid it on his ribs, softly kissed his forehead, and slipped back into bed.

◆

Volodya's ribs hurt almost unbearably. He looked over at Iza, who was wide awake and watching him, but turning made his ribs hurt even more. He saw that her beautiful eye was a swollen, purplish-black mass.
It is my fault. Taking U-Bahn was foolish mistake. He heard Iza laughing softly. "Iza, what is funny?"
"Look at the two of us! We look *so* pitiful."
"How come we are not like guys in movies? They are punched and shot and keep going," Volodya laughed softly to keep the pain in check.
"It's because they're not real people. *Real* people break."
She brought large glasses of water and the bottle of aspirin from the kitchen. "I'm glad you bought the jumbo size," she said with a grin. Iza helped Volodya sit up in bed, then continued, "Today, I'll buy ice packs for us and a heating pad. And I'll check if a compression wrap might be recommended for your ribs. I'll buy some eye patches and naproxen sodium, too."
"You have to also buy newspapers."
"Why?"
"Such attack in U-Bahn will be in papers. I am not worried that I will be identified right away. There are probably many long-haired guys with leather jackets in Berlin, and who knows I am here? Only very few people. But you look like American woman. If there is good security camera footage of you, maybe some police guys will find you. And through you, they could find me."
"I should have thought of that. I'll pick up newspapers on my way to work. Volodya, you should go to a doctor for X-rays."

"No, I am okay," he responded, trying to ignore the grinding pain he felt. *I have no insurance and no money.*

"Well . . . if your ribs don't improve in a few days, you'll *have* to go in. I'll *make* you," she threatened.

Volodya assessed Iza's eye and agreed she should bandage it; it would be best if no one could see how terrible it looked. They had no eye patches, but Volodya fashioned one out of gauze. He sat on the sofa, and Iza laid her head on his lap. He could apply the bandage in that position without putting too much strain on his rib cage. He cut a section of gauze to fit her eye area, then carefully taped it into place. It wasn't as neat as a precut patch, but seeing the white gauze looked better than seeing her swollen, purplish-black eye. He asked Iza to sit up next to him. He kissed her cheek near her eye, saying, "If I kiss it, it will be all better." Iza smiled, remembering she'd said the same thing to Volodya when he burned his hand on the spaghetti pot handle some days ago. Volodya continued, "Now I need cold shower."

Iza smiled coyly, then laughed.

"I will take blueprints to Tony after work," Volodya said. "Can you tell him I will come by his hotel late today?"

"Are you sure you can go there? You're really hurt."

"*You* will not visit Tony today." He knew Tony wouldn't believe she'd gotten a black eye on accident. He'd quickly reason that something had happened after they'd met him at his hotel. Tony had confided in Volodya that Iza's dad's death still weighed heavily on him; he wouldn't allow something to happen to Iza on his watch.

"Volodya, I'm telling people at my work I got this black eye by running into a door. What are you telling your people?"

"Hmm. Maybe some guy tried to rob me, and he hit me in ribs?"

"What about Tony?"

"Maybe he does not notice something is wrong."

"I think he'll notice; you aren't walking or even breathing normally, and you aren't going to be by this afternoon either."

"Iza kicked me?" he grinned at her.
"You better think of a good excuse. He'll know something is wrong."

Volodya left for the data center early, taking the blueprints along in a grocery tote that he held onto tightly, hidden within his leather jacket. He rode the U-Bahn directly to the northeast station on the Ku'damm. Although the aspirin helped to reduce the pain somewhat, by the time he walked into the briefing room, his skin was pale, beads of sweat were forming on his hairline, and he was in obvious pain. He was early for the briefing, but Petro and a few others were there.

With concern on his face and in his voice, Petro asked in Ukrainian, "Volodya, what happened?" Volodya just shrugged and shook his head without answering. Petro kept looking at him with concern. The rest of the Team gradually filed into the room, but no one else noticed Volodya. They were focused on the briefing.

Intelligence reports indicated that Ukrainian troops were holding out against repeated attacks by Russian forces in Avdiivka, outside Donetsk, and in Bakhmut. Troops at the southern front were poised to battle for the strategic Kherson region, which Russia appeared to be reinforcing. However, there were also contradictory indications that *all* Russian troops were evacuating across to the east side of the Dnipro. It was perhaps disinformation and a trap for the Ukrainian military. Iranian-made Shahed-136 drones were targeting critical infrastructure across Ukraine and had targeted Kyiv overnight. Some damage was reported, but there were no fatalities or injuries.

After the briefing, Lloyd, Max, and Dmytro left the room immediately to attend an additional security-review meeting. The remaining Team members slowly moved to their respective workstations. Volodya waited until everyone else was gone, except Petro, who waited with Volodya.

"Volodya, what happened to you?" Petro asked again in Ukrainian so the others wouldn't understand. "You're *hurt*, yes?"

"Some guy tried to rob me and kicked me in ribs." Volodya took out his wallet and showed Petro that he only had €20 and ₴100, plus one credit card. "The guy should have asked first; maybe he would have given me some of his money instead." Volodya laughed softly so that his ribs wouldn't hurt. Petro gave Volodya his hand and helped him out of his chair. The two walked slowly together to their workstations.

Volodya admired Petro; he was like an older brother who actually cared about him, unlike his true brother, whom he'd not heard from since May. In some other circumstance, perhaps when the war ended, and if they were each still alive, he hoped that he and Petro could remain friends. He'd never met Iryna, but he thought he and Iza would probably like her. She liked to cook and bake, and she enjoyed music and art. She'd even worked at a museum. He'd heard this much about Iryna from Petro.

Janie and her team arrived again after the briefing, hauling their boxes into the area where they'd be working on Bobby. Volodya flagged down one of Janie's helpers from the Berlin CIA Disguise group from the U.S. Embassy. "Can you help with leather jacket to remove stains?" he questioned. He lied that he'd stopped at a *Fleischerei* on his way home Tuesday evening, and they'd accidentally splattered his jacket with blood.

The woman looked at his jacket, saying, "We can try. We do have leather cleaner and restorer somewhere in our boxes here." Volodya pulled his Swiss Army tool out of one of the pockets, then discretely removed the grocery tote from where he'd concealed it in the folds of his jacket, before handing over the jacket. The jacket disappeared into the area with Bobby, Janie, and the other Embassy CIA Disguise group members.

The transformation of Bobby was something none of the other Team members had expected, nor something they could have imagined. Janie gave him a wig of long, brown hair in his natural color, pulled back into a ponytail, and a full, heavy beard and mustache. He was dressed in blue jeans with a brown belt, an open-collared white shirt, a brown windowpane-plaid sport coat, and brown boat shoes. He had a wool cap and a medium-length brown topcoat for outerwear. Bobby no longer screamed "Alabama." The others found it amusing that Bobby actually seemed to like his new look. "I was worried they were gonna turn me into a snuff-spittin', knuckle-draggin' hill ape," Bobby told the Americans when he returned to his workstation, "but this look ain't all that bad." The Germans and Ukrainians had no idea what Bobby meant by a snuff-spittin', knuckle-draggin' hill ape, but the Americans from the South roared in raucous laughter, which made the others laugh along.

Before the morning break, Volodya worked on updating maintenance records for the sixteen high-mobility artillery rocket systems—HIMARS—in Ukraine. With a range of three hundred kilometers, precision targeting, rapid-strike capability, and the ability to "shoot and scoot," the HIMARS were proving a formidable weapon for Ukraine in the war against Russia. One of the Team's tasks was to ensure these systems were routinely maintained according to U.S. military standards.

During the morning break, Petro came to sit with Volodya in the canteen. Janie's assistant brought Volodya's leather jacket to him as she stacked some of their boxes for later pick up. "Everything cleaned off from the accident," she told him. "It looks almost new." Volodya thanked her profusely but didn't move from his chair. Petro grabbed the jacket and handed it to him.

Near the end of the break, when everyone else had returned to their workstations, Volodya remained in the canteen area. Atop one of the boxes the woman from the CIA Disguise group had stacked was the long, curly, blonde-haired wig Janie had worn during her presentation on Tuesday. Volodya grabbed it and stuffed it down the sleeve of his leather jacket. *Iza can use this as disguise when she leaves Embassy.*

At the start of their lunch break, Volodya sat together with Dmytro and Petro. The three talked quietly with one another until Bobby slid into a seat beside the three of them. They switched from Ukrainian to English and maintained a lively conversation, with Bobby choosing the topics of discussion. Bobby could always keep their group well entertained, even if they often couldn't understand half of what he said. The distractions helped Volodya dismiss the searing pain in his side. But by early afternoon, he could feel his energy level sinking and the rib pain increasing, despite a steady dose of aspirin.

◆

Iza left for the Embassy at 7:30. Along the way, she purchased copies of the *Berliner Morgenpost* and the *Tagesspiegel* from a newsstand. She'd planned to complete the few final items for the Masters' family and scan through the newspapers, but at 8:15, her embassy phone line buzzed. Iza answered and was surprised to hear Roger's sleepy voice.

"Roger, isn't it like 2:15 a.m. there, or are you traveling somewhere?"

"Yeah, Iza, it's early here. I'm in D.C. I had a crazy dream, and I . . . I needed to call you."

"Oh?"

"Yeah, kid, remember me telling you how I'd go out for a few drinks with your dad like once a month or maybe every other month? We'd call it our 'session.' Your dad and I could talk about anything, kind of like me and you. So anyway, in this dream, we're drinking in one of our sessions, and he suddenly gets real agitated. He tells me you're in trouble, and I need to help you. Iza, it was *so* real. I woke up, and I just like had to call to hear you're okay. I figured you'd be at work there."

Iza was a bit shaken. She didn't want to tell Roger the truth; he'd be upset, and there wasn't anything he could do to help them. "Roger, I'm pretty much okay," she lied.

"Just pretty much okay or really okay?" he questioned.

"Yeah, I'm really okay. But if I'm ever not okay, I'll let you know for sure."

"I'm glad it was just a dream, then."

After a short pause, Roger questioned, "You *sure* you're really okay?"

"Yeah."

"Then I'll go back to sleep. I had to check. You know, your dad would have wanted me to. He really loved you, kiddo."

"Roger, are you still planning to come here this Christmas?"

"Yeah, Iza, for sure. I've been looking for cheap flights. When I know my schedule here and see a good deal, I'll call you to fix the dates."

"You sleep well. Remember, I love you." Iza started to tear up but had to stop herself. She needed the bandage to stay in place, covering her eye.

Iza grabbed the newspapers she'd bought earlier in the day and carried them along as she and Claire walked to the third day of meetings at the German State Department. She hoped to have time to scan them during one of the scheduled session breaks.

"Iza, what happened?" Claire asked as she stared at Iza's eye bandage.

"I guess I'm just having bad luck these days. First food poisoning, now I ran into a door and gave myself an ugly shiner. I decided to cover it up with this bandage so I don't gross everyone out. It'll probably take a couple weeks for it to get back to normal. I hope bad luck doesn't come in threes, or else I'm in trouble."

Claire chuckled; Iza was relieved that she didn't ask anything more.

The meeting of officials from Germany, France, Italy, and Spain once again proved fascinating. Iza got a few strange stares because of her eye patch but largely went unnoticed. Diplomats from Spain and Germany discussed the need to strengthen their alliance and promoted a plan to build a new natural gas pipeline through the Pyrenees to transport natural gas from Spain and Portugal to the rest of the European Union.

The talk broadened into suggestions that the pipeline be built for the future with the option to carry hydrogen. Iza was surprised because, although not an engineer, she'd understood that hydrogen transport required a much more sophisticated system compared with the transport of natural gas. She'd read that hydrogen is reactive and might lead to degradation of the usual types of metals used in natural gas pipelines. She'd also read that hydrogen is a notoriously "leaky" gas. The materials and construction requirements for such a pipeline would be incredibly costly.

In another talk, German diplomats once again defended their proposal for a €200 billion subsidy to businesses and consumers to combat the impact of rising energy prices. France and Italy opposed the plan because such economic resources were not available to them; the French and Italian diplomats complained that all countries needed a level playing field. German diplomats countered that Germany was working hard to improve the energy security of the entire European Union through their initiatives to build new terminals for importing liquified natural gas.

During the first break, Iza couldn't scan the newspapers because Claire remained in her seat next to her, and Iza didn't want to appear rude by ignoring her. Instead, Iza's mind wandered to the meeting with Tony and Volodya on Tuesday evening. She suddenly turned to Claire and asked, "If I wanted to learn something about a German company that's a *Gesellschaft mit beschränkter Haftung*, is there a research group at the embassy that can help me?"

"Which company do you need to learn about, and what do you want to know?" Claire asked curiously.

"No particular company right now. With all this talk about pipelines and terminals, it got me wondering which German companies are involved."

"Yes, there is a Research department at the embassy . . . a library of sorts. They'd help you find the information. I can send you the email address, or you can find them in the internal embassy directory."

"Thanks, Claire. I only wondered, you know, if down the road we'd need that kind of information."

Before Claire could respond, Alex Schröder slid into a temporarily empty seat next to them and glanced over at their padfolios, attempting to read what they were writing. "Claire and Iza, I observed that you are each taking copious notes at our meeting here this morning. Are Germany's plans for pipelines and LNG terminals truly of such interest?"

"Good morning, Alex! Yes, the U.S. is very interested in everything the big four economies are planning to eliminate their dependence on Russian natural gas. It's in our interest, since we're strongly supporting Ukraine in the war," Claire answered pleasantly, while closing her padfolio. Iza took Claire's cue. "I noticed you seemed to be doing some serious writing there yourself just before the break. Anything we should know about Germany's plans from the esteemed Berlin representative of the Bundestag?"

"I simply find the topic fascinating," he said with a smile, slipping out of the seat as the original attendee returned from break to reclaim his chair. "I hope it is nothing serious with your eye, Iza." He nodded, then waved to another attendee as he made his way to his seat.

"Notice he's sitting next to Stephan Gabel," Claire whispered to Iza. "He's another prominent member of the German SPD."

◆

Near the end of the lunch break, Iza excused herself to call Tony.

"Hi Tony, how are you feeling?" she giggled.

"Not bad, Iza. Today's when I'll take my next COVID test. If I test negative, then I just need one more negative test before I'm released from my self-imposed quarantine."

The two laughed together.

"Tony, I wanted to let you know that Volodya will be stopping by your hotel room in the evening with the 'stuff' you need. He wasn't sure on the time, but I told him you'd probably mostly be in your room anyway."

"Yeah, any time this evening is fine."

"How's the presentation coming?" Iza queried.

"Pretty well. I still need to anticipate how he'll respond to some of my questions and decide how I can counter any arguments he makes."

"I'll let you get back to it then. Thanks, Tony." Iza was ready to hang up, but Tony continued.

"By the way, Iza, can you and Volodya get together for dinner with me in an embassy dining room on Friday evening? I'd like to see both of you before I leave on Saturday. I'll ask Volodya when he's here too."

Iza hesitated, thinking of her swollen, purple eyelid. "Sure, we'd like that. I have to get back to the meeting room here. Will you call tomorrow after your meeting?"

"Yeah, maybe not right away, but sometime in the evening."

"Great. Good luck tomorrow."

The meeting restarted, and Iza still didn't have time to look at the newspapers. She thought the afternoon portions of the meeting were just as interesting as the earlier sessions. It was fascinating to hear the diplomats in action and to keep a watchful eye on Alex Schröder. By the end of the day, her eye was throbbing in pain, but she'd made it through perhaps the toughest day. She wondered how Volodya was doing; they'd had no way to call each other. The new secure phone lines at the data center wouldn't be available until late in the week.

It was after 17:30 when Iza returned to Volodya's apartment, still carrying the unread newspapers she'd purchased in the morning. On the way home, she'd stopped at a drugstore to purchase what they'd need for mending their wounds, and, at a music store along her route, she'd also bought a CD of Joaquin Rodrigo's Concerto de Aranjuez, with Serbian classical guitarist Mak Grgić. *I hope Volodya likes the concerto; I remember it's a mix of classical and folk sounds, and he likes folk music. He needs a break from stress, and I do too. The fun at the apple orchard already seems like the distant past.*

Volodya hopped on the S-Bahn from the Ku'damm station, carrying the blueprints for Tony. He slowly walked the remaining kilometer to the Adlon Kempinski Hotel, arriving at Tony's room near the end of civil twilight. He wasn't feeling well; it was too soon after his rib injury to be walking any distance, and his stomach was starting to reject the aspirin he'd been taking.

"Volodya, come in," Tony greeted him—warmly, this time.

Volodya moved slowly into the room, greeted Tony with a firm handshake, then quickly sat in the highest chair he saw and tried to ignore the concerned expression on Tony's face. Volodya had originally hoped to simply hand the prints over to Tony and leave, but he'd thought of some additional questions he needed to ask. He knew Tony might need time to find answers before he left Berlin on Saturday.

Tony laid the blueprints out on the desk at the edge of the sitting area and looked them over. Volodya sat motionless in his chair, biting on his upper lip and frequently closing his eyes, pressing them together in obvious pain. Tony finally looked up from the blueprints. "So, this Kurfürstendamm 23 is the address, correct?"

"Yes," Volodya answered weakly.

"And Iza says this stamping here means 'Top Secret,' correct?"

"Yes, I think so. Tony, is there restroom down hall from your room?" Volodya asked quietly.

"No, I think there's only a public restroom on the first floor of the hotel, but you can use mine in the room here."

Volodya sat for a moment thinking, then walked to the bathroom in Tony's room. He immediately turned on the faucet in the sink and flushed the toilet while he vomited. He sat on the closed toilet for a moment, composing himself, flushed the toilet again, then rinsed his mouth and washed his face and hands in the sink. He hoped Tony couldn't hear him. When he came out of the restroom, Tony stared at him as he walked slowly back to his chair.

"Any more questions about blueprints?" Volodya asked.

"Not about the blueprints, Volodya, but about you, yes. What on earth happened to you?"

Volodya hadn't considered a response, even though Iza had warned him Tony would notice something was amiss. Volodya didn't really feel like answering, so he changed the subject. "Tony, if Iza thinks airport guy works for imperative Energie, can you find out more about company? What do they do? I think GmbH company has to list directors, yes? Who are they? Does place have headquarters in Berlin? How many employees? Anything else interesting about company?" Volodya bit his upper lip and closed his eyes again, breathing slowly and shallowly.

Tony walked around the desk and stood in front of Volodya's chair, crossing his arms. "Volodya, those are good questions, but I won't help you answer them unless you tell me what happened to you. Did something happen to Iza, too? Is that why she isn't here with you tonight?" His speech became increasingly strident.

Volodya sat quietly, carefully thinking about how to respond. "A guy tried to steal from us last night on U-Bahn," he said, choosing his words cautiously. "Iza is okay—just little black eye. He might have breaked ... broken ... my ribs.

That's all. We do not have money, so he got nothing from us. We are both okay. Really."

Tony exhaled loudly, leaned against the edge of the desk, and replied, "What if I don't believe you?"

"Then I will leave. I need to go home." Volodya shook his head and stood up unsteadily to leave. Tony blocked him.

"Sit down," he ordered. Volodya fell back into the chair. "Now you listen to me, Volodya. You tell me exactly what happened to you and Iza, and then we can talk about your questions, and then you can go."

"Please, I tell you truth," Volodya lied.

Tony looked at Volodya with an expression that conveyed both frustration and pity. "I want to trust you Volodya, but honestly, if I hadn't already heard from Iza today, I wouldn't be letting you off so easy. I'll look into your questions. I want to have dinner with you and Iza again on Friday evening at the embassy. I'll try to answer your questions by then, and I'll let you know about the meeting with Kühn tomorrow. I'm calling a taxi to take you home."

"That is okay. I will walk."

"No. It isn't 'okay.' You're riding in the taxi I call. At least let me help you that much." Tony called the hotel's front desk to arrange a taxi, then slowly accompanied Volodya to the curb outside the hotel. They stood in an uncomfortable silence until the taxi pulled up in front of the hotel. Then Tony said, "Take care of Iza and get some rest. I'll see you Friday, hopefully with some answers." He patted Volodya gently on his shoulder and helped him into the taxi. He prepaid the driver and then walked back into the hotel shaking his head.

◆

Iza first paged through the *Tagesspiegel*. "Man in Critical Condition after Subway Attack," read the headline in the Local section of the paper. The article reported that the man's throat had been slit in an apparent robbery attempt, although the victim's wallet and other valuables were not taken. The paper indicated that authorities were looking at security camera footage. They'd tentatively identified a couple exiting the U-Bahn, but as Iza read further, she realized the exit mentioned was where the other couple on the subway train had exited. She paged through the *Berliner Morgenpost* next. "Man's Throat Slit in Apparent Robbery Attempt," read the second headline. The body of the report also indicated that the man's valuables were not taken and that, at present, there were no suspects in the attack. Iza left the newspapers open to the articles on the kitchen table to read to Volodya.

Volodya returned to the apartment at 19:45. Iza took one look at him and helped him into the kitchen. She got the ice packs ready and wrapped them around Volodya's ribs, loosely holding them in place with a compression wrap. She read the newspaper articles to Volodya but didn't ask about the meeting with Tony. She could sense that he didn't want to talk about it. Iza turned on the CD player, and they listened to Rodrigo's Concerto de Aranjuez while holding hands at the table. Iza was pleased that Volodya liked the concerto. She played it a second time, then helped him to bed and brought another ice pack. She then massaged his forehead to help relieve his stress until he finally fell asleep.

Thursday, October 27 (Day 16)

Volodya carefully moved out of bed and retrieved ice packs for his ribs and Iza's eye. He also fetched the wig he'd stolen from Janie on Wednesday. "Iza, you can wear this wig when you leave embassy at end of day. It will make you look different in case anyone watches for you. And see how well Janie's worker cleaned blood stains from my leather jacket."

"Wow, that's amazing! I thought you'd need a new jacket, but the spots don't even show." Iza then quietly asked, "How was the meeting with Tony?"

Volodya frowned and looked downhearted. "I think Tony does not like me so much. Maybe I lie too often or not good enough for him. I always think I am honest man, but maybe that is not true any longer."

Iza stared at Volodya with a sad expression on her face, "I've always tried to be honest too, but now we can't be. We have to protect each other. When this is all over, we'll be honest again; it's who we are."

"Just so we are always honest with each other," Volodya sadly smiled at her. "Do you need help with your eye bandage today?"

"No, these new bandages just stick on; I think I can do it myself."

With that, Volodya kissed Iza and departed for the data center.

◆

Iza purchased newspapers again on her way to the embassy, wondering if there would be updates on the subway attackers and Evgeny Petrov's condition. She didn't have time to look through the papers before Claire arrived at her office door.

The two chatted as they made their way to the German State Department. "What do you think of the meeting so far, Iza?"

"I'm not sure I agree with the German energy-subsidy approach. To me, it seems like energy is *the* principal resource; it defines what an economy is. Printing more euros to subsidize energy prices for companies and consumers doesn't make more energy. It doesn't mean I don't support helping people in need with paying their energy bills. I mean, it isn't acceptable if people are freezing to death or something. It only seems help could be more targeted to those who really need it, and others could be asked to sacrifice more. But I suppose if the German government doesn't do it, it'll turn a lot of people against supporting Ukraine in the war."

"Those are my thoughts exactly."

"What do you think about Alex Schröder's visit yesterday? He seems friendly enough, but something about him is a little disturbing to me."

"He's a schmoozer. It's hard to tell with him. What's his purpose in asking some of the questions he asks? It makes him seem a bit slimy at times. But honestly, he's a politician—and probably a good one. They're all a little slimy, aren't they?" The two laughed in agreement.

During the first meeting break, Iza called the Research department at the U.S. Embassy. "Hello, my name is Iza Carter. I work as an assistant to Claire Daniels in Consular Affairs. We're currently attending a meeting at the German State Department about energy and economic issues. Can you assist me in finding information about a specific company, imperative Energie GmbH? We'd like to learn the nature of their business, the number of employees, the names of company directors, and founding information; actually, whatever information you can pull together." The Research department employee told Iza she'd assemble everything she could find, and Iza would have the information by Friday morning. Iza provided her phone number and email address, then thanked the woman for her help.

◆

Tony entered Wilhelm Kühn's third-floor office promptly at 10:00. The two hugged and exchanged pleasant greetings, then talked about their respective families and reminisced about their previous dinners together. Wilhelm was a tall, thin man in his early sixties. He had a long but straight nose, a somewhat pointed chin, and an otherwise relatively flat, long facial profile. His hairline was receding but with a pronounced widow's peak, and he wore a closely trimmed beard and mustache, all a uniform light gray. His piercing, narrow eyes were an intense, icy blue color. He was always fastidiously dressed, and this day was no exception.

Tony immediately exhibited the German blueprint photocopies, explaining that they revealed the location of an active, top-secret U.S.-German-Ukrainian military operation in Berlin, which could have been, and still might be, compromised. If the prints were to fall into the hands of the Russians, the operation might be "terminated." The prints were planted on an unsuspecting U.S. Embassy employee traveling from the U.S. to Germany. A Russian agent in Germany had already attempted to recover the prints. The agent had nearly killed Tony's embassy employee, but the information contained in the blueprints remained secure. Tony shared his suspicion that there was some connection between the blueprints and *Wilhelm's* agent, who'd been murdered on the evening of October fourteen. This was Tony's reason for requesting more information about the man murdered in the Mitte borough. Tony offered that perhaps he'd not made that clear in his previous meeting with Wilhelm. *Now he'll have to divulge more info since I've said I know it was his agent who was murdered, even though I really don't.*

Wilhelm showed no emotion during Tony's presentation. He simply nodded his head at times as if nothing new were being revealed to him. When Tony stopped, and after a long pause, Wilhelm stated, "Tony, you have presented no information we do not already know here in Germany. Four months ago, these blueprints were copied. But my agents have been working on this 'case' for a much longer time, actually. Since near the end of last year. It seems we have a problem here in Berlin, and you, my friend, also have one in Washington.

"My agent broke into your employee's apartment here in Berlin to recover the blueprints, but he informed his superior he was unable to find them. He was ordered to wait outside the apartment building for your employee to return home when he was murdered. I believe a Russian Embassy employee—Mikhail Dobrynin—was his killer, although I have insufficient evidence. My agent was killed by a single gunshot through his head with a 0.22 LR cartridge. I presume you know who uses this type of bullet."

Wilhelm then stated he had his suspicions about the identity of the U.S. spy in Washington, but he wouldn't reveal who he suspected. He would only say that he had "a top man" working on the case in the U.S. and expected an eventual breakthrough. Tony thought, *I'm waiting to hear back from the Secretary for permission to contact FBI Counterespionage; it'd be a lot easier if you simply told me who you suspect, Wilhelm.*

Tony questioned Wilhelm, "What about these blueprint copies?"

Wilhelm removed his pipe from his desk drawer and pulled out a butane lighter. He lit his pipe, then walked to his office window and opened it. "Ah, Tony, it's a beautiful October day in Berlin, don't you think? It must be nearly fifteen degrees—sorry, about sixty to you—and mostly sunny, with barely a breeze."

Wilhelm suddenly grabbed the blueprint copies and lit the edge of the stack using his lighter. He held the burning papers outside his open window until it seemed as though he might burn his hand. Then he flung the remaining fragments into the air, causing bits of ash to fall beneath Wilhelm's window.

Wilhelm then indicated he'd need to leave soon for a lunch engagement. But he suddenly showed Tony a recent newspaper clipping about a man who'd been brutally attacked in the U-Bahn on Tuesday evening.

"Since he is a foreign citizen and works for the Russian Embassy in Germany, my agency is involved in the investigation." Tony wondered why he raised this subject.

Wilhelm continued, "Unfortunately, the security camera at the U-Bahn station where the attack occurred was not working properly. We were only able to capture two poor-quality still images of the perpetrators. However, I realized anyone who *exits* the U-Bahn had to *enter* somewhere. My people pulled security footage from the cameras further up the line. This footage of the perpetrators matches with the poor-quality still images."

Wilhelm stood at his desk, while turning his computer monitor in Tony's direction. It displayed security camera footage of Volodya and Iza near the entrance to the U-Bahn in the vicinity of the Adlon Kempinski. He then showed the still photos of the two at the U-Bahn station where they'd exited. Tony's eyes opened wide as he inhaled deeply and then momentarily held his breath.

"He, I don't know who he is. But she, I think, is one of yours—Iza Carter, I believe? Perhaps she's the U.S. employee you mentioned in your earlier presentation, yes? You see, just as your CIA knows the identities of our employees here in Berlin, we too know the identities of yours. Iza Carter called me on your behalf some days ago to inquire about our agent who was murdered on the fourteenth."

Wilhelm continued with contempt in his voice, "I personally have no sympathy for the Russian. As I told you earlier, we suspect he's the one who murdered our agent. The Russian had only stepped onto the U-Bahn when the alleged attack occurred. In the footage, as he entered, I saw that he is a large and imposing man. This made me wonder why a relatively small man and a thin woman would attack such a person *precisely* when he entered the subway car. To me, it seemed rather odd." Wilhelm paused briefly and then continued, "I have no doubt the Russian attacked them instead, and they were merely defending themselves. However, the Russian Embassy wants answers. I can make this security footage disappear permanently and am inclined to do so, Tony. *Scheiß auf die russische Botschaft!*"

Tony tried to hide the shock and trepidation that he felt.

"I would be most grateful to you if that were to happen, Wilhelm," Tony responded quietly and respectfully.

Wilhelm set his pipe in a holder on his desk, smiled broadly, and hugged Tony. "It was so nice to see you again, my friend. Next time, I hope it will be under better circumstances."

Tony left the BKA feeling tired, old, and humbled.

When Tony returned to his hotel room, he called for a room service lunch, then phoned the Research department at the U.S. Embassy. "Jeanine, this is Tony Brooks. How've you been?" he began. After the two conversed briefly, Tony said, "Jeanine, I need your help finding some information about a German company—imperative Energie GmbH. I'm interested in whatever you can dig up about them."

"Wow, Tony, you're the second person to ask for research on that company today. I'm already working on it, and I'll have the information to you by tomorrow morning."

"Oh? May I ask who else inquired?"

"Normally, my answer to most people is no. But for you, yes. The woman's name is Iza Carter. She apparently works with Claire Daniels in Consular Affairs."

"Thanks, Jeanine. I'll look for the intel tomorrow morning."

Tony hung up the phone, feeling even more tired and much older.

◆

Volodya's busy day ended at 16:00. He continued to ice his ribs and eventually took a dose of naproxen sodium. Although he was still in pain, the pain level became more tolerable. As he walked toward his apartment, he even stopped to pick up dinner along the way at a newly opened Ukrainian grocery and deli. He purchased potato *vareniki* with fried bacon, onions, and sour cream, a cucumber salad, and a walnut *perekladanets* for dessert.

◆

Iza left the Embassy after 17:30 wearing the wig that Volodya had stolen, a rough draft of her report to Claire completed. She'd checked her phone several times while at lunch, on break at the meeting, after returning to the U.S. Embassy, and finally, on exiting the embassy, but there was no message from Tony regarding the meeting with Herr Kühn. Tony's administrator left a message inviting Iza and Volodya to the dinner with Tony in a U.S. Embassy private dining room at 18:00 on Friday evening, but that was the only message Iza received.

Volodya was waiting for Iza at the apartment, and while they ate and awaited Tony's call, Iza paged through the *Tagesspiegel* and the *Berliner Morgenpost*. But there was no further information about the U-Bahn attack or Evgeny Petrov's condition, which seemed odd to them.

As the evening progressed, and there was still no call from Tony, Iza decided that they shouldn't call him. They'd wait until the Friday dinner to ask their questions.

Iza showed Volodya her eye; the swelling had decreased, and she could partially open the lid. He kissed her face near her eye, then took her hand and led her to the sofa. He turned on the receiver and CD player, and they cuddled together listening to Rachmaninoff's Piano Concerto No. 3 until it was time to sleep.

Friday, October 28 (Day 17)

Iza awoke early and quickly dressed for a short morning run. When she returned, Volodya was still sleeping, but Iza realized that he was having a bad dream. He was sweating and appeared agitated; he suddenly called out, "*Ni, ni!* Stop, stop!"

He awoke to see Iza leaning over him, caressing his face while she sat at the edge of the bed. "Did you have a bad dream?"

"I do not remember," Volodya lied. He carefully sat up in bed and pulled Iza close. He didn't want to tell her he'd had the recurring nightmare about his parents' torture and murder in Bucha. Having her nearby helped calm him and, after a few minutes, to clear his head from the disturbing images in the nightmare.

"Did you run this morning already?" he asked quietly, now smiling at Iza.

"Yeah, I needed to. Stress relief. Are you sure you're okay?"

"Yes, I think so," he said as he carefully got out of bed.

Iza then picked up her clothing for the day and raced to the bathroom ahead of him, laughing and calling out, "I get the shower first!"

After quickly finishing their morning tasks, Iza told Volodya she'd meet him at the embassy plaza at 17:45 unless he let her know he couldn't be there by that hour. Iza pulled on the curly blonde wig. They left for work at the same time, walking in their separate directions, but Volodya stopped and looked back at Iza, watching her until she disappeared from view.

◆

Iza picked up newspapers again on her way to the embassy, and since she arrived early, she had a few minutes to scan them for any updates on the U-Bahn attack. There was no further mention of the incident in either newspaper. *This is so strange,* she thought. *Maybe the Russian Embassy quashed the investigation or someone here in Germany wants to keep it quiet.*

"Iza, I won't be attending the meeting today," Claire announced as she stepped into Iza's office. "I'm taking off later today and then next week Monday through Wednesday. David and I are driving to Bavaria for a little vacation. I didn't mention it sooner because we didn't find a sitter for our wild one until late yesterday evening. It's hard to find a sitter when you have a feral child," Claire said, laughed softly.

"I hope you and David have a fun and relaxing trip."

"Thanks, Iza."

Iza arrived at the German State Department meeting alone. She sat in the same area where she and Claire had been seated previously. Before the meeting began, and while other attendees were visiting with one another, Alex Schröder slid into Claire's empty seat.

"How are you today, Iza Carter?" he asked casually.

"I'm well, and you?" Iza responded, a bit startled that he'd come to sit next to her.

"I'm doing very well today, thank you. Is it now two weeks in this new embassy job for you, Iza?"

"Yes." Iza wondered why he was asking such a question. *Perhaps he just wants to be friendly and make small talk,* she thought.

"I hope you are enjoying your work. Are you also enjoying life in Berlin outside of work?"

"Yes, very much so," Iza answered carefully, now wondering where Alex was leading the conversation.

"And in what neighborhood do you *actually* live in Berlin?" he queried. "There are so many great places to live here."

"In the Mitte," Iza responded, trying to remain calm although her heart was racing. *I'm not about to tell him I'm living in the Kreuzberg neighborhood.*

"Very nice neighborhood," he responded as he looked away from Iza, suddenly sliding out of the chair and waving hello to another meeting attendee. "Enjoy the meeting this morning," he said as he quickly walked to catch up to the other man.

What was that all about? Claire said he's a schmoozer, and Germans are notoriously poor at making small talk. But, did he have another purpose in questioning me about where I live? I've got to tell Tony about this.

The topic of the final half-day session was the hope that the euro zone could stave off recession in 2023. Newly reported third-quarter GDP results showed that Germany had defied expectations by reporting another quarter of economic growth, although consumer prices in Germany rose by 11.6 percent compared with the same period in 2021. GDP growth in France, although still positive, slowed in the third quarter, and slowing trade was dragging down the French economy. Inflation had quickened at a faster rate than expected, reaching a record 7.1 percent. Price pressures were becoming more broad-based, driven by energy, food, and manufactured goods. Italy was already in recession in the third quarter, and inflation there hit an all-time high of 12.8 percent in October. GDP growth in Spain had slowed dramatically in the third quarter as rapid inflation curbed consumption. *I wonder if the poor economic news will soften E.U. support for Ukraine in the war?*

Iza walked slowly back to the U.S. Embassy, feeling somewhat anxious about the forthcoming information from the embassy Research department concerning imperative Energie. She wondered what sort of business a company named "Vitally Important Energy" would be involved in after she'd identified Johannes Brandt, "the suitcase man," as a sales representative for the firm.

A large file from Jeanine in Research was awaiting download when Iza arrived back at her desk. Iza noted that the Managing Director of imperative Energie was Matteo Mehlman, a well-known, previously retired business leader from the German energy sector. Other founding members included Leon Baumann, a former leader of the Nord Stream pipeline consortium, and Stephan Gabel and Alexander Schröder, prominent members of the Social Democratic Party and of the German Bundestag. Iza was shaken to see Alex's name on the list of founding shareholders. *Brandt works at his firm!* Jeanine's notations indicated the four were very active members of the German SPD. The final founding member of imperative Energie was Mikhail Friedemann, a Russian oligarch who remained a close ally of Vladimir Putin.

The business was founded in 2014. The current range in the number of employees was "11–50." Imperative Energie's mission was: "Providing unique cybersecurity services to the energy industry." Several brochures that Jeanine had scanned promised to secure the cyber assets of energy and utility organizations with critical features, such as "provision of complete visibility to the organization's network, comprehensive risk management, integrated threat intelligence, and early detection of attacks to enable timely mitigation before the disruption of critical processes." Iza noted that the 2021 sales of the company were €18 million.

The headquarters of and the city of registration for imperative Energie GmbH were Berlin. Jeanine had listed a phone number and a web address in her notations. Iza's eyes widened, and she audibly gasped when she saw that the headquarters location was Kurfürstendamm 195. She quickly brought up a map of Berlin on her computer and discovered that the headquarters of imperative Energie was, at most, one kilometer southwest of Volodya's data center location.

When she searched online for a view of the headquarters building, she learned that imperative Energie was tucked into a multi-level, glass-walled building along with the headquarters of a number of other information technology firms. The web page for the building management company listed the motto: *Hier arbeiten die Jungs, die das Internet machen.* Iza sat back in her chair and ran her hands through her hair. She hadn't known what to expect, but this information was somehow more disturbing than she'd anticipated.

Iza sat thinking for a moment, then opened her U.S. Embassy new employee manual. She quickly paged to the "business" section and read: "The United States and Germany have one of the most dynamic trade and investment relationships in the world. With its stable political and economic environment and well-developed rule-of-law, Germany is an excellent market for small-to-medium-sized U.S. companies. At the same time, the U.S. is a top destination for business and home to the largest amount of Foreign Direct Investment in the world. *German companies of all sizes profit from this great potential.*" Iza highlighted the last statement and then read on: "Please explore our business pages and find out how we can help German companies grow their business in the U.S.—and beyond."

I need to talk with Tony and Volodya about this at our dinner tonight. Could I visit imperative Energie with someone from our U.S. Embassy Bureau of Economic and Business Affairs? We might be able to learn more about the company from a visit under the guise of offering the firm new business opportunities in the U.S.

◆

Volodya arrived at the data center early for the 7:00 briefing. He sat next to Petro, who'd also arrived early. Petro had just received his new round, gold, John Lennon-style eyeglasses from Janie's team, and he modelled them for Volodya.

Volodya smiled broadly, and he said in Ukrainian, "You look like John Lennon from early seventies, I think."

Petro grinned while removing the glasses. "I think I will wear mine inside. I can look like John Lennon when I come and go from here." The two of them laughed softly. "How are your ribs, Volodya?" Petro questioned with concern.

"I am much better today. At first, they hurt like a hell, but now they only hurt bad."

In the briefing, they learned that Ukrainian aviators carried out twenty-nine strikes during the past day. Twenty-one areas of concentration of manpower, weapons, and military equipment were destroyed at least partially and five positions of anti-aircraft missile systems were destroyed. Independently, Ukrainian artillery and missile forces had struck four areas of concentration of manpower, weapons, and military equipment and a warehouse containing enemy ammunition.

The work of their Team, coupled with the skill and bravery of the Ukrainian military, was gradually destroying Russian logistics and command-and-control centers in southern Kherson Oblast, rendering it impossible for Russia to maintain forces on the west bank of the Dnipro. Everyone on the Team realized that continued patient work would eventually lead the Kremlin to withdraw Russian forces from Kherson City and perhaps even ultimately from Kherson Oblast. It was only a matter of time. Sadly, things were going differently in the Donbas. There, the war was more of a grinding artillery battle of attrition. They'd had some success finding ammunition depots but not as much success as in Kherson.

Volodya and Petro talked quietly with each other in Ukrainian as they worked at their respective stations. Petro confided, "I am tired of killing people, Volodya."

Volodya countered, "Zaluzhnyi says, 'Russians must be killed, *just killed*, and most important of all, we should not be afraid to do it'."

"Yes, yes, I know. Many would happily kill us instead. But I often think, does God forgive me for what I do?"

Volodya sat for a moment scanning his monitor, then replied thoughtfully, "We are not aggressors, Petro; we defend our homeland. Maybe this war is like battle of Rephidim in bible. Like Moses, we fight under banner of God. And maybe then, God will forgive both of us."

The day went by like all others. Find the concentrations of ammunition, drones, personnel, military equipment, and weapons, then send the GPS coordinates to the Ukrainian military command for their choosing.

It had been a warm and mostly sunny day in Berlin—nearly twenty degrees Celsius at 17:30. Iza waited for Volodya on the embassy plaza. She wore her very short black skirt with black tights, greenish-yellow oversized sweater, citrine earrings, and a patch over her right eye while carrying a small gift bag and her jacket. The sweater slipped off her shoulder on the right side, revealing her bare skin.

She could see Volodya walking toward the embassy, favoring his right side and carrying his leather jacket because it was so warm. She saw him search the crowd pouring out of the embassy at the end of the work day to find her. She waved to get his attention, then ran out to meet him, smiling and laughing as she came to him, her curly blonde wig blowing in the breeze. She asked how he was feeling and how his day at work had gone while she took his hand and they walked to the embassy entrance.

As they waited inside at the embassy security station for an agent to help them, she whispered some basic information about imperative Energie but said that she'd tell him more later.

Volodya appeared surprised, "I did not think you could find this information; I asked Tony on Wednesday to get same." Embassy security stopped Volodya this time. They took his Swiss army tool, telling him he could recover it at the station when leaving the embassy. He whispered to Iza, "They did not find it on Monday."

When they arrived at the private dining room—the same room where they'd dined on Monday—Iza immediately set the gift bag on the edge of the dining table. She told Volodya, "It's a birthday gift for Tony's daughter, Greta, for him to take back. She'll be twenty next week."

Tony arrived a few minutes late, again carrying his large, over-stuffed computer bag. Yet he seemed almost a different man. For one thing, he was wearing jeans, a flannel shirt, and casual boat shoes. Iza couldn't recall the last time she'd seen him wearing anything less than a sport coat, an open-collared shirt with dress pants, and highly polished dress shoes. His thick hair, which was typically well-groomed, looked a bit tousled. She also noticed that he carried himself a bit less confidently than usual.

She whispered to Volodya, "Tony looks like he's ready to cut loose tonight."

Volodya whispered back, "What does 'cut loose' mean?"

Iza replied quietly, "He's less controlled than usual and looks like he's ready to have some fun."

Tony greeted the two of them warmly, then sat in one of the club chairs. He didn't mention Iza's eye patch or Volodya's still apparent injury. *Wow, he didn't ask about my eye patch! I wonder why? I thought I'd have to lie to him about what happened to me.*

An attendant arrived to take their drink orders. Iza ordered Prosecco, while Tony ordered a California Cabernet. Volodya asked if they had Nemiroff vodka. The attendant said he thought they might, but he'd check. Volodya asked if he could have the vodka chilled. When the drinks arrived, Volodya was told that his drink was indeed Nemiroff vodka and it had just come from the freezer. It was served in a *very* large tumbler, and the tumbler was nearly full. The three toasted each other, Volodya toasting Tony a bit tentatively. Iza and Tony sipped their drinks, but Volodya drank nearly half of his tumbler of vodka in one swallow. Iza looked at him a bit curiously. *That was a lot of vodka to drink at once.*

After making small talk for half an hour, Iza excused herself to use the restroom. Volodya moved to Iza's chair next to Tony, rubbed his hands together, and looked pensively at Tony. "Tony," he said quietly, stopping to choose his words carefully, "I apologize for lying to you when we met on Wednesday." Volodya continued using Iza's words, "That is not who I am. You see, I worry that you will transfer Iza to embassy away from Berlin, and so I lied. But I think we both want what is best for Iza. You must decide what is best to keep her safe."

Volodya began telling the truth about the U-Bahn encounter with Evgeny Petrov just as Iza walked back into the room. Volodya was facing away from the door and hadn't heard her enter. Tony put his finger to his lips to signal Volodya to stop talking.

Iza slipped back into Volodya's chair across from Tony, wondering why Volodya had moved. Tony replied to Volodya in a kind voice, "Volodya, I understand." Iza looked confusedly between the two but didn't ask Tony what he meant. Volodya raised his vodka tumbler and downed the rest of his liquid courage in one swallow, which made Tony laugh.

They ate salads, a small pasta course, and a delicious smoked pork T-bone entrée. Tony ordered a bottle of Morey-Saint-Denis Burgundy for the three to share with their dinners. When the dishes were finally cleared from the table, Tony ordered each of them an espresso martini for dessert. Then the tone of the evening became serious.

Tony spoke about his meeting with Herr Kühn. "The man murdered outside your apartment building *was* an agent of the BKA. Herr Kühn was aware of the blueprints, and in fact, the agent broke into your apartment to recover them. He couldn't find them, and was apparently awaiting your return from the embassy event when he was killed. Kühn burned the blueprints to ashes. I was so surprised; he held them outside his window and lit them on fire! He told me the originals remain somewhere in the secure possession of the Bundesministerium der Verteidigung—the German Ministry of Defense."

Volodya suspected that Tony knew what had happened on the U-Bahn with Evgeny Petrov. *Why did Tony not question Iza about her eye after I admitted I lied? We were not victims of attempted robbery on U-Bahn. Why did Tony stop me from telling him truth about my lie, and why did he instead say, 'I understand,' unless he already knows?*

Iza summarized what she'd learned about imperative Energie. She named the shareholders who formed the company, including Alex Schröder, and of the strange interaction she'd had with him in her morning meeting. "The business develops and sells cybersecurity software to the energy industry—like to utilities and pipeline operators. Their sales last year were eighteen million euros. And, their headquarters are located very close to Kurfürstendamm 23; they're at 195."

When she'd finished, Iza proposed that she visit the company with someone from the U.S. Embassy Bureau of Economic and Business Affairs. "I might be able to learn more about the cybersecurity business and how Johannes Brandt is involved in the business in his position as a sales representative. I think it would be safe to make this kind of one-time visit, because I just can't imagine a company with as many as fifty employees can be illegitimate. It's not possible that everyone working there could have nefarious purposes, or the company would be known to the German authorities. It was founded in 2014, so they've been in business for eight years. If they've got around fifty employees, their software must be used at quite a few locations around Germany. It *has* to be a legit business. If I went there in disguise, Brandt wouldn't recognize me if he happens to be in the office the day that we'd go."

They then discussed the fact that although the blueprints had been destroyed, the people looking for them had no way of knowing the prints no longer existed. Iza worriedly said, "Someone from the Russian Embassy will continue looking for the information they think I still have—and for me. Even with the prints destroyed, they can still try to get the address from me."

Tony mentioned under his breath, "That 'someone' won't be Evgeny Petrov." Iza didn't hear what Tony had mumbled, but Volodya did. He looked questioningly at Tony. *How does*

Tony know this? Only Iza and I know what happened to Evgeny. The newspapers did not name him.

"Okay, you two. Here's what I've got on my list to do. I'll have imperative Energie studied more thoroughly by the CIA in the U.S. I'm already trying to engage with the FBI Counterespionage Division in identifying the spy in the U.S. I'm still waiting for some special clearances so I can talk to them. And I'll arrange for a meeting between the U.S. Embassy Bureau of Economic and Business Affairs and imperative Energie under the guise of making business connections between the U.S. and Germany."

Tony sat quietly thinking for several minutes as Iza and Volodya looked on. He finally turned to Iza and said, "You know, I've never forgiven myself about your dad. It's a decision I made that I regret every single day. Please understand, I simply couldn't live with myself if something happened to you because of my poor choice."

"Tony, I've grown up. I can make my own decisions and I already have. I plan to stay here in Berlin, and I want to go to that meeting. I mean—I want someone with some experience there along with me—but I want to go."

"I've got the power of my position to transfer you to another of our embassies or consulates in Europe."

"So, you've made *your* decision for me, even though it isn't what I want?"

"No . . . I haven't made any decision yet."

Tony and Iza sat staring at each other for several minutes without saying a word. Volodya said nothing as the impasse in the abruptly tense discussion dragged on. He suddenly realized that the alcohol was passing through his system, and he felt an urgent need to use the restroom. Yet, he didn't want to leave the room without knowing the resolution of their disagreement. Tony's decision would have a profound impact on his life with Iza. He sat pensively and shifted in his chair.

At last, Tony resumed talking. "Iza, I think it would be wise for you to attend the meeting with the Embassy person assigned from the Bureau. I'll call to make the arrangements first thing on Saturday before my flight back to the U.S. I'll make it an urgent request. But I agree you'll need to go in disguise. I don't want them to see your name in the visitor log, and I don't want anyone to recognize you. I'm not worried Alex Schröder will be at any meeting. He's a shareholder partner, not an employee. But if Brandt is there, I don't want him to recognize you. And remember—separate from the meeting that I arrange—you'll have to be exceptionally careful, particularly as you depart from the Embassy every day to ensure you're not under surveillance."

"Thank you, Tony," Iza replied with a smile.

Now realizing that Tony had made his decision, Volodya felt relief, intense worry, and an even more urgent need to leave the room.

The attendant returned to the dining room and inquired if anyone wanted another drink. Tony suggested that, yes, the three of them would order again. Iza requested a small glass of Pedro Ximénez sherry, Tony wanted a small glass of Olivares Dulce, and Volodya ordered another tumbler of Nemiroff vodka.

Tony and Iza moved back to the club chairs while Volodya excused himself to use the restroom; he could wait no longer.

Iza immediately turned to Tony. "Tony, when you get back in D.C., I'd appreciate if you don't tell my mom about Volodya."

"Why shouldn't I? By now, I'd think you'd at least have mentioned him to Elise."

"No. I still haven't told Mom about him. Mom would disapprove of him . . . he's not who she'd choose for me." Iza pressed her lips together, breathed in deeply, and sighed loudly. She said sadly, "Mom's been 'different' toward me lately, Tony. When I was back living with her in the summer, I didn't notice it so much because I was working all the time. She was too, and she also spent most of her free time with Günther. We barely ran into each other. But, since I've been here, I've hardly heard from her. And when we have talked,

I've noticed she's become so dismissive of me. I don't think she loves me anymore. She loves Günther."

"How can you *say* that, Iza? She raised you by herself after your dad died! And Günther is good for your mom. She hasn't had anyone in her life since your dad."

"I know," Iza replied quietly. "It's why I keep trying. Tony, believe me, I've tried to be a good daughter. I'm trying to accept Günther, even though I admit I don't like him. It's just that Mom and I used to be closer than we are now."

Iza's voice rose with emotion. "Her only interest in me right now is trying to hook me up with Günther's son in Berlin, whom I don't really want to meet. Günther keeps pushing her to get me to meet his son. How could I tell her about Volodya? She'd never understand. Even though *she's* never met him, she thinks Günther's son is who *I* need to meet. Mom is absolutely smitten with Günther. It's also one of the reasons I asked you about Günther . . . like . . . what he does for the German Embassy. I just don't think he's who we think he is, and it's hard for me to trust him. Why does he want me to meet his son?"

Volodya returned from the restroom, and Iza's conversation with Tony ended without resolution. The drinks were served, and they continued on with more pleasant topics.

◆

Thirty minutes after the drinks were finished, the three stumbled out of the Embassy, but not before Volodya recovered his Swiss Army tool at the security station.

Iza giggled as she thought to herself that Volodya couldn't possibly be feeling any pain. He seemed to stagger, and his English was not as good as usual as they said their fond goodbyes to Tony. It was still eighteen degrees Celsius, so they carried their jackets. They talked nonstop on their glacially slow walk back to the apartment. Volodya told her in somewhat slurred speech that he'd have the entire weekend off from the data center. He was especially happy not to have work tomorrow because he thought his head wouldn't feel very good in the morning. Iza occasionally stopped to prop him up; she was actually worried he might fall over and re-injure his ribs. But the walk seemed to clear his head a little.

When they got into the apartment, Volodya asked Iza to sit with him on the sofa. He turned on the receiver and the CD player and inserted Rodrigo's Concerto de Aranjuez. He turned the volume low so it played in the background as they sat together on the sofa. "I have something important to tell you," Volodya said. Iza wondered if it was bad news. *Is he being sent back to fight in Ukraine?*

But instead, Volodya began, "Iza, today is two weeks since we meet. You know I have powerful physical attraction to you." He smiled crookedly and winked at her, then continued, "But my feelings for you are so much more. You are my best friend. You make me happy. I already tell you that I love you.

"I think about what lies ahead for us now. I decide that if something happens to you or to me, you might never know completely how I feel for you—that I am *committed* to you. Our partnership is not only about love. Love is not enough. Love gets us through good times together. It is not what makes us weather storm when disaster strikes. That is something different . . . it is commitment and being responsible to that commitment. Commitment means we act with integrity and we take care of each other. I love you, but tonight I tell you that maybe more importantly, I am committed to you."

Iza started to tear up. *He's so drunk, but that's the sweetest, most sincere thing anyone's ever said to me.* "Volodya, your words were beautiful. But you didn't need to tell me you're committed to me. You've already shown me that. You've stuck with me when anyone else would have run away in fear. I'm committed to you too. I can't say it the way you just did; I'm not so eloquent. But I mean it."

Volodya grabbed Iza and kissed her quite passionately, then fell back on the sofa and said, "Iza, I do not feel so well. I think I drinked too much vodka. I needed courage tonight."

"Let me help you to bed," she offered. "I'll get the heating pad for your ribs." The Concerto de Aranjuez ended as Iza helped Volodya walk slowly to the bedroom.

Saturday, October 29 (Day 18)

Iza prepared for an early-morning run, a twenty-one-kilometer route she'd planned a few days earlier. If she kept to her desired pace, she'd be back at the apartment in ninety minutes. Since Volodya wouldn't be able to run until his ribs were more fully healed, she'd have to run alone. Before she left, she saw that Volodya was finally sleeping; he'd likely had a rough night, having thrown off the down comforter several times, awakening her in the process—the result of drinking too much at their dinner with Tony. She looked in the mirror on her way out. *My eye looks better. The skin is sort of bluish-green now instead of purplish-black.*

Volodya awoke to see that Iza and her running shoes were gone. *My head feels like shit; it pounds so bad—but I will not sleep more. I need to enjoy time off these two days with no data center.*

The entire Team had gotten this longer-than-normal, yet still short reprieve, because Lloyd realized their mental health was suffering. They weren't considered combat troops, yet they worked long, tedious hours at their screens. They were remote from the war in Ukraine yet still *very* much connected to it. When all parameters were met, they simply sent coordinates for their kills, be those equipment kills or human kills. One person's decisions could lead to the deaths of tens of people, even if they were the enemy. The Team members all realized many Russian soldiers didn't want to be fighting in Ukraine; what was the purpose of this "special military operation?" Destroying military equipment and ammunition depots was one thing; killing people was quite another. Yet it had to be done, and they couldn't be afraid to do it.

I want to spend whole weekend with Iza. We can do whatever, but together. He checked for a note from her but saw that she'd left nothing. *I will try not to worry; she is running. I will make special breakfast for her.*

He'd purchased *salo* at the Ukrainian market earlier in the week, and the ingredients for preparing *Nalysnyky*—crêpes filled with quark and dill. "How hard can it be to make Nalysnyky?" he asked himself aloud. Volodya had looked up the recipe on his phone before purchasing the ingredients. The recipe hadn't sounded all that difficult; it said it took forty-five minutes to prepare and bake. He pulled up an online video: "Mariya makes Nalysnyky."

After struggling to separate eggs, mix a smooth crêpe batter, and produce perfectly round, flexible, and lightly browned crêpes, Volodya concluded, "Somehow, Mariya, I do not think things go like this for you." After slipping the pan of misshapen quark-stuffed crêpes in the oven, he prepared the fried salo topping. After the skillet of fatty salo had been on high heat for one or two minutes, the fat got hot, and the water in the fat turned to steam, popping streams of fat into the air. Volodya knew grease would be building up on every flat surface of the kitchen. He looked into the skillet. It reminded him of videos he'd seen of an erupting volcanic spatter cone, throwing blobs of lava into the air. The salo chunks were little bits of unmolten rock floating in a sea of lava grease. He pulled the skillet from the heat, carefully skimmed the fried salo chunks out of the lava, and set them aside.

Volodya stacked the now substantial quantity of used dishes and utensils in the sink, then set the table, not realizing his socks were tracking grease around the entire kitchen. Finally, he brewed coffee, something he knew he was very good at doing. He looked down at himself, then around at the kitchen. He'd created a monumental disaster and hoped to quickly clean the mess before Iza returned, but it was too late. He heard the key being inserted into the apartment door lock. Iza's eyes widened, and she gasped as she looked at the kitchen with surprise.

Volodya smiled at her and shrugged. "I hope it tastes better than kitchen looks."

Iza grinned, "Thank you for baking these; they're delicious! Everything's better with bacon." Volodya smiled broadly, feeling the sense of cooking accomplishment that comes from receiving a genuine compliment from a fellow gastronome.

As they were drinking the last of the coffee, Iza asked Volodya, "Do you think Tony knows what happened on the U-Bahn?"

"I also wondered what Tony knows. I apologized to him that I lied about robbery attempt on U-Bahn. He knows something else happened with your eye and with my ribs, but it was not because I told him. And later, you did not hear him say, but he said Evgeny will not be person looking for you. How would he know that unless Herr Kühn told him? Only you and I were there. That means there was surveillance camera footage, and someone saw us. But they could not know who I am, only you. And no one arrested you in last few days, and Tony showed no concern. And if they did not arrest you, they will not find me."

"That's what I think too. Tony has to know, and it could only have come from Kühn. Kühn could easily find me. Maybe he could be a friend to us if we ever need one."

"I think same thing. You still have his phone number, yes?"

"Yeah, maybe I'll put it on speed dial."

◆

Iza and Volodya worked together to clean the kitchen. They washed the floor first, then realized that they'd trapped themselves in a corner of the kitchen with no escape without getting wet socks. They removed their socks and tip-toed across the floor to clean the stovetop and counters. Then they tackled the dishes. At last, the cleaning process was finished. While Volodya was putting away their dishes, Iza grabbed the sprayer on the kitchen faucet and sprayed him in the back, drenching his T-shirt. He had to move gingerly to avoid straining his ribs but now grinned at Iza and yelled out, "This means war!"

They struggled for the sprayer, now laughing and facing off. Iza didn't want to reinjure Volodya, but she didn't want to lose the war either. Volodya got hold of the sprayer, gave a dastardly laugh, and sprayed the front of her T-shirt, drenching her from her neck to her waist. She screamed and backed away from him.

"Hey, I like how that looks on you." He raised his eyebrows and laughed as her wet T-shirt clung tightly to her chest. He sprayed her again in the crotch. Iza ran to the bedroom screaming and laughing, then jumped up and knelt on the bed facing the doorway.

Volodya walked quickly into the bedroom and pushed her down on the bed, saying in his deep voice, "Surrender, Iza!" He carefully lay atop her, alternately kissing her lips and her neck.

Iza yelled back, giggling and squirming underneath him, "*Never*, I *won't* surrender!" He kissed her lips intensely. "Well, maybe I might consider it," she managed to get out between kisses. He kept kissing her. "Okay, Volodya, I surrender." The two of them rolled apart on the bed and lay next to each other, laughing in their wet clothes, yet sweaty and weak from their war.

By this time, Volodya's head wasn't pounding, and his ribs weren't too sore. It was a mostly clear and relatively warm afternoon; the temperature was nearly twenty degrees. They decided to go for a walk, and Volodya chose the route— a route that went by Kurfürstendamm 195. He wanted to see the location of imperative Energie.

"We don't need to walk by there today."

"I only want to see building," Volodya responded with a smile. "Mostly we look in fancy Ku'damm shop windows for fun and maybe get ice cream."

◆

They walked the same route that Volodya took each day to the data center, then looked in shop windows once they'd reached the Ku'damm. The street had some of the most high-end shops in the world: Prada, Dolce & Gabbana, Valentino, Hermès, Chanel, and Gucci. They laughed at some of the fashions displayed in the windows—hardly looks that would fit the two of them. Not that they could afford them anyway. The prices were outrageous for two struggling young adults, or for anyone except the filthy rich, for that matter. But it was fun to see what "society" defined as beautiful.

"Maybe we don't want to be beautiful," Iza said thoughtfully after seeing one particularly unusual women's outfit.

"We are confident people, Iza; we do not need anyone to tell us what we have to look like."

Iza did see one two-piece black, beige, and white plaid suit in the store window at Chanel that she liked, but then laughed at the €10.650 price tag and the fact the store was open "by appointment only." *I think I can live without it,* she thought. *They probably wouldn't let me in the door.*

They eventually came to the address, Kurfürstendamm 195, near the Gucci shop. The glass-walled building looked like any other in the high-end shopping district. Volodya wanted to look inside, but Iza refused. "What if Johannes Brandt is there today by chance, and he sees me?"

Volodya responded, "You wait here by Gucci store, and I will be back in five minutes . . . maybe ten minutes." Iza tried to stop him, but he was gone in an instant. He opened the glass door to the building and disappeared inside.

Volodya checked the building directory at the entrance and saw that imperative Energie was located on the third floor. He walked up the stairway rather than use the elevator. Imperative Energie took up half of the third floor. The interior wall of the business was all glass, which he found unusual for a cybersecurity firm. He could see into the reception area and into a main open work area. It looked as though private offices might be located on the outer walls of the building, where there would be views out over the Ku'damm and surrounding areas. However, there were no interior windows in those offices to offer a view back into the open work area. The furnishings were elegant, having a Danish-modern style and clean lines. He could see the heads of two people moving near the rear of the main work area, but he still thought about trying the door. He reconsidered; this was not the time to make another foolish mistake.

Volodya was about to walk back down the stairway to rejoin Iza when the freight elevator opened. A stocky man about Volodya's height and wearing gray coveralls stepped off the elevator, dragging a janitorial cart behind him. Volodya pretended to look at the building directory as he watched the man roll the cart to a storage closet across the hall from imperative Energie. The man removed his coveralls and hung them in the closet, then pushed the cleaning cart inside, closed the door, and immediately stepped on the elevator and headed down.

Volodya walked cautiously to the closet and tried the door; it wasn't locked. Several pairs of coveralls hung in the closet, but only one held a badge. In his haste, the man had forgotten to take his security badge. Volodya slipped into the coveralls. They were much too large in width, but he wrapped them tightly around himself and tucked the excess into his jeans. He moved the badge from the chest area to his waist. He didn't look like the man who'd just left, but with the badge at his waist, he figured no one would notice the photo.

He rolled the cart out of the storage closet to the entrance of imperative Energie. He placed the badge on the door reader, and the door unlocked, so he pushed the cart into the reception area.

Once inside imperative Energie, Volodya took a microfiber cloth off the cleaning cart and pretended to dust in the reception area. He saw that there was a visitor log, along with a card that listed employee names and phone extensions, but not their titles. He slipped the card into a pocket in the coveralls. Volodya grabbed paper and a pen from the desk, then continued down the main entryway with the cart.

The two men working inside looked up from their monitors and waved at Volodya; he waved back. He quickly drew the floorplan on the paper while pretending to dust and empty waste and recycling baskets. He assumed that the corner office, which would have two banks of glass windows, would be the office of the Managing Director. He noted the nameplate near the door: Mehlman. However, the door was locked, and he was unable to enter using his janitorial badge. Four additional offices were adjoining that of the Managing Director. Those nameplates read: Schröder, Baumann, Gabel, and Friedemann, and those doors were also locked.

He continued working down the hallway in the opposite direction. Another area appeared to be the sales department. He saw a nameplate for Brandt, then several other unfamiliar names. Between these offices, was a large framed map of Germany hanging on a wall. The map was littered with small markers, presumably representing various sites around Germany where imperative Energie cybersecurity software was employed. Volodya dusted around the map while looking at the markers. Some showed locations of pipelines, while others showed electric substations, power plants, or other energy-related infrastructure.

In the center of the office area, there was a medium-sized, glass-enclosed room labelled Demo. While looking inside, he sprayed some cleaner on the glass window and wiped it off. The room held a bank of monitors on the far wall and a control desk fronted by five chairs. A conference table was visible along the side of the room. The room was also locked, and his badge didn't allow entry.

Volodya drew out the remainder of the floor layout on his paper, then started for the exit with the cart. Just then, he heard one of the men working in the main area holler out, "*Scheiße! Komm hier, bitte!*" Even though he didn't understand German, he understood that the man was calling for him to come to his workstation in the main work area. The command "Komm hier" was similar enough to English. He rolled the cart ahead of him and hid the badge in the folds of his oversized coveralls.

"*Ich habe meinen Kaffee verschüttet!*" Volodya saw that the man had spilled his coffee on his workstation and on the carpet. Volodya smiled, then grabbed a small water bucket and rag from his cleaning cart. The man moved away from his station; he and the other man took their coffee mugs to a coffee station across from the work area to refill them. The men were both wearing black uniform shirts embroidered with the company name, logo, and their first names. The name of the man who had spilled his coffee was Markus; Volodya didn't see the name of the other man before he turned away.

Volodya wiped up the coffee from the rug and then from the man's workstation. He saw on the monitor that the man was coding, but he couldn't learn anything without time to study the code. However, he noticed a thumb drive on the tabletop at the far back edge of the workstation, tucked behind the monitor. He didn't know if the drive contained anything interesting—it might even be blank, simply stored at the back of the station—but he swept it into his drying rag and dropped it into his coverall pocket. Volodya then waved to the two men and headed to the exit. He quickly rolled the cart into the storage closet, took his floorplan map, phone list, and thumb drive, and then hung the coveralls and badge where he'd found them. With that, he walked quickly down the stairs and out of Kurfürstendamm 195.

Iza wasn't standing outside of the Gucci store. Volodya scanned around, looking for her, and noticed a clock. It was 16:00! He'd been at imperative Energie for nearly an hour when he'd promised to be gone for only five or ten minutes. He was about to check for her in another direction when Iza came running up behind him.

"What happened, Volodya?" Iza questioned anxiously. "I've been so worried!"

"I am sorry, Iza. I found some interesting things, and I lost track of time. We will look later." He kissed Iza and ran his hand softly across her cheek. "Time for ice cream."

He took her hand and led her to one of the Ku'damm ice cream shops, where they shared a "Brownie Explosion" specialty ice cream creation at an outside table on the terrace in front of the shop. Volodya took the phone list, floor plan, and thumb drive out of his pocket and showed them to Iza.

"Here is list of phone extensions in case you need them later. I made floor plan for you. If you go for demo, you sit on this side of room," he said, pointing to the spot on the plan. "Room has glass windows, but it is hard to see someone along this side of room. Alex Schröder sits here, so avoid going that way or near there. And here is office of Johannes Brandt."

He told her about the map of Germany with the markers showing locations of German energy infrastructure, and that there was a visitor log that she'd have to sign near the entrance at the reception desk. Then he showed her the thumb drive.

"I saw this on guy's desk; he is there with another guy coding something today. He spilled his coffee and asked me to clean it up. Maybe it has nothing on it or is encrypted, but maybe it does. We will check later. I saw his first name is Markus, but I did not see the name of the other guy who was there." They scanned the list of phone extensions and saw that the man's surname was Peters.

He slipped the papers and thumb drive back into his pocket. Iza touched his forearm gently and smiled at him, a sign of appreciation. They walked slowly back to the apartment, still looking in shop windows along the route.

◆

Iza immediately started preparing Ukrainian *pampushki*: pull-apart garlic rolls. As she mixed the dough, Volodya started to prepare borscht. He called it the Ukrainian peasant soup and told her he'd prepared it so many times in graduate school that he could make it in his sleep. In the cramped kitchen, the two kept bumping into each other as they maneuvered about preparing supper. Volodya came up behind Iza as she finished kneading the dough and put his arms around her waist. He kissed her neck. Iza turned around and rubbed a stripe of flour down his nose, then amorously kissed him. She broke away from him, set the dough to rise, kissed him again, then said while grinning, "I'll be back." She went into the bedroom, closed the door, and lay on the bed to call her mom.

Elise answered immediately.

"Iza, how are you?"

"I'm pretty good, Mom. How are you?" Iza asked, trying to sound cheerful.

"Günther and I are going shopping in Crystal City soon, and then we'll go out somewhere there to eat. We're getting some things ready for Costa Rica. I'm so excited! What about you, Iza?"

"I had a great run this morning, Mom."

"Iza, all you *ever* think about is running. You need to find some friends there! You need to think about more than just yourself and your running program. You'll end up alone. Did you call Günther's son yet?" Elise questioned.

"I didn't yet Mom, but I will. I've been busy."

Elise's pleasant voice suddenly became accusatory.

"Busy *running*? You could have called him instead of running. I don't understand why you can't just call him to introduce yourself and say hello. It's not like I expect you to marry him or even date him if you don't like him. I'm only asking you to be nice—for Günther's sake—but I guess you can't *ever* be nice, can you? He's got a great job there. You might actually like him if you gave him a chance."

"Mom, I didn't realize this was so important to you." Iza was very frustrated with the direction the call was taking. *Maybe it's time to tell you that your selfish and not-very-nice daughter already has a male friend and she's living with him.*

"For one thing, Mom, you never told me this guy's name. I realized I couldn't just call him and ask for 'Günther's son.' And for another—"

Elise cut her off. "I'm sorry Iza," she apologized, her voice becoming more pleasant again. "I should have mentioned it before. Günther told me he goes by Johann at work and by Jan with his friends. It's the equivalent of 'John' in English. It's a *very* common name in Germany, just like here in the States."

Iza started again, "Mom, I already have—"

But Elise cut her off again. "I'm sorry, I have to go, Iza. Günther wants to leave for Crystal City now. Let's talk again soon." Elise hung up her phone.

Usually, their recent calls ended with Iza being upset or crying afterward, but this time, although her mom's stinging comments hurt her, she also felt defiant. *Am I really such a selfish person who thinks only of herself? Haven't I ever been nice? I'm not perfect, but I'm not a terrible person either. And if I enjoy running, that's my business. Everyone needs some kind of exercise. We'll only be talking again soon if you make more of an effort, Mom.*

She sat on the bed for a few minutes, composing herself. She didn't want to let the call ruin the evening with Volodya. Iza returned to the kitchen smiling, hiding the hurt she felt inside.

Volodya had the borscht cooking in the large, banged-up soup pot—the same pot he'd brought to her apartment the first time they'd dated after the embassy dinner. "This soup pot had a lot of love," Iza commented as he dropped a final ingredient in the pot.

"It was my mom's . . . the only thing I found when I went to their apartment after I heard they are killed."

Iza came to Volodya and hugged him. "I'm so sorry, Volodya." She didn't know what else to say. She hadn't known the soup pot belonged to his parents.

"Iza, it is okay. But I think we need to make pampushki."

Iza looked at the dough, now nearly overflowing the container. "Whoa!" They started laughing and were soon cutting pieces of dough and forming rolls. After the rolls had risen,

Iza brushed them with an egg wash and put them in the oven to bake while the soup simmered.

◆

They ate the borscht and pampushki, happy to see there were leftovers for another day or two. Following supper, they spent the evening on the sofa, reading and listening to music. Volodya set up the heating pad for his ribs, then chose one of his history books from the pile on the floor. But before he lay on the sofa, he disappeared into the bedroom. After a few minutes, he emerged carrying a laptop and power cord.

"I need to charge battery and hope it works," he told Iza. "I have not used it since end of last year in grad school. Later we can open thumb drive and look together."

Iza had a U.S. Embassy report on energy that she'd wanted to read. The two sat reading on opposite ends of the sofa with their legs intertwined.

After an hour, Volodya slid over to Iza's end of the sofa. "Iza, what happened earlier in call with your mom? I could tell it made you sad even though you pretend to be happy."

Iza pressed her lips together, then let out a loud sigh. "Volodya, I . . . I don't think my mom loves me. Or maybe she's just so infatuated with Günther that she's forgotten she has a daughter who still loves her and who craves her approval."

"All moms love their kids," he tried to reassure Iza.

"My mom's only interest lately seems to be getting me to meet Günther's son in Berlin, who, honestly, I don't care to meet. Günther has been pushing her to get me to meet him. Why? If this guy actually exists, why would I want to meet him? I barely know Günther. Could it be his attempt at being friendly with me? I don't know what to think. But I'm so suspicious of him.

"Tony thinks Günther is great for my mom, and he's not suspicious of him at all. When he says this, I think I must be a terrible daughter who can't accept that her mom has this new guy in her life because I don't like him. Maybe I need to call his son, say 'hi', and be done with it."

Volodya hugged Iza and said, "Let me tell you story. Christmas two years ago, I came home from school to Mariupol just before my parents moved to Bucha. My mom wanted to fix me up with girl who lived next door to us. I told my mom, I do not like this girl. She only wants stud to make her babies with and guy with money to buy her jewelry and nice clothes. And I am nearing end for my PhD. I am so poor; I have no money, only enough for rent and not even enough to eat. I even stop in rooms after meetings at University to eat garnish off of food trays. I lost five kilos. I have to write my thesis and papers for publication to get good job. I do not have time for this kind of thing. And besides, I am waiting for Iza. She and I look for each other. She is person I want—independent, confident, kind, smart, honest, someone who knows how to have fun." Iza smiled at Volodya and held him close.

He continued, "My mom got *so* mad at me; I never see her so mad. She said things that really hurt me—that I am arrogant and aloof because of PhD. I think I am better than people in Mariupol. I explained, no Mom, I just want someone different for my life. This is not arrogance or being aloof. It is just me growing up and knowing who I want to spend my life with. Later she said she is sorry, to please forgive her. I forgave her. I know she only worried about me.

"Maybe it is so with your mom. She thinks she is helping you find friend, and because she likes Günther, she thinks you will like his son. But you look for something different that she does not understand. She worries about you. But you grow. . . grew . . . up, and now you know what you want for your own life."

"I hope that's true. My mom is so absorbed with Günther, but I guess I don't begrudge her the relationship. My dad's been gone for thirteen years. I've been out of the house since I was eighteen. She's been alone for a long time. You and I suspect Günther has some involvement with the blueprints, but Tony doesn't seem to think so. He doesn't know for sure what Günther does at his embassy job, but he thinks it's just some middle-management administrative job. Tony told me he doesn't think Günther would have access to any documents like the blueprints. Of course, he isn't positive."

Volodya retrieved the laptop and thumb drive. He and Iza moved to the kitchen table. He inserted the thumb drive and looked at the contents; there were two files. There was a diagram entitled Attack Phases, Tactics, and Techniques. It listed over one hundred types of cybersecurity attacks and the tactics and techniques that a hacker might use to gain unauthorized access to a system. Volodya scanned through the file quickly and didn't see anything that would be unexpected for a cybersecurity firm to list. The second was labeled "68" and contained multiple lines of code, apparently for whatever 68 referred to—perhaps number 68 in a series of attack modes. Volodya realized that he'd need a lot of quiet time to understand the intent of the multiple lines of code. "This could be something, Iza," he said as he slowly scrolled through the code, "but it will take serious thinking I do not have within me tonight."

Volodya removed the thumb drive, and they decided to hide it in the kitchen.

Sunday, October 30 (Day 19)

Volodya rolled out of bed, slipped on his jeans and T-shirt, and headed to the kitchen. He decided he'd make coffee and then review the "68" file from imperative Energie until Iza was awake.

Iza stumbled sleepily into the kitchen shortly after, barefoot and wearing her long-sleeved running shirt and jeans. She cried out slowly, "Must have coffee." She came up behind Volodya, put her arms around his neck and shoulders, and hugged him. As she continued hugging him, she saw that he was working through the imperative Energie file on his laptop and had already written a full page of notes. "Did you learn anything?" she asked as she rubbed his shoulders.

"I make progress. Nothing to report yet, but I understand what he is doing here," he said as he pointed to several lines of code on the laptop screen. "The "68" I think is very small part of *huge* cybersecurity application—probably millions of lines of code. Maybe some guy is doing upgrade or fixing problem with code in this segment. I think it defends against one way someone attacking infrastructure company's network might try to cause disruption. I see two places where I do not understand purpose of some lines of code, but I am still thinking." Iza looked at the code displayed on the laptop screen; it was an unrecognizable language to her, as foreign as Chinese. She decided that Volodya must be more than a "pretty good" coder.

"Should we visit a museum today?" Iza asked quietly as she continued to rub his shoulders.

Volodya smiled at her, "Yes, Iza. Maybe we want to be outside for some of today too. I saw it might be twenty-two in afternoon and sunny."

Iza took out her phone and sat near him at the kitchen table, searching Berlin museums as she drank her coffee. After a few minutes, she suggested, "What about the Museum für Naturkunde . . . the natural history museum? It says here they have a cool dinosaur exhibit and a big collection of minerals. We could go from there to the Tiergarten and walk the trails in the afternoon."

Volodya shut down his laptop and set aside his notes, now looking intently at Iza. He thought for only a moment and smiled. "It sounds fun, Iza. What am I now?" he said as he bent his elbows and curled his hands to make claws, growling and snarling as he walked stiffly around the kitchen. Iza started laughing, but she didn't really know what he was trying to be. "I am T-rex." He stumbled toward her with an open jaw, turning his head from side to side and snarling loudly. Iza backed away from the kitchen table and fell onto the sofa laughing. Volodya plopped down on the sofa beside her, winced, and grabbed his right side.

Just then, Iza's phone pinged, signaling an incoming text. She and Volodya looked at each other with surprise, wondering who would be texting at this early hour. It was Tony. His text message was simply to call him as soon as possible. Tony answered immediately.

"Tony, what is it there? 3:00 a.m.?"

"Yeah, I'm still awake here. Iza, I wanted to warn you this coming week is going to be busy and stressful for you. I contacted Bill Harmon from the Bureau of Economic and Business Affairs before I flew out yesterday. He's our top rep from the Bureau, and he's the one I've tapped to work with you getting in for a visit to imperative Energie. I told him the visit is urgent but didn't give him a lot of other detail. I just said we need to make this business contact soon, and try to offer them the enticement of a business opportunity in the U.S. He'll be pushing for a time this coming week.

The CIA will be pulling you out of your apartment sometime tomorrow. I need your new address there, and one of you will have to be there late in the evening tomorrow when they drop off your things.

I've got you an appointment at 13:00 tomorrow with the CIA Disguise group. I took the liberty of telling Bill your name is Claire Daniels. That's who you're going to be for the meeting."

"Whoa, Tony, I don't really look a lot like Claire," Iza interrupted, "and I don't feel comfortable trying to impersonate her. That doesn't seem like a good idea to me. And I'm supposed to work all day tomorrow with Jack Malone doing interviews. I can't just leave Jack for an appointment. I don't have the authority to do that."

"Give me your address."

Iza quickly recited the full address for Volodya's apartment.

Tony continued, "I'll follow up with Jack and with Claire. You can work with Jack in the morning, then cut out for the rest of the day. Yeah, you don't look a lot like Claire, but I think the Disguise people can make you look close enough for this kind of meeting."

"Tony, Claire is on vacation until Thursday; I don't think you'll be able to reach her. But . . . say Bill and I get an appointment this week. I'll probably look different enough that Johannes Brandt wouldn't recognize me, but what if Alex Schröder is there? He knows Claire—at least well enough to say hello—so he knows what she looks like. And he knows what I look like."

"That's a risk, Iza, but how likely is it that he'll be there? He's a shareholder partner in the firm, not an employee. That's like being on the Board of Directors for a company. He'd be there for meetings probably only four times a year. And you're going to be there for what—maybe an hour—two at most?"

"It still scares me."

"Honestly, I don't see that as a problem."

"Remember, I'm the one who's going there, not you."

After a brief pause, Iza continued, "Tony, Volodya and I walked past their office yesterday, and Volodya was able to get inside. He found some interesting things for us."

"What?" Tony hollered in an exasperated voice. Then he said in a more hushed tone, "What are you two doing breaking into a business?"

Iza replied quietly, trying to calm Tony down, "We didn't break in, Tony; Volodya was able to walk into their office. He . . . there . . . well, he got in as a janitor doing office cleaning. He's got a floor plan drawn out for me, showing me where everything is located. Alex has an office there. Volodya also got a phone card listing the names and numbers of all their employees. It looks like forty-seven total. The phone numbers are easy; they use the same root number and then end differently, like with a -10 to a -57. I can send those to you. And Tony, he found a thumb drive on a guy's desk, and there's some code on it. Volodya's decoding it to understand what it does. It's not their full software package but a small section of code. He's trying to determine if anything in the code is unusual."

"Iza, might I remind you that trespassing on a business property and accessing their files without permission is industrial espionage. People go to *jail* for that," Tony said as his voice rose in pitch once again.

Iza thought quickly and responded, "Tony, Volodya's in the Ukrainian military. If he has reason to suspect that someone in that company is trying to compromise his country's military operation in Berlin and potentially kill his people, do the same rules apply?"

"That's only your suspicion, Iza. Just because Brandt works for the company, and you don't quite trust Alex Schröder, it doesn't give you the right to steal files from the company. I consider what you and Volodya did—and are apparently still doing—to be something *very* stupid."

"Well, should I secretly drop the thumb drive back there on the visit Bill schedules?"

Tony ignored Iza's question. "I don't need the floor plan, but send me a copy of the phone listing *and* the thumb drive in a diplomatic pouch tomorrow. You can do that after your 13:00 meeting. Volodya needs to stop working on the code; I'll get that taken care of here."

"You're interested enough to have someone *there* look at the file, but *we're* guilty of stealing it?"

Tony again ignored Iza's question and continued, "Once you're through the meeting at imperative Energie, hopefully this coming week, I want the two of you to pull back from your involvement. By then, you may have already done a service to your country, Ukraine, and Germany too. No one got the blueprints from you, and maybe you'll even learn something more in this meeting. But after the meeting, you two need to focus on your *own* safety. Promise?"

Iza pressed her lips together while thinking and, after a pause, replied quietly, "I don't think I can promise that, Tony. I need to see this through until you've found the spy or spies in the U.S. I mean, see it through as much as I can from here, which probably isn't going to be much more anyway. We're trying to be careful; I promise you that."

"Iza, *please*! Look, FBI Counterespionage is already investigating this whole mess from the D.C. end. You'll be safer if you just stay out of this." Iza said nothing.

"Let me talk to Volodya," Tony quickly requested. "Volodya, Iza can tell you about the plans for next week, but I need your help. Once Iza is done with this meeting at imperative Energie, I want you two to pull back on your involvement. And I don't want you looking at the code you found, either. Iza is sending me the thumb drive tomorrow. Your work is *done*. Focus on your and Iza's safety. Deal?" Tony implored.

Volodya sat thinking how he could respond. He didn't want to lie to Tony again, but he also knew he was probably as good at coding as anyone Tony could find. And, he'd already decided he would ask Dmytro, who was one of the best computer specialists in Ukraine and someone who he revered, and perhaps also Petro, for their help if he ran into something he couldn't understand. Volodya could hear Tony's breathing as he awaited Volodya's answer.

Tony finally said, "Well?"

"I will think about what you said. You know, our ability to pull back depends on Russians too; we do not have choice with them. They will keep trying to get what they want. I know these guys."

Volodya could hear Tony sigh loudly as he handed the phone back to Iza. "Iza here again."

"Iza, send me the pouch tomorrow. Bill said he'd call each of us when he has a time arranged for the visit, and we'll do a debriefing afterward. Remember, Bill thinks you're Claire Daniels. In the meantime, call me at any hour if you need help. And don't forget, if you run into *any* problem at imperative Energie, or you feel unsafe, get out, even if it means you don't learn anything. You can call Herr Kühn, too, if you need immediate help. Be safe there, Iza."

"Tony wants the thumb drive. And he wants me to go to the meeting as Claire!" Iza exclaimed after hanging up. "I think that's a bad idea."

"You can send thumb drive to Tony; I already made copy on my laptop," Volodya said with a smile. "I have not met Claire, but Tony seems like smart guy. He must have good reason to suggest this. Now, you and I need to visit dinosaurs."

Since the museum didn't open until 10:00, Volodya and Iza rewarmed leftover Nalysnyky and ate a leisurely breakfast, then took a long and winding walking route to get to the museum. They talked nonstop about everything and nothing, only avoiding talking about the phone call from Tony and Russia's brutal war in Ukraine.

Once inside the museum, Volodya immediately pulled Iza to the dinosaur exhibit. "You know," he told Iza, "dinosaurs were big success one time. They lived more than 150 million years and through three geological eras. They survived one mass extinction and adapted to big changes in environmental conditions. But then their reign ended suddenly. Let us hope that we humans are not on same path."

"How do you know so much about dinosaurs?" Iza questioned.

"I always liked dinosaurs as little kid. They are pretty cool."

Iza shot some funny photos of Volodya with the dinosaurs on her phone camera. In one part of the exhibit, there was a colorful projection of a T-rex on a black-painted wall in a darkened area of the museum. Volodya stood next to the projection, with his head appearing to be in the jaws of the T-rex. At another location, he lay across a granite slab on the edge of a display of enormous running dinosaur skeletons, his eyes bulging and his tongue hanging out of his mouth. Iza lay on the museum floor to take the photo. It looked as though he'd just been crushed underfoot by one of the running dinosaur skeletons. A few passing visitors laughed as they looked at what the two were doing. In yet another area, Volodya sat on a bench, surrounded by predatory dinosaur skulls on display, their sharp teeth appearing to envelop his head.

They passed by a Plateosaurus skeleton, a Triassic herbivore that was both the oldest dinosaur in the exhibit in terms of geological history, and one of the earliest dinosaurs ever discovered, the find dating back to the 1830s. Iza snapped a photo of Volodya looking as though he were taking his Plateosaurus for a walk, much like someone would walk their dog. The two of them smiled as they looked through the silly photos. They spent an hour in the dinosaur exhibit until Iza finally pulled Volodya with her to the area of the museum housing the mineral collection.

"I like rocks," she smiled.

She translated the German sign at the entrance to the display collection.

"It says here that this is the original exhibition hall that was preserved from the nineteenth century, and the display cabinets are mostly historic. There are almost 200.000 specimens, representing sixty-five percent of all known minerals in the world." They wandered the area looking at samples of copper, quartz, gold, silver, and emerald.

It was almost 13:00 when Volodya suggested they walk to enjoy the nice weather. They purchased a large soft pretzel at the museum café to share on their way. When they'd finished the pretzel, Volodya grabbed Iza's hand, and they walked in silence for a few minutes, eventually arriving at the busy Tiergarten. Suddenly, Volodya turned in front of Iza and stopped. He pulled her close to him and kissed her intensely. Passing walkers and runners looked on and either smiled or scowled at them.

"Iza, can we always be happy like this?" he asked, his eyes filling with tears. "I hope you do not mind that I hold your hand often, that I touch your face, and hold and kiss you often. Since I am in military, I have no human contact that is not violent. My parents are killed, and my brother fights somewhere. When I came here to Berlin, I am not allowed to socialize with my guys from data center after work, and all my days are about hatred, violence, and death. For three months, each night, I went home to apartment, and I was alone without friends, and my family are mostly all dead. But then, I met you . . . who I have been waiting to find . . . and I *need* to touch you. I *need* to feel human."

"I like when you hold my hand and kiss me. That's part of being in love. Honestly, I hope we can always feel this way about each other, even after we've been together for a long time—that we never take each other for granted. We'll have to work for it, but you always have to work hard for the best things in life.

"You're a kind and caring man. You've shown me that. What you're doing now in the war is necessary. You said when we first met, it's a job you *need* to do. It's for your country. The war will end someday—soon, I hope. Then you can be the man who you are full-time. I'm committed to help you keep that man inside you; I don't want him to disappear."

They walked slowly around the park and sat on benches or the grass periodically for almost three hours, enjoying the warm sun and the fresh air, talking and laughing, until Volodya finally admitted that his ribs were getting very sore. Then they headed back toward the apartment.

◆

Volodya lay on the sofa with the heating pad on his ribs as he read from a history book. Iza knelt down beside him and showed him the silly photos on her phone of him with the dinosaurs. The two laughed softly but suddenly jumped when Iza's phone rang. It was Tony again.

"Tony, what's up?" Iza asked in surprise.

"Iza, I need to tell you something." He sounded almost breathless and terribly upset. "We went out for an early birthday brunch for Greta's twentieth. She has to drive back to school pretty soon. Anyway, Roger, your mom, and Günther joined us. I sat next to Günther, and he had a couple—maybe three—bloody marys; he was a little tipsy. Your mom, Ellen, and Greta did their girl's trip to the restroom together, and Roger was busy kidding around with Tony Jr. Günther and I got to talking about our kids, and Iza . . . Günther doesn't have a son in Berlin! He said he has two daughters who live near Potsdam. I didn't know what to say. Who is it that he wants you to call?"

Iza breathed in deeply and held her breath. Her eyes opened wide, and her body started trembling. She nearly dropped the phone.

Volodya sat up, "Iza, what is wrong?"

"Tony, can I call you back?"

I need to calm down. How many times has Günther pushed Mom to get me to call his son. At first it seemed innocent—like Mom was hoping I'd have a boyfriend here. She might have thought it'd be cool if I ended up liking his son as much as she likes Günther. But then it got weird. It made me wonder if his son even exists. I think I'm right.

God, this coming week is going to be like a long and difficult race. I need a strategy to stay calm and get myself to the finish line as the winner. But I'm not even at the starting line yet. The race starts tomorrow. Winning means figuring out everyone who's involved in this so someone can stop them.

Iza breathed deeply, then exhaled, repeating the sequence a few times until she regained her composure. Iza told Volodya Tony's news. He ran his hands through his hair. "Jezus."

"I never liked Günther. I think I'm right, and he isn't who we think he is. Can you get the imperative Energie phone list? I noticed this yesterday when we were eating ice cream, but it didn't register in my brain until just now."

They sat together at the table while Iza scanned through her phone looking for the number her mom had given her for Günther's son. Her mom had never told her the son's name until their last call when Iza finally asked for it. She'd told Iza that Günther said his son's name was Johann or Jan—John. She found the phone number her mom had given her, then scanned the list that Volodya brought to the table. "Günther's 'son' is Johannes Brandt—the 'suitcase' man and sales representative for imperative Energie. The phone numbers are identical."

Volodya warmed leftover borscht and pampushki for their supper while Iza called Tony. "Tony, Günther's supposed son has the same phone number as Johannes Brandt."

"What?" Tony said incredulously. "Iza, I need to evaluate what's going on, and I'll have to call you tomorrow after your meeting with the Disguise group. I need more time to think, and I need some rest."

"Remember to find out exactly what Günther does for his job."

Iza and Volodya ate quietly at the table. Volodya reached over occasionally to run his hand over Iza's cheek or to touch her hand.

They went to the bedroom early to get extra sleep, but as soon as Iza was sleeping, Volodya slipped out of the bedroom and restarted his laptop at the kitchen table. He made coffee and continued working through the "68" code for several hours, still getting frustrated by the same two segments in the pages of code. He tried to understand the purpose of each segment, but got increasingly irritated because he wasn't able to understand what the segments accomplished, and he knew that he *had* to understand to help Iza. His frustration built until it spilled over into anger. He crumpled his notes and threw them across the kitchen, then pushed over his chair onto the floor. "Fuck this shit; what you *mean*, guy?" he quietly cursed the writer of the lines of code. But nothing came to him. He didn't want to awaken Iza by getting back into bed, so he dropped onto the sofa, covered himself with throw pillows, and finally fell asleep.

Monday, October 31 (Day 20)

Iza awoke at 4:30, surprising herself that she'd slept so soundly through most of the night after feeling such a sense of fear and unease when they'd gone to bed. Iza saw that Volodya wasn't in bed next to her, and she found him lying asleep under a pile of pillows on the sofa. She dragged the down comforter from the bed, carefully removed the pillows from him, covered him with the comforter, and softly kissed his forehead. She picked up the chair from the kitchen floor, wondering how it had tipped over; then she saw Volodya's half-full mug of cold coffee on the table.

Oh, Volodya, I'm so sorry, she thought as she sat at the table in the semi-dark kitchen. She felt overwhelmed again, then took some deep breaths, turned on her headlamp, and wrote out a list of tasks she'd need to accomplish:

- Jack Malone interviews
- Claire's office
    photos of Claire
    change Claire's phone message with admin
    Claire's monogrammed pen
- CIA Disguise group
    padding, clothing, shoes, makeup and fix black eye, wig, large cross-body purse
    (easier to run with, if I need to), note pad, pens, employee identification badge with
    my altered image as Claire Daniels
- Send diplomatic pouch to Tony (from where in embassy?)
- Call from Tony for instructions
- Call from Bill Harmon
- Volodya (phone numbers for secure data center lines)

- Memorize imperative Energie floorplan
- CIA to drop my stuff at apartment tonight

Am I missing anything? she thought. *I'm approaching the starting line, and the race is about to begin.*

◆

Volodya was sleeping so soundly that he jumped when Iza gently shook him awake, and he wondered for a moment where he was. He and Iza talked through their plans for the day. "Iza, I am sorry. I made little progress last night understanding two segments of code that trouble me. I will ask Dmytro, and maybe Petro, if they are willing to help me. We are not allowed to meet at our apartments or not even to go out for beers, but maybe they will meet me at café after work. I think it is not socializing if we only work to look at code and eat while working."

"Volodya, remember to call me with the new phone numbers at the data center in case I need to reach you there." Volodya dressed quickly and left for the data center.

◆

Iza left the apartment at 7:30, walking determinedly to the embassy. She first checked for a message from Tony, but seeing none, left to meet Jack Malone.

"Iza, how are you?" Jack queried as he gave Iza a quick hug, then did a double take as he looked curiously at her black eye. "What happened to you?"

"I'm so clumsy and in a hurry. I ran into a door a few days ago. Believe it or not, it looks a lot better than it did. Like I told Claire, first bad sushi and now a black eye. I hope trouble doesn't come in threes."

"Say Iza, Tony Brooks left me a message. He said you can only help me with passport interviews until noon today. Then I guess he's got you on a special assignment. Any hint about what you're working on? I'm not the type to be envious, but in your case, I am. It must be something pretty important for Tony to be involved."

Iza laughed softly. "I wish you could take my place, Jack, but Tony picked me for some reason or other."

Iza quickly changed the subject, asking to see the list of interviewees for the day. Jack took her cue and didn't question her further. They worked through the morning with only short breaks between the interviews until it was nearly noon. Iza bid Jack farewell and raced to Claire's office.

Claire's office was locked, but her administrative assistant let Iza inside. "Be sure to lock the door on your way out," she said as she left Iza at the office entry.

Iza scanned the office for photos of Claire—anything that might help the CIA person prepare a good disguise for her. She found three photos: a close-up of Claire's face and upper body, taken after she'd received an embassy award, and two showing Claire standing in groups with other embassy employees, which would give the CIA person an impression of her height and weight. Next, Iza looked for Claire's special monogrammed pen. Claire left it in a holder on her desktop, so Iza took it for the meeting. She'd bring the photos back later in the afternoon, and she'd return the pen after the imperative Energie meeting.

Iza looked around Claire's office. *I think there's something else I'm supposed to do here, but what?* She simply couldn't remember, and she'd accidentally left her task list with Jack's list of interviewees. Iza closed the door, but didn't lock it, and made her way to the CIA Disguise Group Laboratory.

◆

Volodya arrived about ten minutes before the morning briefing. Bobby sat beside him in the briefing room and tried to engage Volodya with some of his latest jokes, but Volodya wasn't in his normal good mood. He smiled at Bobby and laughed when prompted by Bobby's laughter, but his mind was elsewhere.

Lloyd began the briefing. "Russia's defense ministry says it recovered and analyzed the wreckage of drones used to attack the ships of Russia's Black Sea Fleet in Crimea on Saturday. They claim the drones were equipped with Canadian-made navigation modules for an attack that was carried out by Ukraine—get this—under *British* leadership." Lloyd laughed heartily. "I guess they don't know about us yet," he smiled at the Team members.

There'd been another Russian attack on civilian targets in Kyiv, with significant damage to water and energy infrastructure. Fierce and brutal fighting continued in the Donbas. The Russians continued to pull back from Kherson. The continued destruction of ammunition depots and equipment was hastening the Russian pullback.

At their morning break, Volodya sat with Dmytro and Petro at a table, and the three spoke in Ukrainian. "Hey guys, my girlfriend needs help decoding few lines of cybersecurity program for her work at U.S. Embassy. I am close to knowing how this part of program works, but have two segments of code where I do not understand purpose."

But before Volodya could ask if they would help him, Dmytro put his hands up, indicating he wanted Volodya to stop talking. "*You* have girlfriend who works at U.S. Embassy?" he asked incredulously as he started to chuckle.

Petro rolled his eyes at Volodya, and the two sat back in their chairs as Dmytro went into a monologue poking fun at Volodya with his "American" girlfriend. "Are you her little Ukrainian gigolo, or do you prefer them younger than you? Is she beautiful? And if beautiful, then how is it that she is *your* girlfriend? I do not understand. Does she not see what *you* look like? Or maybe she is not very smart."

Dmytro went on with his teasing. Petro could see that Volodya was beginning to seethe with anger. Finally, Dmytro got too personal. "Does she fuck better than Ukrainian girls?" he asked as he broke out in raucous laughter—trademark Dmytro.

Volodya stood up and kicked back his chair. It crashed to the floor. The other Team members looked over at the three of them. Despite his sore ribs, Volodya reached across the table and grabbed Dmytro's shirt by the collar, pulling him forward and tightening the shirt around Dmytro's neck. Petro quickly picked up Volodya's chair, then pulled him back into his seat. "Hey, Dmytro," Petro said calmly while looking Dmytro in the eyes, "why don't you shut up and listen to what Volodya has to say."

Dmytro was so shocked that Volodya had attacked him and that Petro had told him to shut up that he stopped talking. Finally, he offered an apology. "Volodya, I am sorry for making crude comment. How can I help you?"

The other Team members concluded that whatever had happened between the three crazy Ukrainians was over. Volodya calmed down and then asked the two if they'd be willing to meet him outside of the data center on Tuesday evening.

"I will buy dinner at Bleibtreu Café nearby on Bleibtreustraße if you help me look at this code. Besides dinner, café has coffee and even beer or vodka if you want. I will buy for you. Maybe we meet at 17:30? Café is open until 22:00."

The two men agreed to meet Volodya there the following evening, and they all agreed to say nothing further about the meeting nor about Volodya's outburst. Before returning to his workstation, Volodya called Iza from one of the secure phone lines and left her a message with the numbers of the four new secure lines in the canteen.

Iza arrived at the CIA Disguise Laboratory about ten minutes before her scheduled appointment time. Suzanne Teller was ready for her and brought Iza back into their work lab. She looked at Iza's black eye and frowned, then took the three photos of Claire that Iza had fetched from Claire's office, along with the photo from Claire's embassy pass that she'd brought up on her computer, and got to work.

Claire was about two or three inches taller than Iza and was about twenty pounds heavier. Her face was fuller than Iza's, but her legs were slender, similar to Iza's. Her weight was carried more in her torso, with a thicker upper body and waistline, although she didn't have particularly large breasts. Her hips were broader than Iza's. Claire's hair was darker brown compared to Iza's but was also considerably shorter and worn in a severe bob cut. Claire wore a lot of makeup too, including foundation and blush, eyeshadow, mascara—sometimes even false eyelashes—eyebrow filler, and bright red lipstick. She also always wore bright red artificial nails.

Suzanne found an upper body suit that extended from the shoulders to the buttocks, including the upper arms, and fitted it to Iza. "This will make your frame look twenty pounds heavier," she said. Then she brought a bright red long-sleeved suit for Iza.

Iza frowned, "I don't want to stand out that much. I'll look like a beacon."

"A red suit will draw the eye away from your face, making it less likely someone will notice the differences between the shape of Claire's face and yours. It looks like Claire often wears red too."

"I'm not convinced this is a good idea, but you've prepared disguises for people before and I haven't."

With the outfit decided, Suzanne chose some black stiletto heels for Iza. "Suzanne, I never wear heels like this, and I'm not sure I can walk in them." Iza tried them on and stumbled around the room.

"Practice walking in them at home. I need to make you look taller, and these are the kind that Claire wears. See her shoes in this photo you brought?"

Suzanne found a large, black cross-body purse for Iza to use to carry her tablet, pen, and flat shoes, in case she needed to change out of the heels after her meeting, then got to work on her hair. She pulled Iza's hair back, pinned it up, and then fitted her with a dark brown, bob-cut wig. She gave Iza a pair of conservatively sized black drop earrings. At last, she glued on fake nails in a bright red color, layered foundation and blush, added eyeshadow, and thickened Iza's brows. She applied a layer of mascara, then glued on false lashes before applying another layer of mascara. She plumped Iza's lips, then added red lipstick in a shade that matched the red of the suit.

Iza looked in the mirror. "I'm shocked at how different I look . . . not that I like this look on me. It's a beautiful look on Claire; she looks like she could model for a fashion magazine. But I feel like my face is going to crack off. I don't look like Iza Carter anymore. Do you think I look like Claire Daniels?"

"Maybe from a block away you can pass for Claire, but certainly not up close. In our notes here, it says you just have to 'sort of' look like Claire—at least, that's what Tony Brooks said. He said there won't be anyone at your meeting who knows Claire."

Suzanne kept talking as she prepared an employee identification badge for Iza, using her new look photo and the name Claire Daniels. With the identification badge completed, Suzanne took detailed notes on Iza's makeup and clothing preparations.

"I'll need an hour with you before your scheduled meeting to repeat this disguise. Otherwise, you're free to become Iza Carter again, except for those red nails. I'm not redoing those. And remember to practice walking in the heels at home."

After removing the wig and clothing, Iza wiped off the heavy make-up, except for the false eyelashes, then took several packs of make-up remover wipes and put them in the cross-body purse for later use.

It was already 15:00, and Iza ran back to Claire's office, slipped in the open door, and replaced Claire's photos. Once again, she thought, *There's something else I need to do in here.* But nothing came to her, and she needed to send the diplomatic pouch to Tony. She locked Claire's office door, then raced to the mail dispatch office with the imperative Energie phone card and thumb drive.

The process for sending those to Tony by diplomatic pouch was straightforward, so Iza was quickly on her way by 15:45.

Iza dashed to her office again and checked her phone. There were two messages from Tony and one from Bill Harmon. She first listened to Tony's message, sent shortly after 13:00. "Iza, this is Tony. I took a lot of time to think carefully about you going to imperative Energie. I decided it's still a go. I just can't see how Günther would know that you're going to be there, so how's it going to be any different than what we'd planned earlier? I hope the Disguise people are doing good work with you this afternoon. Be extremely careful and remember to get out if anything doesn't seem right to you. But I'm sure we'll talk again in person before any meeting time is set."

At 13:50, there was a long message from Bill Harmon. "Claire, this is Bill Harmon from the Bureau of Economic and Business Affairs. Tony Brooks wanted me to set up a meeting for you with imperative Energie on an urgent basis. I called the business this morning, and this is really short notice, but their marketing person—Kristin Pfeiffer is the name—had a demo cancellation tomorrow morning at 10:00, and she can see you then if you can make it. Unfortunately, I can't make it tomorrow, but I took the appointment since Tony said this is urgent."

Iza nearly dropped her phone; she was stunned that Bill wasn't going to the meeting with her and that she'd be at imperative Energie in less than eighteen hours. She listened on.

"I assigned a new fellow from my group, Derek Thomas, to attend with you. He's only been with us for two weeks, but I think he'll do fine. He's an Ivy-League MBA, and he's got a good mind, so I'm not worried." *Of course, you're not worried—you don't have to go to the meeting with him—I do!*

Bill's message continued, "You're to meet him tomorrow morning at 9:00 near the Embassy entrance. You two can discuss the meeting for thirty minutes beforehand in the lobby, and then I've arranged for a car to pick you up at 9:30. Only call me back if you can't make it. Good luck with your meeting."

At 14:20, there was another message from Tony. "Iza, this is Tony again. I think Bill called you about the meeting tomorrow morning. I'm not too happy about the timing and that he isn't going, but he said he thought my labeling the request urgent took precedence over his attendance. Let me know if it isn't going to work for you to be there tomorrow morning. I'm really sorry about the timing, and I . . . I just hope this works out. Call me with any questions.

"I tried to learn about Günther's job at the German Embassy too, but my contact at the CIA was really evasive. He said he couldn't tell me; I'm not *authorized* to get that information. I've got a call in to another of my contacts. Eventually, if we have to, I can contact the Secretary."

Tony's not authorized? Iza thought. *What kind of job could Günther have that Tony can't know about?*

Iza immediately called Suzanne from the CIA Disguise Group and asked to schedule an 8:00 morning session for Tuesday to get her disguise prepared for the day. "Wow, sorry, Iza. I'm at the other embassy site tomorrow, so I can't help you. Let me take a look at the schedule." Iza waited nervously as she heard Suzanne paging through their appointment book. "Looks like Tina Richards can help you prepare. She's new at the Embassy—been here a couple weeks—but has a lot of theater experience as a makeup artist."

Great, Iza thought with mounting anxiety, *now I'm working with a new person from the CIA Disguise Group and an Ivy-League MBA who's been at the embassy for two weeks. And I'm the one with seniority—two more days on the job than they have! How's this going to work out?*

Iza grabbed the black stilettos and left the embassy an hour early in frustration, pulling on the curly blonde wig before walking out onto the embassy plaza.

When she arrived at the apartment, Volodya was not there yet, so Iza started to memorize the floor plan for imperative Energie, added Volodya's work phone numbers into her phone, and stumbled back and forth across the apartment wearing the heels. She simply couldn't hold her balance on the narrow stilettos, but she kept trying. "Is it better to walk normally or to look taller and walk like a drunk?" Iza wondered aloud.

◆

When Volodya arrived, he laughed and shook his head in disbelief at the sight of Iza trying to walk in the stilettos. He was also surprised by her new employee photo as Claire Daniels, and at her bright red fingernails. "I like my Iza better," he said while smiling at her and rocking back and forth on his heels as he watched her trying to walk.

Suddenly, Iza kicked off the heels, bent her arms at the elbows, curled her hands to make claws, and growled and snarled at Volodya as she walked stiffly around the kitchen and near the sofa.

"What am I now?" she giggled. "I am T-rex with polished red nails." Volodya started laughing too. He removed his socks and squeezed his feet into the black heels, barely able to get his toes inside. He stood on his toes in the shoes and stumbled around in the heels as Iza laughed hysterically.

"*How* do you walk in these?" Volodya asked in an incredulous tone of voice.

"I don't. I stumble around looking like I'm drunk!"

As they waited for the CIA to drop off Iza's belongings from her apartment, she confided, "Volodya, I'm scared to death about this meeting. It seems like everything's going wrong. This Derek guy and I don't have any experience. We're both new employees. And the woman who's supposed to work on my disguise tomorrow is new at the embassy too. I don't think Brandt will know who I am if he's in the office. The disguise *is* pretty good. But what if Alex Schröder is there? Tony thinks there's zero chance that could happen, but like I told him, he's not the one going there.

"I feel like my race started today. I'm still in the middle of the pack or maybe in the rear. Tomorrow, I need to make my move to pull ahead—to find out who's involved with this so they can be stopped. But I'm worried I'm not going to do well the way things are going so far."

"Do not go. Tell Tony you need more time."

"I'm not sure what to do. Tony left another message too. He's not authorized to find out what Günther's job is! What kind of job could he have that Tony—the Assistant Secretary of State for European and Eurasian Affairs—can't know about?"

"Is it possible someone in U.S. already figured out that Günther is spying for Russians and they are trying to catch him, so they cannot give Tony that information?"

"I don't know what to think."

A few minutes later, two CIA employees dropped off Iza's remaining belongings from her old apartment. She didn't have much, but there was enough to fill the area next to the sofa in their tiny apartment: her suitcase, now packed with her clothing and towels; several totes containing more clothing; bedding; her small bedroom lamp; toiletries; and, cooking gear. Iza pulled the framed photo of her mom and dad from one of the totes, looked at it tearfully, then set it back down. When the CIA employees were gone, Iza said, "Do you mind if I just leave these totes and my suitcase packed up here until later in the week? I'm kind of stressed tonight to be unpacking."

"Iza, for me, you can leave stuff packed there forever. You know I do not care about that sort of thing. Let me make us something to eat."

Volodya put his arm around Iza and led her to a chair in the kitchen, then set about making a quick pasta dinner while they continued talking about what tomorrow would bring for each of them.

After their quick supper, they lay together on the sofa. Volodya started kissing Iza, and that was how they ended the evening—laughing quietly and kissing each other. She suddenly understood Volodya's need for tender human contact and realized she needed it too.

Tuesday, November 1 (Day 21)

"Iza, call me after imperative Energie meeting. I will sit near phones at lunchtime and at afternoon break to wait for your call. Be careful . . . do as Tony said . . . leave meeting if you do not like something there." Volodya was visibly worried as he ran his hands through her hair, then held Iza's face between his hands and kissed her. "You can still back out of meeting. If you are worried about disguise, tell Tony you will not go today. And remember . . . I work on code tonight with Dmytro and Petro at Bleibtreu Café; I will be late."

"I'll call you there as soon as I can. Thank your friends for helping me." Iza looked distressed as she watched him leave the apartment.

Volodya sat between Petro and Bobby for the 7:00 briefing. Petro leaned over to Volodya and whispered with tears in his eyes, "Did you hear? Last night Russia destroyed *forty percent* of Ukrainian power infrastructure in massive missile and drone strikes. They are stealing our art from museums. Iryna told me they took everything of value from museum where she worked. They try to eradicate us—our people, our culture—they leave us to freeze in the winter!"

Volodya put his hand on Petro's shoulder, "We need to listen to Zaluzhnyi, Petro. I told you before, and I repeat it again. He says Russians must be killed, *just killed*, and we should not be afraid to do it. I decide I am no longer afraid. I do not ask for this feeling, but I am *full* of hate for Russians. You must find courage, Petro—for your wife and your son—for your son's future. When war is over, we can go back to being people who we were before."

Just then, Bobby leaned over and told one of his jokes—something about sheep and Petro having his head in a fence. They didn't understand his joke, but Bobby's laughter was so contagious, that the two of them laughed together with him. It broke the anxiety that the two felt as they contemplated the destruction of their homeland.

Max, the German Team commander, delivered the briefing: Ukrainian forces continued their interdiction campaign against Russian concentration areas, logistics nodes, and military assets in Kherson Oblast. Ukraine's Southern Operational Command reported that Ukrainian rocket and artillery units conducted 180 fire missions against Russian manpower and equipment concentrations in Kherson Oblast and that Ukrainian aviation struck a Russian stronghold in Snihuriyka in Mykolaiv Oblast. Ukrainian forces also struck Russian ammunition warehouses near Beryslav. They reported destroying the Akhtamar Hotel along the Mariupol-Donetsk City Road, which was housing Chechen troops under the command of Ramzan Kadyrov. The Team returned to their workstations.

Iza was apprehensive about the day ahead. She immediately proceeded to the CIA Disguise Group Lab area, but Tina Richards wasn't there. Tina arrived at 8:15, leaving only forty-five minutes to prepare Iza's disguise.

"Sorry I'm late, Iza. My kid is sick." She pulled the clothing for Iza and ran to get the makeup cart.

"Tina, I just can't walk in these stiletto heels. I practiced last night at home but I end up walking like I'm drunk," Iza implored when Tina arrived with the cart. Tina said nothing, and instead disappeared between two rows of industrial shelving. She returned a few minutes later carrying a pair of black pumps with wide stacked heels.

"I love you, Tina," Iza giggled.

With her outfit on, Tina got to work on Iza's hair and makeup. She pinned up Iza's long hair in small ringlets, then fitted the dark, bob-style wig over her head and pinned it in place.

"I don't like what Suzanne did with your face. I'm gonna do something a little lighter on you. You'll find that body suit is pretty warm, and you'll be sweating. I don't want your makeup to run off your face in a sticky blob."

Tina was efficient and practical. She eliminated most of the foundation, using only a few small dabs to conceal Iza's colorful black eye and went with a couple of compressed powder and blush colors to highlight Iza's cheek bones.

"You've obviously done this before."

"Yeah, I worked ten years as a theater makeup artist. I got good at quick changeovers."

Soon Iza was ready for the meeting, with new eyeliner and the same eyeshadow, mascara, lip plumper, and bright red lipstick that Suzanne had previously chosen. Iza slipped on the stacked heels and, although still a bit unsteady, found that she could walk reasonably well. She grabbed the crossbody purse and looked at herself in the full-length mirror. She wasn't Claire Daniels, but she looked more Claire-like than Iza-like. *Will this disguise be good enough?* she wondered.

Tina concluded the appointment with some words of wisdom: "Bring back what you can after your meeting or wherever you're going, but if you need to dump any part of your disguise, save yourself before the clothes."

Iza hurried down to the embassy lobby, now ten minutes late, wondering if it would be difficult to locate Derek Thomas. As she caught sight of him, she thought, *I didn't need to worry*. Derek was well over six feet tall, with thick, nearly black hair, a cleanly shaven face with a square jaw, perfectly apportioned facial features, and large, dark eyes— the epitome of the tall, dark, and handsome male. He was nervously scanning the lobby, obviously looking for someone who was ten minutes late.

"I'm Iz . . . Claire Daniels," Iza caught herself, as she walked quickly up to Derek with her hand extended.

"Derek Thomas," he replied, shaking Iza's hand. He then continued, "You don't look at *all* like your photo in the employee directory."

"Oh?"

"Yeah, I looked you up in the directory, and your photo makes you look about ten years older—no offense intended. I guess it's better to look younger in person than in a photo." Derek smiled, then launched into work. "So, I did some research on imperative Energie and wondered if you know why Tony Brooks is so interested in the business? And I also wondered, why's he sending *you* there? No offense intended, but I read you're just a manager in Consular Affairs. It seems like an odd assignment for someone with *your* background."

Iza was momentarily dumbfounded by his insightful first question and annoyed by the second. She improvised. "With what's going on in cyberspace in the Russia-Ukraine war, Tony is thinking ahead that reliable energy delivery systems in the U.S. require cyber-resiliency. Our national security and economic prosperity depend on having a reliable energy infrastructure. As I understand, he heard about this business and wondered if they might provide a reasonably priced, performance product for small- to mid-sized utilities. I'm sure someone with *your* background already knows the few big players in this space in the U.S., and our Department of Energy has a cyber program, but he's thinking about those smaller utilities with more limited budgets and less in-house know-how.

"As for me, Tony's known me a long time and he trusts my abilities. My advanced degree in International Relations focused on energy economics; I just attended an E.U. conference on the topic of energy infrastructure development. I guess he was thinking of that when he asked me to attend the meeting today, but I'm not actually positive why he asked. I don't see myself taking a larger role in this if the contact today leads anywhere." *What a jerk—implying that his Ivy-League MBA with two weeks on the job makes him more qualified to attend a software demo than Claire, with ten years of experience in Consular Affairs! Maybe he didn't intend his comment to sound so condescending, but it sure came across that way.*

Iza didn't know if her answers satisfied Derek, as he had an inscrutable face. She explained what she'd learned about the structure of the company, and again, Derek didn't ask any further questions or indicate if her information was news to him or not. Soon after 9:30, a black Mercedes pulled in front of the embassy, and the two were on their way.

After arriving for their 10:00 meeting at imperative Energie, Derek stopped at the lobby directory, but Iza went directly to the elevator and pressed the up arrow.

"Claire, how do you know where we're supposed to go without looking at the directory?" he questioned as he walked quickly to the now-opening elevator.

"No offense intended, but I did my research," Iza smirked, mocking Derek's phrase.

She pushed the button for the third floor and turned right to exit the elevator. Iza observed the glass-paned walls of the business and saw the reception desk near the door. Volodya had told her that the door was locked on Saturday, but it was now open.

"Welcome to imperative Energie," the gorgeous young receptionist purred, handing Derek the visitor log and giving Iza a dismissive glance. While Derek was signing in, Iza scanned the area. It appeared just as Volodya had diagrammed on his floor plan. When Iza looked back at the reception desk to sign in, she noticed a beefy man with a shaved head and dressed in a stylish-looking sport coat and slacks, sitting behind and to the left of the receptionist reading a magazine. She saw a prominent bulge in his sport coat on one side—perhaps a gun. As she signed in as Claire Daniels, she glanced over and saw the man look up from his reading. Although he didn't appear very old, he had a lined and scarred face with a flattened nose, as if he'd been involved in one too many fights in his young life. She decided that perhaps he was their security guard, but a strange-looking security guard at that. The receptionist called their host for the meeting, and Kristin Pfeiffer appeared at the desk to escort the two to the Marketing Department.

"Welcome to imperative Energie," Kristin gushed in English but with a very pronounced and seductive German accent. Iza guessed Kristin was in her early- to mid-forties, with long, thick, wavy blonde hair, blue eyes, a pert nose, and *very* pouty lips. She wore an expensive-looking black Gucci suit, a silky beige blouse, and large gold hoop earrings. Iza grinned to herself, noticing that Derek was impressed by her looks. As they turned left at the hallway T-intersection, Iza glanced to the right and saw that the hallway leading to Alex Schröder's office was dark. She breathed a sigh of relief.

"We will make a stop here in the Marketing Department, then travel on to the Demo Room. And I apologize. Typically, the Sales Representative for your country would be joining us this morning, but he has," she glanced at the date on her Longines watch, "only two days left in your Washington, D.C. He flies home tomorrow evening."

Iza inquired, "What is our Sales Representative's name?"

"Ah, yes, I am sorry. His name is Johannes Brandt. I will give you his card at the end of our meeting today. He's been with us for not quite a year as we try to expand our business to the U.S., but he has a lot of prior experience in cybersecurity software sales. We haven't had any breakthroughs in the U.S. yet, but he's certainly traveled to the D.C. area many, many times. I always tease him that he must have special boarding privileges at Dulles there by now. I'm *sure* he would like to be with us here today."

I'm so glad he isn't with us here today, she thought with relief, *but Kristin just confirmed he's traveled to D.C. many, many times since he's worked here and that he goes through Dulles on his return flights.*

Kristin continued as they stopped at a tall cruiser table in the Marketing Department, "But now, I'd like to give you an overview of imperative Energie: how it came to be founded and a bit about the history of our cybersecurity products, before I give you a demonstration of how our software can combat a professional cyberattack. I won't be covering our other capabilities in the demonstration today, but we do offer threat intelligence services, and system repair services as well. If those are of interest, Johannes will send you further information when he returns to the office."

Kristin continued, "I'm giving you a bit of history here right away because we realize we have a perceptual liability due to one of our former shareholder partners. Johannes has run into this in your U.S. and we feel it is inhibiting our expansion plans. So, I want to be *completely* honest with you upfront. If you've looked at any information about our company before this meeting, I'm sure you've seen the name Mikhail Friedemann. Herr Friedemann was one of the founding shareholder partners for this company when it was formed in mid-2014. I know seeing his name raises, how do you say it—a red flag—for many since Herr Friedemann is a confidant to Vladimir Putin. I *assure* you that Herr Friedemann is no longer a partner of imperative Energie, but as you can imagine, it takes some time to work through the German bureaucracy to remove his name from our founding papers. He's been sanctioned by my country and your country since the unfortunate Russian invasion of Ukraine in February.

You may have also noticed that our Managing Director, Herr Mehlman, and our shareholder partners are all active members of the German Social Democratic Party. This has also raised an additional 'pink' flag for some since the Party has long been known for forging close and mutually beneficial relationships with the Soviet Union, and now with Russia. I don't know if you understand the history of the SPD, but I will expound on it for you only a couple minutes longer. I want you to feel completely confident as you consider working with our company."

Iza observed that Derek appeared to be falling in love with Kristin's pouty lips and seductive manner of speaking.

Derek, I hope you're paying attention to what she's saying, not just to her cleavage in that sexy beige blouse.

Kristin went on, "As Germans, we have had feelings of historical guilt and gratitude toward the Soviet Union and now Russia as its successor state. Most from the West do not realize the extent of our shame from our World War II in the East, where untold numbers of Soviet citizens were killed. Western losses *pale* compared to what my country did to the Soviets in the war. This, and gratitude for our successful reunification of communist East Germany with West Germany, led Germany, particularly the SPD, to feel that we have a moral obligation to ensure peaceful relations with Russia. The SPD also expected that a cooperative and integrative Russian policy would lead to a democratic and peaceful Russia. And, of course, as a result, we came to have a strong reliance on Russian petroleum products, particularly natural gas.

As we all know now, in hindsight, a cooperative and integrative relationship did not work with President Putin at Russia's helm. After Russia annexed Crimea in March of 2014, many in the SPD became disillusioned with the direction of the relationship. Still others continued to push for maintaining close ties with Russia. Two from the SPD who did not trust Russia so much any longer formed this company, along with two who wanted to maintain close ties with Russia. The four realized that there were both reasons to continue to engage with Russia, but also reasons to think again about how much trust we can really have with one another.

"This cybersecurity company was formed to provide cyber intelligence services and cybersecurity protection services in support of German energy infrastructure. Our services *now* offer a hedge against President Putin's Russia, which seems to have more nefarious goals in Germany than had been imagined. However, back in 2014, when the company was formed, Herr Friedemann was invited to join as a shareholder partner as a sign of their desire to continue to engage with Russia. This was a requirement of two of our shareholder partners."

Iza interrupted Kristin. "Are you free to say the two who wished for close ties with Russia?"

"Of course. It is no secret. Herr Schröder and Herr Gabel are the two." Iza's eyes opened wide. *I wonder if they still maintain those close ties. They were sitting together at the E.U. meeting. Energy policies were discussed there. They could share that info with the Russians. Plus, they seemed really interested in these new pipeline and LNG terminal projects. They were supposed to be there as members of the Bundestag representing their constituents' interests, but maybe they were actually there to find new opportunities for their business. What a conflict of interest!*

Kristin then led them to the map of Germany hanging on the wall in the Sales department, which Volodya had mentioned to Iza. She showed them that the colored pins on the map marked the dozens of locations of energy-related infrastructure around Germany where imperative Energie software was employed.

She then continued with her address, the words spilling from her pouty lips. "Our software package is unique in the industry and was developed by the world-renowned computer scientist Herr Doktor Klaus Timmer at the Technische Universität Berlin, along with his graduate students. He was simply a *brilliant* man. He realized there are multiple ways attackers can gain access to an industrial network to disrupt network processes. His goals were both to detect and then to localize attackers' activities in the earliest possible phases. The software he pioneered can detect over one hundred attack techniques. It can respond in real-time, providing unprecedented cybersecurity protection."

Iza questioned, "You used the past tense when referring to Herr Doktor Timmer. Does imperative Energie still employ him?"

"No, it was really a shock for our company, but he died unexpectedly a little over two years ago. He was involved in so many things in his life—such a wonderful man—and one of those was gardening. But of course, in Berlin, we do not have large spaces to garden, so he had his garden on the balcony of his *Eigentumswohnung*. I believe that is called a condominium in the U.S. While he was bringing in his plants in the autumn, he tragically fell to his death from his balcony. But we are fortunate to have one of his former graduate students to take his place in our company, so we have continuity in developing and improving our cybersecurity products. Let us move to the Demonstration Room."

Which Russian pushed him off his balcony? Iza wondered. "May I ask the name of the former graduate student?"

"That would be Herr Doktor Markus Peters, our Director of Software Development." *That's the name of the guy Volodya stole the thumb drive from on Saturday!* Iza realized. *How convenient to replace your professor and mentor in his well-paid job after his unexpected "accident."*

Kristin, Derek, and Iza moved into the Demonstration Room. Iza realized how noisy it was with the open office space and reception area. She could hear bits of conversations, people laughing, and even the receptionist talking. She also noticed the Demo Room was exceptionally warm. She began perspiring heavily with the body suit beneath her bright red outfit and the wig covering her head. Kristin prepared the demonstration.

"I'm going to leave the door open here. It's quite warm in the room. I hope that our noisy programmers don't bother you so much."

"Not at all," Derek responded. He moved his chair close to Kristin's until his leg almost touched hers. Iza sat near the wall, where Volodya said it would be difficult to be seen by someone passing by the room.

"So here we go. In this demonstration, we have an individual attacker trying to gain entrance to a natural gas distributor's system through a secondary vendor of pipeline repair parts. You can see the attacker has compromised the vendor system here. In this case, the vendor does not use our software and is unprotected from cyber intrusions."

Kristin continued on with the demonstration, showing how the vendor had access to certain systems within the natural gas distributor's network in order to check the distributor's inventory of spare parts. This provided a place of entry for the attacker. The demonstration then showed the response of the imperative Energie software to such an attack. The secondary vendor immediately lost access to the distributor's network, the attacker was essentially "surrounded," and the natural gas distributor received nearly instantaneous notification of the attempted intrusion. Kristin went on to show them a second, more complicated example, then ended with another simple example.

It was nearly noon when she finished her presentation, and they'd been in the Demonstration Room for over an hour. Iza was dripping with sweat and felt somewhat queasy. *I'm not a software expert, but this product seems world class. This is definitely a legit company.*

"Is it possible to get a copy of the demonstration software for us to look at later?" Derek asked breathlessly, still sitting close to Kristin.

"Why, of course. This demonstration is a bit older version of only a tiny portion of our software program, which we no longer consider so proprietary. Are there any further questions?" Kristin handed Derek a thumb drive engraved with the imperative Energie name and logo. Iza saw him slip the drive into a pocket in his leather conference folder.

As she looked at her watch, Kristin suddenly announced, "I am so sorry. I have a hard stop at noon for our demo today."

"Might I use my phone in the hallway here to call for our car?" Derek asked.

"Of course. You can step into Johannes' office and close the door if it is too noisy for you to hear in the hallway."

As soon as he left the room, Iza slid her chair over and asked Kristin a question about the software. While Kristin focused her attention on the monitor to answer Iza's question, Iza slid the thumb drive out of the pocket in Derek's leather folder and slipped it into her cross-body purse.

Kristin turned to Iza after answering her question and said, "If you have any additional questions, please do not hesitate to call Johannes when he returns to the office later this week. I do need to excuse myself soon. Our shareholder partners come to the office on the first of every month for a review meeting at 12:30." Iza's eyes opened wide, and she let out an audible gasp. She saw it was already 12:05. Then, Iza heard the receptionist.

"Alex, welcome! I am so happy to see you!" the gorgeous receptionist at the front desk exclaimed. Iza's pulse increased, and her mind raced. *What should I do?* Then she heard Alex's voice.

"*Claire Daniels* is here today?" Iza realized that he must have been looking at the visitor logbook. "I *must* go to see her and say hello. Is she in the Demonstration Room?"

Iza leaned forward toward Kristin and whispered, "This is so embarrassing, but I just realized I started menstruating. I have to excuse myself."

Kristin was about to tell Iza the location of the women's restroom, but Iza was already out the door. Volodya had shown her the restroom location on his floor plan; it was two doors away from the Demonstration Room on the outer wall of the building. Iza opened the door and rushed into the single-stall washroom; there weren't many women working at imperative Energie. She locked herself in the restroom just as she heard Alex making the turn at the T-intersection.

"Where is Claire?" he called out as he walked quickly to the door of the Demonstration Room and peeked inside.

"She had to use the restroom," Kristin replied. Derek returned and picked up his leather folder to leave. He introduced himself to Alex, and the three continued to talk while standing in the Demonstration Room awaiting Claire's return. Iza looked at her watch. Five minutes passed since she'd exited the room. *How long can I wait here?* She checked the window in the restroom, but it only opened a tiny crack to allow fresh air into the room, certainly not enough for her to climb through. *And anyway, imperative Energie is on the third floor. Where would I go even if I could climb out the window? I'm not Jason Bourne.* She anxiously paced around the small washroom, then stopped and carefully listened at the restroom door.

Iza heard someone call out, "Alex, Matteo wants to see you for a minute. He just has a quick question for you before the meeting." She could hear Alex leaving the area.

"I'll be right back. Tell Claire to wait for me."

Iza peeked out from the restroom and saw someone with his head leaning into an office at the far end of the hallway where Matteo Mehlman's office was located. She took a deep breath and exhaled, left the washroom, and then rapidly walked to the exit of imperative Energie through the main work area, avoiding the Demonstration Room. Most of the employees from the main area were getting ready to leave for their lunch breaks, and she mixed with the moving mass of men, but her red suit stood out among their black imperative Energie uniform shirts. Iza got to the exit doorway just as Alex walked past the T-intersection of the hallway.

"Claire . . . Claire Daniels!" he hollered as he walked briskly toward her. Iza turned left out the door and rushed to the stairwell, looking back momentarily to see Alex staring after her through the glass walls adjoining the corridor.

"That doesn't look at all like Claire Daniels," he said as Kristin and Derek joined him near the entrance of imperative Energie. Derek stood utterly dumbfounded, not knowing what to say.

"Have you known Claire a long time, as I have?" Alex questioned Derek.

"I only met her this morning. I just started at the Embassy two weeks ago," he answered in a bewildered tone. He shook hands with Kristin and Alex, excused Claire's strange behavior, and left to meet the car for his return ride to the U.S.

Embassy. Kristin shrugged and returned to her office to prepare for her presentation to the partners.

Alex turned to the man with the shaved head. "Quick. Follow the woman and get a photo of her, or better still, bring her back here if you can," he ordered quietly.

Iza removed her shoes and ran down the stairs to the entrance level of the building, then slipped them back on when she was back outside on the Ku'damm. She rushed into the growing lunchtime bustle but realized that her red suit made her highly visible in the crowd. When she was about a block away from the building, she stopped and looked back toward Kurfürstendamm 195. She saw the beefy man with the shaved head exit the building, look around, and then walk briskly in her direction. Iza panicked. W*hat can I do?*

Iza looked around, and to the left, she saw the door to the Chanel store opening. A woman, obviously a customer carrying several Chanel bags, was now standing in the open doorway with a woman whom Iza assumed was a Chanel sales associate. Iza raced up the steps and pushed past the women into the store, where she quickly walked toward the rear of the sales floor, away from the display windows. The sales associate abruptly ended her conversation with the customer, locked the entrance door, and confronted Iza.

"Excuse me; this store is open by appointment only. Do you have an appointment?" the associate questioned in German.

"I should be on your list. I made my appointment several weeks ago when I was in Paris," Iza lied, breathless with fear.

"Name bitte?" The sales associate looked at her appointment list, seeing that there was no one scheduled until 13:00.

"Claire Daniels."

"You have no appointment; I must ask you to leave," the woman replied, switching to English.

Iza looked toward the display windows and saw the man with the shaved head peering inside.

"But I *have* an appointment, and I want to purchase the black, beige, and white two-piece suit on the mannequin in the display window." Iza remembered the suit she'd seen with Volodya on Saturday, priced at €10.650.

After a short pause, the sales associate responded, "Oh yes ... I *do* see the name Claire Daniels on my list now. Please go to the fitting area, and I'll bring you"—the woman looked Iza over, assessing her size—"a size 34."

"I'd like a size 30."

The sales associate gave Iza a derisive look and shook her head, whispering aloud under her breath, "Women these days! Always trying to fit into something too small for them."

Iza ran back to the fitting area, and the sales associate brought her the suit in both sizes.

"Try the 34 first," the associate advised coolly. "I'll be back here to check on you at some point. Please take your time."

Iza could hear the man with the shaved head pulling violently on the locked entrance door, then heard him pounding on the glass. She peeked out of the fitting room and saw the associate wave to him, indicating that she'd come to the door but not immediately. She was organizing her paperwork from the sales she'd made to the previous customer and didn't want to be disturbed until she'd finished. Iza looked out from a side door in the fitting area. That door opened to a short hallway that led to a clothing storage area and a rear exit to the store. But the exit was alarmed. Iza's heart was racing. She quickly pulled off the wig and the red suit, kicked off the high heels, and ripped off the body suit as the man continued pounding on the glass door. She heard the sales associate call out loudly in German, "If you keep pounding on that door, I won't come at all."

Iza used a handful of makeup wipes to clean off her makeup, except for the eye make-up, which she thought would be too difficult to remove quickly, then pulled the pins from her hair. Her long hair fell in soft waves past her shoulders, looking contented to be free of the wig. She swiftly pulled her flat shoes from the cross-body purse, then stuffed the red suit, wig, hair pins, and used wipes into the purse. The heels and the body suit wouldn't fit into the already overstuffed bag. She tried on the size-30 two-piece suit. It seemed to fit perfectly, but in her haste, Iza didn't notice that the button loops on the front of the suit were designed to allow a slight gap between the two sides of the buttoned suit jacket, leaving a thin strip of her bare chest and abdomen exposed from just below her neckline to just below her navel. Coupled with the very short skirt, it was the seductive Chanel look.

Iza heard the clicking heels of the sales associate as she moved across the wood floor to the front of the store. The associate partially opened the door and inquired of the man with the shaved head, "Yes? You wanted something?"

"My wife is in your store, the woman wearing the red suit. We got separated, and the door closed before I could get inside."

"Come in," the sales associate offered. "Your wife is in the fitting room, but you can wait in the chair near the handbags."

The man walked into the store and sat waiting. Iza was terrified. She couldn't possibly walk out to the front of the store, but she couldn't go out the alarmed rear exit door either. If the alarm sounded, she'd either be caught by the man with the shaved head, or she'd eventually be caught by the Polizei. But an escape through the rear exit door seemed her only possible alternative. She waited in the fitting room, pacing back and forth in the small space, trying to decide the best time to make her dash out the rear exit.

As the minutes ticked by, a buzzer sounded. Iza heard the clicking of the sales associate's heels as she walked across the wood floor toward the exit door at the rear of the store. She disarmed the alarm and opened the door to let in a DHL deliveryman, who was hauling a large load of packages on a dolly cart. The deliveryman pushed the cart toward the front desk area on the main sales floor, leaving the rear exit door propped open and unalarmed. Iza peeked down the rear hallway and, seeing the now-open door, tip-toed quietly out the back exit, carrying her purse, the body suit, and the high-heeled shoes. She tossed the body suit and heels into the back of the DHL delivery van, then walked quickly around the rear of the adjacent buildings until she found a path leading to the Ku'damm. She glanced over her shoulder but didn't see the man with the shaved head, so she kept moving until she was back among the throng of lunchtime pedestrians.

Iza gasped for breath as she continued walking in the crowd. *Tony is going to absolutely kill me when he finds out I shoplifted a €10.650 Chanel suit! But what could I do? That guy didn't look like he was there to wish me a good day.* Her pulse rate eventually dropped, and she composed herself as she continued walking purposefully toward the U.S. Embassy.

◆

The man with the shaved head called to the sales associate as he looked at his watch. "Could you please get my wife? We have an appointment in a few minutes."

The associate walked to the dressing area, checked the room Iza had been using, frantically checked all the other dressing rooms, and then realized what had happened. "Claire Daniels" had run off with a €10.650 suit through the momentarily opened exit door. The associate quickly walked back to the man with the shaved head.

"Your wife left the store," she blurted out. The man turned toward the locked front door, but the sales associate blocked his way and sternly confronted him.

"Your wife left the store without *paying* for her suit. She took this suit in a different size!"

She showed the man the size-34 suit. "You must *pay* for your wife's suit, or I will not let you out, and I'll call the Polizei!"

The man with the shaved head pushed the associate toward the door.

"Don't you dare push me! I am pressing the alarm if you try to leave here without paying for your wife's suit, sir," the sales associate threatened.

The man with the shaved head walked back to the front desk with the sales associate and handed her his credit card, having no idea of the price of a Chanel suit. He didn't want to create a scene, nor did he want the associate to contact the Polizei. The associate ran his card.

"Sir, your card has been declined. Perhaps you do not have a high enough credit limit on this card. You must give me another card."

The man with the shaved head thought for a moment, then called Alex using his cell phone.

"Alex, don't ask questions now, but I need your credit card number," he whispered into his phone as the sales associate looked on. There was a pause on the other end of the line. "Alex, I need your credit card number *now*." The man with the shaved head handed his phone to the sales associate, and she took Alex's name and his card information. After the call ended, the sales associate smiled pleasantly at the man with the shaved head.

"Thank you, sir. I hope your wife enjoys her new suit."

The sales associate let him out of the store just as her 13:00 customer arrived. He rapidly scanned the Ku'damm but did not see a woman with bob-cut hair, so he slowly returned to Kurfürstendamm 195.

Iza checked her watch. It was after 13:45; Volodya's lunch break would have already ended. She'd have to wait to call him until his afternoon break. As she entered the embassy lobby, she saw Derek leaving, perhaps for a late lunch. He looked directly at her but gave no indication that he'd ever seen her before.

Iza rushed to the CIA Disguise Lab to return the red suit and the wig. Tina was preparing for another disguise consultation and was in a hurry.

"I'm so sorry, but I had to toss the body suit and shoes after my meeting. I had to make an urgent exit," Iza apologized.

"Suzanne told me it happens all the time—not to worry."

"Really? People make urgent exits *all* the time?"

"Yeah, an occupational hazard, I guess."

"Can I keep this purse until tomorrow? I need some time to sift through everything."

"Of course, return it whenever you can. There's no rush. Say ... where'd you get that *Chanel*?"

"Oh . . . I just changed into it a minute ago in my office. It was a birthday gift from my Uncle Frank in Chicago."

Iza left the Lab, a bit nonplussed by Tina's comments, then dashed up the stairway toward Claire's office to return her monogrammed pen. Claire's administrative assistant walked with Iza to unlock Claire's door. "Claire has gotten so many calls while she's been out on vacation. It'll probably take her a week just to catch up with her phone messages," she said, making friendly conversation with Iza as they walked the short distance to Claire's office.

It suddenly dawned on Iza that she'd forgotten to ask Claire's assistant to change the message available to Claire's callers; it was what she'd tried to remember to do the previous day as she'd stood inside Claire's office. The assistant was only supposed to indicate that Claire was out of the office but not tell anyone that she was on vacation or how long she'd be away. Claire's assistant continued, "She even got a call just minutes ago from a member of the German Bundestag!"

Iza's eyes widened and she stopped walking. "The person didn't leave a name, did they?"

"Yeah, Alex Schröder. He didn't leave a message, though. At least that's one call she won't have to return. He only wanted to say hello."

"Did you tell him Claire is on vacation until Thursday?"

"Yeah, shouldn't I have said anything?"

Iza didn't answer. *This is turning into quite the mess,* she thought. *I never should have gone to the meeting using Claire's identity. What a huge mistake!*

Iza returned to her office, still frazzled by the events of the day; she sat for a moment thinking.

If I call Tony now, what do I say? Tony, I pilfered the thumb drive from Derek, I shoplifted a €10.650 Chanel suit, and I blew my impersonation of Claire, maybe even harming her reputation at the embassy in the process. Did you know Alex Schröder was there today after all, and he found out from Claire's admin that she's on vacation until Thursday? Did I tell you I got chased by some thug security guy too? And I'm pretty sure he had a gun. Oh, and by the way, Tony, Volodya is still performing "industrial espionage" on the code from the original thumb drive that he stole and that you told us not to look at any longer. Did I forget to mention we made a copy of the software before I sent the thumb drive to you? Sorry. I know people go to jail for all of that, but if they don't, Tony, it's probably because they got killed first!

Iza nervously continued her internal discussion. *On the other hand, Tony, I learned that imperative Energie is a legit business that may be compromised. It seems clear, to me at least, that Johannes is the conduit passing information from the U.S. and Germany to Russia. I also learned that the thumb drive Volodya stole belongs to their Director of Software Development. That guy conveniently happened to be available to replace the world-famous professor who had that job before being thrown off his balcony by the Russians! It might all hinge on what Volodya figures out with the software code. If the software seems secure, maybe Johannes is a lone bad apple in imperative Energie. But if this whole mess also has something to do with their software, there could be way more people involved. And by the way, Tony, I'm scared out of my mind!*

Iza sat dejectedly at her desk, still contemplating whether or not she should call Tony. *With the change to daylight savings time in Europe, but not in the U.S. yet, there's a five-hour time difference between us. It's 9:00 a.m. in Washington. Tony won't be in his office yet. I'd have to call him in his car on an unsecure line.* She made her decision. *Well, Tony, I'm not calling you right now. Later today . . . maybe . . . for sure tomorrow. Yeah, I'll call you tomorrow.* Iza waited and called Volodya instead.

"Hello," Volodya said as he picked up the secure phone in the data center canteen. He didn't identify himself, but Iza recognized his deep voice.

"Volodya, it's Iza." She heard a huge sigh of relief on the other end of the line.

"Iza, I am so worried for you. What happened?"

"There's so much to tell you. I'll wait until we can talk in person. I'm safe for now, and I got their demo software—it's just a segment of the program, but maybe it's useful."

"Iza, can you bring it to Bleibtreu Café tonight?"

"You sure that's okay? I mean . . . with your friends there and all."

"Yes, for sure. I will buy you dinner, too. I never got to do that for you yet, but I got paycheck today—first one in long time."

Iza could almost see the smile on Volodya's face. He hadn't been paid since well before she'd met him. He'd been slowly parceling out cash from his last paycheck and had almost nothing left.

"I'll be there around 18:00. I love you, Volodya."

He whispered, "I love you too, Iza."

◆

Volodya could sense from the anxiety in Iza's voice that things hadn't gone according to plan for her, but he'd have to wait for the details. At least he knew she was safe.

Bobby looked curiously at Volodya, "Y'all got an incoming call?" he asked as the two left the canteen.

"Yes. It was my girlfriend," Volodya grinned. They walked back to their workstations together as Bobby told

Volodya another off-color joke, which Volodya barely understood.

At 17:00, the Team members filtered out of the data center. Volodya picked up his laptop and cell phone from the security monitoring station, then slipped out the door and walked directly toward the Bleibtreu Café, while Petro and Dmytro walked in the other direction, leaving a block of space between the two of them as they continued walking. They each turned left about three blocks from the data center at the same intersection, then met up and walked briskly toward the Bleibtreu Café, Dmytro huffing and puffing to keep up with Petro.

The three converged at the Café entrance. The Café had a cozy atmosphere, with a décor of dark woods, warm colors, and low lighting. Although it was relatively early for dining, the bar was already busy with customers. The three took a table near the front of the restaurant at the end of the bar along a wall. There was a power outlet nearby in case Volodya needed it for his laptop later in the evening. Volodya sat facing the door to keep an eye out for Iza. They ordered three steins of König pilsner, and shortly thereafter, the friendly server delivered their beers.

"Volodya, what is this all about? You need to tell us more about this software and why it is so important to your American girlfriend. Why does she need *our* help? Does U.S. not have good programmers to help her?" Dmytro asked as he took a large draught of beer.

Volodya had thought ahead, knowing that the two men would ask these sorts of questions. He took a sip of beer, then saw Iza enter the Café.

"I see my girlfriend," he said and quickly walked to the entrance. Petro and Dmytro turned in their chairs to see him kiss Iza at the front of the restaurant. Her now-wavy long hair glittered in the low light of the Café, and the eye makeup she hadn't wiped off enhanced her already large and expressive eyes. Volodya looked curiously at the Chanel suit.

"Where did you get suit like *this*?" he raised his eyebrows.

"I'll explain later."

"Iza, do not say anything to Dmytro and Petro about what I will tell them. I tell them why we need their help. I thought about this, and I have idea. You only listen." Volodya then introduced Iza to Dmytro and Petro, smiling to himself because he could see that Dmytro was nearly drooling into his beer stein as he focused on the line of skin visible on Iza's chest.

The server came, and Iza ordered a glass of Prosecco, which he brought to her almost immediately. As she sipped her drink, Volodya started to explain in a whisper, "This is highly confidential and you must keep it so, but I need to tell you this. Iza is field agent for U.S. CIA."

Iza nearly choked on the Prosecco. As she regained her composure, she smiled sweetly at Dmytro and Petro and said, "Excuse me; the bubbles do that to me sometimes." *Of course, Volodya has to tell them I'm a field agent for the CIA. In what other job could I have access to the type of information he'll need to disclose?*

"Iza is assigned to U.S. Embassy in Berlin. Her people found there is spy who sends information from U.S. to Russia using German intermediary guy. The German guy works for company that developed this cybersecurity program that I have small sample of on my computer. This same guy recently tried to pass blueprints of our Team's data center and its location to Russians here in Germany, but Iza was able to find blueprints before Russians did, and she destroyed them."

Dmytro nearly jumped out of his chair, his eyes wide with surprise as he yelled, "What?" Several customers at the bar glanced toward their table. Dmytro lowered his voice to a whisper. "There are blueprints of our data center? What about these Russians?" Petro looked at Volodya in pure shock.

"Dmytro, Petro, let me finish," Volodya continued in a low whisper. "Iza is still uncertain if German guy is only bad guy at this company, or if others there work for Russia. This is important because if this software is somehow compromised, it would allow Russia to cause problems for German energy infrastructure, like interrupting natural gas flow at different places around Germany or damaging electric grid. If Russians can do this, it will maybe make Germany think again about supporting Ukraine in war, including our Team's intelligence operation here in Berlin.

"I already looked at one section of code out of what must be very large cybersecurity program from this company, and I have problem understanding two segments in code. What was intent of coder when he put these segments into bigger program? This is why Iza needs your help and why I do too." By this time, Dmytro and Petro were left speechless by Volodya's revelations.

Iza chimed in, "There aren't any programmers with the sophistication required to understand this software here at the embassy in Berlin, and I'm working against time here. There's no time to get this to Washington. I'm looking to the three of you for help. I know Ukraine has the most talented information technology people in the world. I hope I can count on you."

Iza pulled the thumb drive containing the demonstration software from her purse. "I was able to get this older version of a portion of the software program from the company earlier today by posing as another U.S. Embassy employee; I attended a software demonstration there. When I was about to leave the demo, someone who just arrived there recognized I wasn't the Embassy employee I said I was. I was pursued down the Kurfürstendamm by a man from the company with a gun, but obviously, I got away. I'm still pretty shaken by the whole thing. Um . . . even in my line of work, this sort of thing doesn't happen every day."

The three of them looked at Iza with surprise and horror on their faces, but especially Volodya. This was news to him. Someone with a gun had pursued her down Berlin's most famous shopping street!

Iza questioned, "Do any of you know a renowned computer science professor from Berlin, Herr Doktor Klaus Timmer?"

Dmytro nodded his head yes. "I met him at a conference several years ago—brilliant guy."

"Well, he's dead," Iza said. Dmytro recoiled and grimaced. "He 'fell' off his apartment balcony two years ago. I'm convinced a Russian agent pushed him off. That and poisoning seem to be the Russian ways of getting rid of 'inconvenient' people. Doktor Timmer developed the initial version of this cybersecurity software for the company with his graduate students. I suspect Doktor Timmer was killed two years ago when he refused to go along with Russia's directive to alter the software. Maybe you can compare the two versions of this software—from the earlier version I obtained today and then from the latest version Volodya has on his laptop. I realize I'm not giving you the entire program—you're only seeing small sections of it—but maybe there's something you can learn."

Petro fidgeted nervously at the table while Dmytro sat deep in thought, rubbing his heavy chin, as the server arrived at their table and inquired if they were ready to order. After quickly reviewing the extensive menu, the three men ordered Wiener Schnitzel with roasted potatoes and cucumber salad. Iza ordered salmon with vegetables and another glass of Prosecco. They ate first. Dmytro proffered they could "perhaps" look at the code after eating. However, neither Dmytro nor Petro committed to helping them, but they hadn't said "no" either.

Petro shook his head in disbelief. "Volodya, I want to believe you, but this is hard to believe. Dmytro and I are not involved in this, except if what you say about Russians targeting our data center is really true. But I am unsure. Yet, there is no harm in looking at software code even if what Volodya says is not true, right?" he addressed the question to Dmytro.

Volodya felt dejected. He had always liked Petro and started thinking of him as an older brother figure. Yet he could tell that Petro didn't believe him, and that meant he probably wouldn't help unless Dmytro agreed to help. Volodya excused himself to get them another round of beers at the bar. Iza looked intently at the two men.

"Volodya and I aren't making this up," she said quietly, pleading with them. "This is real. Someone from the U.S. sent the blueprints and the address of your data center to Germany, intending to give those to the Russians. I *know* this is true. Volodya has been living this for the past couple of weeks. I don't know what he told you, but you've probably noticed his rib injury. He was attacked by a Russian agent on the U-Bahn a week ago. I was injured too, but we got away." She took a cloth napkin from the table and wiped the foundation and eyeshadow away from her eye, revealing the discoloration of her black eye. "*Please* help us. If it's at all possible, we need answers *now*."

The server was delivering their meals when Volodya returned to the table with three more pilsners. He looked questioningly at Iza, seeing that she'd wiped off the makeup concealing her black eye. Dmytro and Petro sat quietly, eating their meals.

Petro suddenly offered, "Volodya, I will help you."

Dmytro quickly added while nodding his head affirmatively, "Me too."

Volodya and Iza smiled at each other.

The server cleared their plates, and the four ordered coffee. As Volodya turned on his laptop, Iza moved to an empty table for two next to the Café windows. An earlier customer had left a newspaper there, and she sat reading while the three men worked through the code. Volodya quickly showed Dmytro and Petro what he'd already learned, and the two segments of code he hadn't understood. They loaded the older software code from the demonstration thumb drive for comparison with the newer code that Volodya had. Volodya could tell that Dmytro almost immediately grasped something about the two segments that had baffled Volodya. He knew that Dmytro had a breadth of practical experience with coding that few others in the world could equal. The three continued investigating the program, occasionally talking animatedly among themselves, now in Ukrainian.

It was nearly 20:00 when Iza looked up from the newspaper and absent-mindedly glanced out the Café window toward a nearby street lamp. She inhaled sharply, then held the newspaper in front of her face and peered around the edge. She was almost certain that the man with the shaved head was standing beneath the street lamp in the dim light. Iza crept toward the restaurant door and peeked out the glass-paned window at the side of the door. He was now standing almost directly on the other side of the glass. *I'm sure it's the same man,* Iza thought, *and it couldn't be by chance that he's standing there. He must have followed me, but how did he find me at the embassy? How could he know what I look like? He only saw me disguised as Claire. Was I that careless that I didn't notice him on my walk here? I've been so vigilant!*

Iza approached the table where Volodya, Dmytro, and Petro were sitting. "I'm sorry to interrupt, but Volodya, I need to talk with you."

"Yes?"

"A private talk." Iza was now noticeably trembling.

"Oh."

Volodya left the table and sat across from Iza at the table for two.

"Volodya, that scary thug guy . . . and carrying a gun . . . I think he's a security guard." Iza's voice was cracking, and her body was trembling so severely that her words came out in disjointed phrases. Volodya looked at her curiously, trying to understand what she was trying to tell him.

She suddenly blurted out, "He's standing outside the Café under that street lamp." Iza motioned toward the street lamp with her head as if she were laughing at something with

Volodya. "Lean forward like you're laughing with me and look out the window."

Volodya saw a man with a shaved head standing near the street lamp outside the restaurant, picking his nails with a pocket knife. He saw the man's flattened nose and scarred face.

"Fuck."

"My thoughts exactly. He must have followed me . . . maybe from the embassy . . . but I *never* noticed him. Oh God, I'm *so* sorry, Volodya." Iza teared up as she looked at Dmytro and Petro arguing about some aspect of the code. "How's it going with Dmytro and Petro?"

"We almost finish. Dmytro is *really* smart guy. And he sees this kind of code before."

"What can we do? There's four of us and one of him, but I . . . I'm pretty sure he's still got that gun. Can you see the bulge in his jacket?"

Volodya leaned forward as if he were laughing at something that Iza had said and looked out the window again.

"Yes." Volodya bit on his bottom lip. "Shit," he said as he shook his head.

"So, what do we do? I can check if there's another exit somewhere that we can use—maybe through the kitchen or something. Maybe the three of you can leave safely out the front door. He wouldn't know who you are, and he wouldn't know we're together."

"Or, did he look in window and see us all eating together? I think it is not safe for Dymtro and Petro to leave here out main door, and I will not leave here without you." Volodya thought for a moment. "Iza, can you call Herr Kühn and ask for help? Remember, Tony said Herr Kühn will help you if you need immediate help. You joke and said you have his number on speed dial, right? We have two hours, and then Café is closed."

"I'll try him right now. But I think I only have his office number, and he's probably not at work now. It's late. Let Dmytro and Petro know what's up."

"Get me when you are ready, and I will look with you for different exit."

◆

Iza tried to concentrate on what she should tell Herr Kühn, but her hands shook, and she couldn't scan her phone for his number. She talked quietly to herself, "Iza, you are still in the race; you need to stay calm and make your move." She calmed herself, located his number, pressed call, then waited. She heard multiple clicks on the line and finally heard Herr Kühn's voice at the other end.

"Kühn hier," he answered coldly.

"Herr Kühn," Iza responded anxiously in English, "this is Iza Carter. I'm a friend of Tony Brooks."

"Ah yes, Iza Carter. Somehow, I knew that I would hear from you again one day. And what can I do for you this evening?"

"Before Tony left for the U.S. after his recent visit to Berlin and after he met with you, he told me I could call you if I ever needed immediate help. And I am in *urgent* need of help right now," Iza fearfully pleaded.

"What seems to be the problem, Iza Carter?"

Iza explained, "I'm at the Bleibtreu Café here on Bleibtreustraße with three friends. I don't want to take up your time with a lengthy explanation about why we're here or what we're doing, but in essence, there's a man with a gun outside waiting for us to leave the Café. I think he followed me here from the U.S. Embassy without my knowledge. I noticed him standing outside the Café a few minutes ago, and I think he may want to kill me—or something. The Café closes at 22:00."

"Oh dear, Iza Carter, you *do* have a problem there, don't you?" There was a long pause as Iza heard Herr Kühn writing something, then heard his breathing on the line. He finally responded. "I will call Herr Hoffman with the Berlin Polizei and have him dispatch two cars to the Café. I'll call you on your phone there when I have the exact time. I am thinking the Polizei will arrest the four of you and remove you from the premises to their squad cars. They can then drive the four of you to your homes. But Iza Carter, I do *not* do this for you or for Tony free of charge. I want to hear your lengthy explanation and expect you to be in my office tomorrow morning at the Bundeskriminalamt at 8:00 to give it. I do know where to find you if you do not show up. In the meantime, I will call Tony Brooks with this update."

"Herr Kühn, I ask for your understanding. I haven't had time to call Tony today to let him know what's happened here. I'm to meet with him tomorrow afternoon in a video call to give him an update, and I was planning to call him later this evening as well. Would you please hold off from calling him, at least until after you and I meet tomorrow morning?"

Herr Kühn quickly responded, "I will take your request into consideration, but I must call Herr Hoffman now. I will be back in touch." With that, he hung up his phone.

Iza sat nervously tapping her foot under the table and watching Volodya, Dmytro, and Petro while she continued to tremble with fear, waiting for the return call from Herr Kühn. She saw Dmytro's and Petro's eyes open wide, then saw Volodya shut down his computer and pay the bill. She casually glanced out the window, and saw the man with the shaved head still standing near the street lamp, now scanning his phone.

Iza's phone rang, and she picked up the call immediately. "Kühn here. The cars will be there at exactly 21:00. The officers will enter the Café to arrest the four of you; just wait inside near the entrance. If all goes according to plan, you should be home by 21:30."

"Thank you, Herr Kühn. I can't thank you enough."

"Remember, 8:00 in my office tomorrow, Iza Carter. Good evening."

With that, he hung up. Iza walked over to Volodya, Dmytro, and Petro and told them the plan. She slipped

Volodya's laptop into her large cross-body purse, and the four waited near the Café entrance.

At precisely 21:00, two squad cars screeched to a halt in front of the Café with lights flashing. As the Polizei entered the Café, a small crowd gathered at the windows and on the street outside to watch. The officers handcuffed the four, then took Dmytro and Petro to one car and Volodya and Iza to the second. As they were escorted to the cars, the man with the shaved head snapped multiple photographs of them on his phone. As Iza entered one of the cars, he called out to her from a distance in German, "Beautiful suit; I would recognize it anywhere."

Iza looked in horror at the man. The two squad cars pulled away from the curb and drove off. They sped together for three blocks, then separated and traveled in opposite directions. The officers pulled into a side street, removed the handcuffs from Iza and Volodya, and then drove them to their Kreuzberg apartment.

Volodya and Iza exited the car, and thanked the officers for their help. When the squad car had driven away, Volodya stopped Iza, then swung her around and kissed her. He put his arm around her shoulder, and the two walked slowly up the stairs to the apartment, each breathing a sigh of relief that they'd survived the day.

Volodya walked into the apartment first and turned on the light. "Jezus!" he exclaimed.

"What's wrong?" Iza asked as she walked in behind him.

Their apartment had been vandalized. Clothing was strewn over the bedroom, toiletries were thrown to the floor, the throw pillows on the sofa and the down comforter on the bed were slit open, their contents spilled onto the sofa and the bed, dishes were smashed onto the kitchen floor, even Volodya's CD player and receiver had been thrown off the shelf and his CDs lay broken on the floor. Obscene graffiti covered the apartment walls. Iza stood in shock, looking around the small room, then began crying and came to Volodya. The disappointment on his face was absolute. This had been the only real home he'd had since before his college days, and now the few belongings he had in the world lay destroyed. Most of what he had was secondhand junk, purchased at Berlin flea markets and thrift stores, but these were still *his* things, his only possessions.

"It is okay, Iza. These are just things. I can replace them someday. Who did this though?" He walked around looking in the kitchen, then turned and came quickly back near the sofa.

"Iza, come here," he called. Iza returned from the bedroom to the sofa. The winter jacket she'd given him for his birthday had been thrown to the floor and she'd hung it again in the armoire. "Look here." She looked at the stack of totes and her suitcase, all sitting untouched as she'd left them the previous evening.

"What kind of thief only messes up part of apartment, but not stuff brought here yesterday?"

"A thief who knows he won't find anything in my totes and in my suitcase because he's already searched them."

"Yes." Volodya immediately turned off the apartment lights and turned on the flashlight on his phone. "Bring your phone light too," he told Iza. He started pulling things from Iza's totes and feeling them, then throwing things already checked onto the sofa.

"What are you doing?"

"We need to check through all your things. I think guy has something in your things to track you. Maybe CIA movers did not check before they brought these here yesterday."

Iza joined Volodya on the floor, and they quickly removed everything from her totes and her suitcase, feeling for a tracking device. They found nothing. Then Volodya slipped his hand into the nearly invisible pocket in Iza's suitcase and pulled out a tracking device. He put the device back in the pocket and closed Iza's suitcase, then sat cross-legged on the floor, thinking for a few minutes.

"We have to leave here soon. I have idea. Here is what we need to do. Where is closest U.S. Consulate to Berlin?"

"It's in Hamburg."

"Okay. I will pack us my duffle bag with clothes for few days and toiletries. While I do that, I want you to buy two tickets on last train to Hamburg for tonight."

"Why are we going there?"

"We are not going there. Suitcase is. I will show you later. Go fast."

Volodya rushed into the bedroom, then stuffed his duffle bag with underwear, jeans, T-shirts, Iza's running gear, some of her work clothing, her nightshirt, the heating pad—anything he could find that they might need for a few days. He saw her citrine earrings on the floor shining in the light of his phone and threw those into the duffle bag. Then he saw the packets of condoms on the shelf in the armoire. He threw the packets in the duffle bag. He walked quickly to the bathroom and grabbed any toiletries that weren't lying broken on the floor. He pulled the zipper closed. He grabbed a jacket for each of them; they'd wear the jackets because there was no more room in his already over-stuffed duffle bag.

"I've got us two tickets on the last train to Hamburg; it leaves twenty-two minutes after midnight."

"Take phone, purse with laptop, any money, then we get out of here."

Iza grabbed the cross-body purse with Volodya's laptop, threw in her phone, and then took the duffle bag. Volodya took Iza's empty suitcase with the tracking device inside. They locked the apartment door, then hurried down the stairway to the street level. Volodya walked outside first, scanned around the area, and seeing nothing unusual, called Iza. They walked as briskly as Volodya could with his sore ribs, without running or stopping, toward the Kreuzberg U-Bahn station, carrying the duffle bag and dragging Iza's suitcase along behind them.

As they walked, Iza asked Volodya, "Did you learn anything about the software tonight?"

"Dmytro finds purpose of two segments of code I had trouble with. Like I tell you, he is really smart guy. He has seen this used before, actually by Russians trying to infiltrate company network in Kyiv. Segments provide backdoor into software application. It looks like normal code, but guy makes purpose of code look ambiguous. Mechanism how it works is heavily obfuscated. You can think that maybe it is just some lines of code that guy left in program by accident when he did upgrade or maybe there is some other reason for them. I am sure this program is huge and complex; it was most certainly upgraded and changed many times since 2014. In these kinds of programs, some code is just there, but no longer serves purpose, and new people working on code are afraid to delete it because they are unsure."

"What does backdoor mean?"

"It means the code allows unauthorized access to network that is compromised. It enables attackers to gain access to highly secure systems that are otherwise rigorously locked down and monitored. This kind of backdoor is most often inserted in code by someone who has legitimate access to code. I wonder if that someone is Markus Peters. Creating this kind of application backdoor is practical way to compromise many systems with not much effort, because software users compromise their own systems by installing backdoored software. Then, bad guys can do bad things through backdoor."

"Is there a backdoor in the older software version from the demo?"

"We did not see these two segments in older version. They might be there in entire program, but we did not see them in small section of code you brought today. But remember, full program probably has many millions of lines of code, and we only looked at small sections."

They arrived at the U-Bahn station, and Iza purchased two tickets. They boarded the U-Bahn and sat in silence, then eventually transferred to the S-Bahn, holding hands as the train continued to the main station. At the Hauptbahnhof, they'd need to transfer to the InterCity train between Berlin and Hamburg, using the tickets that Iza had already purchased at the apartment. They had only an hour to spare before the InterCity train to Hamburg was scheduled to depart from the main station. When they arrived there, Iza filled out a luggage tag for her suitcase and affixed it:

Herr Tony Brooks
U.S. Generalkonsulate
Alsterufer 27/28
20354 Hamburg, Deutschland

The train pulled into the station at 00:22. As soon as they were called for boarding, Volodya dragged the suitcase, still containing the tracking device, onto the train, and Iza carried the duffle and purse. They made their way to a luggage storage area, and stowed the suitcase. Then they quickly exited and watched from the platform until the train pulled away from the station.

"Goodbye suitcase. You bring only bad luck for Iza," Volodya called as he waved at the departing train.

◆

They quickly walked to the Meininger Hotel, almost directly adjoining the Hauptbahnhof, and registered for an inexpensive room for four nights. Iza showed her identification to the desk clerk and registered them as Mr. and Mrs. Carter. They made their way to their eighth-floor room, which was small and simply furnished, but, at the moment, looked like the most comfortable place on earth to the two of them.

Iza giggled. "I get the shower first!" Volodya showered immediately after Iza while she hung up some of their clothing and set their toiletries on the edge of a small shelf above the sink in the bathroom. She saw that Volodya had thrown the packets of condoms in the duffle and laughed to herself. *He must have thought those were essential.*

They were exhausted from the stress of the long day, but when they got into bed, Volodya came to Iza.

"Iza, I need you tonight."

"What about your ribs?"

"I know, but I need you. I *really* need you."

Iza looked at Volodya's face in the dimly lit room and saw that he had tears in his eyes. He'd lost almost everything, but he had her.

Iza came to him and rolled the condom on him; he was already aroused. The two moved together as one on the bed, enjoying the relief they brought each other. The stress of the day was released. Afterward, Iza laid her head on Volodya's chest, then eventually massaged his forehead. It was her loving way of giving him another form of stress relief. The two cleaned off, and she brought him the heating pad for his ribs. They lay together nude under the down comforter on the bed.

"I will not go to data center tomorrow," Volodya whispered to Iza. "I will call in to new phone line and hope someone answers before 7:00. I am sick. I think maybe I have COVID. I will check rapid test tomorrow and if negative, I will return next day."

"I have to meet Herr Kühn tomorrow at 8:00. I set the alarm for 6:45," Iza whispered back.

"I will go with you."

Iza whispered, "I love you, Volodya," but he had already fallen asleep.

Iza lay on the bed trying to think about the upcoming meeting with Herr Kühn, but she couldn't concentrate. *It's so peaceful lying next to Volodya,* she thought as she drifted off to sleep.

Wednesday, November 2 (Day 22)

"Hey, Bobby. This is Volodya."

Volodya sat sleepily at the edge of the hotel bed after awakening only five minutes earlier.

Bobby had picked up the phone in the data center canteen, having seen Volodya take an incoming call the previous day on one of the new secure phone lines. It was ten minutes before the morning briefing.

"How y'all doin'?"

"Not so good, Bobby," Volodya responded with a nasal-sounding voice and fake cough. "Is Petro there? Can you bring him to phone?"

"Might could." The line went quiet. Volodya looked over at Iza lying on the bed; she'd fallen back asleep immediately after the alarm sounded but had thrown off the down comforter in the too-warm hotel room. He gently shook her awake and smiled at her sleepy face.

"Hello." It was Petro.

Volodya continued in Ukrainian. "Petro, you get home safe last night? And Dmytro?"

"Yes, yes. And you, Volodya?"

"Petro, my apartment was destroyed last night before we got there. Maybe by Russian guys. I have almost nothing left. Maybe some clothes and few pots and pans."

"Volodya!" The concern in Petro's voice was noticeable.

"We are safe in hotel Petro, but I am not able to come to data center today. I told Bobby I am sick. Maybe I have COVID, and I will test later today. If I test negative, then I will come there tomorrow. Can you make excuse for me?"

"Of course, Volodya. There was a pause on the line, then Petro continued cautiously. "Volodya, I am worried for you. Iza seems like nice girlfriend for you, but maybe her line of work is too dangerous for you to ever have life together with her. I only say this because I care about you."

"Petro, I need to go right now. I will see you tomorrow." Volodya abruptly hung up his phone.

◆

Iza dressed quickly in jeans and her running T-shirt for her 8:00 meeting with Herr Kühn. Volodya would go with her but would remain in the lobby.

"I'm not dressing up for this meeting today. I'm too tired."

"It is okay. You look beautiful no matter what you wear, and you look best when you wear nothing."

As they passed through the metal detector at the Bundeskriminalamt, the security guard called Herr Kühn's administrative assistant, then promptly confiscated their cell phones and Volodya's Swiss Army tool from the pocket of his leather jacket.

The assistant glanced at Volodya and asked Iza, "Is he with you?"

"Yes. Is it okay if he waits here in the lobby?"

"Of course," the assistant responded as she wrote something on a scrap of paper.

Herr Kühn was taking an urgent phone call, so Iza was escorted to a sitting area in his sizable office. Iza noticed that his assistant slipped him the scrap of paper she'd just written on in the lobby, then quickly exited the room.

Herr Kühn is apparently an art lover and a lover of Rembrandt, Iza thought as she perused the sumptuously illustrated art books on the coffee table near her chair. One book was already opened to the page displaying the latter of Rembrandt's two Lucretia paintings, which was Iza's favorite work of Rembrandt. She sat studying the poignant reproduction in the book as she waited patiently for Herr Kühn.

"So, Iza Carter, are you also a lover of Rembrandt's works?"

Iza looked up to see Herr Kühn dragging his chair close to hers.

"Yes, very much so. Lucretia is my favorite of his paintings."

"Yes, the work is one of my favorites as well. Such powerful art makes an impact by leaving us with many questions: What was her motivation? When did she make the choice to do it? How many did she hurt because of her decision? And it speaks by making us search within ourselves for the answers. Be careful you do not end up getting stabbed in your heart, Iza Carter."

Iza's blood ran cold with fear at his commentary.

"I know little about you, Iza Carter. You are a friend of Tony Brooks, and newly assigned to the U.S. Embassy in Consular Affairs. Tell me more. Where do you come from in the U.S., and why did you want to work in Berlin?"

Iza was surprised by his questions. When she'd talked with him on the phone previously, he'd come across as cold and detached—someone who was *strictly* business, even though he'd greatly helped them the previous evening. Now, he actually sounded a bit friendly. But for him, maybe this *was* strictly business, understanding the motivations of the person you intended to get information from.

"I was born in Washington, D.C., but my parents' work at the State Department took us to Europe almost immediately after my birth and then eventually for a short time to the Middle East. My parents knew Tony and his wife for years. That's how I know him. My dad was killed on assignment in the Middle East when I was fourteen. My mom and I moved back to Washington the following year. I'd lived there until three weeks ago. But I always wanted to move back to Europe. I love my country, and I want to serve my country as my dad did, but in a weird way, I've always felt more European than American. And I speak German relatively well—I certainly don't consider myself fluent like a native speaker—but I can get by here. When I applied for a Consular Affairs job with the Department, Berlin was my first choice. I've enjoyed living here . . . I mean the parts where I could live a normal life . . . not this unexpected intrigue I've somehow gotten involved in."

Apparently satisfied with her answer, Herr Kühn went back to business.

"Let us move to my desk area, Iza Carter."

Iza sat in a low chair facing Herr Kühn behind his large wooden desk, feeling like a little girl sent to the principal's office for some unknown infraction. She noticed that he'd started to record their conversation.

"And now, I want to ask you some questions about yesterday," Herr Kühn stated rather coldly.

"I have a question for you," Iza interjected. "How did you know the blueprints were in my suitcase? After the two of you met, Tony told me you already knew about them, but he never mentioned *how* you knew."

Herr Kühn replied icily, "Iza Carter, might I remind you, *I* will ask the questions."

Iza was shocked by both his tone of voice and his response. He began interrogating her as he leaned toward her from across his desk chair.

"Who are Dmytro Melnik, Petro Yurchenko, and Volodymyr Korsun? These men are not on our registry as lawful residents of Germany. Are they Russians? And what were you doing with these three eastern European men at the Bleibtreu Café last evening?"

Iza avoided specifically answering his questions. "We were having dinner together. One of the men is a close friend of mine, and the other two are friends of his, who I met for the first time last evening. I honestly don't know anything about your German registry. Someone from the Embassy must have taken care of my registration for me."

"You have not answered my questions truthfully, Iza Carter. You might want to consider that I have surveillance video of you and your eastern European 'friend' at a U-Bahn station just after you attacked and severely injured an employee of the Russian Embassy. If you are not completely honest with me, I will have both of you detained. I know your friend is sitting in the lobby here as we speak."

Iza realized that his assistant's note on the scrap of paper had informed Herr Kühn that Volodya was with her and that he was waiting in the building lobby.

Herr Kühn continued authoritatively, "I *know* these men were working to decode software for you last evening. *Where* did you find this software code? *What* was the purpose of having *these* men decipher the code? *Why* are you all interested in it?" Iza realized that the Polizei must have questioned Dmytro and Petro about what they were doing at the Bleibtreu Café. They must have been required to give their names to the Polizei. Because their presence in Germany was supposed to be kept secret, Iza knew that none of the three were registered as residents.

"I'm an employee of the U.S. Embassy—a diplomat—and I'm entitled to call Tony Brooks before I give you any information."

Herr Kühn laughed and then responded sternly in a loud voice, "You are not *entitled* to anything, Iza Carter. You will answer my questions, or you'll be detained, along with your friend."

Oh God, I'm terrified! Kühn knows we were on the U-Bahn with Evgeny. Volodya and I guessed we were caught on a security camera somewhere. But I thought Tony convinced him we were defending ourselves—that Evgeny attacked us. Tony didn't seem at all concerned at our dinner on Friday.

Tony said Kühn's a dedicated public servant . . . like dedicated to protecting Germany's security. Why is he interrogating me then? Why does he think I'm a threat?

I think I have a right to call Tony, but now I'm not sure. I should have listened better in that new employee orientation.

Iza decided to answer some of Herr Kühn's questions—at least a few—so he'd let them go. Then she'd immediately call Tony.

"Decoding the software was secondary to my purpose yesterday." Iza wondered if Herr Kühn would accept her answer. He said nothing in reply. She continued, "Earlier in the day, I attended a meeting at imperative Energie. It's a cybersecurity software company here in Berlin. I confirmed the identity of the conduit who carries confidential information between our two countries for the Russian Embassy here in Berlin. I learned that he works for imperative Energie. That's what you *really* want to know, isn't it? Tony told me you had a 'problem' in Berlin, and he's got one in the U.S.

"But I still don't know who in the U.S. is the spy sharing our information with the conduit. And there must be a case officer in the Russian Embassy in the U.S. who recruited the spy there. And there has to be someone here at the Russian Embassy in Berlin who recruited the conduit. I don't know who any of those other people are."

"And *who* is the conduit?"

"His name is Johannes Brandt. He's a relatively new U.S. sales rep for imperative Energie. He frequently travels to the U.S., and he *always* leaves through Dulles in Washington. Washington must be where he normally makes his contacts. In fact, he's flying out of D.C. tonight. But something was *different* with these blueprints. He didn't get them delivered to him in the U.S. The spy in the U.S. must have been suspicious of something. Someone put the prints in my suitcase instead. Someone who knew I was leaving for Berlin. Brandt tried to retrieve them from my suitcase at the Berlin airport, and when he couldn't find them, he sent the Russians to retrieve them from me."

"You admit that *you* brought the blueprints to Berlin?"

"I didn't bring them here knowingly! I didn't know they were inside my suitcase!" *He thinks I carried the blueprints here—that I knew I had them! I don't understand what's going on. Why is he accusing me?*

Herr Kühn got up from his chair and now leaned against his desk directly in front of Iza, crossing his arms. He shouted at Iza, "And *who* is the man with the gun who you say wanted to kill you last evening outside the Café?"

"I don't know his name!" Iza shouted, now getting agitated by the harshness of the interrogation. "It's the truth. He works for imperative Energie. I think he's their security guard, but he doesn't look like any security guard I've ever seen before. He looks like a thug. Tony had me attend the meeting at imperative Energie in disguise impersonating another U.S. Embassy employee. But someone who wasn't supposed to be there and who knows the U.S. employee showed up and realized I wasn't her. I was chased by this guard earlier in the day as I left the meeting, and he must have somehow known I'd gone to the U.S. Embassy. He must have followed me last evening without my knowing. I'm not an agent or a spy; I don't know how to avoid surveillance! I never had training for that."

"You submit you are not an agent or a spy, is that correct?"

"Are you accusing me of something here?"

"Iza Carter, I need to remind you again that only *I* will ask the questions. Moving on, I will ask you once again, *who* are Dmytro Melnik, Petro Yurchenko, and Volodymyr Korsun? Are they Russians? *Where* did you find this software code? At imperative Energie? *What* was the purpose of having *these* eastern European men decode the software code? *Why* are all of you so interested in it?" Herr Kühn's questions kept coming. He kept repeating them as he leaned in ever more closely, tormenting Iza and insinuating that she'd done things she hadn't done. He pressed her to make a confession.

Iza suddenly realized, *Herr Kühn didn't send the Polizei to the Café last night to save us from the man with the shaved head. He only responded because he wanted information from me. He probably didn't care at all what happened to us. He even told me on the phone he wasn't helping me "free of charge." I'm not answering any more of his questions. I have to reach Tony!*

Herr Kühn kept confronting Iza, applying pressure by asking the same questions over and over again in an ever-louder and more demanding voice. He started pacing back and forth around her as she sat silently in the chair. "*Where* did you find this code? *What* was the purpose of having *these* men decode it? *Why* are you interested in it?" He continued tormenting Iza until she could no longer stand the mental anguish he was inflicting on her.

Iza snapped. "Leave me alone, Herr Kühn!" she shouted at him, defiant anger now surging within her.

"Be quiet!"

She suddenly realized the answer to what she and Volodya had been pondering over the past ten days. "You know what?"

"I told you to be quiet!"

But Iza wouldn't stop. "I think I finally figured this out. My friend and I wondered *how* those blueprints got to the U.S. *Who* had access to these highly classified German documents? It had to be someone with authority, because whoever it was even made *copies* to send to the U.S.—*copies* of highly classified stuff about an *ongoing* military intelligence operation! It had to be someone who really wanted to entice a spy with them. What kind of people have access to those kinds of documents anyway? I think it's people like *you*, Herr Kühn. I think *you* fucked up.

"You thought you were *so* smart. *You* put those blueprint copies out there to catch the guy you suspect, but that guy was smarter than you imagined. You thought you could entice him with something *so* secret and *so* important to the Russians, you'd be sure to catch him immediately as he *ran* to pass off the information, and you'd be able to retrieve the blueprints while they were still in the U.S. But the spy held on to them for a while, didn't he? He was suspicious because you made it too easy for him. And then you lost control of your little 'operation,' didn't you? You didn't know what the hold-up was—the blueprints were gone, but the spy hadn't contacted anybody. Then you somehow figured out they'd been hidden in my suitcase and that I'd *unknowingly* brought them to Berlin on my flight. Tony told me your agent broke into my apartment to retrieve them but he couldn't find them. And he got *killed* trying."

Iza could no longer control her emotions, as she continued accusing Herr Kühn. "You were probably *so* relieved when Tony brought those blueprint copies to your meeting last week, weren't you? You lit them on fire and burned them to ashes to save your own ass! But you're responsible for the death of your own agent, and for screwing with my life, and most importantly, for endangering the lives of innocent people working in that intelligence operation. I had *nothing* to do with this, and neither did any of these other people, and you dragged us all into your big stinking pile of shit! You don't care about any of us, do you? I lost my apartment, I lost my friend his apartment and most of his belongings, but most importantly, we almost lost our *lives*! And maybe we'll still get killed!"

Iza's voice kept rising with emotion until she was screaming at him. "But, we're all just collateral damage to you, aren't we? As long as you catch your spy, you don't give a damn about anyone else. Well, *fuck you*, Herr Kühn; I'm not answering any more of your fucking questions." She broke down sobbing for several minutes, rubbing at her eyes to wipe away her tears. The bluish green of her black eye turned purple again.

Herr Kühn remained silent and stood quietly staring at Iza. "Iza Carter," he finally responded in a more hushed, yet still cold voice, "I wish to remind you that in this business we *all* have the potential to become collateral damage. It is the nature of this work." He softly, yet firmly pounded repeatedly on his wooden desk with his closed fist as he punctuated each word with a thump, "The security of Germany is *paramount*!"

Iza stopped crying, stood up from her chair, and walked to the door. "Then I feel sorry for you. I'm leaving, and if you want to detain me, go ahead and try. You *know* my friend and

I didn't attack Evgeny Petrov on the U-Bahn. He attacked us. And I've got diplomatic immunity."

As Iza exited the office, Kühn's administrative assistant inquired, "Should I have someone pick them up in the lobby?"

"No, let them go. If I need her, I'll know where to find her."

Iza ran to the stairwell and raced down to the lobby. She'd been gone almost an hour and a half. Volodya was pacing around the lobby when he saw her burst through the stairwell door.

"Let's get out of here, Volodya," she whispered to him, still wiping tears from her eyes, obviously shaken.

"What happened, Iza? You are crying, and look at your eye!"

"I'll tell you later. We need to leave *right* now."

"I need to pick up Swiss Army tool and our phones. Wait for me."

As they rushed from the building, Volodya suddenly called for Iza to stop. He'd dropped behind her as she ran to the street.

"Iza, come here."

He stared at her jacket pocket as she turned back to him. Unlike him, she was always neat and organized. She always kept the outer pocket flaps on her jacket buttoned closed, but now one was open, and the flap was tucked awkwardly inside the pocket. He reached inside and pulled out a small GPS tracking device. Herr Kühn had intended to track Iza's movements; she was stunned. She realized he must have slipped the device into her pocket as they talked about Rembrandt at the start of their meeting when he'd pulled his chair near hers. They walked quickly to the U-Bahn station with the device in hand, trying to decide where to dispose of it.

Volodya queried as he looked ahead toward the station, "How do I say excuse me in German?"

"*Entschuldigung.*"

Volodya looked ahead to see a businessman dressed in a fashionable suit and carrying a large, open computer bag overflowing with papers. He was exiting the U-Bahn station and walking toward them. Volodya turned Iza in the man's direction, and they walked quickly to pass him. Volodya brushed into the businessman, dropping the GPS tracking device into his open computer bag.

"Entschuldigung."

The man gave Volodya a foul look, then walked on his way.

They took the U-Bahn toward their hotel, then exited after a few stops and kept rapidly walking.

"Let's get some coffee and *Brötchen*," Iza suggested. "I need to calm down just a minute before I call Tony. I know it's around 5:00 a.m. in Washington, but I *have* to reach him soon. I'll have to wake him up."

Iza purchased rolls and coffee at a *Bäckerei* along their route while Volodya stood watch outside the door. They ate breakfast while sitting in the bright sun on a grassy bank of the Spree River in a location where they could see all passersby.

Volodya looked carefully at Iza's eye, then asked with concern in his voice, "What *happened*, Iza?"

"Volodya, Kühn was a *dick*! He interrogated me! Why? He accused me of knowingly bringing the blueprints to Germany, and he tried to get me to admit I'm working for the Russians here in Germany. He wanted to know who you and your friends are. He kept asking me if you're Russians. And he wanted to know why we're interested in the software. But I figured it out. Kühn's the one who authorized copying the blueprints. That's why he burned the copies—to save himself. I'm pretty sure he had those copies brought to the U.S. to catch the spy there. He never expected that those copies would end up back in Germany."

"He thinks we are all Russians or working for Russia? Why?"

"I don't know. I have to ask Tony. Kühn is his friend. Maybe he'll have an idea why Kühn did this to me. Tony told me once that Kühn can be tenacious when he wants to get at the truth. Does he think I'm lying? I'm still shaking so bad.

"But now I'm *sure*—Günther's the spy. I know it. He was smart with the blueprints. He didn't want to make contact with Johannes Brandt as they usually do. The blueprints were probably something bigger and more important than anything else he'd ever found to send over here. So, he needed to be more careful, and he was probably really suspicious too. He knew he and my mom were driving to Vermont right before I left for Berlin. He was at our house the evening before they left. He'd seen my suitcase, and he knew I had it out on the chair in my room—that I was packing. I'd gotten home from work and was in the bathroom showering. He was there waiting for my mom to get home from work. He could have easily slipped them into my suitcase, and *no one* would ever know he did it."

"Then how did Herr Kühn know, Iza? That is weak place in your story. You said before, maybe not right away, but Kühn eventually knew that prints were in your suitcase. He sent his agent—guy who got killed outside your apartment—to recover them on Friday that we met."

Iza ignored Volodya and continued with her train of thought, "The Marketing woman at imperative Energie told us yesterday that Brandt is in Washington now—that he's flying back tonight. It's the same flight I took to Berlin. Maybe Günther has something new for him . . . maybe Tony can catch them together."

"Iza, *please*. Listen to what I say. How did Günther get blueprints in U.S.? If they were brought to U.S. by Herr Kühn's people from Germany, someone had to plan how Günther would find them. What is Günther's job at German Embassy in U.S.? How could they make finding these look legitimate to Günther? No one could just hand him blueprints and say, 'Günther, here is information you might want to give Russians.' Yet you said Tony isn't *authorized* to get information about Günther's job? Why?"

Iza responded slowly, obviously dispirited, "I hadn't thought about how they could make it look legitimate to Günther to find the prints. Maybe I'm wrong about him . . . I don't know."

"No, no, Iza. You may be right about Günther, but there had to be way that Günther found blueprints, where he could not think he was falling into trap. There had to be reason in his job that he would see these and then he could think about taking them."

"Yeah, Volodya, and then, are the blueprints related to the software backdoor? These are both efforts to damage Germany, and probably Ukraine in the process. Is there somebody who's trying to pressure Germany from supporting Ukraine in the war? I just don't know *what* to think. In fact, I *can't* think anymore. I'm *so* tired."

"Hey, Iza, come on . . . smile for me. We will figure this out. I think you are still doing pretty good in your race to find answers."

Feeling calmer, Iza tried Tony's number, but his line was busy—at 5:30 in the morning in Washington, D.C. Iza tried several more times, but the line remained busy.

"Tony, this is Iza. I can't reach you. I need to meet with you earlier than we planned. I'm not connecting in to your debriefing meeting with Derek at 17:00. Can Volodya and I video conference with you at 15:00 from a room at the Embassy? That's 10:00 a.m. your time. Volodya will need an entrance pass, and you'll need to arrange a video conference room for us.

"I met with Herr Kühn this morning, and I urgently need to tell you about that meeting. He interrogated me and it was awful. He also put a tracking device in the pocket of my jacket, but Volodya found it and we disposed of it. We both disabled location services on our phones, but Kühn can still track us using Wi-Fi. We have to turn off our phones to avoid tracking, but *please* leave me a message with the details if this is a go. I'll check at noon my time for your reply. By then, we'll be at a safe location and I can temporarily turn my phone back on. Tony . . . this is important . . . *real* important. We need your help. Call us." With that, they walked back to the hotel.

At noon, near the Hauptbahnhof just outside the hotel, Volodya and Iza together listened to a message from Tony sent at 6:30 a.m. from Washington. He sounded extraordinarily tired, more tired than from simply having been awakened at an early hour.

"Iza, this is Tony. I . . . I hope you and Volodya are staying safe. I finally got authorization from the Secretary and from the FBI Director late yesterday afternoon to contact FBI Counterespionage on this case. I got a full briefing very late last night. I need to warn you . . . you're in this thing deep, Iza . . . dangerously deep. But I think there might be a breakthrough soon—maybe even later today.

And I talked with Wilhelm early this morning. It must have been just after your meeting with him. He told me some of what's been happening, but I'd like to hear more from the two of you. He wasn't particularly open with me about your meeting. From your message, it sounds as though he was pretty hard on you. Let's meet at 15:00 your time by video at the embassy. My admin will arrange everything, and she'll let you know the room later.

"Oh . . . I canceled the 17:00 meeting with Derek. I'm rescheduling to next week; I'll be in Berlin midday Sunday."

Tony was returning to Berlin.

Back in the hotel room, Volodya suggested, "Iza, we should sleep. You are tired and I am too. I will set alarm for 14:00 to give us time to get message from Tony's assistant and to get to embassy conference room."

They lay on the bed in the semi-darkened room, but neither could sleep. Volodya gently rubbed Iza's hand when he asked her, "Iza, what will happen to us?"

"Tonight?"

"No . . . maybe four . . . five years from now."

Iza thought for a moment, then responded quietly, "Well, I think the war will be over, and Mr. Volodymyr Korsun will have moved back to Ukraine . . . maybe to Kyiv . . . but maybe to Kharkiv or Lviv. He'll have a job he absolutely loves at an NGO doing some kind of artificial intelligence programming for . . . I don't know . . . like maybe climate change mitigation or maybe for some clean water program. He'll be the kind and caring guy who he is, and he'll be making a big difference in the world. And if he ends up in Kyiv, he'll have season tickets to the National Symphony Orchestra."

"And what about Iza Carter?"

"I think she'll still be working at the U.S. Embassy," Iza said, then paused. Volodya's heart sank. She put him back in Ukraine in five years, but she thought she'd still be in Berlin.

Iza continued softly, not knowing Volodya had misunderstood her. "I guess it depends on where Mr. Korsun gets his job. She'd be at the U.S. Embassy in Kyiv if he's there, but she'd have to check if there are consulates in Kharkiv and Lviv. She's not sure about that right now . . . hmm. And in five years, she'll probably *still* be suffering, trying to learn Ukrainian grammar."

Volodya smiled as he ran his hand down her cheek. Iza continued, "They'll have a small apartment, but it'll be nice. Even though it's small, it'll have a big kitchen, and a washer, and a big drying rack. They won't have a car, but maybe they'll rent one to go to the countryside to ride horses some weekends. And they'll definitely have bikes."

"What do you think will happen to us in five years?" Iza asked, turning toward Volodya on the bed.

"I think you are right about everything, except by then, maybe you will be Iza Carter-Korsun—if you want to be," he quickly added.

"I'll consider your suggestion, Mr. Korsun," Iza laughed softly as she took her hand and messed up his hair. They lay quietly resting on the bed until 14:00, then left for the embassy, calling for Tony's administrative assistant's message along their way.

◆

As they approached the plaza at the embassy, Iza abruptly grabbed Volodya's arm.

"Volodya, I just saw the man with the shaved head! Look casually to the right, down the street by the embassy. Do you see him?"

Volodya scanned the areas to the right side of the embassy entrance.

"I do not see him."

"I don't see him now either, but I think I did. Maybe it's stress, and I only imagined seeing his ugly face."

They quickly made their way to the video conference center in the embassy and found the room that Tony's admin had reserved. Tony started the meeting promptly at 15:00; he looked very tired, his hair was a bit disheveled, and he appeared dispirited. Iza wondered if she and Volodya looked the same.

"Hi Tony," Iza and Volodya waved and smiled, trying to look cheerful.

Iza started with the description of her day at imperative Energie. It appeared to be a legitimate business—their cybersecurity software was probably world class—but it may have been compromised by both Johannes Brandt and by someone else with a deep knowledge of the software code. Perhaps even others in the company were involved.

Alex Schröder happened to be in the office on the first of the month for a meeting of the shareholder partners. Iza explained, "He stopped by at the end of the software demonstration to say hello and recognized I wasn't Claire. He called the embassy and learned Claire is on vacation until Thursday. I was chased by the security guard from imperative Energie, who looked to me like a gangster."

Iza paused, before continuing contritely, "Tony, I got trapped in the Chanel store on Kurfürstendamm. I went to the fitting room to hide, but the security guard got inside the store, and he waited for me. I had to change my outfit because the Disguise people put me in a bright red suit, and I stood out like a beacon. But I couldn't pay for the suit I changed into with the guy sitting there waiting for me, so I ran out the back exit of the store. I shoplifted a suit—it cost €10.650."

They could see Tony's eyes open wide, but he said nothing about the suit; nothing at all, for that matter. He simply looked at them wearily.

Iza continued, "The security guard followed me from the Embassy to a café last evening, where Volodya and his friends were working on decoding the software application code. Alex Schröder must have told him to look for me at the embassy, and I think maybe the guard recognized my suit. I'm not sure. I never saw the guy following me, Tony. I'm not trained in how to avoid surveillance. I only saw him later when we were already inside the café. We met Volodya's friends there, and the security guard was waiting for us near the exit. He was carrying a gun! Herr Kühn arranged for us to get safely out of the café, but the man took photos of all of us. I don't know why; maybe to show Alex. Alex is going to know *I* went to that demo meeting posing as Claire." Volodya and Iza looked at each other curiously as Tony nodded in agreement, seemingly oblivious to Iza's comment about the man having a gun or about the fact that they'd kept a copy of the software application and had been decoding it.

As Volodya told Tony about his apartment, Iza realized that Tony was only partially paying attention to what Volodya was telling him. He seemed very distracted by something. Volodya finished by telling Tony that whoever installed the tracking device in Iza's suitcase now knew where they were living. They were staying in a Berlin hotel temporarily, but they'd need a new apartment soon and someone would need to recover their belongings, or what was left of them, from his current apartment. Tony nodded his head as if in agreement but still said nothing.

"And Tony, Iza bought us two tickets to Hamburg. We hoped guys would think we traveled to Hamburg instead of staying in Berlin. We sent Iza's suitcase with tracking device to you at Hamburg Consulate by train. We hoped it might confuse whoever installed device. We are not sure if someone from train station will deliver suitcase or if police will get it, but maybe you should know because your name is on luggage tag."

Iza continued, "Tony, I know Herr Kühn is your friend, but he actually *interrogated* me today. I don't understand why he did that. It was awful. You told me he can be tenacious when he wants to know the truth. Why does he think I'm lying? I said some not-very-nice things to him. But I'm not sorry for what I said." Iza sensed that Tony wasn't paying attention at all; his mind seemed to be consumed by something else. As a test of his attention, she said, "I told Herr Kühn to fuck off." Tony simply nodded his head in agreement.

Volodya started to explain what he'd learned about the imperative Energie software, but Tony suddenly interrupted. "I have to take a call here. It's urgent."

Iza frantically inquired, "Tony, before you go, what's the breakthrough? Who's the spy?

Tony continued forcefully, "I'll have to tell you later, Iza. I want you two to stick around the embassy area until 21:00 and wait for me to call you before heading out. I'll call you on your secure office phone line, Iza. And I'll make everything right for both of you—soon. But absolutely *don't* leave the embassy until we talk again!" With that, Tony abruptly closed the meeting to take the urgent phone call.

"That's like 4:00 p.m. in Washington. Maybe they're trying to catch the spy meeting with Brandt around lunchtime or in the early afternoon before Brandt heads to Dulles, and Tony is calling us afterward," Iza wondered aloud.

◆

They had five hours to kill before Tony's next call, so they first walked to Iza's office. After looking around her office,

Volodya sat in her visitor chair and immediately fell asleep, his head bobbing down and snapping upward on occasion. Iza took out her new employee manual and aimlessly paged through it for lack of anything more interesting to do. It was a long wait, and it was so boring that it eventually became a form of stress relief. *This is almost like being on a long plane ride with nothing to do. My brain is turning to mush.* It was nearly 21:00 when Volodya suddenly awoke and moved his chair close to Iza's as they awaited Tony's call.

"Iza, this is Tony." Tony spoke very quietly. He sounded devastated. "Is Volodya there?"

"Of course, he's here."

"Can I talk to him?"

Iza handed the phone to Volodya with a questioning look on her face.

"Volodya, I . . . I don't know how to tell Iza this. We got photos of the spy handing off some classified information to Brandt over the lunch hour here." There was a very long pause on the line.

"Tony?"

"The spy is Iza's *mom*."

Volodya's eyes opened wide in shock, "*No!* Are you sure?" His eyes filled with tears for Iza.

"Unfortunately, yes. She's an interpreter of German and Russian at the State Department. FBI Counterespionage has been watching her. By process of elimination, they discovered *all* the information that's been lost came from meetings where she was there as the interpreter. They took her into custody right after the hand-off today. She hasn't given them a voluntary statement yet, but that might happen tonight. There's no way she's not guilty."

After a long pause, Tony continued, "We still have to determine who her case officer at the Russian Embassy is, but we're sure she's the spy. Kühn's people are picking up Brandt at the airport when his flight arrives tomorrow morning." After another very long pause, Tony said, "I'm devastated, Volodya. I've known Elise for thirty years. She's our close friend. Iza will be traumatized. Oh, God . . . this is overwhelming."

"I am very sorry."

Iza looked at Volodya questioningly. "Volodya, what's happening? What's Tony telling you about? Why are you crying?"

Volodya held the phone with one hand, grabbed hold of Iza's hand, then quietly asked Tony, "What about Günther?"

A long pause ensued. "I just learned this afternoon that he works for Wilhelm Kühn. His assignment was to get close to Elise to try to figure out how she'd been working this."

Volodya sat in disbelief. Iza's mom was the spy! She'd betrayed her country and endangered her own daughter's life. How could she? It was so cruel.

"What's going on?" Iza asked again, frantically looking at Volodya. "What are you talking about?"

"Tony, this must come from you. I will be here to help. . . you know . . . with what happens."

Volodya slowly handed the phone to Iza and put his arm around her shoulder, drawing her near to himself.

"*No! No!*" Iza screamed hysterically into the phone. "It's not *true*. You're making this up, Tony! You're *lying*! My mom wouldn't do that—*ever!*" Iza broke down sobbing.

Volodya took the phone from her hand. "Tony, I will call you later," he said.

"Wait, Volodya! You need to be *extremely* careful. You need to protect Iza, both physically and emotionally. Do you understand me?"

"Yes, Tony, I do."

"Where are you staying?"

"Meininger Hotel Hauptbahnhof."

Volodya held Iza close and listened. She was sobbing. "It can't be true. Tony is lying," Iza said. "This is all made up." Iza's eyes were swollen and red, her black eye now deep purple. After she stopped crying, Iza remembered Herr

Kühn's comments as they'd discussed Rembrandt's painting of Lucretia. She realized that he'd suspected all along that her mother was the spy. And now the truth had stabbed Iza in her heart.

When it was nearly 23:00, Volodya said gently, "Come on, Iza, we need to leave here." He helped her stand up, put his arm around her shoulder, and walked with her out of the embassy.

They walked slowly toward the Moltkebrücke, a bridge crossing the Spree River, in the direction of the hotel. It was a quiet, dark night, and the streets were deserted; there was only a small, waning crescent moon in the sky. Volodya had been using his phone flashlight to light their way in areas where there was no street lighting. He'd heard footsteps behind them on occasion. At first, he thought it was only his imagination, but then he became convinced that someone was walking behind them.

"Iza, I think someone is following us," he whispered.

Iza tensed up and carefully turned to look behind them while Volodya kept them moving forward. She saw the shape of a beefy-looking man walking a short distance behind them.

"Volodya, I think it's the man with the shaved head!"

They picked up their pace, but the man started walking even faster and was gaining on them.

"Should we run?" Iza questioned.

"I am not sure I can with my ribs like this."

"Come on, Volodya; you have to try!" Iza quietly implored Volodya as she started to sprint toward the bridge.

Volodya ran and tried to keep up with her, but his breathing was strained, and the pain in his ribs increased with each expansion and contraction of his rib cage. They could hear the man running behind them, the distance between Volodya and the man shrinking, while Iza was pulling away. They were on the bridge when the man overtook Volodya. Volodya shined his phone light directly in the man's eyes, temporarily blinding him, but the man with the shaved head recovered quickly and came for Volodya. The man had a gun in his right hand. Soon, it was pointed at Volodya.

The man with the shaved head called out to Iza in German, "Woman with beautiful suit, come back here!"

Volodya screamed out to Iza, "Run, Iza! Go!" but she stopped and turned around. "Go! Go!" he implored, but to his dismay, she started to slowly walk back toward them. He realized that in the semi-darkness on the bridge, she couldn't see the gun.

Volodya assessed the man. He was well built but not nearly as tall or as massive as Evgeny Petrov. Volodya had had hand-to-hand combat instruction as part of his basic military training, and he knew he could hold his own for at least a period of time with someone this size, but the man's gun was pointed at him. Volodya had been in a similar situation before in the battle for Kharkiv. He knew that people fighting in hand-to-hand combat didn't typically fight to the death; someone with a gun almost always ended this type of fight. Yet he realized that he absolutely had to try to protect Iza, even if he might die in the process.

Iza slowly approached the two men until she saw the gun pointed at Volodya. She shrieked, "No! No!" as she faltered, then suddenly fell to her knees, sobbing. "*Please* don't take him away from me!" she cried out in terror.

The man with the shaved head was distracted by Iza's outburst and her sudden fall. This gave Volodya his chance. He swiftly grabbed the gun and turned the barrel downward, twisting the man's wrist. He then tightly constrained the man's tricep while sharply twisting the man's forearm behind his back. Volodya's motions were so rapid that the man with the shaved head had no time to respond. He was no longer able to grip the handgun, and it dropped out of his hand onto the sidewalk. Volodya kicked the gun off the sidewalk into the street.

The man with the shaved head fought back. He wrenched himself out of the hold, and not immediately seeing the gun, came at Volodya. They scuffled on the bridge. The man knocked Volodya to the ground and mounted his body. Volodya brought his forearms up defensively to block the man from reaching his eyes and neck, as the man tried in vain to gouge his eyes and strangle him. Volodya curled his lower legs around the man's hips in an attempt to roll over and gain the top position, but he wasn't strong enough to flip the man off of himself.

Iza grabbed the gun from the street, then yelled at the man in German, "*I* have it! *I* have the gun!" as the man continued pummeling Volodya's forearms.

The man with the shaved head stopped pummeling Volodya's forearms momentarily, turned his upper body away from Volodya, and lunged toward Iza. She jumped away from him, enticing him to come after her for the weapon. Iza taunted him loudly in German, "Come and get it—if you can!"

The man suddenly stood and lunged again toward Iza, completely disengaging from combat with Volodya. It was Volodya's second chance. Volodya surged upward and seized the man around his neck from the rear, putting the man into a blood chokehold with his right arm. Volodya braced his left hand behind the man's head and pushed it forward to keep the man from snapping his head back into Volodya's jaw. He then pulled tightly on the man's neck with all his strength, his bicep and forearm compressing the man's carotid arteries. The man struggled and reached back, trying to grab at Volodya's crotch, then his arm, but Volodya held on, dancing out of reach of the man's flailing arms. He was dripping with perspiration from the combat and applying the chokehold. His ribs were screaming in discomfort.

Volodya started counting—ten-to-twenty seconds and the man would pass out. More than twenty seconds, and the risk of brain damage or death was real. The man's body went limp at eleven seconds. Volodya stopped at fifteen seconds and released the man's body to the ground.

"Let's get out of here, Volodya," Iza yelled out as she grabbed his hand and pulled him away from the man with the shaved head.

Volodya felt weak and exhausted, his rib cage stinging from their run and from the exertion of combat, but he was able to walk, albeit slowly. Iza raced ahead of him to the middle of the bridge and threw the gun into the Spree. They heard it splash into the water as the two gradually walked the rest of the way across the bridge toward the hotel.

When they got to the room, they immediately went into the shower together and held each other, washing away the sweat and the fear that they felt. They kissed each other, then crawled into the bed together. Within minutes, Iza was sleeping soundly, but Volodya dressed again, looked at his now-broken and useless phone, then took Iza's phone and walked outside the hotel to call Tony.

"Tony, this is Volodya."

"How's Iza doing?"

"She is sleeping now, but Tony, we need your help with things. I mean *really* need your help. Can you make list to help us?"

"Of course!" Tony replied, sounding both weary and distraught. Volodya could hear him moving papers across his desk.

Volodya continued, "You need to call Iza's work. She will not be in office for rest of week. She will come there on Monday.

"You need to call my work for me, but it is complicated. I will give you four phone numbers. Maybe you can find someone in military to help. I will not be at data center for rest of week. I will return on Monday. It is *very* important to call; I am in military and they might think I am AWOL.

"Next, I need new phone. We also need new apartment. We are in hotel here tonight and two more, then we are out of money. We need apartment in Kreuzberg neighborhood. Small apartment and already furnished. Maybe it will have big kitchen and washer and big drying rack.

"Then someone needs to go through my apartment and clean up our stuff. But *this* time, they need to check *everything* for tracking device *before* they bring it to new apartment. Can you do this?"

"I'll do anything for you," Tony responded, as he wrote down the phone numbers that Volodya recited to him.

"Oh, and one other thing. We were followed tonight from embassy by security guard from imperative Energie. He attacked us on Moltkebrücke across Spree River. I might have killed him," Volodya said matter-of-factly. "Please send Polizei to Moltkebrücke. They need to check if he is dead there or if he lived and got away."

Without waiting for any further response from Tony, Volodya said, "Okay, we will call you tomorrow," and hung up the phone. Then he returned to the hotel room, and collapsed onto the bed.

Thursday, November 3 (Day 23)

Lloyd called together Dmytro and Max before the morning briefing. "I got a call from the Pentagon this morning at an ungodly hour. Volodya won't be back here until Monday. I didn't even know, but he's been working on some special security assignment on our behalf—something to do with an effort by the Russian Embassy here in Berlin to get intel on our location. Are either of you aware of what he's doing?"

Both Dmytro's and Max's eyes opened wide. *So Volodya was telling truth to us,* Dmytro thought.

"Yes. I knew he was involved," Dmytro offered, "but I was under strict orders not to say anything here; we're not supposed to worry the boys."

"At the end of the briefing, I was ordered to announce he's got COVID, but he's already feeling better, and should be back by Monday at the latest. Not a word to anyone," Lloyd ordered.

Dmytro immediately walked to Petro's workstation and conversed with him in Ukrainian, while pointing at Petro's monitor, pretending to discuss an important technical topic.

"Petro, what Volodya told us at Café Bleibtreu *is* true. The Russians in Berlin *are* looking for our location. The U.S. Pentagon even called Lloyd to confirm it. Volodya is helping them now on special assignment."

"Dmytro, I am *relieved* we did not let Polizei take us home to our apartments. At least no one knows where *we* live. It was your great idea to stop in different neighborhood and walk to our apartments once Polizei had gone. After they asked us our names and what we were doing at Bleibtreu Café, I did not trust them. But, is Volodya okay? Is he safe?"

"I think so. Maybe he will tell us more when he comes back here on Monday."

"Dmytro, what do you think about his girlfriend, Iza? They seem to love each other and she is nice girl, but I worry her job is *much* too dangerous. Will he have future with her?"

"They will work something out together, I am sure. But I will talk with Volodya privately on Monday. I will suggest his girlfriend should find different kind of job."

◆

Volodya woke up with a start at 10:00, still dressed in his clothing from the past night, as if he'd fallen asleep the moment he'd dropped onto the bed. At first, he wondered where he was, but then he recalled the fight, which explained why his forearms, right shoulder, ribs, and back were all sore. He looked over at Iza, who was staring at the ceiling, deep in thought.

"Iza, what are you thinking?" he asked quietly, moving closer to her on the bed.

"I still can't believe my mom is a spy for Russia. How could she dishonor our own country—her friends—my dad? She *worked* for our government, and had our government's trust to be honest and loyal.

And then . . . to have endangered you and all the people you work with. Didn't she think about what she was doing? That people could be killed through her actions. I don't know what other kinds of information she secreted away for Russia, but did she hurt other people too? And for what?"

Iza's eyes filled with tears. "Now I realize it was my *mom* who wanted me to contact Brandt; Günther probably put her up to it though. She most likely thought Brandt would get the blueprints at the Berlin airport and I'd never need to be involved. But after she somehow determined he hadn't found them, it sure seems like she didn't care if I got hurt. How could she do that to me? Our relationship hasn't always been the closest, but she was good to me after my dad died. I've been searching my mind, trying to understand. I don't think Tony or Ellen or Roger could have seen this coming either. My mom must love me, right?"

I cannot tell Iza who Günther is. I hope she can believe that he encouraged her mom to do this. It is not true, but knowing what is true will hurt her even more. Volodya reached for her. "Iza, I do not know what to say about your mom; it makes me very sad for you. I can only tell you *I* love you and I will *always* love you."

Iza smiled as she tried to stop thinking about her mom's betrayal. "How can I ever thank you for loving me and for the commitment you showed me last night. I promise I'll make this all up to you someday. I'll replace everything in your apartment that got ruined. I'm sorry."

"No, no. You have no need to feel you owe me something."

Iza gently touched his forearm. "I owe you everything ... I owe you my life."

"In different way, I owe you mine also," he said as he stared into her eyes, no longer feeling despondent about his life.

They hugged each other.

"Volodya, why are you dressed?" Iza asked suddenly. "Were you awake earlier?"

"I forgot, but I promised to call Tony yesterday in evening. I had to go outside near Hauptbahnhof again to use your phone. I made Tony request—long list of things to do to help us, and I asked him to send Polizei to Moltkebrücke to see if I killed that guy. I think maybe I passed out on bed when I got back or something."

"Why do you think the man with the shaved head followed us last night? I thought about it this morning and wonder if he works for someone else, not only imperative Energie. Does he work for the Russians? He took photos of each of us on his phone as we left the Café with the Polizei. Maybe the photos were for Alex Schröder; who knows? But I wonder if he studied mine before he gave them to whoever he gave them to and suddenly realized I'm the woman who has the information the Russians want, not just some crazy imposter at his company's demo."

"I do not know. Maybe we will not need to worry about him if he is dead," Volodya replied, no longer caring if he'd killed a man.

◆

Late in the morning, Tony left a long, detailed message for Iza and Volodya; he'd been working on Volodya's list. Together, they listened: "Okay you two, your absences from work are excused until Monday. Let's see . . . I learned the Polizei didn't find a body on the Moltkebrücke. I directed my admin to locate an apartment in the Kreuzberg borough, and I'll take a look at whatever we find there before making a decision for you.

"I need to tell you more about Herr Kühn, Iza. If you ever have to meet with him again, my advice is to be *completely* honest. Tell him *everything*, even your most remote guess at what he might want to know. There isn't a whole lot I can do to help you in dealing with him. You're in Germany, and in Germany, we play by his rules."

There was a brief pause, then Tony continued with his message. "Pick up Volodya's new phone at *exactly* 13:00 at the Apple store on Rosenthaler Straße. I made an appointment for you."

Iza replayed his message and looked puzzled by his cryptic reference to some unknown future meeting with Wilhelm Kühn. "What did he mean by that?" Volodya gave her an equally puzzled look in return.

Roger had also left a message, likely wanting to talk about her mother. Iza was too overwhelmed by her feelings of grief to talk with anyone other than Volodya and decided to call him at a later time.

◆

Just before 13:00, they walked into the phone store and inquired about an order for Herr Korsun as Tony had instructed. A helpful employee retrieved the phone and handed the package to Volodya. "It's all paid for and your service agreement is set up—same phone number as your old phone. Turn it on and you're ready to go." Volodya unpackaged the phone, leaving the packaging on the counter, and slipped the new phone into his pocket. He and Iza turned from the counter to leave.

Suddenly, a squad car from the Berlin Polizei swerved in front of the phone store with lights flashing; two officers sprang out of the car and sprinted into the shop. The Polizei accused Volodya of shoplifting, and pushed the two into the waiting squad car, then squealed off as nervous customers looked on. "Where are you taking us?" Iza repeatedly asked the two officers, but neither answered. "We didn't take anything!"

The squad car sped into the restricted entry area of the Bundeskriminalamt. The two were frisked, then ordered to pass through the metal detector. The entry guard confiscated Volodya's Swiss Army tool and their cell phones.

Herr Kühn was awaiting their arrival. He ordered the two to sit in chairs arranged in front of his desk. Volodya and Iza realized that the *only* way he could have found them at the phone store was through Tony, which must have been why Tony specified they arrive there at *exactly* 13:00 for their "appointment." His reference to a potential future meeting with Herr Kühn was clear. And, it was also evident that Tony had betrayed them.

"Iza Carter, we meet again," Herr Kühn said coldly.

"Why did you bring us here again?" Iza asked defiantly. "We didn't do anything wrong, and we have nothing to say to you."

"That is not true, Iza Carter. You need to explain many things to me, and Tony Brooks assures me your friend here has *something* he can tell me. Is that not true Herr Korsun?"

"It depends what you need to be told."

"Tony told you where to find us, didn't he?"

"Yes. It would be a shame if Elise Carter's treachery were splashed on primetime news programs across the U.S.—*such* an embarrassment to your State Department. Tony understands that protecting the reputation of your State Department and the security of the U.S. are paramount, just as I understand the same for Germany."

Herr Kühn continued with increasing stridency, "And it would be an even *greater* shame if Elise Carter's only daughter were implicated at the same time, wouldn't it? Iza Carter, you *did* carry the blueprints to Berlin in your suitcase. You already admitted that yesterday. I have your confession recorded."

Iza's eyes opened wide in horror. "I told you before, I didn't *know* they were in my suitcase! I'd never knowingly do something like that! I'm *not* my mother. How *dare* you accuse me! I didn't do anything wrong. I took a new job here, and I flew here to start my job. That's *all*."

Herr Kühn threatened, "I can have you sent back to the U.S. as a persona non grata. And you"—he continued while turning his gaze to Volodya—"I can have you detained for attacking a man on the Moltkebrücke last night and for industrial espionage—for stealing developmental software from a German company. I suggest the two of you will want to be *very* honest with me."

Iza suddenly remembered Tony's cryptic instructions: *"Be completely honest. Tell him everything, even your most remote guess at what he might want to know. You're playing by his rules."*

Turning his gaze back toward Iza, Herr Kühn questioned, "How do you explain *these?*" He spread a stack of photographs across his desk in front of them. They were images of Iza meeting with a man in the dark of night near the Brandenburg Gate. In successive photos, it appeared as if Iza were handing the man a large envelope. "*He* is Ilya Morozov, an employee of the Russian Embassy in Berlin, who we suspect is a case officer for the Embassy—a spy handler. Perhaps he is the case officer for Johannes Brandt. Or is he *your* case officer, Iza Carter?"

As Kühn glared at her while he awaited her reply, Iza looked at the photos in shock. "They're fakes. I've never seen the man in these photos before in my life. That's the truth. I don't have a case officer because I'm not a spy or a conduit for a spy."

"Where did you get these?" Volodya interrupted as he pored over the photographs.

"Herr Korsun, might I remind you, I will ask the questions." Yet Kühn continued, "They were delivered to the BKA by courier yesterday afternoon at 16:30. The courier did not know the source of the package, but these were sent to my attention. My Forensics Lab people are looking at more of these photos as we speak to judge their authenticity."

Volodya immediately noticed two critical details in the series of photos. First, Iza was wearing the Chanel suit in the photos. She'd *only* worn the suit in the afternoon and late evening of the first of November—following her meeting at imperative Energie until their arrival at the Meininger Hotel—because she hadn't stolen it until the afternoon of the first of November. Secondly, the images were obviously, at least to Volodya, doctored images. They were convincing images in some respects, but there were subtle signs that the images of Iza had been altered and combined with the images of the Russian Embassy employee, Ilya Morozov.

"Can I ask question?" Volodya asked.

Kühn nodded.

"Will you believe me if I show you where these images were altered? I think your own guys will see this too and they will show you. I look at images every day for my work, and I need to look very carefully. If I do not, I might kill my own guys by accident."

Volodya continued, "Call Tony right now and ask him. He will know that Iza got this suit in photos on first of November in afternoon. She told him about it yesterday. Tony sent her to imperative Energie to meet with them, but in disguise. However, embassy people gave her red suit and when she needed to run, red color stood out too much. She had to change to something plainer to blend in because she was being chased by company security guard. She ran to first open shop door on Kurfürstendamm, and it was Chanel store. This suit was very expensive, but she had to take it to get away from imperative Energie's security guard. She told Tony she took it. Besides Iza and me, only Tony and now you know that she took it and did not pay for it.

"If you got photos at 16:30 on second of November and Iza first had this suit on first of November, then passing this envelope had to take place after dark on first of November. But look at street and sidewalks in photos. They are very wet. But it did not rain in Berlin during night of first of November.

"Iza, show Herr Kühn your hands." Iza held her up hands for Herr Kühn to see them. "See here, Iza's hand and forearm in photos are not hers. She has long, slender hands and fingers, and this hand in photo is short and fingers are very short. It is not Iza's hand. These photos of Iza were taken by security guard from imperative Energie, who followed Iza to Bleibtreu Café from U.S. Embassy on night of first of November. Whoever altered these photos did not see Iza's hands and forearms because they were handcuffed behind her back when we left Café Bleibtreu with your Polizei. They had to guess what her hand would look like and they guessed wrong.

"And see here, Iza's face is bright in photo, but Ilya's face is shadowed, yet they stand very close to each other under street lamp. The light level on their faces should be same, not one bright and one dark.

"And here, you see very, very slight imperfection on this photo where two separate photos were joined to make one and they could not hide seam so well. I might see more signs of photo alterations too, if I had more time to look. If your Forensics Lab is good, and I think they are, your guys will notice these details."

Volodya suddenly questioned, "But if guys from Russian Embassy made these photos, why would they send you photos of one of their own, Ilya Morozov? That makes no sense."

"It does make sense, Volodya," Iza responded, realizing that she had to defend herself before Herr Kühn. She *had* to make him believe her. Tony had directed her to tell him *everything* she could think of that she even guessed he'd want to know. She would do that, whether he asked the questions or not. "I mean—that these photos were sent to Herr Kühn to implicate this man, Ilya Morozov. They weren't made *by* the Russians. They were made by someone from imperative Energie—like one or more of the shareholder partners. I mean . . . I don't think the partners literally made the photos themselves, but they probably hired someone to do it, and to do it quickly."

Iza looked directly at Wilhelm, fearful of his icy stare, yet determined to prove that she'd done nothing wrong. "When I was at the software demo at imperative Energie, their Marketing Director gave us a little history of the company. She told us the company has a 'perceptual liability' in terms of expanding their business to the U.S., because of one of their former shareholder partners. That guy is Mikhail Friedemann, and he's a confidant to Vladimir Putin. She called it a red flag for them that his name is associated with imperative Energie. The other shareholders had him removed as a partner, but it wasn't until the beginning of this year. He had *eight years* to put his imprint on imperative Energie. Maybe Mikhail made it possible for a Russian from their embassy to recruit employees at the company to work for Russia; Brandt for sure, but perhaps others.

"The man who, by the way, attacked *us* on the Moltkebrücke is a security guard for imperative Energie. We think he's working for Russia on the sly. If the Russians penetrated the company, isn't it to their advantage to have the security guard on their side? The guard can report on all the comings and goings of everyone who works for or visits imperative Energie, and he can follow people after hours if they order him to do that. He followed us last night to the Moltkebrücke. I'm sure he figured out who I am, and he wanted to get the blueprints; he would have killed me if he'd gotten them. He had no way of knowing that you already destroyed them."

Volodya interrupted, "Someone at imperative Energie is working to compromise imperative Energie's software code by inserting backdoor in application code. Russians would naturally want ability to disrupt natural gas supply or damage parts of electric grid in Germany, and since that software protects much of Germany's energy infrastructure from cyberthreats, it offers them chance to have that ability. They are not happy with Germany for supporting Ukraine in their war. But they need guy with very *deep* understanding of how that software works to go into program and create backdoor code."

"Did the Russians recruit one of imperative Energie's best programmers to do that? Their Marketing Director told me their Director of Software Development is a guy named Herr Doktor Markus Peters. He was one of imperative Energie's former—meaning dead—Software Director's graduate students at the Technische Universität Berlin, and one of the main coders who originally developed this security software. Imperative Energie's former Director fell to his death from the balcony of his condo two years ago. I think someone murdered him by throwing him off his balcony because he wouldn't go along with their plans to alter the software."

Iza questioned Herr Kühn. "Doesn't someone like you try to recruit a person to spy who's disgruntled, who has some grudge against their boss or coworkers or their country, or who wants money to support a lavish lifestyle? Wouldn't a disgruntled former graduate student, who didn't get *any* fame or fortune for his cybersecurity software development be a perfect candidate for recruitment by the Russians?"

Iza turned away from Herr Kühn, avoiding his icy stare. "Once Friedemann was gone, the partners probably cleaned out his office files and got some clue what he'd been up to. I'm certain they figured out that the Russians are making hay in their company, and they need to do something about it. But they couldn't come directly to someone like *you* for help, Herr Kühn, because then it'd eventually be public knowledge.

Imagine the headlines . . . '*Security of German Energy Infrastructure at Risk! imperative Energie Cybersecurity Software Compromised!*' They couldn't let that happen. They'd lose all their business.

"How could they clean up the mess without alerting someone like you? They undoubtedly hired a private investigation firm to help them. That firm likely discovered the Russian Embassy's involvement in imperative Energie. But what could they do with someone like Ilya Morozov? The private-investigation firm likely faked these photos because they need *you* to get rid of Morozov now that they've identified him. You guys can send him back to Russia as a persona non grata. A PI firm can't do that.

"These fake photos of Morozov with me were probably photos of Brandt with him, taken by the PI firm. They took Brandt out of the photos and put my image there instead. If the PI firm knows about Brandt, they're looking for a way to get rid of him. But they didn't need to do it with these photos. The Marketing Director told me he's been travelling a lot to D.C. to get new business for them in the U.S., but he hasn't made any breakthroughs. Imperative Energie could let him go for poor performance after he's been there for a year and no one would be any the wiser. They don't need to involve you to get rid of him.

"And why did they insert my image in the photographs with Morozov?" Iza paused for a moment and then replied thoughtfully. "I think one of the partners, Alex Schröder, figured out it was *I* at his company software demonstration. I was in disguise and posing as another U.S. Embassy employee who he knows and he *freaked out*. It was by chance that Schröder was in the office on the first of November and saw me there. He probably got suspicious and asked himself, 'Does the U.S. Embassy somehow know what's going on here in my company'?"

Iza continued slowly, "Alex saw my boss and me at a German State Department energy meeting about a week ago. The big four E.U. governments proposed building new natural gas and hydrogen pipelines between Germany, France, and Spain, and they also proposed constructing liquified natural gas terminals in Germany. I'm *positive* imperative Energie will want to compete for that cybersecurity business once the pipelines and terminals are built.

But when a guy from the U.S. Embassy Bureau of Economic and Business Affairs shows up at imperative Energie for a software demo, bringing a woman in disguise using her boss's identity, Alex probably wondered, '*What* is going on? Is the U.S. Embassy trying to get this business for one of their own cybersecurity firms?' He probably sent these photos to you, thinking that when you saw the photos, I'd become a persona non grata and be sent back to the U.S. He might even be planning to go after the guy from the Bureau and maybe my boss too—to get them sent out of Germany with me."

Iza and Volodya worriedly glanced at each other, their eyes silently questioning, *What more can we tell him to prove our innocence?* At that moment, Herr Kühn's administrative assistant entered the room and whispered something to him. He finally addressed Iza and Volodya. "In my many years of performing interrogations, I have used several techniques to get at the truth. I can use harshness, but I can also give the suspects enough rope to hang themselves. Iza Carter, Herr Korsun, I have discretely recorded your statements here this afternoon—more discretely than in our previous encounter, Iza Carter. Very soon, I will know if you are lying or if you are telling me the truth. You are to remain in my office until I return. There will be a guard stationed at the door here—inside the room—so do not attempt to leave." With that, Herr Kühn excused himself, saying that he'd be back very soon.

Iza frantically and breathlessly whispered, "Volodya, Kühn thinks I'm a conduit for my mom! Will he believe any of what we just told him? What can he find out 'very soon?' Tony said he can't help us here!"

Volodya whispered back, "What does 'making hay' mean?"

"I'm sorry. I'm so upset; I didn't realize I used an idiom. It means someone is making good use of an opportunity. In this case, the 'someone' is the Russians. And the 'opportunity' is to screw Germany so they won't support Ukraine anymore. But there's also a slang meaning for making hay." Iza leaned close to Volodya's ear and whispered, "It means 'to copulate in bed with your significant other'."

Despite the seriousness of the situation, Volodya quietly chuckled and whispered back, "Really? I am sorry, but that is funny." Volodya saw the look of distress on Iza's face. They'd both experienced terror and uncertainty the past two days, but particularly Iza. To learn that your own mother had betrayed her country, and had apparently not cared about the fate of her daughter, had been devasting. So, he suddenly tried to make Iza laugh to lessen the stress she was feeling. "Iza, if I do not take cold shower pretty soon, I will need to make hay with you." Iza was so surprised by his comment, that she broke into giggles and it temporarily relieved the pressure she felt as they awaited Herr Kühn's return.

Volodya sat thinking for some minutes, then turned to Iza, and said quietly and thoughtfully, "Iza, I think I finally understand. *Culture* at imperative Energie allowed Russians to make inroads into company. Maybe at beginning partners thought it was good idea to have Friedemann as partner. He gave them access to big cybersecurity contracts for Nord Stream I and II pipelines—for the Nord Stream Pipeline Consortium and for Russian Gazprom. But then as you said, Friedemann got someone like Morozov to make inroads in company and Russians start to make hay. They turn Brandt and he gives them opportunities to bring information from U.S. and Germany interactions to the Russians. Russians know ahead of time what U.S. and Germany are thinking when they work together. And now that is especially important because of war in Ukraine.

"Then, Russians turn someone with programming skill at company. That guy can give Russian hackers easy access to their cybersecurity software. Russians can hold Germany hostage by disrupting German energy supply.

"And finally, Russians get people like man with shaved head from company to do their dirty work. This is what happens when company leaders are too greedy and not so ethical. They are willing to have few principles. What partners did in having close relationship with Russia was legal, but was what they did moral? Is what they did in best interest of Germany or only in their personal interest in quest for power and wealth?"

"I think you're absolutely right. It's obvious they're motivated by greed."

Herr Kühn didn't return to his office very soon, as promised. After their discussion, Volodya dozed off in his chair, his head bobbing downward and then snapping back to attention on occasion. Iza sat tensely looking around the office under the watchful eye of the guard, who said nothing. She eventually went to page through Herr Kühn's book of Rembrandt paintings to calm herself, as the guard closely followed her movements. She was tormented by thoughts of her mother's betrayal.

After waiting in his office nearly two hours, Herr Kühn finally returned. He formally announced that Johannes Brandt had been apprehended at the Berlin airport on charges of espionage as he exited his late-arriving flight from Washington.

The German Foreign Ministry would imminently declare two additional Russian Embassy personnel personae non gratae . . . in addition to the forty embassy personnel expelled from Germany in April of 2022. Ilya Morozov and Mikhail Dobrynin, a.k.a. Evgeny Petrov, would be required to leave the country within seventy-two hours.

Herr Kühn revealed that he'd just spoken with Tony Brooks. Elise Carter had given a voluntary statement to FBI Counterespionage. She'd identified Maksim Vasiliev and

Boris Kuznetsov from the Russian Embassy in Washington D.C. as her case officer and handler, respectively. They were about to be declared personae non gratae by the U.S. and would be ordered to leave the country within seventy-two hours.

Herr Kühn told them he'd authorized surveillance teams to monitor imperative Energie to determine if the announcement of the diplomatic expulsions from Germany or the news of Brandt's apprehension would filter back to the employees, possibly panicking some of them into making a move.

Finally, the BKA Forensics Lab confirmed that the photos of Iza with Ilya Morozov were manipulated fakes. Volodya let out a huge sigh of relief, so loud that even Herr Kühn allowed himself a slight grin.

Iza felt a huge weight lifting from her, but then, the weight of her mother's betrayal fell back upon her. Her mom had given a voluntary statement. Now there was no doubt. Her mom was guilty of espionage.

Volodya addressed Herr Kühn, "There is still question of software. We found backdoor inserted in version of application code, but has this version reached customers yet? What will you do in order to protect Germany's energy infrastructure?" But Kühn declined to specifically answer his questions.

"Are we free to leave now or do you still plan to detain us?" Iza questioned, the exhaustion and dejection in her voice now palpable.

"Yes," Herr Kühn responded.

"I guess I should have asked those questions separately. May we leave now? Or if not, are you detaining us?"

"Yes, you may leave now. My office will inform Tony Brooks of any updates, and I am sure Tony will convey anything pertinent to you. You must carefully watch if you are being surveilled over the next seventy-two to ninety-six hours. And finally, Tony Brooks requests that you call him as soon as possible after you leave my office." He paused for a moment, then said, "Herr Korsun, I may need your assistance in the near future when my Digital Forensics Laboratory gains access to the imperative Energie cybersecurity software."

As they prepared to leave, Herr Kühn stopped them. "Iza Carter, I am not sorry for how harshly I interrogated you yesterday, nor for any accusations I made against you today. It is my job to protect the security of my country—of our democracy—and I take my job very seriously. I needed to know if you were involved in your mother's treachery. When he and I spoke earlier this week, Tony Brooks assured me that you are innocent. But he also assured me that your mother was innocent. He let their friendship cloud his judgment. In this business, I cannot let that happen."

"Is that how my life is going to be from now on? Am I guilty simply because I'm my mother's daughter?"

Herr Kühn didn't respond to her questions, but instead wearily offered, "You may call me if you are in need of urgent assistance in the coming days, Iza Carter. I wish both of you well."

Iza and Volodya walked slowly out of the BKA building after Volodya retrieved his Swiss Army tool and their phones. They said nothing as they walked three blocks from the building, then rapidly shook out their pockets and felt through their clothing for any tracking devices. Finding none, Volodya spun Iza around toward him, hugged her, and said, "Iza, I think you are in final stretch to learn everyone who is involved in this, so maybe they can all be stopped. You will win your race to accomplish this."

"No, Volodya. My mom ran out from the crowd and tripped me. It doesn't matter to me anymore if I figure it out and win," Iza said sadly. "Maybe I cared at one point, but I don't care anymore." She shook her head, tears welling up in her eyes. "I only want the two of us to stay safe."

Volodya ran his hand tenderly down her cheek. "Iza, you cannot change what your mom did, but power to accept what happened and eventually to become happy again resides within you. And I think you are kick-ass girl. You will be happy again." Volodya quickly added, "Bobby at my work told me that word 'kick-ass'; I hope I used it right." Iza smiled, while tears ran down her cheeks.

◆

As they walked briskly back to the hotel, they eventually came to the Reichstag building. All at once, they were engulfed within a large group of Japanese tourists moving to cross the street from the visitor center to the steps leading to the main entrance of the lower house of Germany's national legislature. It was nearing civil twilight, and the tourists were quickly assembling for a group photo in front of the building on the steps, after having passed through security screening.

Iza glanced ahead and spotted Alex Schröder and Stephan Gabel talking with someone who was blocked from her view. They were standing on the sidewalk, not far from the tourist group. She grabbed Volodya by the forearm, pulling him along with her to remain hidden among the Japanese tourists. They moved to the rear of the group. "It's Alex Schröder and Stephan Gabel," she worriedly whispered. "Don't let them see us!" They watched as the men continued conversing with the unknown person. The crowd cleared near Schröder and Gabel, revealing the man with the shaved head.

"I wonder why they're meeting with him outside of work?"

"Maybe they make extra payment to him for photographs he took of us leaving Café Bleibtreu."

"It wouldn't surprise me."

"Keep head down," Volodya quietly ordered as he saw the two German Bundestag members move. Schröder and Gabel abruptly turned and slowly jogged up the steps, disappearing inside the Reichstag building. The man with the shaved head turned to walk in the direction from which Volodya and Iza had just come. He was wearing a turtleneck underneath his sport coat, likely to hide bruising on his throat. He passed by them, obviously annoyed as he pushed and limped through the throng of the gathering Japanese tour group.

Volodya and Iza stood quietly at the rear of the group, afraid to move. They continued watching until they lost sight of the man with the shaved head. They gazed at each other questioningly.

"Is it safe?" Iza whispered.

They remained at the rear of the group and kept watch in the direction where the man had disappeared from their view.

"What else can happen today? Pretty soon, I'm going to have a nervous breakdown."

The group was ready for their photo, yet Volodya and Iza were still afraid to move. The Japanese tourists were oblivious of the two of them standing at the rear of their group. Iza turned toward Volodya's shoulder to hide her face, but Volodya simply stood at attention, unsure what else to do, while the tour leader took multiple snapshots using several cell phone cameras. The group then rushed up the steps to the visitor entrance.

Volodya and Iza continued cautiously on their way, no longer able to hide within the group of tourists. Iza suddenly giggled inappropriately, considering how narrowly they'd missed walking into the conversation between the two German Bundestag members and the man with the shaved head.

"What is funny, Iza?"

She could barely get out her words as she laughed. "What are those Japanese tourists going to think when they notice an eastern European guy photobombing their group picture?"

Her sudden inappropriate laughter infected Volodya. "What does 'photobombing' mean?" he asked with a chuckle.

"It's a relatively new verb in the English language. It describes the act of spoiling someone's photo by unexpectedly appearing in it." Volodya grabbed Iza's hand and the two giggled as they continued on their way, the image firmly in mind. They didn't notice that the man with the shaved head had turned back and was following them at a distance.

◆

The two eventually returned to the hotel after stopping to buy vodka and *Döner* for their supper. They sat in the room on a small bench near the bed, setting the bags containing their Döner on the nightstand across from them. Volodya had absconded with two glasses from the Meininger cafeteria, and he took them from his jacket pockets. He poured vodka for each of them and they toasted.

"Budmo—let us be."

"Budmo." Iza smiled at Volodya, though the thought of her mother's betrayal saddened her.

"May I offer you our specials for evening?" Volodya inquired in a formal voice, trying to cheer her up.

"And what are the specials on your menu, handsome waiter?"

"Our restaurant serves Döner 1 or Döner 2. You may make your choice," he offered as he held the two bags in front of Iza.

"May I ask the difference between Döner 1 and Döner 2?"

"There is no difference in food—we both ordered our Döner with everything—except one of them comes with special prize."

"Hmm. I'll choose Döner 1."

"Ahh, ding, ding, ding! You are winner! By choosing Döner 1, you get dessert later tonight after your dinner."

"And what is on the dessert menu, handsome waiter?"

"*I* am on dessert menu," Volodya said as he winked at Iza and laughed in his deepest voice. "For dessert, I will make hay with you."

"Handsome waiter, what would have happened if I'd chosen Döner 2?"

After a brief pause, Volodya shrugged and grinned. "You will never know, will you?"

After they'd eaten the Döner, Volodya reminded Iza, "We need to call Tony tonight. Herr Kühn said Tony wanted our call as soon as possible, but we have not called him."

"I really don't want to call Tony, Volodya. I know he didn't have much choice, but he betrayed us . . . sort of. And anyway, what's he going to tell me that I want to hear right now? I need some time to process . . . you know . . . everything."

"Maybe his admin found apartment for us."

"I suppose, but I'm afraid he's going to tell me to call my mom tonight, and I *can't* do that yet."

"I think you need to call Tony. And you said Roger left message too. You need to call him."

They walked out to the Hauptbahnhof at 20:30. The steps leading to the train station were bustling with people on this relatively warm Thursday evening. Iza called Tony first.

"Iza, I've been waiting for your call; I was getting worried that something happened to the two of you."

"Tony, lots of 'somethings' happened to us in the last . . . oh . . . say twenty hours. I could start with our walk back to the hotel last night and end with our walk past the Reichstag building late this afternoon. In between, Volodya and I got attacked by the security guard from imperative Energie. Volodya was accused of shoplifting—thanks to you. Let's see . . . we were taken into custody by the Polizei and then dragged into Kühn's office at the BKA. Just minutes later, Kühn accused me of being my mom's conduit—of schlepping documents to *my* Russian case officer. Volodya and I had to defend ourselves; he was going to detain us! Oh, and I almost forgot. Kühn also told me that my mom gave a voluntary statement to the FBI; I guess that means she's for sure guilty of espionage. Then, we nearly ran into Alex Schröder, Stephan Gabel, and the same security guard who attacked us, when we walked past the Reichstag building coming back to our hotel here. We were only meters away from them! So, all-in-all, I'd say that's a lot of somethings to happen to us," Iza's voice cracked with emotion as she summarized all that had happened.

"You're not angry with me about the phone store, are you?"

"Angry? No." Iza let out a rueful laugh. "Disappointed? Yeah. I guess I understand why you did what you did to us. But it wasn't fun, Tony." She sighed loudly.

"Ellen wants you to call her on Saturday. She wants to talk to you about your mom. Iza, you're going to have to call your mom at some point."

"I knew you'd say that. I'm sorry, Tony. I . . . I'm not ready for that call yet. I know you guys were all good friends for longer than I've been around. But you have to understand, I'm *grieving*. I lost my mom, yet, she's not actually dead. And apparently, she didn't care if I died as long as she met her objectives, whatever those were. That's a *lot* to ask me to process in a day. I'm just a young adult. I already had to deal with my dad's killing as a kid. This is almost worse."

"I'm sorry, Iza. I'll arrange for you to call her when you're ready. Don't think that we're trying to pressure you. Is Volodya there?" Iza said nothing in reply and handed the phone to Volodya, then walked away to sit at the base of the steps to the Hauptbahnhof.

"Hey, Tony."

"Volodya, my admin found a new apartment for you guys. It's in the Kreuzberg borough and it looks pretty nice, at least in the online photos. It's not very big, but it does have a washer and a large drying rack. The kitchen is small, but not tiny. I'll have the CIA people comb through your things at your old apartment and bring everything over to the new place. I'll need your old address; I think I had it at one time, but I can't find it in the mess on my desk. My admin said you'll be able to move in on Saturday; the landlord will meet you there at 9:00 with the keys."

The two men exchanged the addresses. "Tony, my rent was paid for by U.S. government. Can you arrange with new place? And for phone too? I do not get much pay from Ukraine right now, as you can imagine."

"I'll figure out how to do that. Otherwise, how is, um, everything?"

Volodya looked over and saw that Iza was now crying. "We are—um, yes—we are okay, I think. Tony, can you call Roger and tell him Iza will call him tomorrow. I think both of us had lot of stress for couple of days and we need time alone to recover. Thank you for finding apartment for us and for phone and really for everything else. I need to go now."

Volodya turned off Iza's phone and went to sit with her. They didn't see the man with the shaved head watching them from the entrance of the Hauptbahnhof. There were too many people on the steps. "Iza, we need to go to hotel. We need to sleep." He helped Iza up and the two walked back to the hotel room, disappearing in the crowd before entering the Meininger building.

They took a shower together and for the first time, Iza saw all of the bruising on Volodya's body from the fight on the bridge. His forearms were contused from his elbows to his wrists. His buttocks and lower back were black and blue where he'd been forced to the ground during the fight, and his right arm was discolored where the man with the shaved head had pulled violently at his arm as Volodya choked him.

"Volodya, I think it's dangerous to have me as your girlfriend," Iza said sorrowfully.

Friday, November 4 (Day 24)

Iza felt terribly dejected. "Volodya, I need you to hold me. I feel so bad." Volodya reached for her on the bed, pulled her to himself, and then kissed her affectionately. She suddenly recoiled. "Your breath smells like garlic!"

Volodya laughed softly. "I have news for you. Yours does too."

"Döner breath!" The two raced to the sink and madly brushed their teeth and tongues. Volodya breathed out toward Iza. "Now you smell like garlic toothpaste."

"I have idea." Volodya poured them each a small glass of vodka. "We gargle." Iza gargled with the vodka and spat into the sink. Volodya gargled and swallowed. "I cannot waste it. I'm Ukrainian," he said, grinning. He breathed out on her again.

"Now you smell like garlic-flavored vodka." Iza ran back and jumped onto the bed, kneeling on the bedding while facing Volodya. "I guess I'll just have to *suffer*," she said, smiling sadly. "I need you to hold me . . . I need to stop thinking about stuff."

Volodya came to her, and the two kissed each other repeatedly, periodically giggling about their horrid breath. They finally lay on the bed holding hands.

"Volodya, I need to run today. I need to blow off some steam. I can't call Roger until later today anyway because of the time difference. If I get some stress relief from a run, I might have Tony arrange a call with my mother too."

"What does 'blow off steam' mean?"

"Sorry. It means to get rid of pent-up energy or strong emotions. In my case, I've got to get rid of some strong emotions. I need to run far enough and fast enough that I just stop thinking. I'm driving myself crazy."

"Maybe we can find place to go indoors. I cannot run with you yet; I do not want you to run outdoors alone. Kühn said we need to be careful next few days. If we find indoor place, maybe they have stationary bike I can ride. We need coffee; then we can check for place to run."

It was drizzling, so they quickly located a coffee shop in the covered shopping area of the Hauptbahnhof, then scanned their phones in search of an indoor running track. "Iza, this place has rooftop track and bikes too. It is only six kilometers south of us. What do you think? You'd have to run in light rain, but maybe it is okay." He showed Iza photos of the track on the building rooftop.

"That'll work. I need to run."

When they arrived at the gym, they purchased a couple's day pass, registering as Mr. and Mrs. Carter. Volodya chose a stationary cycle in a dark corner for his workout, propped his phone on the upturned bike handles, and read updates on the war as he pedaled with increasing intensity, his anger growing at the stupidity of "Russia's" war. His country was being destroyed, bit by bit.

Iza climbed the stairs to the rooftop track; there was a stunning view of cloudy Berlin from the roof. The light rain temporarily stopped as she ran a few turns of the track at a moderate pace. She then raced at full throttle. A gym trainer raced behind her, expecting she'd run only a lap or two of the track at this pace. But she continued racing, and he eventually dropped off the track and watched her in astonished silence. When she'd finished, she'd run ten kilometers in just over thirty-eight minutes.

They made their way back to the hotel, now much more relaxed from their strenuous workouts. By 14:00, Iza was ready to call Roger.

"Iza, you doing okay?" Roger asked with concern.

"I'm hanging in there, Roger. I guess I need to call my mother—maybe today. How are you?"

"Yeah, kid, I'm okay, but I just can't believe it . . . I mean about your mom. Tony called me last night; he told me most of what's happened to you the past few days, too . . . at least what he could officially tell me. I guess you weren't quite giving me the truth when I called you about my dream last week."

Roger suddenly blurted out, "I talked to your mom yesterday and she . . . she reminded me of something that I thought was all over years ago. I guess it's on her mind right now. I don't know if Tony told you, kid, but your mom is being sedated. She's pretty upset, and I think they decided they needed to do that for her. She's drifting back in time, and then coming back to the present. She knows what she did . . . I mean she's not that out-of-it. But maybe you should wait a few days before you call her. Like, call when they stop the medication."

"What 'something' did you think was all over years ago?"

"Oh, nothing important for you to know," Roger said dismissively, trying to cover his blunder. "Like I said, maybe you should wait to call her, okay?" He then abruptly changed the subject.

"I've got some dates for you for my Christmas visit. But I'll call you with those later; the trip isn't important right now. You are doing okay, right kid? I know this is tough for you. I'll help you however I can. Really, you just let me know and I'm on it."

"Thanks, Roger. I love you. I have to go here, but maybe we can talk about your trip plans next week," Iza said as she felt herself tearing up again. She didn't want to cry on the call with Roger; he'd be upset if that happened.

"Yeah, I'll call you next week. And call me if you need someone to talk to."

Iza hung up the phone. The tears came again but stopped when she saw Volodya smiling at her as he waited for her on the steps of the Hauptbahnhof. Iza recalled Roger's words and wondered, *What don't I know about Mom from the past that Roger thought was "all over" years ago?*

◆

"Iza, how are you and Volodya? Anything I can help with?" Tony offered when she called a short time later.

"Yeah, actually there is. But first, I need to thank you for finding the apartment for us and for everything else. I'm really sorry I didn't thank you yesterday. The past few days have been stressful. We *so* appreciate all your help, Tony. I probably didn't sound like it yesterday, but I know we couldn't have gotten through to this point without everything you've done to help us. And now . . . I have another big favor to ask." Iza continued sheepishly, "Can you reimburse me for our hotel bill here? It's for four nights, and neither of us can afford it right now."

"Sure, I'll find a way to do that. I'll let you know if I hear anything from Wilhelm too; I'm sure it's on your minds—I mean the software and the people still out there. Apart from that, I hope I'll see you two on Monday evening. Will you join me for dinner at the embassy? My admin will get you the details by early Monday. And I hope you both like the apartment; remember to pick up the keys tomorrow at 9:00. In the meantime, call me any time—day or night—if you need something."

"Tony, we'll be standing at the door of that apartment waiting. We've got a lot of things we're going to have to replace from Volodya's apartment, and neither of us has much money available. Thank you for picking up the hotel bill."

Iza hesitated a moment, then asked cautiously, "I've got another thing I need to ask. Do you know something about my mom from the past that I don't know? I just talked with Roger, and he made some comment about how he thought something with my mom was 'all over' years ago."

"Honestly, Iza, I don't know what he was referring to."

"Can you arrange for me to call her later today?"

"Yeah. Be aware your mom is being sedated. Since the FBI took her into custody and she thinks Günther left her, she's been pretty agitated."

"Roger told me that. But I think I'll try to call her. A part of me needs to ask her why she did it. Let me know the time; I'll wait for your message. See you Monday, Tony. Have a safe flight, and thanks again for all the help. Tell everyone I miss them." Iza turned off her phone, still worried that their location could be tracked.

Volodya suggested they sit at a coffee shop in the Hauptbahnhof shopping center while awaiting Tony's message. The cool, damp Berlin weather was chilling, so they drank coffee and talked about everything and nothing. Tony eventually left his message with the time—20:00 in Berlin—and the phone number to call.

They considered strolling to the Kreuzberg neighborhood to locate their new apartment but then decided to avoid the rain and simply walked back to the hotel. Volodya took Iza's hand when they arrived in the room and danced with her to some melody in his head. They had to sway back and forth between the bed and the wall in the tiny space available. As they danced, Iza sought Volodya's advice.

"Volodya, I'm *terrified* to call my mom. What should I say? I thought about Herr Kühn's method of interrogation—asking lots of questions, like, Why did you do this? Were you unhappy with your life? How did the Russians find you? When did this all start? What happens now? When do you get sentenced? . . . Do you love me? But I don't think I can do that. It would make me cry, and I don't want to cry anymore."

"Why not use his other method? Just let your mom talk. See what she has to say, and then you only need to listen."

It was nearly 20:00 when they walked back out near the Hauptbahnhof entrance to a dimly lit area near the top of the stairway. Although the light rain had temporarily abated, there were few people using the stairs on this cool, damp Friday evening. Volodya walked down the steps, away from Iza, to give her privacy while she made the call, but he continued watching her from a distance.

"Hello, Iza. They told me it was you," Elise's voice sounded detached, as if she were mentally in a far-off place.

"Mom, tell me what happened," Iza started, using Volodya's suggestion.

Elise began in a dreamy voice. "Iza, I don't know. Your father and I had such a wonderful life planned . . . just the two of us. We'd be vagabonds, working for the State Department in Europe. He was in D.C. applying for his first appointment to the Embassy in Berlin, and then we figured we'd move across Europe every few years: Paris next. Then London. Maybe Madrid. It'd be exciting . . . even a little exotic. And if we were careful, we'd have enough money for other travel during our time off.

"But before that appointment in Berlin, I unexpectedly got pregnant. Iza, you were a mistake . . . an accident. I wanted an abortion with all my heart. A kid wasn't in my plans. Your father finally went along, and we got the date set but then he went drinking with Roger in one of their sessions a few nights before the date. He asked Roger what he thought about the abortion. Roger told your father it was not his decision to make, but Peter and I should think carefully about it. A kid would definitely cause a huge change in our lives but it wouldn't necessarily be all bad. After that session, your father asked me not to get the abortion. He promised that he'd get a nanny for the baby—that we could still keep all our plans—that everything would work out. So, I went along."

Iza was shaken by Elise's revelation. *Mom didn't want me. I was an "accident."*

There was a long pause, and Iza could hear her mother breathing into the phone. Elise finally continued speaking. "Right after you were born, your father got the appointment to Berlin and we moved. He kept his word, and we hired a full-time nanny for you. Your father doted on you. But we didn't have the money or freedom we'd planned.

And besides, you were such a homely, scrawny kid. You weren't cute like Tony and Ellen's Greta. You were such a quiet child too; I always thought there was something wrong with you. Your father kept his word though. We did move around Europe—Paris, London, back to Berlin—but you were like an anchor around our necks. Everything in our lives revolved around you. I tried very hard to love you, but I just couldn't."

Iza was fighting back tears. *I never felt close to you then, but it didn't register that you didn't love me, because there were so many other people around me who did. I thought it was just who you were.* There was another long pause.

"What happened then, mom?" Iza prodded, barely able to hold her tears at bay.

"Then Peter took the job in the Middle East. It was so much harder for me there. I was alone with little work and there were no nannies there. When your father was killed, my dreams died with him.

Tony tried to help us; he blamed himself for your father's death, but it wasn't his fault. He was only carrying out orders from the higher-ups. And the Department didn't help me. I had to move back to D.C. to find a better job at State. They provided no help finding housing for us. You needed help after your father's murder, and I couldn't afford it. You name it—State didn't help us enough. It made me so bitter."

Elise continued, "I tried again to love you, and I think I did for a time. I gave you riding lessons, I got you into a good school . . . I provided a decent home. I encouraged you to get into cross-country. But *I* never recovered emotionally after Peter died."

Iza's breathing was becoming irregular, and her body was quivering as she tried to tamp down her emotions. The move back to D.C. was the time she'd felt closest to her mother; it was when she felt her mother's love.

"Then, while I continued to struggle, you suddenly became something. You excelled at cross-country running; you started doing well in school and got into American with a scholarship. Then, you got accepted into graduate school. You got prettier with age while I got older and had nothing to look forward to." Elise's voice rose with emotion. "You were off starting your own life, and I was left alone—all alone. It made me even more bitter. I started to *resent* you when you went away to college and grad school."

Elise continued talking quietly. "That's when I met Boris Kuznetsov from the Russian Embassy while I was interpreting for a meeting he was at. He promised me a better life. I'd be able to travel. I could finally buy a Valentino dress, a Gucci handbag, and a sapphire ring. I only had to do a few things for the Russians, and then I'd be free to stop. But they wouldn't let me stop. They threatened me."

Elise paused momentarily, then continued on in a dreamy, sedated voice. "And then I met Günther, and I had someone to love again. We had plans together. But the Russians wouldn't let me go. I had to do something big for them. In the meantime, you got your job in Berlin. You were leaving to live the life I'd planned for myself—what *I* wanted—and what I never had, all because of *you*!"

Iza staggered on the steps. She felt as though her mother had taken Lucretia's dagger and stabbed her repeatedly in the heart. She couldn't stand it any longer and abruptly ended the call without saying another word, turning off her phone.

The light rain started again as she walked unsteadily down the stairs to meet Volodya on the middle landing of the Hauptbahnhof steps. He suddenly ran past her up the steps, and she spun around as he rushed by.

Volodya punched the man with the shaved head in his abdomen as the man charged down the steps toward Iza. The man hadn't noticed Volodya standing behind the pillar on the landing; he'd thought that Iza was alone. Iza froze in a state of shock, overcome by the combination of her mother's rejection and sudden, extreme fear.

Volodya punched the man a second time as he struggled to recover from the first blow. The man with the shaved head doubled over, then lunged toward Volodya. He knocked

Volodya over, and the two tumbled together down the Hauptbahnhof steps toward Iza. Volodya hit the back of his head on the concrete middle landing and lay still, concussed by the blow. The man with the shaved head groggily sat up, two steps above Volodya, disoriented by their tumble.

Iza saw Volodya lying motionless on the landing next to her, and let out a guttural cry. She lashed out at the man with the shaved head with the aggression of a wounded animal. She threw herself at him and clawed at his face with her fake fingernails until he bled from the wounds she inflicted. He tried to push her away but was still stunned from his tumble. She repeatedly punched the man in the groin with her clenched fists, screaming and sobbing. He writhed in agony as he lay on the steps. She picked his head up in her hands and smashed it onto the concrete step, the man unable to stop her as he twisted in pain.

Volodya regained consciousness, sat up, and saw Iza attacking the man with the shaved head, her hair now wet and tangled, a wild expression in her eyes. He crawled up the two steps and tried to pull her away from the man, as the man with the shaved head moaned. Two passing men came running to the man's aid.

Volodya screamed, "Iza, stop!" He held her near to him and whispered, "We need to go back to hotel now. Come with me." Volodya's voice shook her from her dazed state. Volodya grabbed her phone from where she'd dropped it on the steps, and they stumbled away, quickly disappearing into the hotel.

Once in the room, the two sat together momentarily on the edge of the bed. "I thought he killed you . . ." Iza said, her voice trailing off. She suddenly started sobbing, her body shaking as she dropped onto the bed. Volodya lay next to her and held her as she sobbed, overcome by her raw emotions.

I hope man with shaved head was too hurt to see us going into hotel, but did those guys who came to help him see us come here? Will they call Polizei? Do Russians know we are here? We need to leave here soon, but there is nowhere to go tonight. Volodya held Iza for much of the night, unable to sleep as he listened carefully to every noise in the Meininger Hotel. He finally dozed off near dawn.

Saturday, November 5 (Day 25)

Iza lay in bed dwelling on an assortment of her terrifying recollections from Friday evening.

I never should have dragged Volodya into this mess. I thought I killed him last night. I couldn't handle it if I lost him. He probably has a huge goose egg on the back of his head, and it's all my fault. I need to make sure nothing else happens to him. We have to get through this alive . . . or at least he does . . . I love him.

Her thoughts drifted to the man with the shaved head. *Who exactly is he? Did Schröder and Gabel order him to follow us, or did someone from the Russian Embassy do that? Or, did he do it on his own, for revenge? Why didn't we notice him following us after we left the Reichstag? Did I hurt him badly enough that he won't be out there waiting for us, or is there someone else to take his place? How do we get out of here safely?*

Volodya was right. I can't change Mom's betrayal of our country. I can't change her resentful bitterness. Those are her own actions . . . her own choices. I can't force her to love me. The power to accept that and to be happy again resides within me. But it's really hard to admit to myself that Mom doesn't love me.

Volodya awoke and said, "Iza, we need to leave here soon and we need to go out different way. But first tell me, what happened with your mom last night?"

"I will tell you everything at some point, but right now, it's more important that we get out of here safely . . . to our new apartment. I don't know how we can be sure no one is following us though. But we're going to spend the day together setting up our apartment, and no one is going to ruin that for us. How's your head?" She carefully touched the large bump on the back of Volodya's head.

"It hurts little bit, but I will be okay." He smiled at her.

"Let's pack and blow this joint."

"What does that mean?"

"Sorry. It means we're leaving here quickly in search of something better; hopefully, our new apartment . . . and hopefully with no one following us to it."

"Iza, can I take cold shower before we blow this joint? Otherwise, I will need to make hay with my kick-ass girlfriend before we leave." Iza managed a slight smile as she carefully packed the expensive Chanel suit into Volodya's duffel bag. They left the building through the Meininger Hotel cafeteria, mingling with the morning crowd of weekend breakfasters.

It was a cool morning, but the sun was shining brightly. They waited outside their second-floor apartment for the landlord to arrive with the keys, periodically smiling at each other as they rearranged their grocery purchases in the overflowing totes they'd just carried from a nearby market on Oranienstraße. They hadn't noticed anyone following them and hoped they had done a better job avoiding surveillance than before.

At 9:00, Yusuf Celik, the building owner and landlord, promptly arrived with the keys. "Mr. and Mrs. Korsun, I presume?"

"Yes, I am Volodymyr Korsun and this is Iza."

"Pleased to meet you. My first rule is *no drugs* here," Yusuf announced as he cautiously looked over the two of them. Iza realized that her red and swollen eyes, pale skin, the discoloration around her right eye, her unkempt hair from having slept with it wet and uncombed, and their thin bodies all suggested drug use.

Volodya quickly replied, "We are not interested in drugs or smoking. We listen to classical music, and sometimes maybe we play it somewhat loud, but that does not happen often.

We are respectful of our neighbors. You will find us quiet and honest people. And we pay our rent on time."

Yusuf handed Volodya two keys. "I think you will find the apartment quite satisfactory. Your friends were here many hours yesterday and did a nice job preparing it for you. I checked on it myself after they'd gone. If there are any problems with the apartment, I live on the ground floor—apartment 103. Again, very nice to meet you." With that, Yusuf disappeared down the stairway.

"I wonder which friends were here?" Iza asked out loud as they cautiously unlocked the door and peered inside.

"Oh my gosh! It's *so* cool!"

They carried in the grocery totes and looked at their bright, bohemian-style apartment.

"Look, Iza—Denon CD player and receiver—not new, but very nice. And these are *new* speakers! Wow!" While Volodya examined the electronics gear, Iza quickly glanced around the rooms. The apartment had hardwood floors throughout the adjoining living, dining, and kitchen areas and in the separate bedroom; off-white-painted walls; and high ceilings, which made the rooms look larger than they actually were. There were warm red-toned Turkish rugs in the living area, in the small dining area under the table, and near the bed; they were not new but still beautiful. The living area had a long, deep, gray, upholstered sofa with multiple colorful throw pillows in warm red tones strewn about. In front of the sofa was a very long, low wooden coffee table. At the far end of the living area, potted houseplants and herbs in wicker baskets were arranged in front of a wall of windows.

"Iza look, they even replaced my CDs." Volodya excitedly glanced through the CD titles as Iza moved to the kitchen.

The galley kitchen was larger than the one in Volodya's old apartment. One wall had lower cabinets, a large sink, and a gas range, with open storage shelving above. The other had a small refrigerator and additional lower cabinet space. Whoever decorated the apartment had found replacements for all

Volodya's broken dishes and glassware. Nothing was new, but everything was carefully chosen. Volodya's mom's soup pot was carefully stowed in a lower cabinet. Iza opened the refrigerator; a bottle of Prosecco and a bottle of Nemiroff vodka were nestled inside the door. *These must have been purchased on Tony's instruction,* she thought.

"It is perfect place. We cannot thank Tony enough, I think."

Volodya looks so happy. I know it was hard for him to lose all his stuff after losing so much in Ukraine.

"Let's have brunch. I'm starving."

While they ate, Volodya said, "Iza, we need to call Tony today before his flight leaves for Berlin, but we need to be careful going out from apartment. Maybe he has news from Herr Kühn about imperative Energie. We should learn what is happening there. And we need to thank Tony again. This place is unbelievable."

"I'm sorry. I can't talk to Tony today. I know he'll ask about the phone call, and I really don't have enough left inside me to handle that today. He'll be in Berlin tomorrow, and we'll have dinner with him on Monday. Do you think we can wait?"

"I think it is important to know if Herr Kühn has any news. I can call Tony. But maybe you need to tell me what happened last night in your call. What did your mom explain to you?" Iza hesitated as she picked at the fruit salad she'd prepared for their brunch.

"Okay. Well . . . Mom told me she spied for the Russians for the money. She's still angry with my government because she doesn't think the State Department helped her enough after my dad died. And she wanted to travel and buy some fancy clothes—stuff she couldn't afford—and they promised her money. That's why she did it, I guess. It's hard to believe, but . . . I'm not my mom. And then, the Russians wouldn't let her stop when she wanted out."

"Iza, I can see in your eyes there was something more she said to you. Am I right?"

Iza squirmed in her chair, and her voice trembled as she reluctantly answered, "Yeah, there was a lot more. She told me I was an accident. She never wanted me and she never really loved me. She thought I was an ugly kid and too quiet—like maybe something was wrong with me. As a kid, I was an anchor around my parents' necks. Then later, when I did well in school and stuff, she said she *resented* me. Her resentment grew when I got this job in Berlin. She essentially told me I ruined her life by being born." Iza started to cry.

As Iza spoke, Volodya's eyes opened wide in disgust, then filled with tears for her. "You know, Iza, you are beautiful person, on outside, but more importantly, on inside. Elise is sick. She has something wrong in her head. Do not listen to this garbage she said to you. She only tried to shift her own unhappiness into your head to make you unhappy too." He smiled at Iza and took her hand. "You should take nice shower and relax today. We can look more at apartment together, and I will call Tony later. I think whoever picked up CDs bought quite a few extras I never heard before. Maybe you know some of them. Later I will cook dinner for us, and we will listen to music together, okay?" Volodya squeezed Iza's hand and smiled at her again.

Iza tried to push her mother's words out of her head, to stay focused on happiness. "Sure. That sounds fun."

Volodya walked two blocks away from the apartment building to place the call to Tony; he was paranoid that someone would find them at their new apartment. "Hey, Tony. This is Volodya. Are you ready for another long flight?"

"Yeah, not looking forward to it. How are things there? Is Iza there with you?"

"Um, no. Tony, first we are in new apartment, and we cannot thank you enough. I never had anything like this in my life since I left my parents' home. It must be close to forty square meters—and all my broken things are replaced. We are *so* happy. And Iza and I thank you for Prosecco and vodka. That was very kind of you."

"I'm glad it's a nice place."

"Did you hear from Herr Kühn? What is happening with imperative Energie?"

"So yeah, I did hear from him. He said he'd call you, but maybe he was figuring he'd let you two know everything on Monday."

On Monday? Why Monday? Volodya thought.

"Let's see. Morozov and Petrov are booked on a flight to Ankara, leaving tomorrow afternoon. They're still running static surveillance on imperative Energie. They don't see anyone at the company displaying unusual behavior yet. I know they're closely watching Markus Peters; they've got a mobile team assigned to him. Wilhelm seems to think if anyone is going to make a move, it'll likely be within the next twenty-four hours, around when Morozov and Petrov leave."

"What time did you talk to Herr Kühn? Did he mention anything about surveillance on security guard from imperative Energie?"

"I talked with him yesterday; I don't remember the exact time. He didn't mention anything specifically about their security guard, but he's the man who attacked you on the Moltkebrücke, right? Why do you want to know?"

"No important reason. I only wondered."

"Kühn hasn't done anything about the software yet, at least to my knowledge. I'm pretty sure he didn't want to cause an all-out panic amongst imperative Energie employees before apprehending the traitors to Germany. But I have to believe he'll be alerting the Managing Director imminently. The BKA will be investigating their cybersecurity software application, and Kühn's people will need access to the source code."

"Will Herr Kühn's people need my help with software?"

"He didn't indicate that. He has your number, and . . . I gave him your new address."

"What about Alex Schröder? Iza does not trust him."

"Wilhelm didn't say anything about Schröder, but Schröder probably hasn't been at imperative Energie since the static surveillance was set up. I mean . . . it sounds like their surveillance operation is extensive and they're watching everyone."

They did not watch man with shaved head so well.

After a long pause, Tony asked hesitantly, "Volodya, how was Iza's call with her mom?"

"How can I tell you? She broke Iza's heart. Elise was *so* cruel to her. I maybe should not tell you everything I know; maybe Iza will tell you herself someday. But I cannot imagine that Iza will have anything to do with Elise ever again. I will not let Elise near her."

There was a long pause on the line, and Volodya could hear Tony's irregular breathing. Tony replied very quietly and tearfully, with long pauses between his responses. "I'm devastated this all happened. It's just so hard to believe. Poor Iza. Do your best to comfort her, will you?"

"Yes, Tony. I am trying."

There was another long pause on the line. Tony finally wished them a fun afternoon exploring their new apartment, and reminded Volodya that he'd see them for supper on Monday evening.

By the time Volodya returned to the apartment, Iza had showered and fixed her hair. She'd changed into a black tank top and loose-fitting grey sweatpants—clothing she'd left at her original apartment and hadn't had access to until today. She also wore her citrine earrings. Volodya was glad she looked more relaxed, and the color had returned to her face. Iza was leafing through the CDs, and they picked out a few to listen to later.

After supper, Volodya told Iza what had happened the previous day at imperative Energie. Then they listened to music as they cuddled together on the sofa—first Mahler's Symphony No. 5, a lengthy and deep work requiring their complete concentration, and then Rachmaninoff's Rhapsody on a Theme of Paganini, a dramatic and passionate composition. After they'd listened for nearly two hours, Iza told Volodya that she'd found a CD from a very different music genre in his new collection. It was music from the sixties that her dad had always listened to. It would be very different from the classical works they'd just enjoyed, but she'd also appreciated this music and hoped it would appeal to Volodya.

Iza took off her socks and stepped onto the coffee table. She strode across the table in front of Volodya, smiling at him, then announced loudly, "And *now*, for the pleasure of Mr. Volodymyr Korsun of Ukraine, Iza Carter of the United States of *America* will perform a special dance."

Volodya smiled at Iza's silliness. She bowed, then used the remote to start the Brazilian bossa nova piece that was her dad's favorite. It had a haunting, sensual rhythm.

Iza swayed her hips back and forth to the music, smiling at Volodya as she moved her body across the long coffee table in front of him. Her original intentions were to be funny and see if the music appealed to Volodya, but her movement gradually morphed into a sexually charged dance. She ran her hands through her hair, lifting it above her head as she swayed her slender hips while looking at him seductively. Letting her hair fall back slowly around her shoulders, she ran her hands up and down the length of her body and beckoned for him to come to her.

"Iza, you are making me crazy," Volodya whispered as he stepped onto the table to dance with her.

Iza swayed her hips, then closed her eyes. She suddenly saw Elise coming for her with Lucretia's dagger. Iza opened her eyes quickly, terrified by the vivid image she'd seen in her mind. But Volodya was still smiling and dancing with her on the coffee table. She smiled at him again, brushing her body against his, then moved to the far end of the table. She closed her eyes a second time, but again, Elise was coming for her. Her eyes snapped open, but it was still just her imagination. She closed her eyes a third time, and this time, she only saw

Volodya smiling at her. She opened her eyes as she felt his body against hers. Then she jumped from the table and started leading him to the bedroom. Volodya followed her, still swaying his hips to the bossa nova rhythm, and they reached the bed just as the song ended.

Sunday, November 6 (Day 26)

Volodya was laughing softly.

"What's so funny?"

"You are. Last night was fun, Iza." Volodya turned toward her on the bed and reached for her hand. "I love you."

"I love you too. Did you like the bossa nova music?"

He laughed a bit louder. "How could I *not* like it?"

"Hey . . . I was only wanting the dessert you promised a couple nights ago. I wasn't going to let you forget about my prize."

Suddenly, there was a loud knock at the apartment door. Volodya slipped into his jeans and peered through the door viewer. There were two officers of the Berlin Polizei standing outside the door. He cautiously opened it.

"*Heißen Sie* Volodymyr Korsun?"

Volodya called Iza. The Polizei explained Herr Kühn sent them, as he was unable to reach Volodya by phone. Volodya was to accompany them to the BKA. The request was that he bring everything with him relating to a software problem.

"Iza, tell them I need you to come too and that we need few minutes to get ourselves ready. Can they wait for us?"

"They'll wait in their car outside the building."

The two dressed quickly. Volodya organized his notes and grabbed his laptop. In ten minutes, they were ready to go. As they were leaving the building for the awaiting squad car, Iza saw Yusuf peering at them from his apartment door. *Great. First, he thinks we're drug users; now the Polizei come for us.*

Volodya was immediately brought to the BKA Digital Forensics Laboratory. Iza was told she could sit in an unoccupied cubicle in the waiting area fronting the Lab. An agent handed her several newspapers, then explained where the restrooms were located and where she could find coffee. He said she might have a long wait. Iza skimmed through the papers, then refreshed her coffee. She wandered the short, sterile hallway between the cubicle, the entry area doorway, and the restrooms before paging through the newspapers again.

Being inside the sterile security building brought Elise to her mind again. Elise was likely sitting in detention somewhere in Washington as she awaited an uncertain future in prison. Iza tried to push those thoughts from her mind, but they kept returning. She slid down in the chair in the cubicle, nearly invisible to anyone coming into or leaving the area, and continued paging through the newspapers, trying to distract herself.

After what seemed like an eternity, she checked her watch and saw, to her disappointment, that it was only 10:00. Just then, she heard the voices of two men as they entered the hallway and moved toward the doorway leading to the Lab. The two abruptly stopped outside the doorway, just behind the wall of Iza's cubicle. One man's voice sounded nervous and apologetic, while the other man's voice eventually became increasingly strident as he spat out orders to the other. Iza realized that it was Herr Kühn talking with a subordinate. She quietly listened and mentally translated the heated German conversation taking place on the other side of the cubicle wall.

"We went to pick him up early this morning, but only his girlfriend was there. He simply disappeared! I don't know. Our people swear they didn't see him leave that apartment building. In fact, no one left that building since last evening except an old woman. She looked Turkish—you know, with a head scarf and their way of dressing. The girlfriend says she doesn't know where he went. She has a ticket to Ankara, leaving tomorrow afternoon—same flight as Morozov and Petrov—only tomorrow, not today. We brought her here for questioning. But he just disappeared. He's gone. His laptop, his papers . . . things we saw him bring into the apartment yesterday evening . . . all gone.

"You incompetent fools! How could you have lost him? Did I need to do this surveillance myself? Is that what it would have taken? Of course, he would have *disguised* himself to get away. You needed to look at everyone coming and going from that apartment building. It is so painfully obvious. He left there disguised as an old Turkish woman."

Iza heard Herr Kühn pause, then continue. "I want someone at the airport and at every train station and bus terminal in Berlin, now! Look for him—and his undercover persona! Send your description of the Turkish woman to all agents, along with his. He may change his appearance again before trying to leave the country. Everyone will need a good general description of his physical characteristics—the ones he cannot change so easily. And I want a list of every flight that has already left Berlin on Turkish Airlines and on Pegasus going to Ankara—and to Istanbul—starting from the time you lost visual contact with him. And I want a passenger manifest and passport photos of every adult passenger on each of those flights. And I want those in my office by 14:00. Make that noon!"

Iza heard the two men walk in opposite directions; one pushing through the door into the Lab area and the other quickly scurrying out of the Forensics Lab waiting area.

So, Iza thought, *Markus Peters slipped away from the German authorities. And he's likely taken evidence of everything he's been working on with him. I wonder if he's still in Germany or if he's already on his way to Ankara or Istanbul. Or maybe even already flying on to Moscow.*

◆

At noon, Volodya came out of the Forensics Laboratory for a break. He found Iza napping in the cubicle. He whispered as he rolled his eyes, "Iza, these guys are nuts. They go through every line of code in whole massive program line by line—like they are trying to understand entire program. They are too

German. Yes, application backdoors are best detected by inspecting source code or maybe by statically inspecting binary using automated analysis with human review. But I tell them, no matter what we do, application backdoor analysis is *imperfect*. I think we need to search for *these* lines in code, like what I saw in two small segments on original thumb drive from imperative Energie. These are lines of backdoor code Dmytro has seen guys use in past. We can be more specific later if we need to be. It will take us long, long time using their approach, and maybe we do not have so much time."

"Did you talk to Herr Kühn about it? I saw him enter the Lab around 10:00, but I think he left a few minutes later."

"Yes, but he does not understand coding, and he thinks his people know more than I do. I mean . . . they are really smart guys, no doubt. And, they probably do know more than I do. But it will take many days to do this as they want, and it will still be imperfect analysis."

"Can you just go your own way?"

"What does that mean?"

"It means you can do things in the manner of your own choosing, even if that's different from what the others want to do. Will they know if you're not following their instructions?"

"Hmm. I am not sure, but maybe I can do that. Anyway, I get thirty minutes to eat at canteen."

"Volodya, get this," Iza whispered. "Kühn was arguing with one of his people outside this cubicle before he went into the Lab area. They didn't know I was in here. Markus Peters *disappeared*. They're trying to find him again, but he might have flown out of Berlin for Turkey already—and then maybe on to Moscow. And he took his computer and all his papers with him."

Volodya shook his head in disbelief. "Jezus."

After returning from the canteen with their escort, Volodya disappeared back into the Forensics Laboratory while Iza sat wearily in the cubicle with virtually nothing to do. Thoughts of Elise repeatedly came to her mind; she couldn't shake them off.

At 15:00, she again heard the voices of two men as they entered the hallway. She quietly listened, and once again translated the German conversation. She recognized the voices; it was the same subordinate with Herr Kühn.

"We followed him to the Russian Embassy. He went inside, and he's still there. He's got dual Russian-German citizenship. If he's one of theirs, they'll let him stay there for a long time—maybe until we get tired of waiting for him to leave."

"We will wait until we seal his fate. Those are my orders. And *this* time, remember he could leave there in disguise. I do not think the Russians will be so careful with this one though. His kind are easily replaced by others just like him."

"When he does leave, what excuse can we use for detaining him? It might be difficult to prove his connection to Morozov."

After a short pause, Herr Kühn continued slowly, as if he were formulating a plan as he spoke. "He attacked a couple on the Moltkebrücke four nights ago. Detain him for that reason. I can force the couple to testify against him."

Iza's eyes opened wide as she heard the two men again walk in opposite directions. The hallway became quiet. Iza thought, *The man with the shaved head must be holed up in the Russian Embassy. But Kühn was talking about us!*

A few minutes later, Herr Kühn left the Lab. Shortly afterward, Volodya came out of the Forensics Lab for a break. He sat with Iza in the cubicle as she whispered to him, "Kühn was talking with the same guy just outside here before he went into the Lab area again. The guy said the man with the shaved head is holed up in the Russian Embassy, and they're going to wait him out and try to grab him when he leaves. When his guy asked what excuse they could use for detaining him, Kühn said they'd detain him for attacking *us* on the Moltkebrücke! He said he'd force *us* to testify about what happened. I'm going to ask Tony if Kühn can actually do that."

Volodya shook his head again in disbelief. "Iza, I am getting so tired. My eyes, my neck, and back of my head are killing me. They do not want me to leave here, but I have to go to data center tomorrow, and I will need to rest my eyes for work. At least I am going my own way now." Iza massaged Volodya's shoulders, then gently pulled on the base of his head to relax his neck while avoiding the large goose egg. He then disappeared back into the Forensics Lab.

Iza found a pen in the cubicle and started informally doodling on the margins of the newspapers. She drew her rendition of the man with the shaved head having devil horns. Then she drew Alex Schröder caught in a spiderweb with a giant spider coming to suck out his juices. She'd never seen Markus Peters, but she drew her depiction of an old Turkish woman carrying a laptop computer. Next, she drew Herr Kühn with a halo on his head but carrying the devil's pitchfork in his hand. Finally, she drew Elise with Lucretia's dagger in her hand and a heart shape nearby. She drew drops of blood dripping from the dagger and the heart. Iza looked at her works of art, then scrunched up the newspaper pages and threw them in the restroom waste container.

It was 20:30 when Volodya reappeared at the cubicle entrance wearing his leather jacket and carrying his laptop and papers. "Iza, we need to blow this joint. My brain is *so* tired. They want me to stay, but I said no. I need to leave now."

"What happened?"

"I went my own way. I think they are all very smart guys, but maybe I am more practical guy. Their guys are doing same thing now for rest of program. It took me long time to convince them. I found backdoor code in newest application version from second of November in section of code I was given, but not in same section of nineteenth of October version. These guys told me imperative Energie pushes out software updates every two weeks. They do updates one week, then send them out following week because they test everything again before sending out. This second of November version is scheduled to go out on ninth of November. They can still stop it. Of course, we have not examined entire program yet, but this is good sign."

"What about Peters? If he took the software code and all his notes and stuff with him and gets away with it, does his knowledge give the Russians an advantage?"

"Yes. It is always advantage to deeply understand anything you are trying to hack. You then have better idea where application has vulnerabilities. I think imperative Energie customers will need to be very observant for long time—to look for network intrusions. Maybe imperative Energie will use this as 'opportunity' to sell their threat intelligence services."

"Yeah, I can see it now. That'd be something their Marketing Director, Kristin, would be into doing. I can imagine her pouty-lipped customer presentation. Iza mimicked Kristin's seductive accent. "I am so sorry, but we screwed up with our cybersecurity software. Now, please pay us more money to protect you by using our software *and* our threat intelligence services. If you need more information about these services, your sales rep, Johannes, will send it to you from his prison cell."

Volodya grinned at Iza's impersonation. "Now you just need Kristin's sexy beige blouse."

As they made their way toward the BKA exit, Volodya stopped to pick up his Swiss Army tool and their phones. While waiting for BKA security, Iza asked, "Do you think it's safe for us to walk back to the apartment? I *really* need some fresh air, but I'm scared about being followed."

"You heard man with shaved head is in Russian Embassy and Germans are there to guard against his escape. If we do not walk near there, will anyone else know where we are? I do not think so. But we still need to be careful."

Iza suddenly changed the subject. "Volodya, what do you think about Alex Schröder?"

"Iza, I do not know. I am too tired to think about Schröder."

The two left the BKA, strolling back to their new apartment, Volodya with his arm around Iza's shoulder for much of the time. "You know, Iza, I am thinking about Elise, and then I am thinking about my mom and dad. They are all dead in some way. Which is harder? To have parents who were brutally murdered when they did nothing except have photos of their kids, who happened to be in military uniforms? Or, to die like Elise? I am thinking it is much, much harder for you than for me. I have no regrets with my mom and dad. I have only happy memories. Of course, I am heartbroken, and my life will always be changed without them. I am even thinking maybe my mom looks down on us now and says, Volodya, you were right not to date that neighbor girl from Mariupol. And then I wish my mom could have met you."

Volodya stopped walking and turned in front of Iza as he quietly said, "But you have to deal with different feelings, and it makes me very sad for you. I promise to help you though. I have strategies I use when I am depressed about my mom and dad, and maybe those will comfort you too. It will take long time for your heart to heal, I think. Hopefully I can always be here for you—that Russia's war will not take me away."

Volodya kissed her. Then the two continued cautiously on their way.

Monday, November 7 (Day 27)

"Iza, I am leaving for data center," Volodya gently shook Iza awake.

"I'll call you at your morning break if I can. Maybe by then I'll know the details of our dinner with Tony at the embassy. I hope Kühn calls Tony with an update. It'd sure be nice to know we don't need to be looking over our shoulders any longer."

"I think Russians will leave us alone. They got two more guys expelled from their embassy, and their spy ring is broken. They will need to lick their wounds for little bit, I am guessing."

"I hope you're right."

Iza left soon after Volodya. She brought the Chanel suit to change into for the dinner but added her black tank top to the tote bag, not wanting to show any skin on her chest when wearing the suit jacket with nothing underneath.

Iza first stopped at the CIA Disguise Lab. Tina was sitting near the entrance reading a book as Iza walked in to return the cross-body purse.

"Hi Tina, busy day today?" Iza smiled as she set the purse on a nearby table.

"Actually, no. And that's even considering that Suzanne is at Clayallee all day. But last week was a different story."

"Can I ask a favor then? Can you get these red nails off for me? A couple broke off already, but I've never worn fake nails before, and I'm not sure how to remove the rest of them. It's not my look."

Tina worked to remove the nails while she continued chatting.

"Yeah, this past Friday was a blast. Suzanne and I got to move and then decorate some guy's apartment. Someone really did a number on his old place. The higher-ups gave us a decent budget for the job. We hit a few of the Friday flea markets and some electronics stores—stuff like that. Then we called in our moving guys and hit the new location. The guy's girlfriend must have been moving in with him around that time because there was women's clothing strewn around and some empty totes nearby. Anyway, it was too much fun. Suzanne told me she never got to do something like that before, and I'm too new to know the difference. I hope the guy likes his new place; I thought it turned out pretty cool."

"I'll bet he really does, and his girlfriend probably does too."

Tony sat deep in thought at his desk in the Berlin U.S. Embassy. It was early, but he hadn't been able to sleep. Later in the morning, he'd meet with Claire to clear up the mess he'd created by authorizing Iza's impersonation of her . . . at least as well as he could clear it up. Then, in the early afternoon, he'd meet with Bill Harmon and Derek Thomas from the Bureau of Business and Economic Affairs to clear up that mess.

His thoughts wandered to the FBI Counterespionage briefing he'd had the past week. It was still all so unbelievable to him that Elise—their friend of thirty years—had betrayed her country. How could that have happened?

Certain high-level American and German diplomats began to notice that the Russians seemed aware of their intentions following various confidential meetings. At first, everything was nebulous, and the information the Russians gleaned was of relatively minor importance—the date of an upcoming meeting or some general, yet confidential, comments made during meetings between the U.S. and Germany. That began to occur in late 2021. After Russia's war against Ukraine commenced on February 24, there was a perceptible uptick in the flow of information and in the importance of what was leaking. Then, when the Americans and Germans began their early discussions of sanctions against Russia and of what to do to decrease Germany's reliance on Russian petroleum products, particularly natural gas, the spigot fully opened. The Russians knew in advance what was being discussed, and they responded accordingly.

FBI Counterespionage and the German Bundeskriminalamt stepped up their fledgling investigation. By mid-May, they'd determined that the interpreter, Elise Carter, was the common denominator in all of the meetings from the U.S. side. But how to catch a spy? And, just as important, how to catch her contacts along with her?

Wilhelm Kühn suggested they plan to pass some extremely sensitive information to Elise. It had to be information so enticing that she'd literally run to pass it to whoever her contact was. After consulting with the U.S. Department of Defense and the German Ministry of Defense, they decided what that information would be. The bait was physical blueprints identifying the location and layout of a top-secret military intelligence operation in Berlin, providing critical targeting information to the Ukrainian military in Russia's war against Ukraine.

The BKA and FBI Counterespionage were convinced that Elise was too inexperienced to take the necessary precautions. She'd err, and be caught as she handed over the prints while they were still physically located in the U.S. Now, they only needed to get the blueprints to Elise, and it had to be believable—at least, believable to an inexperienced spy.

It appeared to be a clever plan. A joint meeting held at the State Department in Washington between State Department and Defense Department officials from both countries was arranged for June 1, 2022. Elise was the chosen interpreter and translator for the meeting. They'd discuss the intelligence operation facility using the German prints. The U.S. side would request a copy of the prints so Elise could write her translations from German to English on the four pages of prints as various aspects of the facility layout were discussed. The copies were to be prepared using a large-format copier located in the Technical Services Department at the State Department. Since the original prints were labeled "Top Secret," and Elise had the appropriate clearances to work with such documents, she'd be the person preparing the copies. They'd send Elise to Technical Services with a Marine guard escort, then watch from a carefully hidden closed-circuit TV camera near the copier. The Marine guard would wait in the Department entry to escort her back to the conference room.

When the meeting occurred, as expected, Elise made two sets of copies, carefully folded them, and then hid one set inside the copier for later retrieval. Following the meeting, Elise requested permission to search for a thumb drive she'd inadvertently dropped "somewhere" near the copier. She recovered the extra set of prints as she'd crawled along the floor near the copier and had slipped them into her leather folio case. They had the proof they needed.

Elise was under twenty-four-hour surveillance. Her work phone was tapped, and her cell phone calls were monitored, but nothing happened, and a month went by. They knew she had the copies, but they needed to catch her passing the prints to her as-yet-unidentified contact, and she wasn't making any move to do that. She must have become suspicious. Obtaining the prints, in retrospect, must have seemed too easy to her.

Wilhelm sent one of his top agents, Günther Kohler, to take on the task of "befriending" Elise to learn more. He'd met her in mid-June at a State Department meeting and had instantly gone about charming her. He'd become more than a casual friend. He'd been able to search her belongings but to no avail. U.S. Counterespionage had searched her State Department office to no avail. They'd continued monitoring her calls to no avail. Where were the prints? It was extremely dangerous for these to be unaccounted for. They wondered if she had somehow already passed them on despite their surveillance.

The fully opened spigot had abruptly stopped leaking, and everything was quiet into early October. Finally, Günther decided to take a more aggressive approach. He planned a vacation with Elise—a short trip to Vermont—ostensibly to view fall colors. Günther knew that Iza was leaving for Berlin to begin her job in Consular Affairs at the U.S. Embassy. He'd surmised that Elise would somehow send the blueprints with Iza as her unsuspecting courier, but he'd searched Iza's suitcase the night before the trip to Vermont and hadn't found anything.

It was on the Friday of their trip to Vermont, where the two were having brunch that Günther made the breakthrough. When Elise briefly left the table to say hello to a former coworker seated at a nearby table, Günther scanned her cell phone. He glanced at a text message sent during the early afternoon of October 11, as he'd later discovered, to a burner phone. The message was: *blauer Koffer* 952. When Elise returned to the table, he was scanning his phone. He searched the flight numbers for flights leaving Washington Dulles near the time he knew Iza had flown, then saw the number—Flight 952, leaving Dulles direct to Berlin—blue suitcase.

The BKA sent an agent to retrieve the blueprints from Iza's apartment in Berlin that Friday evening, but the agent hadn't found them in her suitcase, and as he'd waited for her to return to her building, he'd been murdered. Their operation was at a dangerous standstill, with the prints still missing.

The spigot dripped again near the end of October. U.S. Counterespionage and the BKA quickly scheduled an early-November meeting between the Americans and the Germans to discuss their conclusions surrounding the Nord Stream natural gas pipeline sabotage; the under-ocean pipeline segments between Russia and Germany were destroyed in several mysterious explosions in late-September. The Russians would be interested in hearing their conclusions from the investigation. Elise was the interpreter at the meeting.

On November 2, in her meeting with Wilhelm Kühn, Iza revealed the name of the spy's German contact—Johannes Brandt. She'd also disclosed that Brandt always flew back to Berlin from Washington Dulles. Wilhelm Kühn and U.S. Counterespionage would be ready this time. And they were.

As Tony ran through the briefing in his mind, he had to admit he was both mentally exhausted and perplexed. *Why Elise? Why* did you do it? Did you think about Iza? You put her in mortal danger. Your own daughter.

"Welcome back, Iza," Claire said as she peeked into Iza's office and smiled warmly. Iza wasn't sure of the excuse Tony had given for her absence, nor if he'd talked with Claire yet about her impersonation at imperative Energie, so she proceeded cautiously.

"How was your vacation, Claire?"

"It was a much-needed break for the two of us. I hate to go right to business, but I need you to assist Jack with interviews again today. I told him you'd be there at 9:00 sharp."

Iza was relieved that Claire hadn't asked her any other questions, yet she probed, "Claire, did you know Tony is back in Berlin this week?"

"Yes. In fact, I'm meeting with him at 9:00."

"Tell Tony I said hello."

Iza was relieved that Tony would soon meet with Claire to clear up the mess caused by her impersonation. As Claire walked out of her office, Iza grabbed her things and ran off to meet Jack, wondering what would happen the next time Claire ran into Alex Schröder. She didn't think Tony could clear *that* up.

Volodya smiled as the room filled ahead of the morning briefing. The message that he'd come down with COVID must have made a strong impression on the other Team members.

Only Petro sat next to him, while the others piled up along the wall at the opposite side of the briefing room.

Petro questioned in Ukrainian, "Volodya, what happened? I was not supposed to know, but Dmytro told me you were assigned to special security project by U.S. It must have something to do with software that we looked at and Russians finding our location here. Can you tell me more?"

"I am sorry, Petro. I would like to, but I am under orders to divulge nothing. But I can tell you I think we are now pretty safe here. My girlfriend did good work for us."

"And is this girlfriend right for you? Iza seems *very* nice, and I can see that she makes you happy and that you love her. It showed on your face at Café. But her job is very dangerous, yes?"

"It will be her former job, Petro. Iza realized CIA field agent job is much more dangerous than she originally thought it would be. She interviewed for another job at U.S. Embassy in Consular Affairs, and she believes she will get it. That is still stressful job but no guy with gun will chase her in that job."

Lloyd reported that Ukrainian troops were massing for an offensive in the direction of Kherson Oblast. The Russians were retreating, and Kherson City would likely be liberated from Russian occupation in the coming few days.

Russian military leadership had thrown the 155th Naval Infantry Brigade into an incomprehensible offensive near Pavlivka in Donetsk Oblast; the brigade suffered losses amounting to over 300 killed or wounded, with the loss of half its equipment within the past four days.

Commander-in-Chief of the Ukrainian Armed Forces General Valeryi Zaluzhnyi stated that Ukrainian forces destroyed 278 aircraft already in the war, while for comparison, the Russians lost only 119 during ten years of war in Afghanistan. Russia would be unlikely to replace these aviation losses quickly since the losses outstripped their capacity to manufacture new airframes.

These were all areas wherein their Team contributed to the outcomes through their careful work. Lloyd concluded the briefing: "Let's get out to our workstations and kick some Russian ass."

Volodya prepared his station for the day ahead. He felt tired from his work at the BKA the previous day, yet invigorated by the news that the work of the Team was making a difference. He thought, *This war is far from over, and who knows how it might end, but for now, things are looking up for Ukraine. And Zelenskyy says we will win next year—I will do my part to make it so. Sláva Ukrayíni!*

It was 16:30, and Iza hadn't been able to call Volodya with the evening dinner plan. She hadn't even had time to check her office phone for the details; she and Jack had been so busy that they'd missed lunch. She raced back to her office.

"Hello," the familiar deep voice answered.

"Volodya, I'm so sorry. I had interviews all day with Jack, and I couldn't even check my phone. The dinner is at 18:00. I'll meet you near the embassy entrance at 17:30. Is that okay?"

"Yes, Iza. I will meet you there. I am *really* hungry; I forgot my lunch today."

"I'm starving too. I didn't get to eat *anything* all day. We were so busy! See you soon."

Volodya noticed Iza in the Chanel suit right away as he walked through the mass of employees leaving the embassy. He also smiled when he noticed she'd worn her black tank top underneath the suit jacket. The two walked to the private Embassy dining room, the first to arrive for the dinner. They were again in the same dining room as for their previous dinners with Tony.

"Let's check out the menu before Tony gets here. I'm so hungry, I could probably eat the menu."

The two looked over their options.

"Look, Volodya; they've got king salmon from Alaska on the menu tonight!"

"I really do not care for salmon."

"But you've probably never eaten Alaskan king salmon before, have you?"

"Probably not. Is it that good?"

"You *have* to try it. And look what it comes with! That's what I'm having."

"Hey, Iza, did you notice there are four place settings at table. Is that mistake or is someone else coming tonight?"

Iza's eyes opened wide and she responded excitedly, "I wonder if Ellen came with Tony. He didn't say anything, but maybe it's supposed to be a surprise for me."

The two wandered the room, looking at the framed prints on the walls. Tony was fifteen minutes late. When the door finally opened, Tony entered the room accompanied by Wilhelm Kühn.

Both Iza and Volodya gasped. After grudgingly greeting Herr Kühn, Iza asked Tony if she could talk with him privately about an embassy topic of concern before their dinner. The two left the room while Wilhelm and Volodya sat across from each other in the upholstered club chairs. Volodya stared intently at Herr Kühn but said nothing; his unease was tangible. Herr Kühn said nothing either, and eventually he walked around the room, viewing the framed prints of Berlin landmarks.

◆

When Iza and Tony were alone in the hallway, she angrily rebuked him as tears formed in her eyes. "Tony, you've got to be kidding! You can't expect us to have dinner with *Kühn*."

"I thought you'd want to hear the latest from him on imperative Energie."

"Weren't you listening when I told you how harshly he interrogated me, or how we had to defend ourselves from his accusations? He accused me of being a conduit for my mom!

And in case you forgot, I'm already dealing with her betrayal, and I will be for a long, long time. Do you think I want to sit here tonight and get indigestion while pretending to be friendly with that guy? I've got feelings too, Tony. And so does Volodya. He dragged Volodya to their Lab yesterday for hours but didn't even thank him for his help."

"Iza, please. Give him a chance. He's only doing his job. It's nothing personal."

"To *you*. To Volodya and me, it's very personal."

"Please, Iza. Do it for me, okay? It simply isn't going to be as bad as you're imagining."

"That's so easy for you to say, isn't it? Nothing is as bad as *I* imagine it, right? Even my mother telling me I was never wanted—that I'm an accident—wasn't personal. I just imagined her rejection when she told me she resented me and was sorry I was born. I'm just supposed to keep taking it because none of this shit is personal."

Tony looked at Iza with a stunned expression. Volodya told him that Elise had broken Iza's heart, but he thought it was all related to her betrayal of her country. He had no idea Elise had rejected her own daughter too. Her actions *had* endangered Iza, but he simply couldn't believe that she'd done so intentionally. Now he knew the truth.

"Iza . . . please forgive me . . . I don't know what I was thinking! I honestly thought you and Volodya would want to hear about the investigation directly from Wilhelm. Now I realize that I've been sitting safely in my Washington office, only hearing snippets of information from the two of you about what you've actually been going through in Berlin. I truly don't know the details of what happened in the nine days since I returned to D.C. This isn't fair to the two of you. But now it's too late. What can I do? Uninvite Wilhelm when he's already sitting in the embassy dining area?

"I'll figure something out," he said as his eyes pleaded with hers for forgiveness. He suddenly offered, "I'll lead the conversation with Wilhelm so you and Volodya can avoid talking with him as much as possible. And . . . I'll try to speed up the dinner. But I do want to hear what Wilhelm has to say about the investigation." Iza gave him a disgusted look, then turned and ran down the hallway crying.

◆

Volodya was both relieved that Tony had returned to the room and distressed that Iza had not. The three men sat in the upholstered club chairs at the small table for before-dinner drinks.

Iza returned to the room just as the attendant came to take their drink orders. Tony ordered Chassagne-Montrachet. Wilhelm ordered a German Riesling. Volodya asked the attendant to recommend a good pairing with salmon, and he ordered an Oregon Pinot Noir. Iza ordered a tumbler of Nemiroff vodka. As he caught sight of her eyes, Volodya observed that she was extremely upset and had been crying. *Be careful, Iza,* he thought.

Tony and Wilhelm made small talk while Volodya tried to politely interject a comment when appropriate. Iza said nothing as she uncomfortably squirmed in her chair. Wilhelm told them the history of the German Mosel wine region, where the grapes used in the production of his Riesling were grown. Wilhelm then expounded on the history of all of the wines of Germany. He seemed almost friendly.

Suddenly, Wilhelm turned toward Tony, "Tony, Herr Kohler returned safely to Germany today. I was able to debrief him this afternoon."

Iza was shocked at the mention of "Herr Kohler" and immediately blurted out incredulously, "Are you talking about *Günther* Kohler?"

"Why, of course, Iza Carter. Günther is one of my top men at the BKA. He was working on the investigation in Washington." Wilhelm was preparing to continue with his discussion of Herr Kohler's work.

Iza was traumatized. This news was not something she'd expected. Volodya's eyes opened wide as he breathed in deeply then rolled his eyes at Tony while shaking his head, his eyes pleading, *Make him stop!* Tony had told Volodya about Günther, but Volodya hadn't been able to bring himself to tell Iza about him.

Tony abruptly changed the subject, directing an innocuous question about German white wines to Wilhelm. The drinks arrived, and the conversation turned back to wine. Volodya glanced at Iza and saw the horror on her face. She drank half of the full tumbler of vodka in one swallow. *Oh, Iza, do not do this,* Volodya thought, his face showing his helplessness.

Wilhelm spoke again. "Markus Peters escaped to Ankara by disguising himself as an old Turkish woman. He took the 5:00 flight from Berlin to Ankara yesterday morning. My people were duped by his disguise, but we recovered."

Wilhelm's piercing, icy blue eyes were now focused on Iza. "We determined which flight he was on, and I alerted Turkish authorities to arrest him. They were to hold him on charges of espionage until we could have him extradited back to Germany. But the Turks arrived at the gate too late. The passengers had already deplaned from the flight."

Iza became increasingly uncomfortable as Wilhelm highlighted the word "espionage" while continuing to focus his accusatory gaze upon her. She was overcome by her emotions, yet tried to hold everything inside.

Wilhelm continued his story as Iza fidgeted in her chair and nervously drank the remaining vodka from her tumbler. "The Turkish authorities remained at the airport, watching for him or for the old woman. They searched passengers on all flights leaving for Moscow. But Peters changed his appearance once again. For the flight to Moscow, he disguised himself as a middle-aged businessman, complete with a very legitimate passport—the passport of a recently murdered Russian businessman. He simply walked onto the plane bound for Moscow and was gone. It was already too late when we learned about the dead man's passport. I failed Germany."

Volodya was surprised by Herr Kühn's admission of failure. He came across as arrogant and demanding of his subordinates, yet he took personal responsibility for the escape of Markus Peters.

The attendant revisited the seating area, and noticing that Iza's tumbler of vodka was empty, quickly returned with another. Wilhelm revealed that the man with the shaved head was holed up in the Russian Embassy. Iza nervously sipped vodka from the second tumbler.

Kühn told them he'd met with Matteo Mehlman, the Managing Director of imperative Energie, a second time. Mehlman was reluctant to reveal too much to his customers about the software backdoor until Kühn threatened him with going public. No application upgrade would be sent out on the ninth of November. Customers were warned to remain attentive for network intrusions for an extended period, and imperative Energie offered three months of free threat intelligence monitoring to each location.

Finally, Wilhelm divulged that there was no indication that others working at imperative Energie were involved, but he would stay vigilant.

"What about Alex Schröder?" Volodya questioned. Iza took another sip of vodka as she listened intently.

"After the shareholder partners employed a private investigation firm to look into Friedemann's files, they became aware of issues within their company. However, we have no evidence to prove that they knew in advance about the Russians or about the involvement of others within their company. It is, however, very possible, Herr Korsun, that Herr Schröder could be more deeply involved with the Russians. But at present, there is no way for me to prove it one way or the other. He is simply someone who I will keep my eye on."

Iza emptied the second tumbler of vodka.

As the four moved to the dining table, Volodya squeezed Iza's hand and tried to engage and encourage her as he whispered, "Iza, you won the race. You identified almost everyone involved and most of those guys have been stopped. That was your goal. You are hurt pretty bad in process of winning . . . but you still won." Iza gave a slight smile yet seemed distraught by the prospect of sharing dinner with Wilhelm Kühn.

Volodya and Iza ordered the king salmon, while Tony and Wilhelm ordered the smoked pork T-bone. Tony ordered Veuve Clicquot for everyone in celebration. Volodya took a sip of the Clicquot to be polite but realized that he needed to be alert for work the following day. He left the remainder untouched. Iza drank her entire glass of champagne while waiting for their dinners to arrive, then took Volodya's glass and drank his as well. She sat quietly at the table, neither looking at Wilhelm nor at Tony. The look of misery on her face was heart-breaking.

"Iza, this king salmon is delicious," Volodya said, again trying to engage Iza in conversation to keep her mind off the unwanted dinner guest. Iza smiled sleepily at Volodya. She ate the delicious salmon but only picked at the side dishes, having lost her appetite when Wilhelm Kühn arrived for dinner.

The conversation turned to the current state of democracy around the world. Volodya realized that this usually would have been a topic of great interest to the two of them, but Iza was not going to engage in conversation with Wilhelm, and at this point, he didn't think that she could, even if she'd wanted to. As the discussion evolved, Volodya comprehended that Wilhelm was a man who passionately loved his country—the country Germany had become after the Second World War—and that he intended to protect the security of the democratic Germany he loved. Volodya concluded that Wilhelm was a true German patriot—albeit a strange and complex man—but he was certain Wilhelm never had evil intent, as he and Iza had earlier believed.

After the dinner plates were cleared, the group stood. Volodya could see that Iza was unsteady as she attempted to move from the table. Tony left the table with Wilhelm, and the two strolled around the room, deep in discussion as they admired the framed photographs of Berlin.

Volodya approached Tony and quietly said, "Tony, Iza and I have work tomorrow, and we have to be alert. I think we need to go. Thank you for nice evening. Before you leave Berlin, will you have dinner with us at our new apartment? I am thinking on Friday evening."

"I'd *really* like that. I can't commit yet, but I hope it will work out. Let me know the details, and I'll confirm my schedule with you on Wednesday."

Iza still stood, slightly swaying while holding on to the dining table. Volodya grabbed their jackets and her tote bag, then put his arm around her and directed her toward Tony and Wilhelm. Volodya offered their goodbyes.

"Iza Carter, Herr Korsun, I wish you a pleasant evening," Herr Kühn intoned. Iza simply smiled wanly at the two men. Tony hugged Iza, but she looked away from him and gave no hug in return.

◆

"Iza, I think we will take U-Bahn," Volodya said after observing her unsteady gait. "There will be no Evgeny waiting there for us tonight."

Volodya put his arm around Iza's shoulder, guiding her to the U-Bahn station while he held her upright. Iza belched, then excused herself.

"Volodya, I think the salmon tonight was bad. I feel like I'm getting food poisoning or something. I feel so lightheaded. Do you feel sick?"

"Not yet, Iza. Maybe I will not feel so good later," he said sympathetically, knowing that it was not the salmon but the alcohol. He knew that by tomorrow, she'd also realize it was not the salmon. But he felt terribly sorry for Iza—for the unimaginably terrible week she'd just suffered through—and for the long future of grief she'd need to endure.

Volodya was relieved that the U-Bahn station was near their new apartment. Iza was having more trouble staying upright, and he knew that he couldn't carry her with his stillsore bruised ribs. He hung up her jacket on the coat rack when they got into the apartment while Iza rushed to the bathroom and vomited. He came to her and held her long hair back as she continued vomiting.

"Volodya, it was the salmon. Look, pieces are even floating in my vomit."

"Yes, Iza, I am sure it was bad salmon," he said as he held her close and comforted her while he ran his hand through her hair.

Nineteen Days Later . . .
Saturday, November 26 (Day 28)

Volodya could see the size of the bouncing speck on the horizon increase as he made the final turn into the home stretch to complete his ten-kilometer run. The speck finally transformed into Iza, vigorously running in place to stay warm on the cool, humid Berlin morning.

"You did great!" Iza smiled broadly as she bounced up and down at the street corner. "That was two minutes faster than your last run."

"But I am still many minutes behind you."

"You just started running again. Don't be so hard on yourself!" Iza encouraged Volodya.

He'd recently restarted his running program after his bruised ribs had recovered. That was a positive. But he'd also had a rough couple of weeks dealing with Russia's war in Ukraine. Russia had continued to target and destroy civilian infrastructure in Ukraine, including that of the recently retaken city of Kherson. It promised to be a difficult winter for his countrymen. The fighting in eastern Ukraine had ground to a bloody stalemate, and the late autumn *bezdorizhzhya* hadn't helped the situation. He'd mentioned something about reprogramming a long-distance drone that was going well; he couldn't tell her any details—only that perhaps she'd read about it in the papers in early December. But that had been stressful work for him; there was no room for error.

The difficult situation in Ukraine was disheartening, and Iza noticed he'd lost some weight from worry. His sweatpants had started to hang loosely on him. She hoped the fun day she'd planned for them would boost his flagging spirits and increase his appetite.

She'd had difficulty dealing with thoughts of Elise and of that future too, but she was making slow progress toward acceptance. She'd prepared herself for the reality that healing would take a very long time, so any good day was a prize. She'd at least had a few good days over the past couple of weeks. Volodya had been so kind to her, and she felt blessed to have him as both her committed friend and her love. She prayed that the war in Ukraine wouldn't take him away from her. Her work at the embassy had gone well. Her one-month new-employee review with Claire had been very positive. And Roger had made his plans to visit over the Christmas holiday—a visit she was genuinely looking forward to.

They'd heard nothing more about imperative Energie or the Russians in Berlin. Although Iza had talked with Ellen several times, Tony had been busy with other European business at the State Department. He hadn't called in twelve days with any update, and they certainly were not going to call Wilhelm Kühn.

Iza grinned deviously at Volodya. "How about we race to the newsstand? Loser buys chocolates and newspapers for the winner. I'll even give you a head start."

"Why do I not trust you?" Volodya looked at Iza with suspicion.

"Moi?"

"Yes, *you*," he grinned.

"Okay. You start ahead of me. I'll yell, "Ready, set, go," and then you start. I'll count to five, and then I'll come after you. Fair enough?"

As Iza yelled "set," she ran up behind Volodya, pulled down his sweatpants, and raced ahead of him, looking over her shoulder and laughing at his incredulous expression as he scrambled to pull them up. She eventually glanced back, and saw the form of a man slowly jogging in the distance far behind her.

Why did I suggest that we race? Even though he's been doing incredibly well with his running program, he's been so frustrated that he's not back in peak condition yet. I only meant to be funny and tease him, but now he's jogging far behind me like he's totally discouraged. I'll go to the newsstand and buy him his favorite chocolate bar for when he gets there.

Iza continued along the two-kilometer stretch to the newsstand with regret, but stopped short when she saw Volodya nonchalantly leaning against the window at her destination. Her jaw dropped open in surprise. She walked the remaining block to where he stood, suddenly realizing that the man she'd seen slowly jogging in the distance far behind her had not been Volodya. Instead, it was apparent that Volodya had found a shortcut to the newsstand, and he'd raced at high speed to get there well before she did.

"Mr. Korsun, you cheated," she said, trying to stifle a smile, as she joined him in front of the newsstand.

"*I* cheated? I think you said whoever got here *last* buys chocolates for winner. I am pretty sure I have been waiting for you here for at least couple of minutes. That means I am winner."

"Grrr," she growled at him while grinning.

Volodya carefully examined each type of chocolate at the newsstand for maximum effect before making his choices as Iza picked up copies of the *Berliner Morgenpost* and *Der Spiegel*, the weekly German investigative newspaper.

The two walked briskly back to their apartment, then sat drinking coffee while Volodya read news from his phone and Iza read *Der Spiegel*.

"These are most delicious chocolates I have ever eaten," Volodya kidded, slowly unwrapping each chocolate in front of Iza.

But Iza was engrossed in reading a particularly interesting article:

A dual Russian-German citizen was found dead earlier this month outside the Russian Embassy in Berlin, it has emerged.

The man's body was discovered on the pavement on 10 November by police guarding the Berlin compound. He had apparently fallen from an upper floor, but it was unclear how.

The Russian Embassy called the death of the man—who has not been officially named—a "tragic accident". Germany's foreign ministry confirmed the man's death but would not give further details. The Bundeskriminalamt in Berlin has not publicly commented on the death, which was reported for the first time on Thursday.

Reports say the man was 35 years old and was listed as an employee of the German software firm imperative Energie.

The Russian Embassy did not agree to a post-mortem examination following the death. In a statement, the Embassy said "procedures related to repatriating the man's body to his homeland were promptly settled with responsible German law-enforcement and medical authorities in accordance with current practices".

It said it considered "speculations which have appeared in a number of Western media" over the man's death in the past twenty-four hours "to be absolutely incorrect".

Iza gasped and grabbed Volodya's forearm "Listen to this!" she exclaimed. She translated the article for him, still in shock over what she'd just read.

"That is end of man with shaved head," Volodya said quietly when she had finished.

"Who believes he just 'fell' out an Embassy window?"

Volodya came to Iza, kissed her, then held her close. "Iza," he said softly, "it's over. We are free."

"I hope you're right."

After rereading the article several more times, Iza abruptly announced, "I made plans for us for later today. I got us a tour of the Reichstag. We always said we wanted to see it. Then, guess what?"

"Are we going to eat somewhere?"

"You get partial credit. I got paid yesterday and made reservations—we're going to Clärchens Ballhaus. I signed us up for salsa dance lessons at 18:00 and made a dinner reservation for later. I know you have work tomorrow, but I think we can get back here at a reasonable time. The dance lesson is only an hour."

"Iza, that sounds *really* fun."

"And, as a special surprise, I bought you this," Iza said as she ran to the bedroom and came back carrying a dark brown corduroy sport coat. "It's secondhand, but I liked the color. Try it on."

"Hey, Iza, it fits perfect. Do I look like professor?"

Iza laughed softly. "Yeah, you look like a handsome professor—someone I want to salsa dance with."

Volodya wore the corduroy sport coat and a T-shirt with his jeans, while Iza wore the Chanel suit—without anything underneath the jacket. She curled her hair into beach waves and even applied a bit of eye makeup.

"You look beautiful, Iza. I want to dance with you."

◆

Promptly at 15:30, the two arrived for their 16:00 English-language Reichstag tour. A large group of Americans was waiting at their tour time.

Their tour guide explained that this would be the final tour of the day because the Bundestag had been called into a special late-afternoon Saturday session to discuss the provision of weapons to Ukraine.

In the hour-long tour, the guide described the history of the Reichstag building, then expounded on the principles and organization of Germany's democracy. Volodya had many questions; the guide eventually requested that he hold his questions until the end of the tour.

When the tour ended, Volodya remained in the gallery talking with the guide, while Iza left the room to stand in line for the elevator to the base of the glass dome on the Reichstag rooftop. The guide had already explained that climbing the circular rampway to the top of the twenty-three-and-a-half-meter-tall dome would be the highlight of everyone's tour.

As she awaited Volodya's return, Iza noticed two men exiting a room, then walking quickly down the hallway in the direction of the stairs leading down to the main hall of parliament. Much to her horror, she realized that one of the men was Alexander Schröder, and his path would take him immediately past her. She backed up, standing close to the crowd of Americans awaiting the elevator to the dome, but it was too late. Alex had seen her.

He walked directly to her, grabbed both of her hands in his, then squeezed them tightly as the other man continued on to the main hall. "Iza Carter, how nice to see you," he said, squeezing her hands ever more tightly. His icy blue eyes gazed directly into hers, and his smile was strained and sinister. "And I am very pleased to see that you are *still* enjoying your beautiful suit. I hope that you also enjoy your tour."

With that, he broke away from her and continued toward the main hall. When he was just out of sight, Volodya emerged from the gallery and joined Iza in line.

"Volodya, do you have the hand sanitizer?" Iza distractedly queried as she continued to look in the direction Alex had walked. *How does he know about this suit?*

"Yes, do you need it?"

"Yeah, I do. I just touched something really slimy."

They got to the dome in time to look out at the 360-degree view of Berlin during the last of civil twilight as the sky began to clear slightly over the city. The view was breathtaking. They excitedly climbed down from the dome and quickly walked to the Ballhaus. The salsa dance class was about to begin.

The two instructors walked them through the eight counts of the basic salsa dance—forward and backward dance steps with weight shifts between legs at each count and pauses at counts four and eight—one, two, three, pause, five, six, seven, pause. They then demonstrated the proper placement of their hands and arms. Volodya put his right arm around Iza and placed his hand just below her shoulder while Iza brought her left arm onto his shoulder. They held their opposite hands together at Iza's eye level, leaving some space between their bodies. They then counted out the steps and pauses, shifting weight between legs with each count and mainly moving from their hips and legs rather than from their upper bodies. It took a few tries until the motion became second nature. Next, they learned to move side-to-side with the same counts. Finally, the instructors added the music. Iza and Volodya were oblivious of the other dance students. They had the motions down and moved easily back and forth, then side to side across the dance floor, smiling at each other as they moved together as one to the salsa beat.

Printed in the USA
CPSIA information can be obtained
at www.ICGtesting.com
LVHW091526131223
766381LV00004B/32